Th...

closer
than you
think...

D0864616

Teresa

Nov 2009

PORTENT

Praise for PORTENT:

'The pace is terrific . . . the details satisfyingly rich . . .
shows why James Herbert is at the top of his league'
London Evening Standard

'Rich in drama and research, PORTENT is a highly
professional piece of suspense writing'
Publishing News

'PORTENT contains an apocalyptic vision of a new
beginning for Mankind'
Starburst Magazine

'Classic Herbert. Skilfully paced, it escalates gently,
instilling tremors of unease, ripples of foreboding, waves of
panic, until Herbert has you hooked and squirming'
Daily Mail

About the Author

James Herbert is one of the world's top writers of horror fiction and has been described as one of the most influential and widely imitated authors of our time. His novels such as THE FOG, THE DARK and THE SURVIVOR are already hailed as classics of the genre, while his more recent bestsellers, THE MAGIC COTTAGE, HAUNTED, SEPULCHRE and CREED, have enhanced his reputation as a writer of depth and originality.

Novels by James Herbert
Published by New English Library

THE RATS
LAIR
DOMAIN
THE FOG
THE SURVIVOR
FLUKE
THE SPEAR
THE DARK
THE JONAH
SHRINE
MOON
THE MAGIC COTTAGE
SEPULCHRE
HAUNTED
CREED

JAMES HERBERT
PORTENT

NEW ENGLISH LIBRARY
Hodder and Stoughton

First published in Great Britain in
1992 by Hodder and Stoughton Ltd

Copyright © 1992 James Herbert 1992

New English Library edition 1993

*The characters and situations in this book are entirely
imaginary and bear no relation to any real person or actual
happenings.*

The right of James Herbert to be identified as the author
of this work has been asserted by him in accordance with
the Copyright, Designs and Patents Act 1988.

This book is sold subject to the condition that it shall not, by
way of trade or otherwise, be lent, re-sold, hired out or
otherwise circulated without the publisher's prior consent in
any form of binding or cover other than that in which it is
published and without a similar condition including this
condition being imposed on the subsequent purchaser.

No part of this publication may be reproduced or transmitted
in any form or by any means, electronic or mechanical,
including photocopying, recording or any information storage
or retrieval system, without either the prior permission in
writing from the publisher or a licence, permitting restricted
copying. In the United Kingdom such licences are issued by
the Copyright Licensing Agency, 90 Tottenham Court Road,
London W1P 9HE.

Printed and bound in Great Britain for Hodder and Stoughton Paperbacks,
a division of Hodder and Stoughton Ltd,
Mill Road, Dunton Green, Sevenoaks, Kent TN13 2YA.
(Editorial Office: 47 Bedford Square, London WC1B 3DP)
by Cox and Wyman Ltd, Reading, Berks.
Photoset by Rowland Phototypesetting Ltd,
Bury St Edmunds, Suffolk.

British Library CIP

Herbert, James
    Portent
    I. Title
    823'.914[F]   PR6058.E62

    ISBN 0-450-58885-8

*One must have chaos in oneself in
order to give birth to a dancing star.*
FRIEDRICH NIETZSCHE

*Truly, it is in darkness that one
finds the light, so when we are in sorrow,
then this light is nearest of all to us.*
MEISTER ECKHART

Mystery suicide of 7,000 penguins

THOUSANDS of penguins have stampeded to their deaths on an island over which the ozone layer has been seriously damaged.

Experts are baffled by the mass suicide of 7,000 King penguins on the uninhabited sub-Antarctic Macquarie Island.

DAILY MAIL – *MONDAY, JUNE 25, 1990.*

Penguins Stampede and Die

HOBART, Tasmania, June 24 – Thousands of king penguins at a rookery on Macquarie Island stampeded, leaving 7,000 penguins dead and officials said today that they were investigating the mysterious occurrence. "We don't know at this stage why they stampeded," a spokesman for the Australian State Parks Wildlife and Heritage Ministry said. "We have not observed this type of behavior before." Macquarie Island is between Australia and Antarctica and is administratively part of the Australian Island state of Tasmania.

NEW YORK TIMES – *JUNE 25, 1990.*

Towards the next millennium . . .

PRELUDE

Midnight.

He had lain awake in the darkness for many hours, but now he rose from the narrow bed and went to the door. There he paused. A shiver ran through him.

Had it begun? Was this the moment he had both dreaded and craved for so long?

He dragged the door open, the effort slow, reluctant, as though night-demons outside awaited admission. But it was only the chill breeze from the lake that pressed by his thin body.

He stooped to go through, his fingers brushing the ridges of the rough wood as he passed. He did not stray far from the open doorway.

His face lifted towards the sky and he listened to the far beating of wings. Was the eagle also aware? Was that the reason for its desolate cry? Had the sensing come sharp and clear, piercing the brooding with a thrust that caused almost physical pain?

He breathed in the night air as though it were precious,

11

*something rare. As indeed it had become. He sank to his knees
and felt the coarse grass, gripping it in his frail fists as if he
might fall from the Earth itself.*

He offered his prayer and it was to the soil beneath him.

Forgive, he pleaded.

*But deep in his soul he knew it was too late. The cancer
would be cleansed – it would be torn – from its host.*

And mankind was the cancer.

*In despair he wept, and the night, so callous in its indiffer-
ence, offered no comfort.*

He stirred from the weeping.
   He raised his head, straightened; yet he remained on his knees.
   There was a new, a different, awareness within him.
   Somewhere, another knew of this midnight's moment.
   And this one gloated.
   For this was her time too.

QUEENSLAND COAST, AUSTRALIA – *the Great Barrier Reef*

It was a calm sea of varying hues – blues, greens, even indigo where in the distance the continental shelf dropped away – and the sun seemed bleached by its own heat. The Pacific swells barely ruffled the surface here on the inner side of the great reef and the floating pontoon, with its thirty-metre-long catamaran moored alongside, rested easy in the water. A short way off an amphibian had landed, two of its passengers already slipping from the airplane's floats into the tepid sea, their bright diving suits as florid as any marine life they might find below.

A semi-submersible lazily moved away from the broad platform, heading with confidence towards the hidden coral canyons, its occupants watching from the vessel's steel and glass tank below the waterline, excited so far by anything that moved in the turquoise gloom. It wasn't long before these human observers inside their dry aquarium thrilled to the sight of damsel and impossibly vivid blue and yellow clown fish; when an orange-headed olive sea-snake flicked by, the vessel all but rocked with the commotion from within.

On the decks of the catamaran, day-trippers lunched on seafood platters and cheap wine, most of them keeping to the shaded areas or moving down to the roofed section of the broad raft, content to watch the nearby snorkel divers or just ocean-gaze.

Further off, one of the bright-garbed aqua-divers slipped down into the cooler depths, the shadow of the amphibian hanging above him on the sun-drenched ceiling like some giant water skater waiting for smaller prey. He paused for a while, waiting for his diving companion to descend, and looked about him, deciding upon a direction.

Neville Schneider III – Snidey to his friends, just Snide to those who weren't – was not, in fact, the third of anything: he was born, bred and laid in Melbourne, the single son of a single parent (maternal), but he liked the American flavour of the added numeral. As a successful self-made man in the footwear trade, he felt entitled to any title he chose. III was good. It spoke of lineage. Lineage implied respectability. And it was a not quite legitimate denial of illegitimacy. Anyway, nowadays he *felt* like a III.

He looked trim enough for his forty-seven years in his yellow and purple wet-suit, with his slight paunch held in check by the sponge rubber and his bald head nicely sealed in by the tight cap. The total exhaustion he had felt after every dive was beginning to ease, so he must be toning up. And there was no doubting that his nightly bedroom workout back at the hotel was improving nicely – Sandie and Cheryl would vouch for that. Pity neither one liked getting her hair wet – things could have been even more interesting down here.

Something nudged him, interrupting his thoughts. Barry,

his diving instructor and paid companion (and dole-bludger, if truth be told), arrived beside him and Schneider quickly indicated with a straight hand the way he wanted to go. A curled finger and thumb 'okayed' him and both men finned off, their movement smooth and easy through the water.

Schneider loved the feeling of near weightlessness, although he was still a little scared of the seemingly infinite liquid-space all around him and exactly what he might meet in it – yesterday a reef shark, white-tipped fins like tiny snowcaps, had glided by, mercifully indifferent to him (Schneider had been reassured later that humans honestly weren't the shark's favourite food, no matter what certain movies insisted). For a short time, at least, he could feel free from the domestic and business burdens. Jodie could spend two weeks humping the garbo or any drongo she liked for all he cared, and the shoe business – *his* shoe business, *his* shoe *empire* – could hoof it on its own for the same time. A fortnight of rest and recreation was what the doctor had ordered and 'scubing' was part of the recreation. Just one part of it. Another two parts were sunning themselves around the pool back on Hayman Island. When they'd fried enough, Sandie and Cheryl would spend the rest of the afternoon prettying themselves up for the hero's return. Schneider was that hero. And by God, he felt like one splashing about down here in the deep. Macho stuff this, no mistake.

Barry had gone on ahead and was pointing at something in the coral, no doubt keen to earn his considerable retainer as instructor and guide. Schneider caught up and nodded in slow motion when he saw the multi-coloured spiral gillworms nestling in the rocks. Like a kid's painting, he thought, spiky sploshes of uncontrolled colour, with no precision and no design.

For a moment or two Schneider was struck by the sensitivity of his own soul.

He twisted away, motioning to Barry to get on with it.

Crikes, he'd turn into a purse-carrying poofter if he went on like this. These little beauts were okay, but it was excitement that he was after. Well, maybe not quite. If he was going to be honest with himself – and he was the only person he could be truly honest with, although even then not all the time – it was the *idea* of aqua-diving in the big ocean that he liked, something to drop into the conversation at Jodie's next bollocks-boring dinner party, or to the boys in the bar at the next footwear convention. With some slight embellishments, natch.

What was that!

Strewth, only Barry grabbing his ankle to show him a new find. It'd better be good. Oh great, an over-sized seashell with a thorny sprig sticking out of it. Maybe he was paying Barry *too* much. What the heck was the gink doing now? He was pretending to stuff something into his mouth. Oh yeah, I get it. The shell was eating the prickly stuff. Big deal. Now if it was a man's leg the thing was pigging on, that might be interesting.

Schneider stiffened as a dark bulk appeared from the gloom. He clutched his guide's shoulder and stabbed a finger towards the moving mass, ready to flee but wanting Barry to cover his retreat when he did so. The other swimmer shook his head in exaggerated motion. He put his hands to his mask and mimed an inspection of the coral around them.

Schneider breathed a sigh of relief into his aqualung and nodded understanding. It wasn't a whale or a huge killer shark making its ponderous way towards them but the semi-submersible he'd seen on the surface earlier, filled with tourists who didn't have the guts to actually get into the water and take a decko at the wildlife down here. He grinned – a difficult thing to do with a mouth full of rubber – and pushed himself off the reef to head towards the odd, window-walled vessel. The other diver saw his client's intention and remained where he was, content to watch. Let the dingbat have his fun while he could. Barry had worked for his kind many times before – big, loud-mouthed, and basically unhealthy; coronaries queued up for these guys.

Schneider set a course that would take him directly beneath the creeping semi-sub, hoping that if he kept in line with the steel bow he wouldn't be noticed. Surprising how much easier it was to swim underwater than on top. *Nearly there, little ways further and I'll be underneath. Just wait till I jump up and bash that glass with me fist. That'll scare the shit out of the buggers . . . Jesus!*

He flinched as something soft struck his mask. *What was it? Only a fish, you dill.* A damsel, all electric blue with a dash of greeny-yellow. *And there goes its mate. Look where you're going, you little sprat. Okay, maybe not a sprat, but not a mackerel either. Wonder what they taste like . . .*

He whirled as a shoal of tiny fish bumped him, their impact almost as soft as snowflakes, but startling all the same. *What was going on? Christ, his own colours were bright enough to be seen. Bloody hell, more of them!* The whole sea was alive with racing fish . . . fish, and other things, things that looked like eels, others like snakes, and more things that looked like flotsam, except they were moving in one direction, speeding out to the deeper ocean. There was one of those bloody great turtles . . . *Jesus, how could it swim so fast?*

Schneider was buffeted not just by the sea creatures, but also by the currents they caused. He turned in the water, flapping his arms, trying to stabilise himself. *Where was Barry, why wasn't he rushing to help him, what the fuck did he think he was being paid for?*

And then the waters became still once again. Save for one or two stragglers, the sea seemed empty. In fact, much more empty than before . . .

Above him, and just a few metres away, he could make out the blurred images of the semi-sub's passengers, their grey faces pressed against the toughened panes. They looked almost comical, but Schneider did not feel like laughing. There was something weird about the stillness all around him.

He realised he was sinking and used his fins to prevent himself going any deeper. Only a few feet down and it was so much darker.

A movement beneath him caught his eye. Something else was rising from below.

Another fish? Too bright, it was too bright.

A diver, it had to be another diver, a diver using a flashlight. Did Barry carry a flashlight? Maybe it was one of those marine scientist blokes on his way up. Maybe he or she caused all the commotion in the first place. Oughta be a law . . .

Wait on. It was a light all right, but nothing with it, no one holding it. Just a light . . . a round light, size of a tennis ball . . . travelling on its own. One of those luminous fishes that hung around on the ocean bed? But it wasn't *that* deep here.

Getting closer. Closer. And it was pure white, and bright . . . But no, there were colours around its edge, like a soft rainbow . . . shimmering . . . Fascinating.

It passed by him, floating upwards.

Schneider watched its progress, craning his neck, his eyes bright behind the mask. A pale glow, almost like moonlight, washed over the semi-submersible's lower deck, and blood-less spectral shapes observed through the glass.

The globe grew fainter as it approached the water's sur-face, not because it had dulled, itself, but because it had to compete with the blanketing sunshine above.

Then it broke through and all that Schneider could see was the gentlest of glows, still rising, becoming smaller, becoming lost, until, finally, it was gone.

Schneider remembered to breathe.

He floated in the weighty silence.

Tell 'em about *that* at Jodie's next dreary bash, he thought.

Even though dulled by the tremendous volume of water around him, the rending *craaack* that came from behind was like a massive thunderclap, brutally raw in its impact, deafening in its intensity. He turned before the full force of disrupted water hit him, his hands instinctively reaching for his covered ears, and saw Barry lifted from the coral as though jettisoned. The diver twisted and squirmed, fighting the currents to gain control of his own body.

From Schneider's position, it was difficult to make out exactly what was happening, but he could see coral breaking away and tumbling like boulders, with flurries of bubbles bursting from the reef itself.

As his own body was buffeted by the sudden surge, he witnessed the most horrific thing in what was to be his comparatively short life.

With a boom that might have come from a hundred cannon, fragments of living polyps shot towards the surface like blasted shrapnel, tearing through the other diver's body as though it were no more than papier-mâché. Barry – or the main part of Barry – disappeared in a great swirl of red, while other pieces of him flew upwards with harder fragments to explode into the sunshine above in a furious fountain of blood, coral and flesh.

Schneider screamed into his air tube.

Just before the whole of the coral reef in his vicinity erupted with a violence that pierced every floating thing above – semi-submersible, amphibian plane, catamaran, pontoon, scuba deck and swimmers – splitting every object, soft and hard, with equal ease, tearing them into a million pieces, he managed to curse his doctor, who had ordered this bloody holiday in the first place.

Then Neville Trevor Schneider III's number increased a thousandfold.

OVER THE GULF OF MEXICO

'Coffee, Doc?'

'Uh?' James Rivers turned from the small window, his thoughts still on the interesting cloud formations, mainly cumulonimbus, in the distance.

The stocky, mustachioed man leaning over him raised the beaker he was holding an inch or so. 'Coffee. Gonna be your last chance before the shit hits us.'

Rivers nodded and took the plastic beaker from Gardenia, wincing as the hot liquid burned through to his fingers. He sipped quickly, then switched hands, managing a smile as he did so. The bastard was still having fun with him.

'What altitude are we going in at?' he asked loudly enough to be heard over the droning of the aircraft's four engines.

'Haven't decided yet,' the other man replied, taking a glance at the monitors ranged in front of Rivers. 'I'd kinda like to go in low, say 5,000 – we'd get more info that way –

but I guess it's up to the pilot. Ten thousand would be a lot safer. How's your stomach?'

'It'll take whatever you decide.'

Gardenia scratched his balding head. 'We've had some bad ones over the past few years – Hurricane Gilbert was the first of them back in '88 – but this one's heading up to be the worst. Check those readings.' He stretched over the narrow desk to peer through the double-layered polycarbonate windows, forcing Rivers to press back into his seat.

'Surface wind looks to be eighty or ninety knots right now.' Gardenia's eyes squinted through thick, horn-rimmed glasses. 'That's soon gonna change, though. Hey, what has three humps and sings "Stormy Weather" through its asshole?'

Rivers shook his head, although he had an idea what the answer would be; these jokes had been doing the rounds for two years now, ever since the disaster.

'An Iraqi camel.' Gardenia clucked his tongue, as if embarrassed himself. 'Yeah, I know, bad taste. But the crazy bastards shouldna' messed with things they didn't understand, 'specially after they got the crap beat outa them in the war. Jeez, take a look at that up ahead. Don't hold onta that coffee too long, Doc, or you'll end up with a hot pecker. We're in for a bumpy ride.'

Rivers looked past Gardenia at the distant weather. The clouds were even blacker and more angry than a minute ago. They moved as though they were boiling.

'You been through one before, Jim?'

Rivers was glad that Gardenia had dropped the 'Doc' – doctors of physics weren't used to being addressed in that way – but the other man's sudden serious tone was hardly relaxing. Thom Gardenia, despite his crassness, pretended or otherwise, was chief scientist for Hurricane Research at the Miami-based National Oceanic and Atmospheric Administration (NOAA), and certainly no fool. His manner might well

23

have been his way of dealing with his own tenseness, a tenseness felt by all members of this particular mission. After the devastation Hurricane Zelda had left behind in Jamaica, everyone on board was aware that this storm was unprecedented. Its power was not just awesome – it was indescribable. Rivers' throat, to use an expression Gardenia himself might use, felt as dry as a mummy's jock-strap.

'I've flown missions in our own C-130 Hercules, but never into anything like this.' He took a sip from the beaker, glad of the coffee's heat. For a moment there a chill had run through him that had nothing to do with altitude – most of the scientific team wore shortsleeve shirts, and crew members were in light, blue uniform overalls.

Gardenia's stubby hand clamped his shoulder. 'Don't worry, buddy, we've never lost a Brit yet. You may even enjoy it.'

The NOAA aircraft momentarily dipped a wing and Gardenia's fingers dug hard. His other hand grabbed the edge of the fixed desk. 'Just a coaster ride, Doc.' He grinned, his porcelain-coated teeth rendered even whiter by the thick black moustache above.

Keeping the coffee level, Rivers stared down into the deep waters below and wondered how this one had started. Over Africa? Winds colliding near the Equator, producing low pressure zones? Six out of a hundred might evolve into storms of something like this magnitude, air drawn in and spinning, the Earth's own rotation driving it faster, giving it power so that as it drifted it picked up moisture from the warm sea, eventually pulling up energy into the atmosphere from the ocean itself, feeding the storm, the clouds becoming ever more turbulent, forming an inner wall that would become the hurricane's core, its centre, the eye.

'Jamaica and the tip of Cuba are wrecks,' Gardenia remarked as the aeroplane straightened again, 'and it's still only a category four. Let's hope it'll wear itself out soon.'

'What was the last satellite eye measurement?'

'Twenny-five, twenny-six miles across before it made land-fall, about ten now it's back over the ocean. It appears to be reducing rapidly.' His forehead puckered. 'Let's see . . . we're around twelve miles away right now, so I figure it'll be more like seven or eight miles across when we reach it.'

'It's shrinking that fast?'

''Pears to be.'

'And we go straight through.'

'Uh-huh. Our pilot doesn't like to manoeuvre too much in that kind of space, particularly when it's getting smaller all the time. There's some hard convection inside the eye, and it's pretty intense around those walls.'

'Thunderstorm updraughts?'

'You got it.'

Rivers decided to risk a scalded throat and finish the coffee before the aeroplane took a beating.

A figure in sweater and chinos came along the aisle towards them. He rested an arm against the bank of monitors where the British climatologist was seated.

'Need to take over, Jim. Our skipper's playing it safe and going in at 10,000.'

Rivers rose, taking the drained beaker with him, and Joe Pusey, the flight meteorologist, slipped into the seat. 'Strap yourselves in, guys, things are gonna get rough.'

The climatologist took a seat opposite, placing the beaker by his feet. As an observer from the British division of the Intergovernmental Panel of Climate Change, he was not directly involved in this particular operation; he could only sit back while the American scientific officer and his team gathered data and relayed it back to the Hurricane Centre on the mainland. Their prime purpose was to pinpoint the storm's exact centre so that its progress and direction could be charted by the forecasters and warnings to coastal and inland areas could be issued. Probes and sensors mounted on the outside of the plane recorded air pressure, humidity, temperature and wind speeds, while radar showed wind and rain patterns, necessary for predicting the height of the storm surge and assessing potential damage when Hurricane Zelda struck land again.

The message that a particularly severe storm was on its way across the Caribbean had reached Rivers at the Hadley Research Centre in Berkshire only yesterday and the hasty flight to New York and then another going south had left him a little travel-worn. But all tiredness had left him now: his mind was sharp, his senses heightened.

Along the cabin the small team of researchers and crew members were busy at consoles or computer keyboards, the young meteorologist on Rivers' right now engrossed in the instruments before him, logging readings and conferring with the aircraft's pilot through the headphones he had donned. Everyone had been courteous enough and friendly in a distracted way – even Gardenia's frequent jibes were good-natured – but Rivers felt like an outsider, a 'dude' with no real field experience, a desk boffin who'd never 'ridden the wind', 'tagged the typhoon'. Well, the truth was slightly different, but there was little point in correcting their assumption. He was there as an observer, nothing more than that.

The plane bucked and Gardenia hurriedly strapped himself into a desk-seat in front of the climatologist. He turned to give a thumbs-up. 'Hold tight, buddy. S'long as we don't have any altitude excursions this'll be no worse than a jeep ride over a rocky road.' Rivers nodded, but didn't return the grin. He was more concerned with the array of monitors before Joe Pusey. He leaned over as far as he could. The meteorologist noticed his interest and tapped the headphones he was wearing; then he pointed to a pocket at the side of Rivers' seat. 'Use the cans,' he called.

The climatologist dipped into the pocket and drew out a

pair of headphones; he adjusted the thin microphone arm when the set was comfortable over his ears.

'We all keep in communication at this time,' he heard Pusey say.

The aircraft lurched and another voice, the pilot's, came through. 'We're into the storm, gentlemen, as you may have noticed. Okaaay . . . we're taking her up to ten thou' and we have approximately eighteen miles to get to the eye wall itself. Once inside, I'll endeavour to orbit if that's any use to you.'

'We'll locate the centre and drop a windsonde while you pass through.'

'That suits me fine. I can make as many passes as you want.'

Rivers opened a notebook he'd taken from his pocket; although he'd be provided with a copy of the mission's records later, he wanted to set down his own observations. The plane pitched again and this time his body strained against the seat-belt. A series of bumps followed.

'This baby's *rough*,' a crew member remarked calmly.

'Yeah, a bad one,' said the pilot. 'We've got some 200-knot gusts here.'

Rivers made a note beneath other information he'd already gathered. Minutes passed and the buffeting became harder, almost constant.

'Making some corrections now so's we hit dead centre,' came the pilot's voice.

'We need to find zero winds, so let's condition one.'

'Check. Hang onta your sick bags, fellahs.'

The aeroplane began to rock violently, fierce rain drumming against its fuselage and lashing the windows. Rivers glanced out on his side and saw only grey, driven clouds, a sombre fury moving at incredible speed. His hand clutched the seat's arm-rest when a particularly powerful updraught lifted the aircraft as if it were no more than flotsam on a wave. His pen fell to the floor and he stamped a foot on it before it could roll away. The plastic beaker he'd placed on the floor earlier had tipped over and was turning a semicircle. He reached down to pick up the pen and as he did so everything became blissfully calm.

Muted cheers rang through the headphones and the cabin, itself, brightened. Rivers' tension eased when he straightened and looked back out the window: white-capped waves circled below, the sea a deep, almost peaceful, blue. The wall of the eye seemed pale and undisturbed in the sunlight from above.

'Looks around twelve miles high,' someone said.

'Yeah, and perfectly clear all the way down,' someone else replied.

'Okay, let's locate the centre,' advised the pilot.

'We're right over it,' Gardenia said.

'I'll mark it.'

'Jeez, we've hit a new low for aircraft surface pressure – 892 millibars.'

'No, it was close to that back in '69 with Hurricane Camille,' came in Gardenia's voice again. 'Gilbert in '88 was around the same if I remember correctly. It's unusual for tropical oceans, though.'

'Wind's running on the south side at 138 knots, and, lemme see . . . 186 knots on the north.'

'They weren't kidding when they said this one was a rogue. It's gonna do a lot of damage when it makes landfall again.'

'Shit, it's gotta be a category five.'

'Going on past experience, I'd say it'll cut a swathe of at least forty miles wide.'

'Hey, we're already halfway across. The eye's shrunk considerably. What would you say – six or seven?'

'Less,' said Gardenia. 'I figure five miles across.'

'We're down 879 millibars. Can the pressure drop that fast?'

No one spoke for a few seconds.

Rivers listened to the drone of the aircraft's engines, his unease mounting. Moisture had made his thumb stick to the page of his notebook.

Gardenia's voice came back on. 'Let's send down the windsonde.'

A blue-uniformed crew member at a console just ahead of the scientific officer swivelled in his chair, the round, taped tube in his hands, ready for the drop. He opened a small raised flap in the aircraft's deck and pushed it through.

Rivers leaned against the window to glimpse the windsonde as it fell.

'This can't be right,' someone said.

Rivers turned his head to see Joe Pusey staring at his monitors in bewilderment.

'What is it, Joe?' asked Gardenia, and Rivers detected an edge to his question.

'Air pressure's sunk even lower. I make it 878 millibars.'

'Can't be correct, Joe, I've never known it that low.'

'Come and take a look for yourself.'

'You boys want me to stay inside for this?' It was the pilot who had spoken.

'What?'

'We're nearly through. I'm gonna have to bank fast if you want me to stay inside the eye. It's shrinking fast.'

Rivers saw Gardenia whirl in his seat and look out at the huge wall of clouds looming up. He turned his head, left and right. 'It's shrinking.'

'Like I said,' came the pilot's dry reply. 'Make up your mind quickly, Thom.'

'Keep us in.'

The wing on Rivers' side dipped sharply and he could just make out the tumbling windsonde as it caught the light on its way down to the sea. Then they were in cloud again, the greyness closing around them like thick fog. The aeroplane shook with the effort of turning and the winds that threw themselves at it.

'Sorry, gentlemen, guess the eye has shrunk more than I figured. We'll be back inside in a minute or so.'

'It's closed in to under five miles,' said Gardenia excitedly. 'Maybe four, Thom.'

'Outstanding.'

'Kinda scary.'

They soon flew back into sunlight, the aircraft still banking hard.

'I don't get it.' Gardenia's voice.

'It's definitely smaller.' That was Pusey's, not a trace of tension in his tone. 'It's collapsing in on itself.'

The plane began to level, but before it had completely, Rivers spotted something. His eyes narrowed.

At first he thought it might be the windsonde still falling, but quickly realised that would be impossible – it would be in the sea by now. Besides, this thing was rising.

'Does anyone else see what I do out there?'

'I got all the interest I can handle right now, Doc,' Gardenia responded.

'Wait, I think I see too,' a crew member came in. 'Over to the left. Lost it now. It's beneath the plane.'

'What was it?'

'A light.'

'A reflection from the sea.'

Rivers cut in. 'No, it was travelling upwards. It was quite small.'

Others began looking out their windows. Apart from engine noise, there was silence again.

'*I see it!*' someone shouted. 'There, coming up from the centre.'

Rivers caught sight of it again, a round light, closer now, rising steadily against the eye's centre downdraught of warm air, no longer a pinpoint but a definite shape.

'Hey, c'mon,' Gardenia chided. 'It's ball lightning, is all. We got exceptional meteorological conditions out there. It's interesting but it's not what we're here for. Joe, I'm coming over to take a look at your monitors.' He removed his headphones and unbuckled his safety belt.

'It's level,' a crew member said. 'And rising.'

Gardenia made his way to the meteorologist's position.

Rivers' gaze followed the tiny ball of light; he was fascinated. It was pure white, with an undetermined edge.

'Tinkerbell,' he said under his breath.

The light passed on, heading towards the top of the hurricane's calm inner circle, to the lower stratosphere.

Events suddenly moved very fast.

'The eye's closing in!'

Without his headphones, Gardenia hadn't heard the warning from the pilot. He was leaning over Pusey, studying the bank of monitors. Everyone else immediately looked out their windows.

'It's three miles across.'

'I'd say two – and getting smaller.'

'We're nearly out.'

'Oh shit – look up there, above us!'

Rivers leaned hard against the clear plastic and peered upwards. His breath momentarily lodged in his chest.

The smooth swirling clouds that formed the cylindrical shape of the storm's eye were turning inwards, looking black and angry, roaring from above to fill the calm space below.

The aircraft rocked and Gardenia clutched the back of Pusey's seat, looking around in surprise.

'Get back to your seat,' Rivers advised him.

But it was too late. The windows filled with darkness and the plane suddenly dropped as though struck from overhead by a giant hammer or, as Rivers immediately thought of it, an avalanche of hostile weather.

Gardenia hit the ceiling, his neck snapping with such

31

sharpness that the sound could be heard over the storm's thunderous boom by anyone in close proximity. His instantly limp body did not fall on to the deck, for the cabin had tilted as the pilot battled to keep control: the dead man dropped over Rivers, pressing him against the wall. Anything that wasn't fixed – books, logs, keyboards and small instruments – flew across the cabin, while bigger machinery strained against their mountings.

Rivers struggled to push Gardenia's body away from him and looked towards Pusey. The meteorologist was clinging to his desk with both hands, his safety belt holding him in his seat; he was staring frozenly at the instruments before him, at the dials and radar images as though it were they and not the raging storm outside that held all the horror of the crew's fate.

Then the world turned over and Rivers found himself hanging from what had been the floor.

Over the tumult of sound that came through the headphones and from outside them, the scream of the aircraft's straining engines, the shrieking rupturing of metal, he heard the pilot's shouts.

'We're going down, we're going down, we're . . .'

BRITISH COLUMBIA, CANADA – *eight kilometres north of Naramata*

Annie Devereux peeled away a section of spruce bark, taking care with the thick-bladed knife not to damage the tree itself. The distant buzz of chainsaws and mechanical tree shears intruded upon her peace, for to her they had become the sounds of encroachment rather than productivity; she hummed a tune to neutralise the noise.

The old coastal Indians of British Columbia, the Kwakiutl, would chant a prayer as they stripped a cedar of its bark for dishes and buckets, or to cover their pit houses:

Look at me, friend!
I come to ask for your dress
For you have come to take pity on us;
For there is nothing for which you cannot be used . . .

The day was coming, and sooner rather than later, when the scavengers would learn to feel that same gratitude.

She examined the wood. 'No bugworm,' she said aloud, adding under her breath, 'thank God.'

Tossing away the piece of bark, Annie tilted her head and looked through the high treetops at the sky, breathing in deeply, pleasurably, as she did so. The breath emerged again as a sigh.

Fifteen years ago, when the Ministry of Forests had first employed her as a silviculturist, nearly half of British Columbia's ninety million hectares had been covered with forests, mainly softwoods but with hardwoods to the northeast; now those forests, most of them established after the Ice Age, were ailing, while the good growths were shrinking, being eaten away by the avaricious timber traders, despite so-called federal controls. Even the new growths were failing, mere shadows of their gloriously abundant predecessors. Yet still the ravagement continued.

Competition from the consistently over-productive Brazilian market meant profits by excess, and even foreign currency fluctuations – the decline in value of the Swedish krona and the French franc, and worse, the dramatic fall of the Japanese yen – worked against Canada's competitiveness. In these times only quantity could guarantee viability.

She touched the naked wood of the pine, the flesh beneath the hard skin, and its moistness was almost sensuous. Annie turned away, closing the knife and slipping it into her anorak pocket.

Oh, to go back to the gangbuster days of cross-cut saws and steam donkeys, when teams of oxen were used to haul logs over skid roads greased with fish oil instead of yarded from the falling site by mobile steel spars, when log booms were sorted and steered downstream by men with stout poles and steady nerves instead of by boom boats and tugs. And now the trees – the hemlock, the spruce, the Douglas fir and the balsam fir, the pine, the cedar – were being genetically cloned. Also, scions from 'plus' trees, those of superior quality and disease-free, were crossbred under scientifically controlled conditions, and satellites watched over the timberlands like sky nannies, while computers judged merits and planned regrowths. Yet still the NSR – the 'not satisfactorily restocked' – areas were increasing, and the old growths were degenerating. More and more the seedlings were not taking, while the old established trees seemed to have wearied.

She kicked forest dust and sank her hands into her pockets. Annie walked on through the woodland, the muted sounds of machinery still following, as if taunting her, telling her that progress was progress, and regress was regress, and after that there was nothing at all.

She came upon a small clearing, a circle of trees and undergrowth that might have been formed by human hand had it not been so ragged. There, lying across it, was a fallen pine, one that had succumbed to years rather than disease. Part of it was rotted away, its powder spilling to the forest floor, but Annie found a place between leafless branches to sit upon.

'My friends,' she addressed the trees around her, 'you're in trouble. But I guess maybe you know that.'

She stooped to pick up a piece of bark from the soft forest rug; her face was solemn and her thoughts distracted as she broke it into little pieces. Annie Devereux was forty-one years old, and already her features were lined and coarsened by exposure, fresh winds and harsh weather the one disadvantage of spending most of her working life – as well as her leisure time – in the great outdoors. Not attributable to such lifestyle, though, was the prematurely greying of her short and otherwise dark, curly hair.

There had been only three serious, and sexual, relationships in Annie's life so far, two if the clumsy high school romance with a boy one year her junior and at least one foot smaller (the school geek, in fact) were to be discounted. That had lasted all of six months, and was a blessed relief to them both when it had ended (school was out and love with it). Louis followed three years later, a tall, serious man whose mission was to save the world, and the one she was to marry. They met in Saskatchewan's Kelsey Institute and were wed before the two-year Renewable Resources course was over; ten beautiful years had followed, a sharing of common interests and uncommon love – the latter was too intense, too fervid, to be termed common. Their mutual enthusiasm for the protection and preservation of the environment led not only to the professions they'd followed, but also to an indulgence in nature itself, with journeys to Canada's lonely outer regions in a constant study of fauna and wildlife and the private planting of seedlings whenever on fieldwork for the ministry. And as they shared their love of nature, they shared their own love with nature.

When they could, when it was possible, when the mood was on them, they made love in the open air. By a lake,·in a forest clearing such as the one in which she now lingered, in the tall grasses – even on the snowy slopes of the Northwest Territories where their vacation cabin was not too far away for a hurried retreat and when appropriate holes had been torn in their clothes beforehand to minimise frostbite. Louis, from Quebec but only gently Gallic, had been a large man, unlike her first lover, yet a graceful one, his big hands as sensitive as a surgeon's and as strong as a faller or chockerman's. Mercifully his death had been swift, the cancer taking him with no half-measures and no respites, only with startling and rapid selfishness.

Three weeks and his diseased lung had persuaded its healthy brother-lung to join in the plunder. Another week and the ravagement was complete. Now, five years after his death, the big man's atrophy seemed like the blinking of an eye to Annie, but it was never the frail and wasted thing lying on that sweetly sour-smelling hospital bed that she remembered; it was always the big man with his black bushy beard and small brown smiling eyes that remained in her thoughts.

So here was her third relationship, her third lover, spread all around her. The rocky hills, the timberlands, the streams and lakes, the snow-capped mountains beyond. And it was her lover in the true sense, for on more than one moonlit or moonless night, it made no difference, she had bathed in the chill waters, lain naked and damp on the forest's yielding carpet; she had taken a random tree as her mate, reaching her arms around the coarse trunk, raising her legs so that the roughness was against her thighs, the protrusions between her legs, holding herself there, thrusting against the hard, still tree, crying out to the night sky, both in ecstasy and in sorrow, finally sinking to the earth, to lie there and whimper for her lost lover.

Now this lover, this once fertile land, was dying too, but slowly, the drama of its death more subtle, the pains more insidious, less evident – or merely less acceptable.

It's too late, Louis. You always maintained there was a chance for revivification, but then you were always the optimistic one. Too few people spoke up, and too few listened. Even so, should we feel angry? Didn't we two doubt your own disease? In that first week, didn't we deny the diagnosis? In the second, didn't we think – hope, pray? – that the horror would take itself away, would leave you alone, go off and terrorise someone else, someone (a shameful prayer, this) more deserving? Lung cancer, sweet Louis, and you never once held a cigarette to your lips. Hard, so hard, to appreciate the irony.

She blinked and her eyelashes were moistened. Surely not tears, not after so long? She had thought the weeping was done. Annie straightened, realising her head had been bowed. Oh Louis, why this terrible sadness today? For you? The mourning was always there, but the worst had been put aside three years after your death. For the forest itself, then, a grieving over the decaying timberlands. Or perhaps these tears were for herself.

Annie closed her eyes and the tears broke free to dampen her face.

A shuffling noise roused her. She turned in time to see undergrowth nearby swaying, obviously disturbed by some small creature that had wandered too close before noticing her presence. It had fled.

A wise move, little friend. We humans are not to be trusted.

A sound to her left, much louder. Something was crashing through the forest, a deer or elk, a sizeable animal judging by the commotion it was making. Now a fluttering of wings. Annie looked up, startled, and saw the flock of birds taking to the sky, the wings flapping against upper branches, beating at the air.

My God, it can't be me. Surely I couldn't have disturbed them.

Because of her tears, her eyes were not quite focused, and the shiny object that caught her attention was like a sparkly glimmer, a diamond catching the sun's rays. She drew a handkerchief from her jacket pocket and dabbed at her eyes, feeling shamed and inconvenienced by the tears. If one of the fallers had come upon her . . .

With clearer vision, she looked again at the bright thing.

'Oh,' she said quietly.

It was beautiful.

She dared not move, lest the tiny light be disturbed.

It glowed among the trees, no more than twelve or so metres away from her, hovering like some wonderful firefly, the shade of the forest enhancing its brightness.

Annie's hand slowly went to her face, an involuntary action as her mouth opened in wonder. The light, floating at shoulder-height, was of the purest white she had ever seen, yet it did not dazzle. There seemed to be a faint shimmering around its edge.

Her hand reached out as if to touch the light.

It began to rise, an easy, almost languid, movement.

Then it began to dance.

Now both hands went to Annie's smiling face. Dark thoughts left her and she suddenly felt joyously happy.

The sounds of machinery, the occasional human shout, came to her from afar, but there was no reality to them; they belonged to another dimension. The light, gently weaving to and fro, flitting between the trees, was the only reality.

Annie Devereux took a step towards the bewitching glow and its movement stopped. Annie froze, afraid she might scare this tiny phenomenon away. What was it, oh Louis, what was this strange and wonderful thing?

The light began to rise again, smoothly avoiding boughs, ascending, it seemed, towards the high treetops. But then it began to move from tree to tree, touching the thinner limbs, bouncing off them like some ethereal pinball.

A small, uncertain laugh escaped Annie. She followed the light's motion, her eyes shifting with its seemingly haphazard pattern, her body tensed like an excited child's. The light swooped delicately and brushed against a slender branch, flicking instantly towards another.

This latter one sparked.

The light touched another, and this one flared briefly.

Annie's smile wavered.

The light fluttered amidst the branches of a different tree and there were more sparks, as if a flint had been soundlessly struck against stone. This time a flame appeared. And as other limbs were brushed against, then they too burst into flame.

'No . . .' It was a low wail of pleading. 'Nooo . . .'

The flames grew and began to spread.

The light flew more swiftly, flitting from tree to tree, igniting branches, kindling new fires. Annie turned with it as it worked its way around the trees. The timber was dry, combustible, ready, just ready, to flame.

A whoosh of fire from behind caused her to wheel around. The flames now had a life of their own, feeding off their burning neighbours, catching flying fragments, the blaze growing. She shouted as if to warn the trees themselves.

She staggered backwards, almost falling, for the conflagration had already become fierce and was spreading fast. She knew she had to get down into the valley so that the Forest Service could be alerted by field telephone. My God, the blaze was growing so quickly, the trees catching one after the other in swift succession, and the light, the light . . . where was the light?

There. Before her. Near the trail that had brought her here to this spot, touching the overhanging branches, kindling them. Annie cried out when she realised what was happening.

She ran towards the rough path, but it was too late. A billow of flame exploded from one tree to another, cutting off her escape. She whirled around, then around again. The fire had encircled her. Every way she turned the trees were blazing. She made a break for it, but a burning branch crashed in front of her as if deliberately, a conspiracy between fire and forest to thwart her.

Annie stumbled backwards. Her arms went up to protect her face from the heat, her skin already beginning to tighten and blister. There was no escape. The fire had fanned out beyond this circle; it was spreading at an unbelievable rate. It was as though a solid wall of flame had been erected around her.

She clawed at her shirt collar as the oxygen in the air was swallowed up, and she sank to her knees, aware that there was nowhere to run, no place to hide from this furious heat.

It pained her to keep her eyes open, but she wanted to see it again, wanted to look upon the light once more.

And there it was, quite still, made pale, a faint star, by the fire that engulfed it. It was no longer a wondrous thing to her.

Annie retched, began to choke.

She attempted to rise again, unwilling to submit to this awful fate. But it was no use. Her strength had gone. As she crumpled to the smoking forest floor, her hair beginning to smoulder, she thought of her dead husband. Louis' image was smiling.

And as the heat and lack of pure air overwhelmed her, Annie's grimace of defeat and pain was not unlike a smile itself.

1

'We're going down, we're going down, we're . . .'

Rivers' eyes snapped open and all dream-images vanished.

He lay there on the bed, only half covered by the sheet, his body damp with perspiration, his mind momentarily numbed.

'Oh sh . . .' he murmured and swept the cover away. He limped towards the open window, falling to his knees before he got there, a hand reaching up for the thin bars to haul himself closer. Rivers breathed in the humid early morning air, forcing calmness upon himself, the throbbing pain of his injured knee bringing reality into sharper focus.

'It's over,' he told himself, hands straining against the metal bars. 'You bloody fool, it's over . . .'

His forehead rested on the edge of the sill for a few moments before he turned and slumped to the floor, his back resting against the wall. He stared at the rumpled bed as fragments of his dream joined as a whole. He began to tremble.

Only the persistent pain roused him from the bleak reverie.

Rather than get to his feet, Rivers slid himself back to the bed; still on the floor, he took the pain-pulser from the bed-side table. Adjusting the setting to HIGH, he pushed the blunted point of the instrument into the hollow beside his knee-joint, finding the conductor-implant there and pressing the pulser's button. It took no more than a few seconds for the pain to ease, but Rivers let the current run for a full minute before switching off.

Supporting himself with his good leg, he lifted himself on to the edge of the bed and looked down at the puckered burn scars of his left thigh, then at the neater surgery scars of the knee itself. Without thinking, he flexed the fingers of his left hand, the tendons still stiff after all these months, the flesh from inner wrist to elbow still an angry and wrinkled red. Nothing, he reminded himself. Nothing compared to what the other two survivors had suffered . . .

He straightened his slumped shoulders, running both hands down his face to shed the last of the tiredness. Busy day ahead, got to get going. Oh God, he hated these heavy duty, three-day international conferences. What conclusions did they hope to draw? That everything was fine, no problems, it was all an ecological misunderstanding? A bad phase the planet was going through? Things'll be fine in a year or two, the climate would settle down. Then there were the alarmists to cope with, the scientists or conservationists whose vanity or moral outrage, perhaps even their ignorance, caused them to exaggerate the problem, even encourage the most pessi-mistic view. How to deal with them? Difficult when they were closer to the truth than the moderates. At least the foreign delegations were limited in members and the conference itself was deliberately low-key; nobody wanted a repeat of the previous year's débâcle in Geneva, when squabbles had erupted into actual violence and made world headlines. Rivers gave a shudder, then reached for the walking-cane leaning against the end of the bed.

He limped down the hall to the bathroom and looked longingly at the bath as he hung the cane on a clothes-hook behind the door; he stepped into the shower cubicle. Ironically, before the ban he had preferred to shower rather than wallow in a tub of water dirtied by his own body. Forbidden fruit, he chided himself. But the tell-tale water meter would never let him get away with it. Roll on winter – so long as it brought rain.

He shaved while he showered, the solraz slow, in need of a recharge, and watched the breakfast news on the two-inch TV dangling from the shower pipe. Water droplets glided over the tiny anti-mist screen as if in mockery of the migrants crossing the parched desert wastes of mid-Africa. When the pictures switched to a snowstorm in Syria, he turned off the set. No doubt the other channels would be showing more of the same and it wasn't his idea of a bright start to the day.

Rivers was at the kitchen table drinking his second cup of coffee and smoking his first cigarette when the telephone rang. He glanced at his watch: 7.40. He didn't have much time for conversation.

The sensor was on the sideboard with his keys and he stretched over for it without rising. He pointed it at the phone-vox discreetly mounted in the wall opposite and pressed RECEIVE.

'Rivers,' he said, resting his cigarette in the Air-Pure ashtray.

'Mr James Rivers?' It was a male voice, full and rich, though slightly wheezy, as if the caller might be prone to asthma.

'Who's calling?' he asked.

'You don't know me, Mr Rivers.'

'Then how did you get my number? It's not listed.'

'Uh, no. Quite. But we have mutual acquaintances.'

Rivers retrieved his cigarette and drew on it. 'Name one,' he said.

The other man took in a small breath before he spoke.

'That isn't important for the moment. I'd very much like to see you, Mr Rivers.'

'Look, I don't mean to be rude, but I'm in a hurry this morning. How about at least telling me your name?'

'Yes, of course. I'm sorry. It's Poggs.'

Although it was too early for humour, Rivers managed a smile. The Dickensian name somehow suited the voice.

'Hugo Poggs?' the other man said hopefully, as though the climatologist might have heard of him.

It did sound familiar, but Rivers couldn't remember just where he'd heard it before. 'I'm supposed to know you?' he said.

'Perhaps not.' There was no evident disappointment. 'I have to meet with you to discuss a matter of great importance. And possibly of great urgency.'

Rivers took time to sip his coffee. 'Life insurance?' he said.

'I would say your life is somewhat charmed, wouldn't you?'

He understood the reference. 'That isn't something I want to talk about . . .' He heard the man take in another breath.

'Nor I, Mr Rivers. May I give you my number so that you can call me back when you have more time?'

'I see no reason to.'

'If I mention one word it might help you decide.'

'It still sounds like life insurance.'

There was a pause. 'In a way, that's not too far from the truth.'

Rivers realised his fingers were crushing the butt of his cigarette. It was the dream, still getting to him, making him tense. It had nothing to do with this stranger. 'I'm waiting,' he said impatiently.

'Tinkerbell.'

He stared at the vox as if it were Poggs, there in the room with him.

A second or two went by before he pressed the MEMO button on the remote unit.

'Give me the number,' he said.

2

Rivers opened the Renault's door and flicked the cockroach off the driver's seat and on to the pavement. He crushed the insect with his foot before it could scurry away, an act that even the Animal Liberation Front wouldn't have complained of nowadays.

'At least my day hasn't been in vain,' he told the mulched remains on the concrete.

After a swift inspection he took an environment-friendly can (not friendly to roaches and their kind, though) from the glove compartment and sprayed the vehicle's interior thoroughly. He closed the door and smoked a cigarette while he waited for the chemicals to work.

How had this man with the silly name known? he wondered as he leaned against the car. And *what* did he know about Tinkerbell? When the critically damaged research aircraft had crash-landed ten miles outside of Galveston and he had been pulled from the wreckage, one of only three survivors, apparently he had repeated the name over and over again.

Tinkerbell, Tinkerbell, Tinkerbell . . . And that had been all he'd said for those first two weeks of recovery.

It had taken that long for him to come to his senses, and at least half that long again for him to remember what the name meant. That was when it became an Official Secret.

A passing neighbour, wearing a white shortsleeved shirt with striped tie and dark knee-length shorts, his briefcase the only heavy thing about him, gave the climatologist a curt 'good-morning' nod. Sun protection cream smeared the man's bare parts and on his shirt pocket he sported a Sun Alert UV self-adhesive badge whose photo-sensitive chemicals would denote the sun's strength throughout the day by changing the colour of its dyes. Rivers returned the nod, unsurprised at the man's caution.

How had this Hugo Poggs found out about Tinkerbell? And what was he implying? That name, Poggs . . . It meant something to him, but for the life of him he couldn't remember what. He'd heard it at some time, or perhaps read about the man somewhere. No matter, it'll come.

He tossed the half-smoked cigarette into the dusty road and pulled open the car door again, allowing the worst of the fumes to waft out before climbing in. After a quick check for any more bugs lying on their backs kicking air, he switched on and drew away from the kerb.

Even at that early hour, the sun was beating fiercely and as he passed his neighbour, a City broker of some sort he seemed to recall, Rivers contemplated pulling over and offering him a lift to the station. The businessman – Simpson or Timpson was his name – used to drive a maroon Jaguar saloon to his office every day, but since such gas-guzzlers and their drivers had become social pariahs, he had taken to using public transport. Rivers drove by – the hell with it, let him walk, there were too many other things to mull over this morning.

The breeze through the open windows soon cleared the

last dregs of the insect-spray; he closed them and let the air-conditioning take over.

The main conference at Bracknell was expected to take up most of the morning and then, after lunch, would break up into smaller meetings in various parts of the massive Meteorological Office building and the nearby Hadley Centre. No doubt these would go on well into the evening, perhaps even into the night. His own briefing wouldn't take long – all the scientists and representatives present would be only too aware of the planet's chaotic weather patterns and their adverse effects on the environment. He and his colleagues, however, would be expected to come forward with calculated predictions on how the current irregular patterns would evolve and settle into an 'established constancy' (he grinned at the latter term, one that the US National Center for Atmospheric Research had recently come up with). Accurate paradigms devised from extensive scientific research and computer models were necessary if world governments were to prepare their countries for unnatural disasters and Rivers was unsure if his organisation could deliver. Such predictions required evidence and information that had some kind of form, some kind of rule, no matter how complex; unfortunately, no such consistency or principle seemed to exist as far as the weather was concerned. The flutter of a butterfly's wings in Massachusetts might cause a tornado in India. Who would even know that butterfly had taken wing? All that the various working groups could offer was possibilities; and since the climate changes had become so erratic – and often, so violent – over the past few years, even possibilities were based mainly on calculated guesses. The truth was, the world had fucked itself up and nobody – scientists, climatologists, meteorologists, and little old men with seaweed, *nobody* – was able to say just what lay in store for the human race during the next few decades. Nor even the next few weeks.

49

A sharp crack jolted him from his thoughts. Something had struck the car.

He kept driving, aware of the probable cause. Blame the government, he mentally advised the stone-thrower: the present motoring restrictions were the politicians' idea, not his. At least it made the route through the city a little clearer, although a wary eye had to be kept out for the legions of cyclists and the taxi-tandem operators, many of whom seemed reckless beyond sanity. And the air itself was just a bit more acceptable to breathe, which was something to be grateful for.

Rivers headed for the M4 out of London.

The number of worldwide organisations attending the conference hosted by the UK Meteorological Office was considerable, ranging from the Scientific Committee on the Problems of the Environment (SCOPE) of the International Council of Scientific Unions to the Royal and Linnean Society (Evolution and Extinction); from the Intergovernmental Committee of the UN Environmental Programme and the World Meteorological Organisation to the Norwegian Institute of Scientific Research and Enlightenment (NIVFO); from the United Nations' Food and Agricultural Organisation, to the Institute of Terrestrial Economy. Just reading through the attendance list had made Rivers' head pound.

Part of his address to the delegates – no more than five minutes, the whole report – dealt with the merits of the new Cray X-MP Mk IV, inarguably the world's most impressive weather forecasting computer, a twenty per cent improvement on its predecessor. The machine would soon be linked to other compatible computers around the globe, sharing knowledge instantaneously with every member nation of the 1993 World Environment Pact (WEP), and might even persuade those countries who, for reasons of their own (usually commercial), were not party to the agreement to join. The Cray X-MP Mk IV had the capability of identifying weather problems long before they reached crucial stage, and in some cases might even assist in solving those very same problems. This was technology at its most advanced and sophisticated, just one of science's contributions towards the Earth's increasing environmental difficulties. Rivers didn't mention the Massachusetts butterfly.

After lunch, prearranged working groups wandered off to various departments around the building while the main conference continued, some of them adjourning to the Hadley Centre for Climate Predictions and Research building where discussions, arguments – and even insults – went on into the night.

Rivers was among one of the latter groups, and it was not until 11.30 p.m. that he managed to steal away to a quiet office and make the phone call.

3

He shifted his leg, the ache having begun only twenty minutes out of the city. Twice so far he'd stopped the car to walk around, mindful of the physiotherapist's advice to exercise the injured leg as much as possible, to stretch the muscles and tendons, never allowing them the chance to contract and weaken. He'd cursed her to her face for the pain the exercises caused, and then to her memory over the past few months, but had also sent her a bouquet of flowers – an expensive item these days – from time to time in appreciation of her insistence and persistence. In a year's time, she promised, the cane will be gone and a slight limp and the tendency for the left leg to tire easily would be his only reminder of the accident. She hadn't mentioned the physical scars. And he hadn't mentioned the mental scars.

The summer drought had left the countryside wearied; the grasslands were seared brown, the tree leaves were brittle dry. Even the cattle in the fields he passed looked listless and thin. The last decent downpour had been fourteen weeks ago, even though the skies were often cloudy, seeming to threaten rain, but never delivering. Today was clear, the sky pallid, offering no respite from the sun whatsoever.

Passing through a small Dorset town, two hours or so into the journey, a policeman had stepped off the pavement to flag him down so that he could take a closer look at the drive-time sticker on his windscreen. Forgeries were common and the fines for such had recently been increased enough to sting hard. When the officer noticed the Ministry of Defence stamp (the public generally was unaware that the Meteorological Office was an Executive Agency within the MoD) he straightened with a smart salute. Rivers had nodded back gravely, suppressing a grin until he was away again and the policeman was scrutinising other traffic passing through his quiet little town. Because higher road taxes, punitive on high-performance cars and lorries, had had only small effect on fuel consumption and pollution, the government had pushed through a Bill restricting vehicle usage, save for haulage and essential services, to alternate weeks. Blue-licensed vehicles for one seven-day period, orange-licensed for the next. The price of those licences alone (they had to be updated every quarter) was enough to deter the casual driver and together with the extortionate cost of fuel itself, the flow of traffic on Britain's roads eased enormously, and the public transport system at last began to make huge profits. It was a radical approach, but one that worked well enough for other countries – apart from North America, whose civil rights campaigners had easily swayed the Senate vote – to adopt the same system. Ironically, if the policeman who had stopped Rivers' car had not been colour-blind (no longer an obstacle in joining the force) he would have seen that the climatologist's windscreen was sporting a *green* sticker, which allowed him access to the roads at any time.

Another forty minutes of driving and he was nearing his

destination. Rivers pulled over into a farm track by the side of a quiet lane, this time to consult the guide Poggs had given him – 'Easy to get lost in our neck of the woods,' he'd told the climatologist over the phone. As Rivers picked up the piece of paper with the directions from the passenger seat, he realised that the daylight had dimmed considerably. Glancing out the side window towards the sun, he saw dark clouds filling half the sky, a tremendous, dramatic mass that, had they not looked so ominous, might have made him smile with relief at the thought of the rain they carried.

Instead he frowned, wondering where the hell they had arrived from. No storm weather had been forecast as far as he knew.

Rivers reached for the carphone and pressed a digit. He watched the lumbering clouds in the distance while waiting for the number to dial then ring.

'G23,' he said when it was answered. 'Jonesy? It's Jim.'

'Don't you know it's Sunday? You get to rest, remember? No, we don't know how it got here, if it's that bloody great cloud bank you rang about. I've been on to Central *and* Observations, even gave Short-range a shot. None of them had a clue it was on the way until it showed up on the satellite a little while ago.'

'It had to start some place, and it had to have had time to build like that. It's hard to believe we're in a drought and nobody noticed this looming up. No wonder the public's lost all faith.'

'Yeah, yeah, I know, but that's not our department, is it? All they can tell us is that turbulence off the south coast is the cause.'

'God knows we need some rain, but this doesn't look friendly.'

'Stay inside is my advice. When it breaks – and it's got to soon – an umbrella won't do you much good.'

'I'm already out.'

'Then good luck. At least the gardeners will be happy, not to mention the farmers. I suppose we all should.'

'Depends on the damage it does. Like I said, it looks mean.'

There was a short silence. 'Let's be optimistic,' Jonesy said.

'Right. Listen, a full report tomorrow. I want to know where it started and the precise volume of rainfall when it's over. Also a record of the PPI and RHI changes as it travels.'

'I thought you were on leave this week.'

'Get it to my address.'

'Done. Now get under cover and enjoy the rest of your day. At least the conference is finished and the Met Office won't be fielding awkward questions from our overseas friends. A mother of a storm on its way after one of the longest droughts in the UK's history, and nobody forecast it. It's almost as embarrassing as the '87 hurricane.'

When Rivers replaced the receiver he looked back at the approaching storm clouds. Now he could see the movement in them, the swirling vapour, the leaden darkness massing at their base. He stepped outside the car to feel the atmosphere. It was unpleasantly muggy, the kind of heavy heat that needed a shower to dispel it. Well, more than a shower was on its way, perhaps a deluge that would bludgeon the very earth. Rivers was only too aware of what was happening to the rest of the world.

He got back into the Renault, checked the directions once more, and went on his way.

It hit like a force from hell.

One moment the skies were sullen with threat, the next they had spewed their wrath. The rain came with such violence that his car's windows were instantly flooded. Rivers stabbed the brake, too hard, too fast, and the car slewed across the lane in a screeching skid. He felt the front wing jolt, but barely heard the crunch over the downpour. His upper body lurched forward when the car dipped and came to an abrupt halt, the seat-belt biting into his stomach and chest, but mercifully locking him there, keeping him from the glass in front. Pain shot up his injured leg and he gasped and clutched his kneecap. He had stamped his foot reflexively, holding himself rigid before the impact.

'Oh, shit,' he muttered, thumping the steering wheel with his other hand. The pain was like fire, spreading both ways, up to his groin and down to his ankle. Fire . . . He scrabbled for the seat-belt buckle, his fingers clumsy, too hasty. He couldn't feel the release, his fingers were numb, his arm . . . his arm was burning . . .

Rain drummed on the metal over his head, lashing against the windows, a grey, running sheet.

'*Christ!*' he shouted, then mentally told himself: *You're not in the plane, you're not going down! Take it easy, there's no danger.* His forehead was damp with perspiration as he fumbled with the release button.

At last the belt unclipped and slid back just as a fresh wave of pain made him cry out. Now he clutched his leg with both hands. *Going down, going down, going down . . .*

Rivers was aware of where he was, that there was no danger, the car wasn't badly damaged; but the dead body of Gardenia was crashing around the cabin, eyes rolling in its head and mouth grinning crazily, a corpse mocking the living because it knew what was coming, what was next, what it was like to die . . . Rivers knew where he was, what had happened, yet his throat still tightened to scream.

But the door pulled away from him before the sound came and a hooded figure was peering in, the face beneath the hood drawn with concern. His senses fluttered and the interior seemed to spin.

'Are you all right?' the woman said.

The car became still again. His senses quietened. But his body would not stop trembling.

'Your leg. Have you hurt it?' Her voice was raised so that it could be heard over the beating rain.

He stared at her uncomprehendingly. Water dripped from the plastic cape she wore as she stretched across him to see if there was any damage.

She turned to him, their faces close, her body protecting him from the pelting rain outside. Even though her face was in shadow, he saw that her features were soft, and even though her eyes appeared black in the dimness, he could tell that they were gentle.

'I can't see anything wrong,' she said. 'Can you try and move your leg?'

He wanted to explain, but his words were mumbled. He grimaced and tried again. 'It's okay. I took a knock to an old injury.'

She smiled and he blinked at her. He could smell the rain, its freshness, on her and somehow her presence subdued the nightmare.

'Do you think you can move?' she asked.

'Uh? Oh – yeah, I can move. It's whether the car can.'

'It'll be stuck for a while, I'm afraid. You ran into a shallow ditch.' He noticed she had a soft American accent. 'That was a spectacular skid, by the way. Luckily you just managed to scrape by a tree, although your right wing is going to need a little straightening.'

'You saw it happen?'

'Ringside seat. It was wonderful, but I won't ask you to show me it again.' She patted his shoulder. 'Come on now, let's get you to the house.'

'I didn't know I was near any houses.'

'You're not – not that near, anyhow. I'm afraid you're in for a hike. Think you can make it?'

He looked over to the passenger side. 'I'll need this.'

Rivers reached for the cane, which had slid over to lean against the opposite door. 'I'll manage,' he snapped brusquely when the woman took his elbow to help him from the car.

She stepped back, but her face showed no surprise or resentment when he stood. In fact she gave him a small smile and her words were friendly. 'You're going to get mighty wet,' she told him.

He already was. The rain had soaked him the moment he'd left the car. He looked upwards, eyes blinking against the torrent, and saw only a vast greyness above, with no breaks at all. Unexpectedly, the rain was almost tropical in its warmth.

He slammed the car door shut and turned back to her. 'How far?' he asked.

'Far enough for you to need assistance in these conditions,' she replied. 'The track's going to be pretty squishy by now.'

'Let's see how I get on.'

'At least lean on my shoulder, okay?' The rain bounced with force off her bright yellow cape and she had pulled the hood forward so that much of her face was in shadow again.

'I'd better take a quick look at the damage first.'

'No need. It's minimal, only a scrape, a little dent. Got your keys?'

He nodded.

'Then hang on.'

He did so, and although her shoulder was small beneath his hand, it was firm enough.

The track was more than 'squishy'; it had already become a quagmire. Ironically, it was the woman who slipped first and he grabbed her arm to hold her steady. She twisted helplessly and he found both his arms around her, her body close against his own. It was a strangely intimate moment, brief yet potent.

'You were supposed to be helping me,' he said.

She appeared flustered and moved away, her face lowered

58

so that he could no longer look into her eyes. 'Sorry,' he thought he heard her say over the noise.

They went on, awkwardly, now both clinging to each other for support, the rain lashing their bowed bodies, increasing in intensity rather than diminishing. The drops were like thousands of tiny water bombs flailing their heads and shoulders, exploding as they struck, weighing them down with their force. The water was cooler, but only slightly so, and vapour rose from the ooze beneath their feet as well as from the foliage on either side of the track. Again the thought of a tropical downpour crossed Rivers' mind.

The pain in his leg increased as they continued their awkward journey. Then he fell, going to his knees, dragging the woman down with him. He slipped again as he tried to rise, once more pulling her down. She rolled on to her side, the cowl falling back from her face, her dark shoulder-length hair immediately bedraggled. To his surprise, she was laughing.

'I haven't . . .' she panted '. . . I haven't had so much fun . . . so much fun in a long time.'

He wiped the dampness from his own face, which provoked more laughter from her. Rivers looked at his hand and realised he had just smeared mud over himself.

'It's okay,' she said, struggling to get up. 'Your mud-pack's already being washed away.' She gave a whoop when she slipped again.

The climatologist stooped and picked up the cane that was sinking into the mire. He dug the end deep into the soil and levered himself upright, grateful that the earth beneath the soaked top layer was still firm. He reached for the woman. 'Take it nice and steady. Dig one foot in and put all your weight on it.'

She did as instructed and joined him, apparently still happy. Her hair was flat around her face and her eyes sparkled with inner humour. He could not help but smile back. 'Shall we try again?' she suggested.

'How much further?'

'A ways yet. Think you can make it?'

'I don't intend to stay here.'

'Let's lean.' This time she put her arm around his waist and tucked her shoulder into his. His own free hand went round to her other shoulder.

As they trudged onwards, embankments rose up on either side of the track, while trees formed a rough canopy over their heads. Even so, the rain tore through the branches, its impact lessened only slightly. Tiny rivers were running down the steep slopes, taking clods of sodden earth with them in miniature landslides and leaves, twigs, even small branches were dropping from the flimsy covering overhead.

'What is this?' she shouted over the downpour. 'I know the weather's become freaky, but rain like this? It's impossible.'

'Keep telling yourself that – maybe we'll get to your home quicker.'

She tugged the hood to one side so she could look at him. 'Do I get the feeling you're not enjoying this as much as I am?'

He skidded, but kept his feet this time. 'I'm smiling, aren't I?'

'As a matter of fact, you're not. It's more like a grimace. Is your leg hurting bad?'

'Yeah, it's hurting bad. But I'll manage.'

He swore under his breath as another slip kindled fresh fire in his knee joint.

Rain lashed them with renewed strength as they emerged from the trees' cover, forcing them to bend against it, each step seeming to take a greater effort.

'This ground was rock solid only a little while ago,' she shouted close to his ear.

'The rain's getting into the cracks and undermining the topsoil. It'll sink a lot deeper if this goes on much longer.' Suddenly there was pain so intense that it brought him to a jerky halt. He gasped, his head raised to the skies, his teeth clenched.

'Let's find some shelter and rest,' she said hurriedly, her eyes filled with concern.

'Shelter?' He looked around.

'The trees are thicker away from the track. They'll give us enough cover, I'm sure.'

Rivers knew he would never reach the house in this condition; even when his injury wasn't screeching pain, it was throbbing it. The car was a long way behind them now, perhaps even as far as the house was ahead. At least if they found some shelter he'd be able to swallow a couple of painkillers. 'Just show me where,' he said breathlessly.

'We have to get up there.' She pointed towards the embankment. 'Can you climb?'

Shit, he thought. 'I'll give it a try,' he said.

They lurched over to the rise on their right side, making for a dip, a gulley where rainwater washed down.

'You first,' she called. 'I'll support you from behind, then you can pull me up.'

Rivers wasn't keen on the idea of this attractive Samaritan pushing his butt, but agreed it made sense. He reached for the top of the embankment, while thrusting his cane into the soft earth of the gulley. The ascent wasn't easy, but with a lot of effort and a lot of pushing, he made it to the top. Once there, he knelt on his good leg and extended the cane down towards his helper.

She grasped the end and her eyes searched for something else to grip with her other hand. It gave him another brief chance to study her upturned face, to take in the paleness of her skin, the cleanly defined lines of her lips, and again, the softness of those eyes. Rivers wondered at himself.

He pulled hard as she began to climb, drawing her steadily towards him as she dug deep into the flowing mud with toecaps and her other hand. She had almost reached the top,

Rivers using his free hand beneath her shoulder, when the loosened earth he was perched on crumbled away, throwing him forward so that he cannoned into her, sending them both slithering down the short slope into the quagmire below.

The woman gave a little scream as they tumbled, not one of fear but of surprise, and when they landed, Rivers half over her lap with his face in the mud and she herself sprawled flat, she uttered a curse that was directed at the heavens rather than their own ineptitude.

Rivers lifted himself from the mire and when she saw his face, her anxiety turned into a grin.

He, on the other hand, failed to see the humour in the situation at all, and was about to remark on that very fact when lights approached through the thick blanket of rain.

The vehicle moved smoothly and at a steady speed along the track's slithery surface, tyres occasionally sinking where they travelled through flooded ruts and dips, the engine quiet under the sound of the rainfall. Its bonnet joined the windscreen almost seamlessly, forming an aerodynamic wedge from bumper to roof, and with the all-around windows and dark green bodywork glistening sleekly in the wet, its bullet shape and furiously glaring headlights, it gave the appearance of an advancing beast rather than an automobile.

It stopped beside the sprawled couple and the driver's window lowered slowly.

The friendly, wrinkled face that looked down at them instantly dispelled any sinister illusions Rivers might have had. The voice was familiar when the man spoke.

'Can I offer you a lift, Mr Rivers, or are you having too much fun down there with my daughter?'

4

'Welcome to Hazelrod.'

Hugo Poggs glanced over his shoulder at Rivers, who was beside his yellow-caped 'rescuer' in the eight-seater Toyota Previa. The woman next to Poggs turned in her seat to look directly at Rivers. Her face was round, plump rather than fat, and her greying hair was pulled back into a girlish braided ponytail. Her pale blue eyes regarded him with some amusement. 'I had no idea climatologists brought their own weather with them.'

This aroused a low, throaty chuckle from Poggs as he guided the vehicle from the rutted track into a broad, cobblestoned courtyard where wood and brick outbuildings and an old stable block were overlooked by a large and much deteriorated Georgian house. A short, burly man in a green oilskin coat and Australian ranger's hat waved at them as he dashed across the yard towards one of the sheds carrying a metal bucket.

'Feeding time,' Poggs remarked as he drew the Toyota to

a halt as close to the three front steps of the house as possible. He switched off the engine and leaned a stout arm over the back of the seat to appraise Rivers. His cheeks were ruddied by tiny veins and his chin sunk almost completely into the flesh beneath it. He was a heavy man and when he spoke he had a habit – or perhaps it was a necessity – of taking a short breath first. 'I suggest we get you cleaned up and into some dry things before we make the introductions.'

The pain in Rivers' leg had subsided a little, but he relished the idea of painkillers and a quick, hot shower. He regretted having left the pulser back at home, but then he hadn't thought it necessary for the journey; besides, plugging in was a practice he was trying to ease out of. He climbed out into the rain.

The downpour had weakened, but it still bounced off the cobblestones and the roof of the Previa with considerable force. Poggs' daughter scrambled out to join him, and he briefly wondered if he had mistaken her accent over the noise of the storm, for Poggs himself appeared to be the quintessential English gentleman, down to his tweed trousers, check Viyella shirt and woollen tie (no doubt the matching tweed jacket with leather elbow patches had been discarded in consideration of the heatwave) and the deep rich tones of his breathless voice. He wanted to thank her for her help, but she turned away as a child of about eight leapt out from the backseat and buried herself under her cape. He hadn't had time to notice the little girl before, and now he saw there was another child, this one a boy in T-shirt and shorts, clambering out the other side to be gathered up by the ponytailed woman and hurried around to the steps of the house. They disappeared through large porch doors with whoops of feigned panic.

'Let's you and I follow at a more dignified pace,' suggested Poggs as he eased his portly figure from the vehicle.

'I think I left my dignity back there in the mud,' Rivers replied.

Together they headed up the steps, Rivers limping badly, Poggs seemingly impervious to the rain. Passing through the windowed porch where a rusting doll's pram and two child's bicycles competed with wellington boots and a stack of dried-out fire logs for space, the climatologist found himself inside a spacious high-ceilinged hallway where a broad staircase led up to a first-floor balcony. There were open doorways on both sides of the hallway and through the nearest he glimpsed a large room, whose every inch seemed crammed with furniture and ornaments. Between sofas and armchairs lay scattered floor cushions, and in one corner he could see a tall fig plant. He looked around the hall for Poggs' daughter, but there was no sign of her. The two children, both around the same age and strikingly similar, were astride an old, paint-chipped rocking horse just by the inside front door. They had the blackest hair he had ever seen, almost gypsy-like with its twisted curls and depth; yet their skin was fair and their eyes a startling shade of blue. They rocked to and fro in perfect unison and with a quiet intensity, taking no notice whatsoever of the stranger in their midst.

'Let's have you out of those wet things, Mr Rivers.' The plump woman with the braided hair had appeared from a doorway on his left and was advancing on him carrying a large white towel. To his relief she dropped it over the heads of the two children and began to rub vigorously, ignoring their squealed protests.

'I think it would be wise,' Poggs agreed. He pointed a pudgy finger upwards. 'Bathroom's third door along the landing. Shower's not the fiercest in the world, but it'll get rid of the muck. Leave your clothes outside the door and we'll supply you with some fresh ones.'

'No, look, I'll be okay . . .'

'Nonsense,' interjected the woman in a tone that brooked

65

no dissension. 'Up you go and we'll see you in a little while. Plenty of time to talk later.' She continued to towel the squirming children.

'My car . . .'

'No one will run off with it,' assured Poggs. 'If you let me have the keys I'll have it brought up here. We'll soon get it out of the ditch once the rain stops.'

There was no point in arguing, not that Rivers felt inclined to: he felt dirty and uncomfortable, and he had to do something about the pain. 'It's kind of you,' he said.

Poggs shook his head and unexpectedly his demeanour seemed weary. 'It's entirely selfishness on our part.' He held up a hand to stay the question Rivers was about to ask. 'When you're in better shape, Mr Rivers. If you don't mind my saying so, you look like something the cat dragged in and was in two minds whether to chuck out again.' He chortled at his own remark, while the woman gave him a scolding glare.

Rivers climbed the stairs and on the turn he looked down to find the family watching him. Even the two children, whose eyes were so vividly blue they seemed blurred from that distance, were gazing up at him from the rocking horse. The adults quickly looked away and became active, the woman lifting the boy and girl in turn from the horse, Poggs wandering off into one of the side rooms. Puzzled, not just by their attention, but as to why he had been invited here in the first place, the climatologist made his way to the landing, then counted the doors until he reached the bathroom. Even more puzzling was why he had accepted the invitation.

Rain squalls beat against the bathroom's tiny window as he closed the door behind him. There was no key in the lock and no catch, but Rivers was too tired and uncomfortable to care. He took out a small container of dihydrocodeine from his damp jacket pocket and went to the sink. He swallowed three with water from the tap, hoping the house had an effec-

66

tive purifier in its tank, then shed his clothes and ran the shower until it was lukewarm. He stepped in and closed his eyes, his face held up towards the jets.

As he soaped his body, the flowing warmth, together with the tablets, began to ease the pain, and it was with some reluctance that minutes later he turned off the shower and grabbed a towel from a rail by the bath.

Perhaps it was because of the rain drumming on the window that he didn't hear her knock; he was only aware of her presence when she spoke.

'You didn't leave your clothes outside.'

He had been drying his face, the long towel covering most of his body, and he froze in surprise. She was leaning round the partially opened door, a bundle of fresh clothes held on one arm.

'These should fit you,' she said with a pleasant, unembarrassed smile.

Her gaze shifted to his scarred leg and he saw her flinch before quickly looking away. He moved the towel so that the injury was out of sight. 'Can I take them?' she asked.

'Take them?'

'Your wet clothes.'

'Oh.' He nodded towards the bathroom stool where they were draped.

She offered the clothes she was holding, then realised his awkwardness. There was amusement once more in those soft brown eyes. 'Sorry. You get used to immodesty around here, especially with the summer heat. Let me swap these for those.' She picked up the sodden clothes and left the dry ones on the stool. 'My name's Diane, by the way. I'm glad I saw the storm coming and decided to stroll down the track to look for you. It's so easy to pass by. If I'd known you were going to dump your car I'd have brought along another raincoat.'

'So it wasn't by chance.'

67

'We've been waiting for you all morning, Mr Rivers. Poggsy took the tribe off to church and left me to keep an eye out for you.'

'Poggsy?'

'Hugo, my father-in-law.' She wondered why he made a small sound of understanding, but went on. 'Poggs is such a silly name, we decided to make it sillier. He pretends not to, but I think he enjoys it.' She stopped halfway out the door. 'Come down when you're ready. You look as if a stiff drink will do you the world of good, and knowing Poggsy, he'll be only too ready to join you.'

He stopped her as she was about to go. 'Do you know why I'm here?'

Her soft brown eyes fixed on his. 'I do. And I just hope you can help.'

'Help? I don't understand.'

'That's the problem. None of us understands. But you might be the link that enables us to.'

As she closed the door a sudden fiercer gust of wind and rain shook the window behind him.

5

The rain had ceased by the time he left the bathroom and the hall below was filled with sunlight, the glow from the polished wood floor almost dazzling. Rivers narrowed his eyes against it as he descended.

He felt a lot better, his body freshened, the pain in his leg under control. The loose corduroy trousers and twill shirt he wore were comfortable, the shoes only one size too large; he wondered who they belonged to. Halfway down he noticed one of the children was astride the rocking horse again and watching his descent.

It was the girl, the top of her dark hair blazed red by the sun through the porch windows, and even though her small face was in shadow, the extraordinary blueness of her eyes was still evident. 'Hello,' he called softly, smiling to show he was friendly enough.

Without a word the girl slid from the horse and skipped into the room Rivers had caught a glimpse of earlier. There were voices coming from there, so he made towards it.

Hugo Poggs was in one of the bulky but comfortable-looking armchairs, while the woman with the braided plait, whom by now Rivers assumed to be Poggs' wife, occupied a corner of the sofa with the little girl's brother snuggled up close to her. Diane sat in a stiff-backed chair with the black-haired girl settled at her feet. He guessed the burly man eyeing him suspiciously from a window seat behind the others was the one in the oilskin who had dashed across the yard when they had driven in. He was a thick-set, strong-looking individual, with a girth that threatened his shirt buttons. Rivers nodded at them all from the doorway.

'Ah, feeling better?' Poggs enquired cheerfully.

'A lot better. You've been very kind.'

'Nonsense. It's you who have been kind, making this long journey to see us on the strength of a phone call. Please come in and join us – we've saved a comfortable chair for you.' He indicated an empty armchair facing his own. As Rivers stepped over cushions to reach it, Poggs took out a pipe and tapped the contents of its bowl into an ashtray.

The boy lifted his head from the ample bosom it rested against. 'Grandad . . .'

Poggs scowled without rancour. 'Forgot,' he mumbled, slipping the pipe back into his breast pocket. He brightened. 'Sun's well over the yard-arm, Mr Rivers, so how about a little something to fire your inners, torment your liver? Or as an alternative, you might try some of Mack's home brew. I can't be responsible for what *that* might do to your liver though. Send it into catatonic shock, I shouldn't wonder.'

The man by the window grinned broadly, refusing to rise to the bait; he gave the impression of having heard the jibe many times before.

'A whisky would suit me fine,' said Rivers, reaching the armchair.

Poggs approved heartily. 'Good man! I have an excellent

brand.' He struggled to the edge of his chair and for a moment it looked like the effort might defeat him.

'Stay where you are, Poggsy, we don't want you busting something.' Diane was already heading for the sideboard at the other end of the room on which there was a silver tray filled with liquor bottles. The girl trailed after her, glancing round once on the way, presumably to make sure Rivers wasn't following.

Poggs grunted appreciatively, winking at the climatologist as he settled back again. 'The Macallan, Diane. In honour of our guest.'

The room was light and airy, with two floor-to-ceiling-length windows on one side, and another to his left overlooking the cobblestone yard. With the sun shining through and sitting among this family of friendly people, Rivers wondered at his own disquiet. After the sinister phone call, he had at least expected a serious, perhaps even traumatic, meeting with this man Poggs, with himself as the interrogator. Now he had been thrown off course completely, the advantage all the other man's.

'We need to talk,' he said to Poggs. 'Alone.'

'Of course. But I want you to know us first.' Poggs fixed Rivers steadily with his somewhat rheumy eyes. 'I want to reassure you that we are all fairly normal.'

Rivers shifted uncomfortably in his seat. 'I . . .' He cleared his throat and started again. 'I don't have too much time. I'll have to get back soon.'

'After you've travelled so far?' It was Poggs' wife who spoke. 'Surely not? Be a little patient with us, Mr Rivers; you'll find it worth while, I promise.'

'This isn't quite what I expected.'

Poggs laughed at that; but he was the only one to do so. 'I'm sure it isn't, my friend, and I'm sure I'm going about this in utterly the wrong way. However, I wonder how far your investigations into these freak weather conditions have progressed? Have you discovered any pattern, any conformity? Has the Met Office with its satellite observation capability and weather stations, with its COSMOS computing complex and worldwide climatological database, has it made any headway at all in discovering the real cause of our present extreme climate changes and the chaos they've brought about?' He leaned forward a little in his seat and, had his chin not been undermined by the flesh beneath it, it would have been jutting. 'After all, global warming cannot be blamed for everything, can it? So what theory has your own working group come up with, Mr Rivers? Do you have any answers at all?'

Diane stood in front of the climatologist, a tumbler of whisky held towards him. 'We're all very concerned,' she said, as if apologising for Poggs' forthrightness. 'So much is happening so fast.'

He took the drink. 'You're not alone in being worried. But I think I should tell you right here and now that I can't give you any information.'

'I know you're bound by the Official Secrets Act, but any help will be mutual. You might find we have more to give you than you us,' said Poggs.

After taking the second whisky over to Poggs, Diane perched on the arm of his chair. The little girl went round to the back of the armchair and leaned on it, her head resting on top of her joined hands. She continued to watch Rivers gravely.

Poggs raised his glass and said, '*Slainthe.*'

Distractedly, Rivers replied, '*Slainthero.*'

The gesture seemed to please the other man. He sipped the malt Scotch with relish. 'Initially, I'd like to discuss your experience before the American research aircraft crashed.'

Rivers stiffened. 'I'm sure you followed the news reports and the various newspaper "insights" afterwards. Didn't they tell you all you need to know?'

'Superficially, yes. The accident certainly attracted a great deal of media coverage.'

'Air crashes do. But that's not why I came here. I'm here to find out what *you* know about Tinkerbell.'

'All in good time,' said Poggs in an irritatingly benign manner. The girl leaned forward and whispered something in his ear. He patted her cheek, then returned his attention to Rivers. 'Our little dryad tells me you're afraid of us.'

Rivers almost choked on the whisky. 'Is there any reason I should be?'

'None at all, although it's only natural that you should be suspicious. After all, you must wonder at our motives. Perhaps that's what gives you fear, and that's something I wish to allay. In most ways, Mr Rivers, we're a very normal family.'

'And in others?'

'Hmn?'

'You said in most ways you're a normal family.'

Poggs chuckled. 'May I call you James?'

'No.'

'Ah.'

Rivers finished the Scotch and felt better for it. In this he agreed with his host: whisky was better with its challenge mildly subdued. He balanced the glass tumbler on the arm of his chair, fingers arched over its rim.

'Another for our visitor, if you will, Diane.'

Before she could rise, Rivers shook his head. 'Thank you, but no.' A small numbness had set in the centre of his forehead, perhaps as a result of combining pills with alcohol. 'Either we talk privately, or I leave now.'

Poggs drew a wheezy breath. 'Oh dear, this is not going the way I planned.'

The plump woman leaned across and squeezed his hand. 'Tact was never one of your strong points, Hugo, and I don't quite understand why you're making such an effort this time. With the way things are in the world today, and given his

73

profession, I'm sure our visitor is a very busy man.' She turned to the climatologist, a no-nonsense expression on her face. 'Firstly though, if only for the sake of good manners, it's time we introduced ourselves to you. *Then* you and my husband can get on with the business at hand.'

'There's no need.' He hoped his own expression conveyed impatience to leave.

'No, there's no need, but as your car is presently stuck nose-first in a ditch, there is time. Now, I'm Barbara Poggs, and as they've nicknamed Hugo Poggsy, I have to suffer Bibby. You can blame that on our grandchildren.' She tapped the boy's head and he grinned up at her. 'Diane you've already met, and sitting by the window over there is Mack – that *is* his name, not an abbreviation – and without him to help us with our livestock and market garden – we're self-sufficient here, Mr Rivers – we'd be lost. He's also very good at fixing things, from electric irons to barn roofs and he lives in an apartment above the old stables opposite. You'll have noticed he's a very quiet man.'

She ruffled the boy's hair and gestured the girl to come over to her. She did so without hesitation, snuggling up tight and reaching round to touch her brother's arm.

'The children are our little wood nymphs – dryads, you heard Hugo call them – this one is Eva and this one is Josh, although in the great tradition of nicknames, Eva insists on being called Minnie. Heaven knows why, but I suspect a certain cartoon mouse has something to do with it. Fortunately, Josh is quite happy with Josh.'

She huffed a breath of relief. 'There, done. And now, to break a habit of – oh, a day or so – I shall have something strong too. Diane, a more than average-sized gin and tonic, if you please, and why not join us yourself, dear? I'm sure with the lashing you took in that dreadful storm you're ready for a reviver.'

Diane rose from the arm of the chair. 'Thank God you took

74

control – Poggsy was making an awful hash of things.' She weaved her slim figure through the furniture to the sideboard again. 'How about you, Mack? Want to forgo your home brew for once and try something civilised?'

Mack shook his head, his attention averted from Rivers for only a moment. The climatologist was puzzled by the man's attention.

Bibby gently pushed the two children from her. 'You two go off and play now. Put on your galoshes if you go outside – it'll be very wet and muddy out there.'

It had been a long time since he had heard the word 'galoshes' and somehow the word relaxed Rivers a little. It was hard to imagine anything sinister about anyone who would use such a bygone term. Or maybe the malt Scotch and the pills were mellowing as well as numbing his brain.

'If you'll give Mack your car keys he'll haul it out of the ditch with a towrope,' she went on. 'As for me, I shall take my g-and-t into the kitchen and prepare lunch. I'd *like* you to stay for lunch, Mr Rivers, but the decision is yours.' She rose to take her drink from her daughter-in-law. 'If you believe nothing else, please believe that we are not your enemies.' With that she strode to the door, followed by her small troupe of children and handyman.

Her last words had startled Rivers. Enemies? Why should they be? Why should they suppose he thought they were? Unease stirred again.

'Are you sure you won't have that refill?'

He looked up at Diane, who had brought the Macallan over. There was amusement in her eyes, but it was not mocking. 'Not such a bad idea,' he said, handing her the glass.

She poured, then left the whisky bottle beside her father-in-law.

Poggs took a wheezy breath. 'I suppose there's no gentle way of leading you into this,' he said to Rivers. 'Perhaps that was my mistake in the first place. I really only wanted you to feel comfortable with us, but it seems I've achieved the opposite. If I may, I'd like to take you next door to my study. Perhaps there I can begin to explain why it was so important that we meet.'

Rivers sipped the Scotch, looking thoughtfully at the other man. Again he tried to remember where he had heard Poggs' name before, but infuriatingly, it wouldn't come to him. 'Okay,' he agreed, rising from the chair. 'Since I've come all this way, and since I'm more than a little intrigued, I'm willing to hear you out.'

Poggs rose too, an odd mixture of relief and anxiety on his face. 'Please bring your drink through,' he said, leading the climatologist to the door. 'I've a feeling you might need it.'

6

Diane followed them along the hall, and past the stairway; as they stopped outside a closed door and Poggs fumbled in his pockets for a key, she gave Rivers a fleeting smile, perhaps of encouragement.

'I didn't get a chance to thank you properly,' he said.

'Like I said at the time, it was fun,' she replied. 'I wouldn't really want to do it again though.'

Poggs opened the door and went through, but Rivers lingered a moment. 'Are you part of this?' he said to the woman.

'I'm sorry?'

'Part of this game Poggs is playing. This petty mystery.'

Her jawline hardened. 'Oh, it's no game, I can assure you of that. But it is a mystery.' She pushed by him and entered.

He hesitated before going through himself.

The room, like the sitting room they had just left, was light and airy, but this one was untidy with books, papers, stacked journals, and files. A long trestle table stood near its centre, barely a square centimetre of its surface clear of paper debris, while on a corner desk stood a word processor and fax machine. A sizeable beaten-leather chair was positioned at the trestle table, its back to a high French window, outside of which were sun-scorched lawns and vegetable patches. Shelves stocked with files and reference books filled two walls, while a third was covered in cork squares that served as a floor-to-ceiling notice board. This was almost entirely overlaid with press cuttings, clipped magazine articles and typed sheets of paper. Some of the cuttings were marked with red felt-tip. By the window on the fourth wall was a large map of the world, which was studded with coloured pins.

Poggs was waving a hand at the paper-littered cork wall. 'Take time to look through these if you will, Mr Rivers. You needn't study them – I'm sure you're more than familiar with most of the reports and articles. I feel it might be useful if you, uh, digest them *en masse*, as it were, perhaps gain a global perspective.'

Rivers turned quizzically to Diane. 'Please,' she said.

By now it wasn't a question of humouring the old boy – Rivers was genuinely curious – but something deep inside him was reluctant to get involved. Apart from the fact that these people were complete strangers to him, his own professional code of conduct could allow no collusion with them. Was Poggs aware of that? Did he realise that Rivers was a member of one of the British working groups specifically set up to investigate the climate phenomena of the past decade? Maybe not, otherwise he wouldn't be suggesting these cuttings might provide a 'global perspective' – he'd know he already had such a view. Still, a quick revision, courtesy of Hugo Poggs, wouldn't do any harm. Placing his glass on a corner of the trestle table, he walked over to the wall-size press collage.

Every report concerned environmental or climatic disasters of some kind or other, from floods in Bangladesh to drought in America's Midwest. He read the headlines mostly, occasionally glancing at photographs and their captions, or skipping through a paragraph or two included in a typed account. There were stories of hailstones and chronic frosts in southern Australia that destroyed the continent's finest vineyards, starvation in the Horn of Africa, devastating hurricanes in the Caribbean, the Pacific Basin, and even in England. There were earthquakes in Armenia, San Francisco, Italy, Japan and more recently the second great Alaskan earthquake, this one having flattened the city of Anchorage and its neighbours Portage and Whittier.

Two volcanic eruptions were clipped together: the first was the massive explosion of a broken fissure in Heimaey, a member of the group of small islands just off the coast of Iceland, which had exceeded the damage a similar eruption had caused in 1973 by obliterating the port town completely and turning the harbour into a solid mass of frozen lava; the second was the eruption of Mount Merapi in densely populated central Java, its disgorged superheated gases and ash descending on villages for miles around. Beside these there was a smaller report of an undersea eruption on the Great Barrier Reef off Australia's north-east coastline, a baffling catastrophe that had killed 128 tourists and holidaymakers.

He skimmed through a lengthy typewritten study on Poland's industrial pollution problem, where in Upper Silesia acid snow had ruined streams and rendered pine forests into slopes and valleys of blackened skeletal stumps, where immense poisonous clouds had formed over towns such as Zabrze, Chorzow, Katowice, to drift and join, staining the very air with their effluent filth – sulphur dioxide, bituminous substances, lead, zinc, magnesium, an endless list of destructive emissions – corrupting the atmosphere, inflicting diseases, turning cities like Krakow into ecological disaster zones. The land itself was spoilt, its waters made toxic. Even though the facts were familiar to him, Rivers could not prevent his anger rising.

Next to this was a feature cut from a magazine, its grim colour photographs a testament in themselves to the folly of the human greed or perhaps desperation, which had turned the Aral Basin, the once fertile heartland of what had been the Central Asian republics of the USSR, into one vast waste, where a whole sea had vanished, where the soil was so full of salt that nothing would grow on it, where the air itself degenerated everything it touched, from human tissue to buildings, where mothers' milk was too poisonous for their infants to drink, where physical deformity and mental retardation were commonplace.

Rivers moved on to the next yellowed news item, no longer conscious of Poggs and Diane, who waited patiently, allowing him to read without interruption. Diane eventually moved to the tall window and stared out at the dampened lawns and hedges. Steam was rising, creating a low grey mist, as the sun warmed the earth once more.

The climatologist read of the deadly morbilli virus that had spread throughout the Mediterranean and even to the coastal shores of England, attacking the brain and nervous systems of the seal and dolphin, so that their corpses drifted in packs on the seas finally to be washed up on to the beaches and rocks. Scientific opinion differed on whether manmade pollution had caused the sickness or had merely weakened the creatures' immune systems to such an extent that they were susceptible to it. One thing *was* certain, however: the warming of the seas and oceans had enabled the epidemic to spread more easily. Species like the blue whale, the right whale, and the humpback were now down to between one and two per cent of their previous population despite the grave warnings of conservationists in the late '80s, and all sea mammals and sea birds, even those in Arctic and Antarctic regions where men rarely set foot, had accumulated large doses of pesticides, mercury and other polluting elements in their systems.

He came upon a relatively small item concerning the mass suicide of thousands of penguins at the beginning of the decade. A report next to this dealt with the relocation of endangered species such as the elephant, hippopotamus, rhinoceros, giraffe, to new game parks in the more favourable climes of Spain, Italy, southern France and North America.

His anger was fading to a bitter kind of depression as he read on. The warnings had been there for years, but few governments, if any at all, had listened. Eventually they had been forced to take heed because of the increasing disasters and adversities that had befallen virtually every continent and country, and even then they listened only grudgingly.

Of the twenty-five million square kilometres of tropical rain forests that had once covered the planet's land surface, there was now little more than eight million left, despite the United Nations' Deforestation Limitation Agreement of 1995. Another resolution universally agreed upon and actioned by separate governments was the inclusion of catalytic converters into every automobile engine produced during and after 1993; the manufacture of low-petrol-consumption cars was also encouraged by special tax concessions, and grants were awarded for further research into the *still* unpopular battery-powered automobile (the latter pleased the fancons – the fanatical conservationists – only moderately, for they claimed pollution caused by nuclear and fossil-fuel power plants in the making of batteries to run these vehicles more than negated the benefit derived from them). However, the introduction in the UK of punitive tax registration fees on existing and newly produced high-performance automobiles, together with the Alternate Week Road-Use Act, 1996, caused minor riots and protest marches throughout the cities during the first few weeks of its enforcement. Now there was also a 'carbon' tax on fossil fuel use, plus a ninety per cent grant scheme for the installation of solar panels on private dwellings, fifty per cent on business premises, and a twenty-five per cent grant on wall and roof insulation for older buildings, domestic or commercial. The phasing out of chlorofluorocarbons was proceeding steadily, as was the reduction of carbon monoxide and nitrogen oxide emissions from power stations and factories, while conventional coal-burning power stations were being fitted with low nitrogen oxide burners. But it was all small fare against the immense damage already caused to the planet and its atmosphere since the beginning of the industrial age, and, even so, not every country was in full accord as to the extent of that damage, or the methods to reduce it. As an ecological 'activist' was quoted as saying in one of the more recent newspaper cuttings: 'Too little is being done too late by too few.'

Rivers paused and looked towards Hugo Poggs, who by now was sitting in the old leather chair at the trestle table, the whisky glass held distractedly in his plump hand, its contents almost drained.

'Please continue,' Poggs urged.

Rivers saw no reason not to. Besides, although depressing, the compilation laid out before him held a morbid kind of fascination.

He read of the insect infestation of the northern hemisphere, the spread of diseases such as malaria and yellow fever across Europe, North America and Canada, the increase of asthma, bronchitis and other respiratory problems in both hemispheres, and of animal diseases like Bovine Spongiform Encephalopathy, which two years ago had returned to the United Kingdom and wiped out over a third of its cattle herds. He moved on: last year a cyclone had hit the Bay of Bengal claiming 13,000 lives and destroying over four million homes; Algeria's entire annual rainfall had fallen in one afternoon, while the USA's western corn belt had been ravaged by the worst drought America had ever experienced; the waters of the Nile were slowly drying up, ruining Egypt's irrigation system and reducing hydro-electric power from the Aswan Dam by a calamitous eighty-five per cent; the same was happening to the contaminated waters of the Euphrates; in the defeated state of Israel, 300 Israeli POWs had frozen to death in open prison camps during the region's coldest night on record; a forest fire in British Columbia had destroyed two million hectares of prime woodland; a party of six tourists were lost in a blizzard on Grand Canary Island, their frozen bodies found floating three days later when the snow rapidly melted.

He stopped when he came upon a caption that said: HURRICANE ZELDA DEVASTATES JAMAICA. Another clipping was tagged below it, a photograph under the headline of a wrecked aeroplane, recognisable only by its tail and one broken wing, the main structure a tangled mass of blackened metal. Rivers felt chilled as he read the words. MIRACLE SURVIVAL OF THREE. Included in the article were pictures of the two crew members and of Rivers himself, all stock shots obviously released from their files. The one of him was ringed in red.

He turned, a different rage inside him now. 'What is this?' he said tightly. 'Just what the hell is going on here?'

Poggs raised a placating hand. 'Look at some of those other cuttings that are marked,' he said calmly.

'What?'

'Mr Rivers,' said Diane, 'please. Our concerns are the same as yours. We're not trying to trick you, we're not into anything devious. Just do as Hugo asks, then hear us out.'

He needed a cigarette, but remembered he was wearing another man's clothes. He shook his head, confused and frustrated by these people.

'What do you have to lose?' Diane said simply.

He mentally shrugged. She was right – there was nothing to lose and maybe, just maybe, there was something to gain. Precisely what, he had no idea, but he was going to find out in the next ten minutes, or, so help him, he was out of there, car or no car. A walk to the nearest phonebox would do him no harm at all.

He returned to the board and glanced over the display of cuttings once again. Those marked with red pentel were the earthquake in Alaska, the eruption on Australia's Great Barrier Reef, the cyclone in India, the forest fire in Canada and, of course, the plane crash that he, himself, had survived.

'So you've singled out certain disasters,' he said, still studying the news cuttings for a clue of some kind. Finally giving up, he rounded on them again. 'What's the point?'

Poggs leaned forward on the table, elbows resting on scattered papers, fingers curled around his whisky glass as if it were a communion chalice. 'The point is that in every one of those incidents eyewitnesses claimed to have observed a tiny ball of light just before the tragedy occurred.'

Rivers was momentarily surprised. Then his mind moved back into gear. 'Luminous phenomena aren't uncommon, especially around the time of earthquakes and suchlike. There's nothing unusual about such sightings.'

'Admittedly there are numerous forms of, as you say, luminous phenomena that defy geophysics, many of them to do with tectonic events. I can give you a long list of the variations, if you like, from the piezoelectric effect to chemiluminescence, but I fear I would try your patience even more. In this case I'm talking of a peculiarly different kind of light, a single floating orb that was witnessed before each of those occasions marked. One of the witnesses, a woman who was airlifted from the forest fire by a Fire Service helicopter, described it just before she died. It seems that even though her body was charred black and she should have been dead long before they got to her, there was what could only be described as a wondrous look in her eyes. The woman told her would-be rescuers that she had watched a "fairy light" a moment or so before the blaze. A single "fairy light".'

Rivers spoke the word quietly: 'Tinkerbell.'

He walked to the table and picked up what was left of his drink. He eyed Poggs coldly. 'How did you know I even mentioned Tinkerbell? There was a clampdown – no news service or journal ran that part of the story.'

Poggs smiled and he almost appeared abashed. 'I suppose, er, you could say we were reliably informed.'

'No more runaround,' Rivers warned.

'The children told us,' Diane said quickly. 'Josh and Eva.'

He switched his gaze to her. 'The children . . . ?'

'Yes, my friend,' said Poggs, sitting back in his seat. 'They pointed out your face to us in the newspaper. They were very excited. You see, they have seen this mysterious light, too. In fact, before each of those disasters you see marked on the wall behind you.'

THE CARIBBEAN SEA – *1,094 fathoms below sea level*

The information-gatherer skimmed along the seabed, avoiding rocky protrusions, rising over smaller mounts, the onboard computer re-routing its direction completely when any obstacle proved too difficult to negotiate. The compact metal body was generally ignored by the life around it, although a few minutes before a blue marlin, suffering from misguided overconfidence, had tried to club it to death with its long, pikish upper jaw, giving up only when the hard-shelled alien, apparently oblivious to attack, had moved into deeper waters.

It had been a long voyage for *Dolphin V* (so called because this model was a direct descendant of the original *Dolphin* of the late '80s), for it had begun off the coast of North Africa where it had slipped from the mother vessel, the RRS (Royal Research Ship) *Arthur C. Clarke*, into the choppy waters of the Atlantic. From there the information-gatherer had made its way across the ocean floor like some roaming missile of the deep, navigating its way over the Mid-Atlantic Ridge via the Vema Fracture until it reached the warmer regions of the Caribbean. Its intention was to traverse the Aves Ridge and eventually rejoin the mother vessel somewhere in the deeper waters of the Venezuelan Basin.

Frequently during *Dolphin V*'s lengthy exploration it had risen from the depths, although never quite all the way to the surface where the waves were far too rough and too dangerous for such a sensitive instrument; from its position below the surface, it had released small radio-capsules which bobbed to the top and floated there waiting for a satellite to pass overhead. When that happened, the radio-capsule beamed information into space, which was then directed back to dry land. The main tasks of *Dolphin V* were to measure the strengths of currents and storm intensities as well as to take the temperature of the water and to note its salinity; but by far the most important charge of this mission was to send back information on plankton presence at each stage of the journey. The importance of these minute sea-dwelling organisms that drifted between the poles and the Equator was immeasurable, for they absorbed carbon dioxide in the colder parts and released it on reaching the tropics, creating an even balance in the Earth's atmosphere. However, the planet was warming, the icecaps were melting, and the amount of CO_2 had increased alarmingly: and the oceans' plankton was behaving strangely.

Scientists and governments alike were desperate to know just how well or how badly the plankton was coping at this point in time.

The little machine had braved the fierce storms of the deep, those colossal surges and titanic tides that were a thousandfold more powerful than any storm in the atmosphere, intrepidly gliding onwards and never resting. It hungered only for data and so much did it gather that it was not until recent years that computers had been devised that were capable of absorbing it all.

Now it had reached a less harsh environment and even the unfriendly blue marlin had been left far behind to search for frailer prey. *Dolphin V* sank with the seabed's natural gradient.

But as it travelled onwards something stirred beneath its hard underbelly. Great swirls of sand eddied upwards, creating murky clouds through which myriad shoals of bright-coloured fish swam frantically. A three-foot-long albacore bumped into the cruising machine, stunning itself almost into senselessness. It spun round in a full circle, then recovered enough to join others of its kind in a dash for clearer waters. A team of three barracuda, halfway through their feast of king mackerel, decided the main course was over and took flight also. The remains of the five-foot-long mackerel sank to the sea floor where it vibrated as though still in a death spasm.

A low rumble began to build from below and time-eroded rocks started to crumble and break. The deep waters became turbulent; they seemed to boil in agitation. Old currents were re-directed, new ones initiated. Surface waters became choppy. *Dolphin V* was buffeted in the undersea storm, yet barely faltered in its course; unlike the sea creatures around it, the machine had no fear.

A fissure in the rock below the seabed of sand and sediment began to open, a seismic fault where none had existed before; the massive rending sound was dulled only slightly by the waters above. The split stretched for thirty miles or more and pressure from beneath the top layer forced a canyon wall of almost that same length to rise slowly like some immense and fantastic monolithic slab, its face sheer and dark, the sound it made a deep grinding roar.

Dolphin V was tossed into a spiralling dive by the maelstrom, then dashed repeatedly against the newly risen wall, its toughened shell finally breaking and the complex inner circuitries smashed. Tiny parts sparked momentarily before dying, and within seconds the machine was rendered useless, a piece of junk metal that continued to be pummelled by the incredible forces around it. Soon it disintegrated completely, its separate pieces falling away to drift like flotsam.

The vast displacement of the sea floor shifted the sea itself, causing a seismic wave, a *tsunami*, that rushed outwards, gathering pace as it went, rapidly reaching a speed of 450 miles an hour. The wave grew higher and higher as it reached shallower waters, and before long it had become massive.

It headed towards a nearby chain of islands.

GRENADA, WEST INDIES – *a hillside overlooking St George's Harbour*

Nello Kwame Lewis brought his gleaming minibus to a shuddering halt on the verge that ran alongside the dusty, potholed road. As the vehicle was doorless – as well as windowless – and because it was never a habit of Grenadians to switch off their engines unnecessarily, it took him no time at all to jump out and stomp over the short, tough grass to a spot that gave him a clear view of the harbour below. But he was in no mood to enjoy that view's idyllic beauty, the turquoise and cerulean sea washing lazily into this Caribbean haven, the brilliantly white passenger liner moored by the customs dock, the schooners and tiny dinghies tied to iron cannon posts on the Carenage side, the white sails of yachts gliding effortlessly to and fro from the lagoon; and overhead, a sky so blue – apart from a vague grey patch in the far, far distance that seemed to touch the sea itself – it would have made a postcard look phony. Nello was too vexed and perhaps too familiar with the everyday scene to appreciate any of it.

'Mahn,' he said aloud, throwing his Epcot cap (left behind in his bus by one of last year's tourists) to the ground, and following it himself in almost the same movement. 'Mahn, this girl makin' me ignorant!'

He picked up a rotting piece of tree bark and tossed it down the hillside, the sudden exposure rousing the sluggish gecko that had been resting in its shade into stone-like tension. The wide staring eyes blinked twice before the lizard slithered off to safer regions.

'He jus' a pippial clerk wit' a manager belly. Everythin's turned ol' mas', mahn.' He was telling the breeze that the real object of his hatred was an insignificant man (who was, in fact, a clerk) with a paunch stomach.

Nello drummed his sneakered heels into the earth, which perhaps was not quite the expected behaviour of a twenty-three-year-old male who owned his own minibus called LOVE ME STYLE and made a good, although by no means prosperous, living taxiing locals from one side of the island to the other and tourists to anywhere they wanted. He was also considered to be one of the island's rising stars at slamming a dom' and, until now, had looked like being chosen to represent Grenada in the next Eastern Caribbean inter-island dominoes pairs championship, which was to take place in Barbados. This, too, was a source of his rising frustration, for that same 'pippial clerk' who was stealing Nello's woman – or intended woman, to be more accurate – had thrashed him mightily in a dominoes play-off only last night.

'*Don' make me vex, mahn!*' he yelled down the hillside towards the customs building in the distance.

Nello, normally a bright spirit with an easy-going nature, was trembling with rage and bitterness, by now a truly unhappy young man. Even when the bus HEAVEN SENT went by and its driver, Norris Hercules, both his friend and neighbour, honked its horn and waved through the empty windscreen, he was too preoccupied to wave back. He even ignored some of the passengers who, lazy with a day's work done, hailed him from the glassless windows.

'*Fire one later, Nello,*' called the unoffended driver. '*Maybe some o' that mountain dew, eh mahn?*' The mention of illegally distilled rum sent his passengers rolling with laughter. 'Oh Grey, Nello play lougarou today,' Norris said to the nearest one.

He was told to relax. 'Hold strain, Norris, mahn, an' watch the road. You a covetous driver.'

Norris smiled broadly and swerved the bus into a pothole at the 'road hog' insult. 'You put goat mouth on that,' he admitted, sending his passenger and those nearby into paroxysms of laughter.

Dust stirred up and left behind by the brightly painted bus drifted down to settle over Nello's head and shoulders. He appeared not to notice, his gaze directed balefully at the tiny customs building below.

'Everythin's turned ol' mas',' he repeated. And he was right: for him, everything *had* become confused for, until six days ago, Angella was his intended woman and the whole village of Boca, where they both lived, knew that; but he'd caught her giving Clyde A. Jelroyd, the 'pippial clerk' in question, the sweet eye – a wink – at the weekend carnival in St George's. Unfortunately Angella worked weekdays in the town's Government Post Office, which was no distance at all from the customs building where that obsocky Dougla (part African, part East Indian) Jelroyd shuffled papers and bounced his rubber stamp, and twice since that carnival night Nello had caught her and this bloated pig strolling the streets together. The first time, despite having a minibus full of passengers, he pulled up across the junction of Green Street and Tyrrel Street to remonstrate with them both. They had proclaimed innocence and '*Don't mamaguy me!*' is what he'd retorted, at the same time raising a fist to 'lick down this locho' – knock down this low-life. Only the arrival of a policeman had prevented him from so doing right there and then, and only the complaints of his irate fare-payers and the cacophonous honking of the traffic his misparked minibus had been holding up for the last ten minutes forced him back into the driver's seat – and a good thing too, for the policeman might well have taken a smack along with the locho.

'Oh woman, don't you know this mahn have keeper and outside child?' he had wailed at Angella later that night. But Jelroyd's common-law wife and illegitimate child didn't appear to bother her at all, because three days later Nello had seen the two of them together again, on this occasion walking hand-in-hand through Market Square. Once more he'd abandoned his minibus, full of tourists this time, and raced across the square to confront the perfidious couple, but this time he had lost them somewhere in the crowded side street. (Or so he thought. In fact they had spotted his blundering approach from 300 yards away, his head bobbing up in the crowd every few feet, and had dodged out of sight into the Straw Mart. Clyde had bought Angella some shell jewellery while they waited for Nello to pass by, which she had accepted with a bashful giggle and a look in her eye that hinted at some foolin' aroun' later on.) When Nello returned to LOVE ME STYLE fifteen minutes later it was empty of tourists, with traffic in both directions in uproar and a constable busy taking down his registration number. That had been less than half an hour ago (twenty minutes to sort out the traffic jam) and he was still seething with the injustice of it all – the unfaithfulness of his sweetheart, the loathsomeness of his rival, the fickleness of his passengers, the wrath of the policeman and, of course, the traffic violation ticket. Oh mahn, this was one grey day.

A tailor bird flew up the hill and past him, wings flapping madly as though it had to get somewhere fast.

Nello concentrated hard on the faraway customs building,

imagining Clyde A. Jelroyd inside, having parted from his, Nello's, sweet thing, thinking of the kiss they would have shared before going their separate ways. In his mind's eye, he could see the customs clerk taking tea with the other office creatures, who would be working late because of the passenger liner's arrival, gloating at how he had not only stolen Nello's woman, but had thrashed him at the dom' also, and no doubt would be replacing him in the championship tournament.

Nello sucked his teeth, drawing a patois 'cheups' sound of contempt. There was a low malevolence in his eyes as he stared down at the harbour. 'I get the obeahwomahn on you,' he said almost as a deep growl. 'She do you bad t'ing fo' brutalisin' me life. She send the jumbie to be blammin' on your door.' He managed a grin, although it was far from pleasant. 'Me tantie is obeahwomahn, she do me fo' right.'

Nello had always lived in fear and awe of his aunt, and he was not the only one on the island to do so. She was a rake of a woman, who relished her own reputation as a witch and who never let one day pass without casting a spell or brewing a potion. At any time she could be found giving bush or herb baths against illness or bad luck, or taking an unborn and unwanted child from a young maiden who had 'swallowed the breadfruit', or putting a curse on an enemy of any eager and preferably affluent payer, or fulfilling traditional requirements such as keeping Mama Maladie, the evil spirit, away at Christmas time. Even to this day, as a grown man, he dreaded visiting his tantie without Mama and Papa and, if possible, with at least two of his brothers and three of his sisters along for the treat.

Yet last night after the domino match which he had so disgracefully lost, and charged with rum alternated with one or eight too many Caribs, he had taken the windy road up through the hills to her shack. Unfortunately, there was no way he could force himself to tap on that old corrugated iron door which, unlike most of the islanders, she always kept clammed tight. Instead he had sat in his minibus, wide eyes watching the small lighted window, quailing in fear. And Tantie had come to the window and stared right back. For a while he thought she might be putting the maljoe, the evil eye, on him; then she'd waved and he couldn't be sure if it was an invitation, or her way of telling him to get the hell out of her face. He had scooted, scratching the sides of the minibus on bushes and trees as he'd executed a tight seven-point turn on the narrow track. He was sure he heard her rollicking laughter all the way back to his village.

The rustling of a nearby fern, followed by a frantic scrambling, disturbed Nello from his thoughts. A wood slave, perhaps the same lizard he had roused earlier, broke free and darted up the hill and across the rutted road into the thick undergrowth on the other side. Nello clucked his tongue at the creature's 'chupidness' and returned his attention to the harbour. A sudden breeze that carried with it an unusual chill caused him to shiver.

'Jook monkey, jook monkey, monkey conkaray. You giving me fatigue, Jelroyd, an' me tantie be giving you the maljoe. She make me deal las' night only.' And Nello had just about convinced himself that this was so. Last night he had slept in his bus rather than wake his parents by lumbering through the house at such a late hour, and as he'd lain there in the darkness, the echo of the obeahwoman's laughter still in his head, Nello *knew* that she *knew* why he had gone to her shack, even though they had not spoken. That his woman was making a fool of him was 'old talk' – gossip – in the village, and Tantie would never turn a blind eye to that, she would never fail a member of the family. She would cast her spell, brew her potion, chant her bad-wish.

'You sick 'fore too long, Jelroyd!' he shouted.

He jumped when a flock of bananaquits flapped low over his head, their *see-ee-ee-swees-tee* call strident and somehow shocking in the languor of late afternoon. He craned his neck to follow their flight and as he watched their black bodies become tiny in the distance, he became conscious of the chill breeze on the back of his neck, a chill that set his skin to prickling. He faced the ocean again and his brow furrowed into heavy ridges as he observed the approaching greyness.

At that precise moment, Nello could not quite comprehend exactly what he was seeing, for there were no rain clouds – the sky was a perfectly clear blue that faded to azure near the horizon – and the greyness was from the sea itself, a kind of swelling that gently sloped away at either end. Before he could think too hard on this, something else distracted him.

Floating directly in front of him, level with his own face and nine yards or so away, was a shining light. It was round like a cricket ball, and about the same size too, and its edges were blurred like the sun's. It hovered there above the incline, and although it was not quite still, its position was fairly constant.

Nello cried out and covered his eyes with his hands. *'Oh Mama, mais non,'* he moaned, and wondered if the jumbie, the boobooman, had been sent to haunt him instead of his rival. The breeze from the ocean, now rising like the strong Christmas wind, snagged on his shirt.

He peeped through his fingers and the day-star was still there as if *it* were studying *him*. But what was looming up behind this hypnotically weird light could not now be ignored, for it began to dawn on Nello just what this vast grey swelling out there on the ocean was.

'Oh Grey,' he muttered under his breath. 'Oh goodness, oh mahn, oh Mama.'

The wave stretched at least fifty miles from end to sloping end, but its height could not be judged from that distance. But it *was* high, Nello could tell that.

He began to rise, and the ball of light rose with him, keeping level with his face. He discovered the strength wasn't in his legs and he stumbled, almost slipping down the hillside. He grabbed the tough grass blades, steadying himself, rolling forward once and clutching at the grass again, so that he was outstretched, flat on his back, watching the swiftly approaching wall of water.

Somewhere in the town below a church bell started to peal. Another joined in. He thought he could hear human cries, but a new sound was beginning to dominate all others, a continuous hissing, like the surf rushing into shore, this sound never breaking, growing louder as the huge dark mass rolled towards the island. Yachts, motorboats, dinghies and schooners were gathered up like driftwood and carried along as it loomed over the harbour.

The sound had become a low, thunderous rumble, and what seemed like hundreds – *thousands* – of birds streamed by over Nello's head, while animals – lizards, rodents, opossum and even an armadillo – scurried past him, squealing and grunting their panic.

'*I did not mean fo' this, Tantie!*' Nello beseeched, hands joined together and raised towards the still blue skies.

The wave was seventy – *no, it was a hundred!* – feet high, and it broke over the harbour smashing boats and buildings alike, pushing the great white passenger liner up on to the dock to flatten the customs building and everyone inside, including Nello's arch-rival in love and dominoes, who had indeed been taking tea and gloating to his colleagues over his supremacy at both games. Clyde A. Jelroyd heard the bells, he even heard the shouts outside, and then he had heard the curious rushing, rumbling sound, and when the wall opposite exploded inwards, he heard his own scream. But not for long did he hear the latter, for soon he was as flat as the Customs and Excise Regulations book he kept on his desk and had already discovered that infinity has no sound at all.

Nello watched in absorbed horror, failing to notice that the little light had disappeared.

As the tidal wave tore through the harbour town, smashing everything in its path, be it concrete buildings, timber frames, metal, glass, or human flesh, he wept wretchedly. For the third time that afternoon, he wailed, *'Oh mahn, oh mahn, everyt'ing's turned ol' mas'!'*

7

They had talked through the afternoon, breaking for a late
lunch, then continuing into the evening. Now it was dusk and
still they went on, the topics ranging from the change in
rainfall patterns to the drastic reduction in the world's food
production, and from the methods of selection forestry to the
threats of toxic hazards (Rivers learned that Hugo Poggs
was a major contributor to the original volumes of *Dangerous
Properties of Industrial Materials*, known more succinctly as
Sax by the scientists and environmental health specialists,
who still referred to the tome to that day).

It was soon plain to the climatologist that his host's knowledge of the global crisis was wider ranging: Poggs had conducted detailed studies of every disaster, both major and
minor, over the past few years that was environment-related,
these as diverse as the widescale spread of infectious diseases and the lack of snow for skiing in the Alps. It had slowly
dawned on him where he had heard Poggs' name before:
some years ago, this man's paper on 'soft engineering' –

working with nature, rather than against it – had been widely acclaimed both for its sound premise and its cost-effectiveness. Later he had predicted the rise in the levels of the planet's oceans because of global warming, listing the countries whose lowlands would be swamped as well as the islands that would disappear altogether. At the time he had been labelled a 'climate hypochondriac', even a 'geophysical Cassandra', and there were enough scientists and fellow-geologists who disagreed with his calculations for Poggs to earn himself media, and thus public, scorn.

The fact that this prediction, and others he had made around the same time concerning the future condition of the planet, were proving to be correct of late might well have won him considerable esteem from those same detractors had it not been for one further and quite astounding hypothesis he had presented to the world. From then on Poggs had been dismissed as an eccentric, albeit a rather brilliant one.

Little had been heard of the man since, hence Rivers' only vague recollection of the name when Poggs had first called. Yet during their discussions throughout the day, he had heard nothing from the man that might have been considered remotely 'eccentric'; however, so far they had not touched on the subject of 'luminous phenomena'.

Poggs had listened as well as talked, showing a keen interest in Rivers' own opinions on the climate and environmental changes which were, of course, backed by the unique amount of data available to him in his capacity as a senior scientific officer at the Meteorological Office.

At no time had the climatologist felt under pressure, for although Poggs and his daughter-in-law asked many questions, none required answers that might have been deemed 'official secrets'. He had begun to relax with these people and indeed, had been keen to take on certain information that his own special working group had either overlooked or had paid scant attention to because of data 'overload'. An example was the variable but widespread warming of the Alaskan permafrost (a gauge that changes temperature more slowly than the air and thus often provides a more accurate measurement), a factor that Poggs had determined through his own researches and one which Rivers' own department had inexcusably neglected, perhaps because further evidence of global warming was hardly necessary. However, it was important as far as maintaining complete and precise records was concerned.

When Poggs' wife joined them again the night was closing in, and shadows in the garden were merging into the natural gloom.

'The mites are abed,' she told them, switching on a lamp and giving the climatologist a brief but warm smile. 'And waiting for a kiss and a cuddle from Mama. They've already had a chapter, Diane, so don't let them kid you otherwise.'

Diane stood and brushed out the creases in her denim skirt. 'I won't be long. Mr Rivers, we'd be pleased if you'd stay over. Believe it or not, there's still plenty more to talk about, and we'd hate to think of you driving all that way back to London tonight. Besides, even though Mack's given your car the okay, you don't know that it won't give you problems on the journey. Much better in daylight hours if it does, don't you think?'

Rivers glanced at his watch. 'I didn't realise it was getting so late. Thanks for your offer, but no. I've, uh, I've got things to do tomorrow.'

Poggs eyed him almost cautiously. 'Now we should discuss the curious orb of light.'

There was a sudden awkward silence in the room.

'I was wondering when we'd get around to it.'

Poggs cleared his throat, a gruff, rumbling sound, and thrust his unlit pipe between his teeth.

'I guess we wanted you to know us a little better before we mentioned it.' Diane's tone was apologetic.

'We don't want you to think we're completely mad, you see,' explained Bibby with a mischievous glint in her eye.

He returned her smile. 'So far you've convinced me that you're not *wholly* insane. But then there's more than just one topic we've avoided.' He turned to look directly at Poggs. 'I seem to recall that several years ago you upset the scientific establishment with a certain public proclamation. I've been sitting here trying like hell to remember what it was exactly, but it's no good, it won't come to me. What I do know is that it didn't do much for your credibility.'

Poggs chewed the end of his pipe for a few moments, his thoughts reflective, a faint smile on his lips.

Diane opened the door. 'At this point I think I'll see to Josh and Eva. I won't be long.' They listened to her footsteps recede down the hall.

'Of course you're referring to the Mother Earth hypothesis. Hardly a proclamation on my part. In fact, it's an age-old concept, but one that was first advanced in scientific terms in the early '70s by a rather brilliant man called James Lovelock, who concluded that the Earth is not merely a haven for life, but is alive itself – or *herself*, if you prefer – a single organism where life-forms and the environment continually interact to maintain a life-preserving equilibrium. Lovelock and I were like-minded on many issues in those days, although it has to be said that he regarded the effects of toxic pollution with less gravity than I. Rather than spend money on a catalytic converter for your car's engine, plant a tree, was his line.' Poggs huffed a short laugh. 'I have to say, he had a point. He also regarded nuclear power as a benign energy, much to the annoyance of purist conservationists, and I went along with him on that one. Unfortunately we disagreed fundamentally on his GAIA theory.'

'GAIA . . . ?'

'The Greek Earth goddess – a fanciful name for a serious idea.'

'And your disagreement?'

'Ah. Well, first let me set out what we both subscribed to, namely that the Earth is, in itself, a regulatory system, alive and ever-watchful.' Poggs was quick to notice the mild irritation on the other man's face. 'No, I don't mean "alive" in the sense that we in this room are alive. There are other definitions.'

Rivers nodded noncommittally: it wasn't a point worth arguing at that moment.

Poggs continued. 'As far as we know the Earth's atmosphere has always been unstable, full of gases continuously reacting against one another until, you might have expected, they reached their own compromise, finally interacting to bring about an equable and enduring atmosphere. Yet this has never happened, there has never been any such movement towards that stability; and just as well – it could have led to the cessation of all those organisms the *instability* supported, including mankind itself. Instead, the turmoil in the atmosphere goes on, while we humans lead our daily lives unaware of the conflict, mainly because the oxygen content and temperature have remained pretty damn-well constant over the past few millions of years. We – Lovelock and I – agreed that *something* was working to organise and, of course, re-organise all of this, our conclusion being that the organiser was one vast organism: Mother Earth, itself.' He rested back in the big leather chair, allowing Rivers time to take it in.

'I can see why the pair of you were at odds with your fellow-scientists,' Rivers remarked. 'It's a little subversive, isn't it?'

Poggs chuckled. 'And so science should be. Isn't that the essence of radical discovery – a non-acceptance of the laid-down rules?'

Bibby, who had taken Diane's seat by the window, spoke with mild impatience. 'Poggsy, dear, I think our guest would rather you got to the point than indulge in waggish

103

profundities. I'm a little worn out myself – no, dear, not because of your never-less-than-brilliant discourse, but because of this dratted humidity.'

'You're quite right,' her husband conceded. 'I must admit to feeling rather drained myself. D'you know, I think we could do with another storm to clear the air.'

'Heaven forbid it should be like this morning's,' she groaned, fanning herself with a sheaf of papers she had picked up from the corner of the trestle table.

'Now, yes, to get to the point, as Bibby so *tactfully* suggested. Well . . . well, where was I?'

'I think you were getting to your fundamental disagreement with the GAIA theory.'

'Yes, and the reason the scientific establishment took further umbrage at me. God knows, they were upset enough by Lovelock's hypothesis without me adding my tuppence-worth. Poor chaps thought I was more bonkers than Lovelock.' He chortled at the thought, the laugh ending in a wheezing cough.

His wife frowned anxiously.

'You see,' said Poggs, regaining his composure. 'You see, according to Lovelock the Earth acts to stabilise the environment for its *own* survival, rather than the survival of the organisms that live upon or below its surface. Certain processes will always take over to rid the seas of pollution and to negate the harmful gases in the air. It's a perfectly natural procedure for GAIA, an innate function of its own self-preservation programme; and Lovelock places no significant importance on human life as far as GAIA is concerned, and believing that it's we who may well be the species to suffer while other, tougher, life-forms will survive.'

'Hugo . . .' Bibby warned.

'Yes, yes, I'm coming to it.' He shook his head at her prompting. 'It is, and always has been, my contention that in some metaphysical way the Earth acts' – he tapped the table before him with his pipe stem for emphasis – 'to sustain mankind itself.'

Rivers reached for his last cigarette and lit up, oblivious of the disapproving frown from Bibby. Poggs sucked fruitlessly on his empty pipe and waited for a comment.

Tense once more and inexplicably resentful (perhaps it was the realisation that the long, uncomfortable, and eventually hazardous journey had been wasted after all), the climatologist exhaled a stream of grey smoke before speaking. 'That's quite a bizarre declaration from a scientist.' It had taken an effort of will to put it so mildly.

'Oh, I don't know,' Poggs replied affably. 'From geology to geophysics to metaphysics doesn't seem such a peculiar progression to me. It depends on what one has managed to absorb along the way, I suppose. And if one is *willing* to progress.'

Bibby waved the air in front of her to clear the trail of smoke that had drifted towards her. 'I'm not surprised at your cynicism, Mr Rivers. As a matter of fact, we've learned to accept it from all quarters. As well as causing a serious schism between my husband and James Lovelock, it also damaged his reputation as a geologist of note and as a Fellow of the Royal Society. Ridicule is not an easy thing to live with, especially if one's motives are sincere.'

Rivers tapped ash into the saucer thoughtfully provided by Diane earlier in the day and twice emptied since. He felt a cold pressure building up inside, a mounting rage that he had difficulty in controlling. 'I'm sure it isn't. But sincerity doesn't compensate for lack of hard evidence. Can you present me with anything to support this . . . this notion? As you've obviously failed to convince your peers, I presume not.'

'There are things I can tell you . . .'

'Firm evidence?'

'That's impossible in a hypothesis of this nature.'

Rivers started to rise. 'Yeah, I guess it must be. For a

while there you almost had me hooked. I thought I was dealing with reasonable people, and I admit, I was interested in most of what you had to say. But now . . .' He held up a hand in a gesture of frustration. 'Now I'm not so sure. I came here hoping to learn something important, because believe me, I've looked into the whole business of light phenomena since my accident and I've found nothing to explain what I saw that day inside the storm.'

He stubbed out the remainder of his cigarette. 'So what do I get from you? A belief that the Earth and its people are all part of the same complicated bundle, no real difference between us.'

'That isn't quite what I meant,' interrupted Poggs.

'Never mind – it's close enough. Next I suppose you'll be asking me to join some quasi-religious cult as a means of finding the true light. Come on, is that what this is really all about, a weird kind of mystic symbolism that just might support your own beliefs? Sorry, but to me it's bullshit.'

'I don't understand your anger.'

And in truth, neither did Rivers himself. 'Call it frustration,' he said, making towards the door.

Bibby rose swiftly. 'Mr Rivers, we honestly didn't mean to . . .'

'Sure,' he said, stopping for a moment. 'No doubt your intentions are honourable enough in your own minds, but what you have to understand is that I don't have time for all this. Things are too desperate, too bloody serious, for this kind of absurdity.' Maybe it was tiredness, maybe it was the painful throbbing in his leg that had started twenty minutes ago; he only knew he had to get out of there, away from these people and their Mother Earth nonsense and kids who saw lights thousands of miles away. Enough was enough.

Poggs remained seated, but his voice was anxious. '*You've got to listen.*'

Rivers' grin was unpleasant. 'Oh no I haven't.'

He yanked open the door and limped down the hallway, his footsteps harsh against the polished wood flooring. The pressure was now pounding inside his head, so that his steps quickened and his teeth clenched together as if to suppress a groan. His intention was to find Diane so that he could get his own clothes back – dry or damp, he was changing into them and getting away from Hazelrod and back to the squalid city where at least the insanity was mundane. He gripped the bottom stair-post, swinging himself round to make the ascent.

But somebody was already on the stairs, about halfway up and descending slowly. There were no lights on at the top, and the hallway itself was only dimly lit.

'Diane . . . ?' he said, one foot on the first step.

She had the children on either side of her, their small faces ethereally pale in the gloom, their bodies tight against her. Diane stopped when she saw him and her voice was hushed and not quite steady, as if she were forcing a calmness that would not frighten the children further. For their fear was evident in their wide staring eyes.

'They've seen the light again.'

It was at that precise moment when glass from the windows of the porch and front door and those beside it shrieked inwards, thousands of jagged shards imploding into the hallway like blasted shrapnel, the scream of their bursting the only warning.

Instinct alone caused Rivers to duck, otherwise his exposed neck and head would have been pierced by the fragments; as it was, hundreds of tiny pieces penetrated the tough material of the corduroy trousers and twill shirt he wore, their force diminished before they reached his skin.

He cried out from shock rather than pain, and collapsed against the stairs to lie there, arms over his head for protection. All around the house could be heard the sound of smashing glass, as if some terrible gale was swirling around outside and breaking through every window.

The two children screamed and cowered with their mother on the stairway, Diane hugging them close, protecting them with her own body.

The window on the landing above crashed inwards as if dealt some tremendous blow from outside, sending a cascade of glittering fragments that fell over the heads and shoulders of those who crouched below. Poggs' wife, who had followed Rivers to the doorway, dropped to her knees behind the door itself as the study's long windows caved inwards, and only the high back of the leather chair saved Hugo Poggs, himself, from the deadly spray.

Glass streaked down the hallway from the window at the far end, spattering on to the floor in a leaden shower when its force was spent.

Hunched and trembling, they listened to the smashing of glass that came from other rooms in the house.

Yet they did not hear the sound of a storm. Nor of any wind. For outside the air was perfectly still.

NEW ORLEANS, LOUISIANA – *Vieux Carré (Old Square)*

It hurt. Oh Divine Mother, it hurt.

She shifted her vast weight in the wicker chair; the inter-weaved cane creaked, the cushions seemed to sigh. The tiny perfumed handkerchief, her Sunday lace and lavender one, was used to dab moisture from her forehead and neck, the lace soon sodden and the scent soon tainted.

She levered herself up, hands gripping the curved arms of the wicker chair and testing their ability to endure to the limit. A rotating fan hummed rhythmically over her head as she crossed the floor, but it was the draught caused by the passing of her huge body and not the cooling air currents that stirred the net curtains enclosing the room's huge bed.

Street noises distracted her and she went to one of the long windows, pushing open its heavy green shutters. She stepped out on to the narrow wrought-iron gallery, while daylight, bright and too eager, rushed past her into the room to be subdued by shadows that did not seem ordinary, so dense and unyielding were they. And outside on the gallery, the afternoon's brightness scarcely made the woman's eyes narrow, even though she had come from such an umbrageous chamber; they stared unblinkingly, dark and protuberant, into the crowds that strolled through the colonnade below.

A tourist, as loud in attire as he was in voice, noticed her and stopped; he nudged his wife and pointed upwards, exhorting her to catch a slice of *real* old New Orleans. His wife shuddered at the sight though, and hurried him on, dragging him by the elbow, never once looking back.

The woman on the balcony breathed in the sultry street-stale air, her fists tight around the filigreed iron of the gallery's rail, and rocked away the soreness inside her head. To and fro, back and forth, a steady rhythm that gradually relaxed into a mild, almost imperceptible, swaying.

Her gaze fell upon a single black child and would not let him go as he weaved his way through the jostling Sunday strollers and sightseers. The boy came to a halt and looked around him as though someone had called his name. Slowly he turned his head in her direction; he looked upwards and his jaw slackened.

The boy quickly joined his hands at his chest in supplication, then bowed his head.

She let him go, her thoughts on other matters, but she had enjoyed the momentary contact.

The boy sped away, forgetting his original destination, re-routing himself back to his own home where he fell into his surprised mama's arms.

He would dream badly for the next seven days.

The woman returned to the darkened room, closing the heavy shutters behind her. Then it was her eyes she closed, and with her black clothing and dark skin she became a shadow among other shadows. Yet had anyone dared to enter

110

at that moment, they would immediately have been aware of her presence, for they would have heard her rumbling breath and they would have smelled her sweat. *If* anyone had dared to enter.

She gave a small moan.

It had hurt.

And she did not understand.

She had sensed the threat and had directed her thoughts to the 'place' – *oh show me where, Great Mama, oh show me WHERE*. The pressure had been almost unbearable, her mind had been flayed; but she had not wavered, she had not retreated, *and it had hurt, it had hurt*.

She had felt the breaking, the shattering of light fragments, the pleasure of that, but then the pain.

This sensing was unlike the others, and she could not understand why it had weakened her so.

But she was aware that the situation must be remedied. Soon – and of this she was sure – she would know how.

8

Although it was not many minutes past eight o'clock, the sun was already drying the sodden land, creating lazy vapour clouds that drifted low to the ground. There was no sharpness to the day, no keen edge to it; even the bird calls sounded listless and unconcerned. The sky was a hazy blue and the greens of the hills around the shallow valley where Hazelrod sheltered were of muted greens.

Diane led Rivers through the orchard beyond the gardens, explaining the husbandry system of the small-holding as they walked. He listened politely, but his mind was on other matters, namely the bizarre events of the night before.

The grounds around the house had been deserted – or at least Poggs and Mack, armed with a shotgun, had found no signs of intruders when they had investigated once the bizarre storm had abated. The conclusion last night had been that an unusual wind, perhaps a twister, had encircled the building, driving inwards to shatter windows, while disturbing nothing outside – outbuildings, trees, fences, or anything at all that

112

should have been vulnerable. No one had argued the point –
at least no one had suggested otherwise.

And no one had been seriously hurt, although it had taken
some time for Diane to pick out small splinters of glass that
had penetrated the heavy trousers and shirt worn by Rivers.
His cuts were few, and mainly on the backs of his hands,
although there was one gash along his cheekbone that had
required some treatment. She, too, had cuts on her hands
and two small slashes on her forehead; her hair was full of
glass fragments from the landing window above where she
had crouched with the children but, because of her protection,
Josh and Eva were unscathed. They were dazed, but there
were no tears and, apparently, no deep shock.

Poggs and his wife were also unharmed, although Bibby
was badly frightened – more so than any of the others. Those
terrible seconds it had taken her to reach the screaming
children, that cold eternity of trepid haste, had taken their
toll: her deathly pallor was still dreadful to see that morning.

Next to the orchard was a pasture divided by a low fence
where on one side cows grazed and chickens pecked at the
earth, while on the other sheep and geese mingled.

'Your own food factory,' Rivers remarked, leaning on the
field's gate and watching the animals.

Diane shook her head disapprovingly. 'It's a cynical
description, but I guess it's right. We keep pigs over on the
other side of the orchard, ducks too.'

'Ducks with pigs?'

'No. There's a pond and a small stream.'

'Like I said . . .'

She smiled. 'We also keep bees. But pigs are best – great
cultivators, and not a scrap of 'em gets wasted.'

'I hope you don't have pet names for them.'

'As a matter of fact, the children do.'

'So what d'you tell Josh and Eva when it's time for Porky
to get chopped?'

113

'It's the country, Mr Rivers, and this is a working farm, small though it is. Sure, we get sentimental about some of the animals, but there's a natural law that prevails here and the children understand it.'

'I'm not criticising. So what do you grow? You've got, what – five, six acres?'

'Ten, much of it woodland. Well, we grow wheat, barley, oats. We also go in for runner beans, French beans, broad beans, and oh yeah – peas. Then there's carrots, fodder beet and kale. Not much of any one thing, you understand – most fields are divided into half-acres.'

'Just the few of you look after all this?'

'Mack's worth three good men. We hire help in the busy times.'

In the distance one of the cows was moving through the rising steam, its legless body seeming to float above the ground.

'It sounds like you're ready for the siege,' Rivers remarked, watching the spectral shape.

'Siege?'

He turned to face her, one elbow still resting on the gate. 'When it's all finally gone wrong. When we've screwed up the world badly enough for the food supply to become critical for every country.'

'You really are a cynic.'

'I know what's happening.'

'Doesn't everyone have an idea?'

'There are plenty of pessimists around, but people generally like to avoid bad news. Their own governments work hard to encourage that.'

'No one can avoid what's plain to see.'

'What can be seen is only half of it – you know that. Most people imagine we still maintain some control.'

'You paint a black picture.'

He gave a short, scoffing laugh. 'I thought that was the

one thing we were agreed on – the bloody disastrous state we've brought upon ourselves.'

'There has to be a way of changing things. At least we're trying to find answers.'

There was a hint of wickedness in his smile. 'I thought you were trying to take care of yourselves.' He waved a hand at the land around them.

Her face tightened with anger. 'That was never the idea. We came here ten years ago when it was pretty much the same set-up, only the man who owned the place had died and his widow had problems keeping it running. Poggsy needed somewhere quiet and roomy enough to continue his researches and we all liked the notion of becoming self-sufficient. At that time we had no idea things were going to get this bad – our intention was just to live our lives without adding to the world's ecological problems. We also happen to think Hazelrod's a great environment for Josh and Eva. Would you bring up your own kids in the city if you had a choice?'

'I don't have any. Kids, I mean.'

'I know that.'

'And what else d'you know about me?'

'Not that much about your personal life. Apart from being a physicist, you've a degree in Computing Sciences. Your full title is Higher Scientific Officer and you've been with the Met for – what? Fourteen, fifteen years now? And during that time you've been involved in such research as the physics of cloud and precipitation, airflow in the lowest kilometre of the atmosphere, the measurement of rain and cloud by radar and from satellites. Exciting stuff like that.'

She gave him a stiff smile. 'For the past few years, though, you've become involved in more significant matters. The global climate and the development of numerical models to represent and predict atmospheric processes, for instance. It appears that certain people who control government purse strings were finally alerted to the climate problems the world was facing and decided to spend money where it was desperately needed.'

She looked towards the misty hills, as though her thoughts were distracted. But he discovered that was far from so.

'This is the interesting part,' she went on. 'You don't work from the Met Office itself, nor from the more specialised Hadley Centre. No, your particular working group, along with two others, operates from a more covert establishment somewhere just outside London. It goes under the guise of an ordinary outstation, or an experimental site, just one of the many dotted around the country. You and your special team are directly answerable to the Met Office's Chief Executive, who also happens to be the UK's Permanent Representative at the World Meteorological Organisation in Geneva. He himself is responsible to the Secretary of State for Defence, no less.'

Rivers was bemused rather than angry. 'I suppose it would do no good to ask where you got this information from.'

'Poggsy still has contacts within the system. Tell me something. The research plane that crashed with you on board – you weren't there as just a casual observer, were you?'

He didn't answer straight away. Instead he now looked towards the grey-green hills. 'I'd been storm-chasing for over a year,' he said after a while. 'Through the Indian Ocean, to the Pacific, to the Atlantic, hoping to discover some kind of pattern, no matter how vague or how general. But there wasn't – there *isn't* – any; at least, none that we've managed to establish. We know the causes, we have an idea where they'll strike, but we still don't know *when* they'll start.'

'Why would it help? There's nothing your people can do to control them.'

'Who knows? Maybe one day we'll be able to. For now we'd settle for long-term advance warning.' He brushed off a large fly from the back of his hand and the insect flitted away, buzzing vehemently. Rivers noticed a tiny spot of blood on his skin where the fly had been gorging itself. He wiped it with a handkerchief. 'Why bother to find out so much about me, Diane? Surely it can't be that important to you.'

'I guess we wanted to know what kind of person you were, and if we could trust you.'

'You trust me? That's a little cockeyed, isn't it?'

'Not if we were going to tell you about the children.'

He looked sharply at her, his eyebrows raised. 'You thought I might have harmed them?'

'We're sure they're in danger of some kind. You saw what happened last night.'

'A freak wind. It had nothing to do with the children. Any one of us could have been hurt by flying glass.'

'The malevolence was directed towards them.'

'Malevolence? Oh boy.'

'They've felt it before – we all have. But last night was the first time it positively manifested itself.'

'Why do I get the feeling I should have left when I intended?'

'You were in no condition to drive last night. Before the . . . the incident, or afterwards.' She looked him squarely in the eyes and he saw the fierceness of her determination. 'Why are you trying to resist us? Why can't you take us at face value?'

He couldn't help but laugh. 'Do you have any idea at all of your "face value"? Any normal person couldn't help but take you for a bunch of weirdos.'

Surprisingly, she laughed too, and her smile was genuine when she said, 'I don't think I'd blame them. And I wouldn't blame you in the least for thinking so. Mysterious lights, psychic children . . . welcome to the funny farm.' She indicated the cows and the geese. 'Literally . . .'

It broke the frostiness between them and Rivers felt some

of his tenseness easing. His doubts, however, and his disquiet, lingered. 'You really believe Josh and Eva have some kind of paranormal power?' he said.

'I know they do. They've proved it many times.'

'How?'

'Oh . . . small things. Finding missing objects without even looking. Knowing exactly what the other is thinking or doing when they're apart. Seeing things they couldn't possibly see through their own eyes . . .'

'I don't understand.'

'A few weeks ago Eva was playing with her dolls in the kitchen when she ran across the room and threw herself into my arms. She was crying, but managed to tell me that one of the sheep was caught in the barbed-wire fence around the field and was cutting itself badly trying to escape. We found the poor creature over in the far field, tearing its coat to shreds as it tried to pull itself free.'

'She hadn't seen it from a window?'

'No way. The field is screened from the house by trees.' A bee flew between them, its drone full and resonant in the sultry air. 'And y'know, Josh wasn't far behind us. He'd been with Mack in the cow-shed when he'd had the same – vision, I suppose you'd call it – as Eva. There are other examples – like I said, mostly small things. But they're convincing all the same.'

'I've read about disturbed children –'

'They are not disturbed, Mr Rivers.'

Her annoyance cut into him.

'In every way they're perfectly normal kids. But they have a gift that none of us understands. Maybe they're the children of a new age, or maybe a throwback with powers we all possessed in a bygone time.'

'If that's so, if they really do have some kind of paranormal power, then it could be that they, themselves, caused those windows to shatter last night.'

118

'So what became of the freak wind you mentioned earlier?' she challenged.

'I'm not dismissing that possibility.'

'Huh.' It was a small, derisory sound.

'But on the other hand, it's not unknown for the troubled thoughts of . . .' He hesitated, not quite knowing how to state it. 'Overwrought children?' he suggested tentatively. Her expression tightened, but he went on. 'To, uh, manifest themselves in a physical way.'

'Josh and Eva are *not* overwrought, Mr Rivers. Far from it. But they are sensitive to certain things.'

'Okay,' he said placatingly. 'I meant no offence. Just try to look at it from a stranger's point of view.'

Her body seemed to relax and the faint, almost playful, smile was back. 'We're not being very fair to you, are we? You get caught in the English version of a monsoon, crash your car, spend hours listening to our diatribe on global warming, very nearly get cut to pieces by flying glass – and now you've got spooky kids to contend with. You must be wondering if you've wandered into the Twilight Zone.'

He didn't laugh, nor did he smile. 'It'd crossed my mind.'

She laughed for him. 'We're not crazy, believe me, we're not.'

'If . . .' he began. 'If the children are . . .'

'Look, why don't you use the word intuitive? It might sit with you more easily.'

He nodded. The word was almost acceptable. 'If they *are* intuitive in the way that you say they are, then how long have you known?'

'We've been aware that they're a little unusual since they were, oh, I guess since they were around a year old. Since we adopted them, in fact. As babies they had a way of communicating with each other that –'

'Wait a minute,' he interrupted. 'You're not their natural mother?'

119

'Josh and Eva were Romanian orphans.'

He wasn't sure why he was quite so startled, for the two children bore little resemblance to Diane herself. Even her hair was dark auburn, rather than black. And her eyes were slightly almond-shaped, whereas theirs were wide and rounded. He'd assumed they favoured their absent father. He was about to comment when a distant shout caught their attention.

They turned to see Hugo Poggs hurrying through the orchard towards them, his stride laboured and his face red with his haste. Even from where they stood they could hear his wheezing breath.

'It's just been on the news, Mr Rivers, Diane.' He slowed a little so that he could catch his breath. 'Grenada . . .' they heard him say. 'It's terrible . . .'

He stopped in front of them, one hand reaching for Diane's shoulder as if for support. He drew in deeper breaths, gradually gaining control. Rivers winced at the rasping sound coming from his throat.

'Forgive me,' Poggs said at last, his face beginning to lose its alarming hue. 'Must get back to smoking m'pipe. Only thing that'll save me.' He cleared his throat and dropped his hand away from his daughter-in-law's shoulder. 'The children were right. A tidal wave . . . a massive tidal wave . . . struck Grenada last night, their late afternoon. According to the radio, the island has been devastated, ruined. It took the full force of the first wave, then the others that followed. Oh dear God . . .'

Rivers felt a coldness invading his mind as well as his body. It couldn't be . . . He thought the children had been dreaming, had suffered a nightmare, no more than that. He hadn't even bothered to check with his own office whether any bad storms or conditions had been reported or noticed on incoming satellite data. Christ, he thought it would have been irrational to do so.

Something, a compulsion, made him look back towards the house.

The two small, dark figures stood near the centre of the orchard. They were hand-in-hand, perfectly still.

They were watching him.

9

Pilgrim Hall was discreetly set in parkland high on the broken ridge of hills that stretched through the home counties of Surrey and Kent to the east coast, known as the North Downs. To the south were green vales and hilly woodlands, parts of these now toned an unhealthy brown, while to the north was the vast concrete sprawl of Greater London. On this humid, sunny day, something odd tainted the atmosphere, lending the faintest yellowish cast to the air itself; it was neither a smog, nor a heat haze, but something brought by high winds from the far south. It was sand that sullied the sky, sand carried from the Sahara Desert by the sirocco, a wind that before had only managed to reach the shores of the Mediterranean and the islands west of Africa, but which now strayed as far as the southern regions of England itself. It rendered the light peculiarly oppressive, lending an eerie, almost crepuscular, tint to the landscape.

To avoid the city, Rivers had taken the eight-lane orbital route, eventually leaving it for the narrow lanes that led to the top of the Downs. He passed through steep woodlands in the hillside before reaching the high point that was the long ridge itself, and it was not too far from there to the discreet entrance of the woodland park. The tar and gravel road ran straight for some way before curving sharply towards a small cluster of single-storey structures, interspersed with satellite dishes and antennae, all these dominated by what had once been an elegant Georgian house, complete with white porticoed entrance. Other less classically designed appendages sprung gracelessly from its sides; these attached working 'sheds' housed various experimental models, computers, consoles and a magnetic tape library databank.

He parked the car in the shade of Pilgrim Hall and, after wiping a hand across the windscreen and examining the fine dust left on his palm, limped to the columned entrance. His skin was sticky from the heat even before he reached the air-conditioned coolness of the building's foyer.

There was no reception as such, but an open door with a plastic ENQUIRY sign served the purpose. A secretary looked up from her typing as he passed the doorway, her eyes magnified owlishly behind blue-framed glasses.

'Mr Rivers? We didn't expect you today.'

'Can't break the habit.' He paused by the door. 'Is Jonesy in?'

'He did the weekend shift, but he'll be back tomorrow. Oh, he left this package for me to bike to your home this morning.' She picked up a large brown envelope from the corner of her desk. 'I rang you earlier to make sure you'd be there for the delivery, but there was no reply.'

He was momentarily puzzled, then remembered he had asked his assistant to get details of yesterday's storm to him. He took the envelope and turned to go.

'By the way,' the secretary called after him, 'Mr Sheridan is here.'

Rivers slowed for a step or two. Why should the Research

Director be there at Pilgrim Hall? Usually the mountain had to go to Mohammed. He quickened his stride, the rubber tip of his cane tapping dully along the tiled hallway, a suspicion beginning to grow in his mind.

Ahead of him the slim figure of a girl was emerging from a room marked G23. Celia's hair was an untidy mess of lacklustre curls and she wore her usual expression of absorbed concentration. Her face was painfully thin, almost gaunt, but even so the Met Office had once considered her pretty enough for the so-called 'glamour' side of weather forecasting, the coveted television slot after the evening and lunchtime news programmes. It had been a mistake, for Celia Jar had been ill at ease under the gaze of millions of viewers and noticeably uncomfortable wearing brisk power suits and coiffured hair. It was Rivers who had rescued her from such high-profile trivia, realising her potential as a dedicated researcher when she had come to him one day in a desperate search for more serious meteorological pursuits. Happy now in casual clothes and conscientious studies, she had proved to be an invaluable member of his team.

She stopped dead when she saw him, and her mouth opened in surprise.

'Hello, Celia.'

'This is your week off. Why are you here?' She seemed almost irate with him.

'I get the feeling I'm not welcome today.'

'I didn't mean . . . Jim, Sheridan's here. He's in your office.'

'In *my* office?'

'With Marley.'

Adam Marley was the head of Working Group Two, a pallid, stooped man whose colleagues had dubbed him the Ghost.

'What're they up to?' Rivers kept his voice steady as anger rose with the suspicion.

'I'm not sure. They gave me a grilling earlier this morning.'

His frown asked the question.

'They wanted to know about our programmes and future projections.'

'I gave Sheridan a rundown last week before the conference. And I flatly refused to give any short-term or long-term projections until we've gathered more data. What the hell's he playing at?'

She blinked up at him, biting anxiously at the corner of her lower lip. 'He's impatient, he wants results. I told him he'd have to speak to you.'

Celia was not a natural rebel and he knew it would have been daunting for her to stand up to the Research Director, particularly with Marley's Ghost present; the latter, who shared the same rank as Rivers and who regarded their separate projects as competitive rather than cooperative, tended to treat the lower ranks with ill-disguised disdain. He touched her arm and managed a smile to go with the gesture.

'I suppose Sheridan knew Jonesy was away today?' he said.

'He didn't ask for him.'

No, he wouldn't; Jonesy was cantankerous at the best of times. 'Don't worry about it. Probably the men from the ministry have been on Sheridan's back since last week's World Conference looking for results that we can't provide.'

Yet, to be fair to Sheridan, he had always staunchly supported his three divisions – Atmospheric Processes Research, Short-range Forecasting Research, and Extended-range Forecasting and Climate Research – against any brickbats thrown by the Chief Executive and his Meteorological Committee or the Ministry of Defence itself. Rivers had even witnessed Sheridan's admonishment of the Meteorological Research Sub-committee, a distinguished body of scientists, high-powered industrialists, and senior officials from certain government departments, when it had the audacity to question the need to spend money on a particular area of climate research.

Yet why the invasion of Rivers' office, the third degree on a member of his staff? And of course, it had been the Research Director himself who had insisted on Rivers taking a week's leave. Concern for his health? Or something more?

Celia was looking unhappier by the moment and he realised his grip on her arm had tightened. He let go, embarrassed. Could be that Sheridan was right: maybe he did need a break. A few months ago he'd have taken such interference in his stride. (Then again, a few months ago – before the crash – the situation probably would never have arisen.)

'Uh, let me have all the information on yesterday's tidal wave, will you? Do we know the extent of the damage?'

'Reports are still coming in, but they're estimating anywhere between 2,000 and 3,000 dead. St George's took the full impact of the first wave.'

'Yeah, I heard on the radio.' He felt tired and depressed. Such a casual waste of life. No warning, no chance for people to get to high ground. 'Where did the surge begin?'

'Approximately sixty miles south-west of the Windward chain. A seismic disturbance in the oceanic crust.'

That perplexed Rivers. 'Are there fault lines in that area?'

'Not until now. Part of the floor moved upwards and caused the shift in the sea. The third and fourth waves were the worst – over 125 feet by the time they reached Grenada, according to preliminary reports.'

'Christ. What was their length?'

'Between sixty and seventy miles.'

That might explain their height, for such tides could sometimes stretch for more than 200 miles; the more compact the waves, then the higher the elevation – at least in most cases. Of course, the sheer and sudden violence of the break could have accounted for its force.

'Intervals?' he asked.

'Approximately twelve minutes with the earlier ones. They stopped just two hours ago, the last only a few feet above normal sea level.'

He stroked his chin with the corner of the envelope the receptionist had given him, lost in thought.

'Jim?'

'Uh? Sorry – what is it?'

'Mr Sheridan?'

He let out a small, resigned huff of air. 'Yeah. Mr Sheridan. Get me all you can on the tidal wave and bring it along to my office.' He handed her the envelope. 'Keep it with this.'

'Jim, you don't look good.'

'I didn't shave today.'

'It's more than that.'

He tapped the envelope. 'Soon as you can, Celia.'

She watched his back as he limped down the corridor. Then, still chewing at her lower lip, she went back into the room marked G23.

'What on earth are you doing here?'

Sheridan was seated behind Rivers' desk, an open file in front of him. Marley was leaning over him as though they had been studying the enclosed documents together.

'Something important you needed to know?' Rivers said coldly from the doorway. He noticed the other buff-coloured files scattered around the desk. Even some of the drawers of the metal cabinets beyond the desk had been left half open, as if hastily raided.

Sheridan closed the file and leaned back in the chair. He seemed irritated rather than abashed. 'You're supposed to be on leave,' he said.

'I wanted information on last night's tidal wave.'

'Just another disaster, Jim. Nothing unusual about that nowadays.'

Marley had moved away from the desk and was now leaning an elbow on one of the grey filing cabinets. 'Are you all right, Rivers? I must say you look as though you need your vacation.' He had an annoying habit of speaking with a perpetual faint smile, so that there always seemed to be a hint of mockery contained in his words.

Rivers ignored him. 'What's the idea, Charles? I brought you up to date with our progress last week.'

'You might call it progress, but unfortunately the Chief Executive has a different view. Remember, it's Sir Spencer who has to take the flak from not only the Defence Minister, but the PM himself.'

'You know the problems . . .'

'Of course I do. And I'm also aware that ours is not the only agency dealing with those matters. However, the Met Office does have a reputation to maintain – we are, after all, world leaders in climate prediction and research. Frankly, the Meteorological Committee and the Research Sub-committee were somewhat embarrassed by our presentation at last week's conference.'

'So I'm the whipping boy.'

Sheridan was genuinely startled. 'Of course not. My God, that isn't what this is all about. It doesn't hurt me to tell you that you're one of the most highly regarded scientific officers we have. But the accident, Jim . . .' He waved a hand helplessly over the desk as though disconcerted by his own insinuation. He dropped his hand despondently on to the file. 'I believe you are not yet fully recovered. The air crash took more out of you than you care to admit.'

'The work hasn't suffered.'

'I'd agree if it were providing more accurate forecasts and perhaps some realistic solutions to our problems.'

'We already know what we should be doing. We've known for half a century.'

'And virtually every country in the world is doing its damnedest to rectify the situation.'

'A little late in the day.'

'Yes, I agree. But at least the will is now there.'

'Yet we're still plundering the world's resources. There's still no real control over that.'

'Energy is something we can't do without, I'm afraid, and no government will allow its country's industries or let its people's well-being suffer due to lack of it.'

'Then there will never be any single solution.'

'I don't believe the Research Director is suggesting there might be,' Marley put in smoothly.

Right on cue, thought Rivers. Marley must be loving this.

'Of course I'm bloody well not.' Sheridan's angry glare was directed towards Marley. He returned his attention to Rivers. 'Look, Jim, I want to play it straight with you, okay? It's fairly obvious to all of us that you haven't yet got over that dreadful experience three months ago. It's not surprising – you were lucky to get out alive.' He held up a hand again, this time to ward off Rivers' protests. 'Look at you now. You're ready to drag me over the desk and yell in my ear that you're fine, there's nothing wrong with you, you've never felt better. You're ragged, Jim, don't you understand? Oh, you've disguised it well, but your nerves are stretched to breaking point. And we know your leg injury is still causing you a great deal of pain. Do you think we don't read our staff's medical reports? Why the hell do you imagine I ordered you to take a week's leave? If we could have spared you longer, I'd have made it a month, perhaps even more than that. The fact is, we didn't allow you enough time to recover. It's the mental scars as well as the physical that have to mend, don't you see?'

Rivers forced a calmness upon himself. He leaned on the

cane and studied the floor for a moment or two. 'You think I'm heading for a breakdown, is that it?' he asked Sheridan in a tone that held challenge rather than sought affirmation.

The Research Director groaned aloud. 'Certainly not. But I'm aware that you're not functioning as well as you used to. Marley here tells me –'

'Ah.'

'I was about to say that Marley tells me he's prepared to take over some of your projects if you're willing. Nothing devious about that, just a colleague extending a helping hand. You'd offer the same to him, I'm sure.'

'Is that why you're going through those' – he indicated the scatter of files on the desk – 'and why you've been questioning my staff?'

Sheridan did not bother to hide his impatience. 'We were bringing ourselves up to date. Yes, yes, I know you spoke to me last week but I thought Marley and I could decide together just what he could take on.'

'Actually, I'm not sure that I agree with some of your conjectures, Rivers.' Marley was sifting through the files with a thin hand, presumably searching for one in particular. 'The influence of sea surface temperature changes on seasonal variations in the tropics, for instance . . .'

'Shut up, Marley.' Rivers leaned on the desk and spoke quietly to Sheridan. 'My people are good enough to continue our set projects in my absence. One week certainly wouldn't make any difference. So come on, Charles, say what's on your mind.'

Sheridan hesitated for no more than a second or two. 'I've already said it – you're not providing us with any answers, Jim.'

'At the moment there aren't any. We need more time, more examples . . .'

'More catastrophes? The world can't wait.'

'I didn't realise it was depending on me alone.'

'No need for sarcasm. All I'm saying is that I've decided

to ease your burden a little, direct some of your work else-where. I think Marley here is more able to cope at this point in time.'

'And if I don't agree to it?'

'I'm not offering you a choice. I don't mean this unkindly, but I want you to leave immediately. Go home and rest. Better still, take yourself off somewhere, somewhere relaxing, where you can forget all this for a while. Give your mind – and your body, for God's sake – a break. We'll talk again on your return next week.' His gaze was unwavering. 'Until then I want to see neither hide nor hair of you. Is that clear enough?'

Rivers straightened from the desk; there was a tightness in his chest that begged release. He fought against his anger again, but Marley's half smile almost tipped the balance.

Sheridan's tone was conciliatory. 'Jim, you're not yet ready to continue your work. I made a mistake, I thought getting you back into the stream of things would be the best therapy for you. But I was wrong, and I think it's time you realised it yourself. Never mind the physical pain you're still in, it's your mental state that we're' – he hastily corrected himself, not wishing to give the impression that Rivers' soundness of mind had been a topic of general discussion – 'I'm concerned about. The trauma of seeing those men die like that . . .' He was stopped by the sudden panic in the other man's eyes, a skittish wildness that quickly passed, yet left Rivers distant and emotionless.

Disturbed, Sheridan cleared his throat and began to say something more.

Rivers' smile cut him short; it contained no warmth at all.

'Okay,' Rivers said. 'I'll stay away. But events are escalating rapidly, Charles, and the world might not be quite the same at the end of the week.'

He left the two men staring uncertainly at the empty doorway.

131

10

Now why in the hell had he said that? Christ, Sheridan already thought he was in the throes of a nervous breakdown and now he'd provided him with further evidence.

Rivers yanked open the car door and slumped into the driver's seat. Shit! What had possessed him . . . ?

'Jim?'

Celia peered through the glass. Wearily he switched on the electrics and pressed the window button.

She wiped a wisp of hair from her forehead and leaned closer to him. 'What happened with Sheridan and Marley?'

'Nothing much,' he replied more laconically than he felt. 'They seem to think some of our projects might proceed faster without me, that's all.'

She shook her head, a mixture of denial and indignation. 'That's –'

'Forget it. They could be right.' His fingers massaged the area above the bridge of his nose. 'Things have been slipping by me for a while now.'

'You haven't given yourself time to recover.'

'I'm not an invalid, Celia.'

She didn't respond.

Rivers gunned the engine, then looked back up at her. 'Play along with Marley and don't let him get to you. He knows his stuff. Tell Jonesy the same.'

'Can I come and see you at home?'

'I'm not sure I'll be there. I might just take off for a few days.'

'If you do, I'm owed some leave . . .'

He paused before shifting into reverse. 'The agency can't afford two of us to be away. There's too much going on. It's a nice offer though, Celia.'

She avoided his gaze. 'It's a serious one.'

Her hand was resting on the door panel and he briefly put his own hand over it. Then he reversed away, swinging the car round to face the long drive.

'Let me know if anything exciting happens,' he called out to her. Dust rose from the ground as the car shot forward. Within minutes he was part of the steady flow of traffic pressing into the capital.

He shivered as he turned down the car's air-conditioning from HIGH to LOW. And again he asked himself the question: Why had he said such a ridiculous thing to Sheridan? And why had it been said with such conviction? The feeling – the certainty of his doomsday warning – had left him the moment he set foot outside the research centre. Yet the thought lingered . . .

Because of its eerie yellowish cast, the bright sunshine somehow added little cheer to the shop-lined streets. Pedestrians, many of them in T-shirts and shorts, with faces, arms and legs shiny with sun-blocks, several of them wearing

Sun Alert badges, moved indolently along the litter-strewn pavements; a group of teenagers squatted against a brick wall, drinking from cans, their separate cordless headphones tuned into one miniature cassette-player, their limbs twitching listlessly in time to the private beat; a woman with bare fleshy arms wheeled a solitary child in a twin pushchair, the empty space beside the sleeping toddler perhaps the cause of her melancholy. Some shop windows were grimed with dust, while others, like the one displaying thin, wall-mounted 3-D television screens, were darkened by slender iron bars, warning signs that the current through these was switched on twenty-four hours a day prominently displayed on the glass. A giant billboard was so cluttered with pirate posters for new bands and underground magazines that the original glossy advertisement was disguised beyond legibility.

Rivers was relieved when he crossed tramlines and joined one of the Red Routes through the city, for traffic flowed more smoothly in these designated main arteries and would quickly take him away from the depressingly drab quarters. Not for the first time he wondered what London would have been like had not the 'alternate-week' system for vehicles been introduced: no doubt by now the city would have developed into one huge car park where nothing on four wheels could move more than two miles per hour.

Tower Bridge loomed up ahead, its dignity long since diminished by the garish red, white and blues of its painted girders. Traffic slowed, as if each driver was wary of the split in the old bridge's middle section; the tyre sounds took on a different tone as vehicles crossed. To the right lay the over-developed docklands area, its offices and abodes still half empty despite various government business incentive schemes and initiatives over the past ten years or so. Amidst the new-dawn architecture stood the Canary Wharf Tower, at one time the tallest tower block in Europe, and now a landmark to apathy. The constant cycle of recession had speeded up, the wheel turning ever faster because long-term investment in the swift-changing world was not merely unattractive, but nowadays deemed extreme folly. To the left was the Tower of London itself, rendered almost incongruous in these times with its backdrop of skyscraper buildings, these bastions of the city's financial quarter. Below, the Thames flowed sluggishly, its depths thick with sludge once more, the brief return to purity a decade before having become a folklore memory.

The route led him into the City itself, the capital's fiscal focus, the pecuniary precincts, through which the world's money continued to flow. The ambience changed dramatically in these canyons, for here the pace was brisk, the attire less casual. Shirts might have been shortsleeved, but they were complemented by ties; even when short trousers were worn, they were of suit material. The women were bolder in dress, their light summer-wear contrasting brightly against the dull concrete environs.

It was drawing towards the end of the lunch-hour and the streets were busy, diesel taxis everywhere, vans, buses and automobiles crawling along at moderate pace. Like a tarnished monument to self-aggrandisement, the Lloyd's Insurance building rose high ahead, its steel and chrome architecture rendered even more unappealing by blemishes and grime. The conduits and piping of the building's exposed 'innards' were in an even more wretched state than the once silvery ramparts, their surfaces rust-stained and blackened. God only knew what was in the atmosphere to cause such deterioration, thought Rivers, but an architect's dream had degenerated into an occupier's nightmare. Unfortunately, massive insurance losses over recent years due to environmental damage and natural disasters, together with the escalation of crime-related claims and general incompetence had seriously eroded the corporation's financial base (and Names, those outside members whose money covered all risks, were almost impossible to attract nowadays), so that the 'cleansing' of the building itself was a low priority. There were some who took satisfaction in the knowledge that the Lutine Bell, rung whenever a ship was lost at sea, had rung metaphorically for Lloyd's itself.

Rivers slowed to a halt, allowing a group of giggling office girls trapped in the centre of the road to cross. One waved a thank you and was nudged by her companion, who cheekily stuck out a tongue at him. He managed a smile, then closed the gap between his car and the one in front when the girls were through.

Lights ahead had stopped the traffic's flow. He checked the computerised TIME-WAIT indicator set in the lamppost by the side of the road and turned off the engine when he saw that the lights would be on red for three minutes, fifteen seconds, just over the limit for engine-running in congested city areas. The hydrogen-powered vehicle was *still* having teething troubles.(or so it was alleged: Rivers wondered how much bribery and sabotage by the big oil companies had delayed the mass-introduction of the water-drinking fuel-cell engine). He leaned forward to press the radio button, then decided against it: he'd had enough bad news. He slumped in his seat and rested an elbow on the doorframe, his fingers scratching the stubble of his chin. What to do with himself for the rest of the week? Take Sheridan's advice and get away somewhere? Leave the problems behind, give his head a rest. Not such a bad idea at that. Find somewhere quiet, peaceful, let the world get on with its own predicament for a while. After all, he was only one, insignificant doctor of physics, so what difference would it make to the global plan? Besides –

Jesus! His hands gripped the steering wheel. *What was that?*

He looked around. People in the street had stopped dead. They, too, were looking around, bewilderment on their faces. A woman nearby clutched at her partner. The man said something to her, probably a reassurance that everything was all right, although his own expression was hardly convincing.

It came again. A kind of lurch. As if the earth itself had given a small hiccup.

A paralysing coldness rushed through Rivers and his knuckles whitened as he clutched the plastic steering wheel even more tightly. His eyes blinked against a sudden glare, but there was nothing bright before him; the image – a round ball of light – somehow had appeared on the retinas of his eyes without being physically present. It was a thought, he quickly rationalised, a strong memory induced by shock. But so real. And so swiftly gone.

The people were beginning to move again, looking askance at one another, shaking their heads in disbelief. Someone laughed, but there was a hollowness to the sound. One of the girls who had just passed before Rivers' car started to cry. An elderly man, smartly dressed in a dark blue messenger's uniform, rested a hand against the side of a building to steady himself. Rivers noticed that the green digits of the TIME-WAIT indicator were flashing rapidly.

A low, ominous rumbling began.

He felt it rising through the floor of the car, rocking the suspension, causing the bodywork to vibrate. The initial sound was familiar, the kind of deep heavy rolling noise that a lorry passing through the night might make, but its increasing intensity – and subdued violence – was unworldly. Rivers understood what was about to happen, for he had studied recordings and films of earth tremors many times during the last few years; but nothing had prepared him for the sheer unnerving violence of the earth's sudden shift. The car began to tremble as the rumbling from below swelled to a deep roaring. The lamppost nearby began to oscillate. People out there in the street became unsteady on their feet; some reached for the nearest support. He saw huge plate-glass windows beginning to warp.

Then something pushed hard against the floor of the car, an abrupt, powerful shove that lifted him from his seat, only the seat-belt preventing his head from hitting the roof. Screams and yells came through the closed windows. Men and women sprawled on the concrete pavements, while others clung to posts or pedestrian barriers. Another wave shook the ground and Rivers' car was shunted into the vehicle in front. He jerked back into his seat and, amazed, watched the roadway outside ripple. Vein-like cracks began to appear in its surface.

The world seemed to settle once more, and the rumbling softened; but the lull did not last long.

The fearsome sound deepened, became a thunderous abyssal roaring that shook the landscape and sent people reeling for the second time. A van in the opposite lane tilted crazily as the road rose beneath it. The driver hastily slid the door back and scrambled out, crawling away as fast as his hands and knees would take him. The van failed to topple, but settled back on top of the fresh-risen mound. The glass wall of an office block's reception area further along the street split from top to bottom as people inside fled through the wide doors next to it. More poured from other doorways, panic-stricken, afraid of being caught inside collapsing buildings.

The trembling of the earth continued, its awful sound almost drowning the human cries. Some drivers and passengers were leaving their vehicles, perhaps wary of becoming trapped inside them, but Rivers stayed where he was, realising what could happen next.

It sounded like a heavy shower or hailstones striking the car's rooftop at first, then larger fragments of glass began to fall. Pieces of masonry and metal bounced off the road and pavements. Larger sheets of glass, popped or shaken from distorted frames, shattered against concrete and bodies alike. His windscreen became an instant myriad of spiderweb lines as a missile exploded against the toughened glass. Still the ground thundered.

Rivers flinched every time something heavy clattered against his metal shelter, yet he was mesmerised by the scene outside. Through the side window he watched the panic as people desperately sought cover, some heading back inside the buildings they had just left, while others clung to anything solid or crawled into doorways. Many lay prone, knees curled up to their chests, their faces buried into their hands.

A man and a woman – the same two he had noticed earlier – came stumbling towards his car. The man, dressed in a beige, lightweight summer suit, shouted something at him, perhaps an appeal to open one of the passenger doors. For a second or two Rivers was motionless, too overwhelmed by what was happening – and its implications – to move. But the terror on the couple's faces galvanised him into action and he reached over his seat to pull at the door handle. His fingers froze on the latch as a huge sheet of plate glass, dislodged from an office tower's upper windows, smashed on to the pavement outside.

But before it had shattered into a million fragments, the toughened glass had sliced into the running man's left shoulder and scythed through the length of his body. Bizarrely, the woman held on to her companion as the rest of his body toppled away, and she looked into the eyes that still flickered with astonished life. The remaining portion of human flesh soon crumpled, leaving the woman clawing at her own face in shocked disbelief.

Glass mixed with blood had spattered the car's windows, a sickening split-second after-effect. He watched as the woman slowly sank to her knees beside the cloven corpse. Another sheet of glass smashed to the ground close by, missing her by only three or four feet, broken pieces flying lethally outwards. Water burst through the fissure in the roadway, a high-pressured fountain that drenched anyone in close proximity. Droplets pattered against the rooftop over Rivers' head.

The car was shaking again, and this time he held on to both seat and steering wheel to steady himself. Screams and the clattering of falling stonework merged with the deep rumbling from below, creating a nightmarish discord that was as potent as the juddering movement itself. In the distance, he could see the great tower building of a national bank swaying as if gently rocked by phenomenal winds. From somewhere further down the street there came a muffled explosion, soon followed by black plumes of smoke spewing out of vents in the ground.

Rivers felt a queasiness in his stomach, a feathery shifting as though the car were skidding on sheet ice; he swallowed hard, afraid he would be sick. The excessive shaking suddenly reduced to a kind of rolling vibration, but this lessening only increased the pandemonium in the street. Those who had fallen scrambled to their feet and began running unsteadily in all directions. More poured from the buildings, sweeping aside those who were trying to return. A red cab tore down the road from the opposite direction in which Rivers' vehicle was facing, mounting the kerb when it reached the angled van that was blocking the way. Sparks flew when metal grated against the wall as the cab squeezed past the obstruction without dropping speed. The driver yanked the wheel hard in a bid to get back on the road, but he was unable to avoid the office workers streaming out on to the pavement and into his path. The crowd scattered, but there were too many and the vehicle was moving too fast. The cab ploughed into them, sending bodies tumbling in the air, bumping over others who had fallen. It slewed back on to the road, tyres screeching on the now wet surface, and smashed into the side of a bus. The cab door flew open and the driver fell out, his eyes wide with panic; he scrabbled around on his knees as if seeking a place to hide.

A *thump* from the front of his car diverted Rivers' attention. He turned to see the distraught woman whose companion had been so hideously killed leaning over the bonnet, her face a red mask of blood. He could see a long sliver of glass protruding from her forehead, but he couldn't tell if it was pain or terror that made her drum her fists against the metal. Rivers pushed open his door and got out.

The noise, now unhindered, swept over him, an assault that heightened his own dread. A young man lay in the gutter only a few feet away, screeching but making no attempt to flee. A lamppost groaned as it tilted at an impossible angle. Someone – it could have been a man or a woman so hysterical was the voice – called a name repeatedly, while other voices wailed for help. The jutting façade of a nearby building began to crack, fissures starting at its base and stretching upwards, branching into dozens of jagged lines as they ascended, sharp cannon sounds announcing each fresh break. Another explosion, this time from somewhere far away. Smoke billowed from one of the side turnings.

The vibration from beneath the ground felt even more strange to Rivers now that it was coming up through the soles of his feet; it seemed to run through his whole body like a continuous but painless electric current. It was impossible to think straight, for the fact that London itself was undergoing an earthquake was difficult enough to come to terms with, and the shuddering of the ground and the noise and mayhem around him induced panic rather than reason. Something struck his back – it might have been a piece of glass or it might have been stonework – and jolted him enough to get him moving.

Rivers ran around to the other side of the car and dragged the woman off the bonnet. Although she did not resist, her body was rigid with tension and he was forced to handle her roughly. Yanking the passenger door open, he pushed the bloodied woman inside. Rather than risk going back to the driver's side, he went in through the rear passenger door, then reached over the front seat to the woman, shoving her down and covering her head and shoulders with his own body. Missiles rained down, some of them heavy enough to dent the roof over their heads.

The woman's screams reached a new pitch when something smashed into the side of the car, almost tipping it over.

Rivers fell into the well between the front and rear seats and for a short while everything became dark and mercifully quiet . . .

HARBOR FREEWAY, LOS ANGELES, CALIFORNIA

Tina Ziggy, real name Barbra Zeigerfield, was in a hurry. Unfortunately, the traffic she was in wasn't. The sight of cars, trucks, and even trailers, backed up on the Hollywood Freeway ramp ahead caused her pretty, California-sun face to grimace. *'Shitshitshit. Move, you mothers, move!'* The traffic took no notice.

The old Chevy pick-up next to her played country. Loud country. The executive on the other side silently bawled out one of his minions on his carphone, the windows of his Mercedes shut tight against the heat and fumes. He caught Ziggy watching and gave her a wink, certainly not angry at her. Now a little wave, phone still glued to his ear, as his car inched onwards. A smug smile, too. The pick-up in the other lane was moving off now. Bye-bye, k.d.lang (still the cream after all these years).

'Fuck you,' muttered Tina.

Feel like shit, she told herself. The Xanax and the Norpramin worked okay, they kept her off the coke, but she was gaining weight rapidly, and was for ever constipated, and she was tired all the time. Tired, but at least she slept most nights. And the craving was going. As were most of her friends. But who needed them? Actors were lunkheads, more interested in their own shadows than other humans. Scratch an actor, hear them squeal. Cokeheads most of them, her set anyway. And worse. Her breed, the next-generation brat-pack, were known by the Inner Circle as the smack-pack. Drugs, fuckin' and rock without the roll (new era low-rock). Peacocks and cockpleasers (and *that* went for both sexes). The hell with them all. No more screw-ups with body or head. Brody was outa the picture – *her* picture, anyway. Let him fuck up someone else's iife. The new River Phoenix? Hah! Somebody oughta let Brody know there was nothing wrong with the old one. No more punch bag for his disappointments. And no more dumb actor boyfriends for her. Be yourself, Zig, old bean. From now on be – what was the word? – *discernin'*. Yeah, that was the one. Use it today. *Discernin'*. Yes, Mr Leiberwitz, oh Mighty Producer, god of all you pervert, I'm looking for more *discernin'* parts, parts that I can *breathe* in. Good. *'Fuckin' good.'*

Movin'. Traffic's movin'. Her open-topped Bug hopped forward. Shit, calm down, girl. You still got time to be early. Take a Valium or two. Or three. Everything's gonna be fine. Today's the day of the big break. She could feel it in her crotch.

Music blasted her ear again as she drew level with the pick-up. The driver, a square-jawed hunk sporting a straw stetson leered down at her, giving her the tongue. She gave him the finger and he turned to his good buddy next to him and said something. The other creep leaned over to look. He panted like a dog, tongue touching his unshaved chin. Tina concentrated on the road ahead.

Thankfully her lane was shifting and she was able to draw away from the two goons and their noise. Hell of a day already. And a miserable bitchin' day it was, too. Lookit the sky. Dark, the California sun under wraps for once. Creepy dark. Not nice. Least it wasn't cold. Fuckin' weird, though.

Tina pulled the sides of her A-shape skirt – split in the front almost to the pubes (the arrow points the way, Mr Leiberwitz) – over her tightless thighs, today not willing to give even a peek away for free. Nothing was for free any more. Lessons had been learnt. Free spirit didn't have to mean free fuckin'. No more, did it. From now on she was gonna be discernin'.

Oops. Hollywood Freeway, Downtown/4th Street. Gotta get over to the exit ramp. Gotta get through this shit on the right first, though. She could see the Dorothy Chandler Pavilion in the distance, the place where they gave away the Oscars and her ultimate destination. Not today, though. But soon. Or eventually. She glanced up at the overhead freeway. At least the traffic on Hollywood was movin' faster. Not far to Universal once she was up there. She waved her arm over the side and flashed her indicator. Come on, gimme a break, lemme in, you bastards. She had to get to the studio early for make-up and wardrobe – this screen test was the real thing. And if Mr Producer, O Lord of all he lusts after, wanted to 'spend time' with her, then so be it. Anythin' for art. *Anythin'*. But nothing for free. No more. She'd make that plain.

Tina needed this part. So what if it was second fiddle to the second fiddle to the leadin' lady who was only token female interest anyway. It was a good movie. It had a real story. And she – if she got the part – got to die before it was over. That was always great. Memorable. Even though it was down at number seven on the serial killer's list.

'Let me in, you motherfuckers!'

The truck with the two cowboys swerved dangerously close, the goons grinning down at her, the driver's buddy almost on his lap now. Clint Black mocked her with his macho bullshit song.

'Come on, guys, gimme a break,' she appealed. 'I gotta get somewhere.'

Texas blew her a kiss. Returned the finger too. KZLA wished her a good day.

Tina put her foot down to make up ground she'd lost trying to pull over, but a Pontiac hauled over in front of her, stealing her space. A Nissan closed up behind.

She swerved towards the pick-up again, threatening to ram it, her face hot with rage. *'I don't need this, you . . .'* She didn't bother to finish: they knew what they were.

'Going somewhere special, hon?' The counterfeit cowboy nudged the hat brim off his forehead with a knuckle, eyes and face wide with mock concern.

'Yeah, up your ass if you don't move outa the way.'

'You mean thet, babe? Ooeee.' He dug an elbow into his smirking companion.

She changed her tack. These dorks wouldn't be threatened. 'Please, boys. I'm in deep shit if I don't get off this freeway.'

'Little girl, ma heart's bleedin'.'

'Fuck you.'

'Ooh, say it's true.'

She banged her horn in frustration. The man in the Nissan took up her plight and banged his horn too. A mean look from Straw Hat quietened him.

Tina looked ahead. A little more space there. She jerked forward, but the pick-up stayed with her, keeping her blocked in.

Okay, okay, stay cool. She'd swallow the whole fuckin' bottle of Valium when she was through this. No, that was bad news. She'd do the screen test like a robot.

'Ahhh . . .' she wailed, eyes beginning to swell with dampness.

The cowboy leaned further out of his cab, left hand flat against the door panel. He opened his leering mouth to say something, when his buddy tugged at his checkered shirt and pointed through the windscreen.

'Lookit,' Tina heard the man shout over the music. 'Lookit over theyar.'

Straw Hat squinted like a true Plainsman as he followed the direction of his companion's pointing finger. 'The fuck is it?' he said slowly.

Despite her anger, Tina looked too. Her pencilled eyebrows rose in surprise.

A small light was dancing across the car rooftops.

'St Elmo's fire,' she heard the cowboy say from some way off.

'Naw,' argued the other one. 'Ball o' lightnin'. Lookit the sky.'

She also looked up.

The sky was darker. Swollen.

'Purty thang . . .'

She looked at the light again. It was, it was truly pretty. And because her eyes were still damp with frustration, it seemed to have a corona of mystical colours. An acid flashback? she asked herself. No, couldn't be – the two dorks were seeing it as well. And the other drivers. Some were poking their heads out of side windows, craning their necks to watch the skittish light, while others in open convertibles like hers just sat and wondered.

The light skimmed over the metal roofs, sometimes dipping to touch the hoods. From one to another, sometimes bouncing, reminding Tina of one of those round balls that used to skip along the words of a song at the kids' movie matinees. But different. This kinda . . . sparkled.

Somehow it lifted her spirits. The screen test didn't count

for much. Nor did the Valium. And nor did Brody. The light was so bright, and so . . . so happy. She smiled, a pure smile of joy, a smile that had been alien to her lips for too long. This thing was better than uppers, it made her feel so light, so full of sunshine.

But now it was becoming more erratic. It swooped and rose, veered and whirled. It hovered and was still one moment, was moving swiftly through the air the next. Someone leaned from their car window as it flitted by like some dazzling butterfly, but it easily avoided the man's fingers.

The traffic crawled onwards beneath it and soon Tina was close enough to judge its size. And its simple beauty. It was pearly white with an incandescent aura of subtle pastel shades (it *did* have a kind of corona, although the tears in her eyes had exaggerated its depth). The light itself was no bigger than a baseball, no smaller than an apple and it skipped over the rooftops like a child might skip over stepping stones.

Oh glorious, Tina thought, *gloriouuusss* . . .

Something splattered heavily to the ground between her Bug and the offensive Chevy pick-up, its dull mushy force breaking through the rapture. She had jumped in her seat.

She stopped the car (it was almost at a standstill anyway) and unbuckled her seat-belt, then stretched across the passenger seat to see what had landed with such a sickening thud. Texas Straw Hat was leaning out further and looking behind to see, the noise heard even over Tanya Tucker. Together they gawked at the space between vehicles.

It appeared that a block of ice had fallen to the ground and smashed itself into little pieces.

They looked up at each other, both leer and animosity vanquished by their surprise.

'Musta been from a plane,' the cowboy said in what had to have been a studied drawl. 'I heard 'bout thet kinda thang.'

He peered up at the sky, searching for the miscreant aircraft. 'Comes from theyar jahns . . .'

Tina had not followed his gaze; she had turned back to the vibrant light. But it had gone, disappeared.

She sighed with disappointment. What had it been? A ball of electric, is all. No, a dancin' star, she preferred to think, a good omen. *Twinkle, twinkle . . .*

'Oh!'

She had jumped in her seat again. A different kind of noise this time, a more of a . . . more of a *splatt!*

Tina mouthed another little '*oh!*' when she spotted the straw stetson on her passenger seat and the Texas cowboy's broken head dangling against the side of the pick-up's door, a single stream of blood dribbling from it. His good buddy was tugging at his shoulder, unsure of what had happened, only wondering why his partner was slumped out the window like some damn drunken fool.

'C'mon, Carl, let's git movin'.'

No good. Tina could tell by the bloodied dent in his head that ol' Carl was dead. *Daid.* The poor fool shoulda never left Texas, or Arizona, or whatever fuckin' cowpoke state he came from 'cos in LA he'd copped a headache he was never gonna get over.

She laughed and didn't know why – it sure as hell wasn't for the fun of it. Jesus, this guy was dead. *Daid. Daid* for sure. Her giggle turned into a sob. Oh shit . . . it was turning into a bad luck day for her . . . and a worse one for him . . .

Something bashed into the sloping front of her car. Her eyes widened at the indentation it had left.

'Oh Gaaahd . . .' came a moan as the buddy discovered the problem with his partner.

And a loud scream from Tina as another block of ice smashed her windscreen. How many johns did this plane have?

More struck the Camaro that had just drawn alongside her.

The driver looked out of his window as if accusing her of the damage. He mouthed something inaudible.

Then the sky was *full* of falling ice.

Tina howled loudly as a hailstone as big as a football and not dissimilar in shape landed on the straw stetson next to her. She pushed herself away from it, rising in her seat, as though it were something alive and horrible. A blow to her shoulder numbed the whole of her arm.

The sound of hammering was all around as the huge hailstones pummelled the Los Angeles traffic. They fell in all shapes and sizes, as icicles, cones, great stars, and uneven spheres – a lethal downpour of iced rain. Metal buckled, glass shattered, and those drivers in open-topped convertibles cowered low with arms over their heads. Over the sound of thudding hailstones and Patsy Cline from the pick-up, Tina could hear the collisions of cars overhead on Hollywood, the traffic there caught at a smarter moving pace.

She raised her good arm just in time to deflect a blow to the head. But now that arm was numbed and she could barely lift it. She had to get under cover, into another vehicle or underneath her own Volkswagen. She tried to rise again and managed to kneel on the seat, despite her useless arms. But the Nissan behind bumped into her and she fell over the back of her seat, her long naked legs trapped by the steering wheel, her back arched. Wind was knocked from her when an iceblock, this one the size of a telephone directory, hit her midriff. She felt as if a steam-hammer had punched her belly.

In her convulsions, her legs worked loose and she fell into the back seat. A glancing blow to her forehead caused her to see many more balls of light, this time exploding ones, rainbow-coloured. And as her body was beaten by the stones of pure ice she began to forget about the pain and to think about the one shining light.

Until this faded too, and there was no more, there was

nothing at all left, and Tina shed her body and went off in search of something new, something infinitely more peaceful than earthly success would be. It was a pleasant enough last thought.

11

The pain was bad. Really bad.

Rivers leaned against a wall, waiting for the daggers that sliced into his leg to blunt, for the hurting to peak out. A woman passed by, wary of him, making no offer of help. Perhaps she had her own worries, friends or relatives caught up in the traumatised sector of the city. Or maybe she thought he was just another street bum, gone on cheap liquor, a fugitive from social order. He looked the part, clothes torn and bloodied, dust in his hair. But the earth tremor had left others in a worse state; some of them it had left dead.

He straightened, the pain hardly diminished at all, the thought that he had not far to go giving him added strength. One more block, he told himself. One more block and he'd be home. Whether or not he'd be able to climb the steps to his front door was another matter.

Strange how dusk-like it seemed out on the streets, even though it was only late afternoon. It was as if all the city's dust had been shaken into the air to mix with the still lingering sirocco sand, washing the sky a golden red, with the sun a muted fireball above the rooftops. The excited faces of the people who cluttered the streets were sanguine in the glow, belying their frightened mood. Many seemed to be in a state of shock, while others filled pubs and bars, spilling out on to the pavements, as if to celebrate their survival. The city had taken on an air of vibrancy, a mixture of fear and nervous hilarity, as everyone debated the unbelievable. *An earthquake had hit London.* Already newscasters were playing down the event, explaining to the public (no doubt urged by the appropriate government department to do so) that Great Britain underwent thirty-three earthquakes a year on average, so the event was not as spectacular, or even as unexpected, as one might imagine. Nevertheless, the impact of this one could not be denied – location alone gave cause for the gravest concern. This one had to have had a magnitude of at least 4.1 on the Richter scale, and scored at least 7 on the Modified Mercalli scale, Rivers thought, an assessment he had been unable to verify as yet. All lines to the Met Office were blocked when he had tried to get through earlier, even those special numbers which only the privileged agency members held. That there had been no warnings, no softer seismic disturbances prior to the main tremor, was not that unusual; but it was worrying. The quake itself had lasted only a few minutes and so far there had been no aftershocks. Now he wondered if there would be any at all.

From the damage he had observed as he made his way through the streets, he had been close to the epicentre, just above the focus point, when the earthquake had struck. None of the buildings that he had seen had sustained serious structural damage, although several would require urgent maintenance and many windows would need replacing. Roads were cracked and even buckled, but no holes or chasms had opened up, and he'd heard that a water surge along the Thames had wrecked several small craft. Inevitably public transport and communications had been badly disrupted, with subways and overground railways closed until walls, bridges and tracks had been thoroughly examined and all signalling checked. The traffic light system had been knocked out in a large area of the city by a power cut, further hindering the efforts of the police to clear the snarl-ups.

When Rivers had regained consciousness in his wrecked car he had found the woman with the bloodied face slumped against the front passenger seat, the vehicle itself tilted at a crazy angle, almost on its side. The rumbling in the ground had stopped; in fact, everything was unreasonably quiet. He had clambered up the rear seat and pushed open a door.

People were standing around the street, most of them, it seemed, in a kind of daze. Some were weeping – men as well as women – while others just stared in amazement. Then the noise began – shouts, calls, vehicles being started up again, the crunching of shattered glass as people crossed the road. The chatter had become a clamour as people poured from the buildings.

Rivers turned the corner into his own road and breathed a sigh of relief. The long journey through the city had drained him of energy, but without a car and with public transport in chaos there had been no choice but to walk home. The pain-killers he always carried had scarcely taken the edge off the ache in his leg, and by now he was limping badly. A red slash of congealed blood across the back of his hand stood proud of the minor cuts he had received the night before; his cheek-bone was already turning a purplish-blue from a blow he assumed he had received when he blacked out in his car. His jacket was slung over one shoulder, his shirt sodden with perspiration and he leaned heavily on the cane as he doggedly limped on.

Rivers closed his eyes for an instant in relief when he saw the steps leading up to his home further along the road. Oh for a cool drink and a tepid shower, in that order. But would he have enough strength left to make it up those bloody steps?

He stopped only thirty yards or so away from the front steps, his leg almost giving way under him. Come on, this is ridiculous, he told himself. He hadn't walked miles through the crowded streets in this strength-sapping heat only to be beaten this short distance from his own doorstep. 'Bastard,' he muttered, referring to his leg.

Ahead a car door swung open and someone stepped out. 'Diane?'

She came towards him, unsmiling.

'Are you okay, Jim?'

She wore a white shortsleeved blouse and light, pleated skirt.

'What are *you* doing here?'

'Are you okay? You look terrible.'

'It's been mentioned.' And that had been *before* the earth tremor.

'You look as though –'

'I've been through an earthquake?'

'Were you hurt?'

'Scraped a little. Nothing serious. Tell me why you're here.'

'Let's get you inside first.'

'Diane, I'm not sure . . .'

She slid under his arm, grabbing his waist. 'Don't be an idiot. Come on, lean on me and let's get up those steps.'

'At least it's not raining this time.'

She gave a short laugh. 'Storms and earthquakes. We meet in dire circumstances.'

'You sound very English.'

'That's what living with Poggsy and Bibby does for you.'

'And your husband.'

'Yeah, let's not forget him.'

He glanced at her in surprise and saw resignation rather than anger in her expression.

They passed the car she had been sitting in, a battered red Ford with an open sun-roof. 'I thought you travelled by minibus,' he remarked as they reached the steps. He gritted his teeth, ready for the climb.

'We only use that for all the family. On my own it's more economical to use that old thing. You ready?'

He nodded and they began the brief ascent. Rivers suppressed a groan as he used both Diane's shoulder and his stick for support.

'Can you make it?' she asked, trying to take more of his weight than he would allow.

'If we stop I'm done for.'

'A couple more to go.'

'Where's your husband, Diane?'

She ignored the question until they were outside the front door. Rivers leaned against the frame, giving himself time to recover his breath and for the pain to subside a little. 'My physio would tell me this is good for me. She'd probably make me go back down and do it all over again.'

'I know that kind of sadist. I worked as a nurse a short while before I got married. Tony's dead, by the way.'

'Tony?'

'My husband, Poggsy and Bibby's son.'

'I'm sorry.'

She shrugged. 'I am too – a little.'

Rivers looked at her quizzically, but she offered nothing more. He dug into his trouser pocket for his keys. Two locks had to be turned before the door would open.

It was blessedly cool in the hallway and both of them breathed a sigh.

'You own the whole place?'

'Just the ground floor. Basement's empty at the moment and two guys share the top.'

'No more stairs then. Good.'

He swayed unsteadily and Diane was by his side again, a hand clutching his elbow, her body firm against his.

'You really are in bad shape.'

'It comes and goes.' It was said with more levity than he felt. He pointed to a door along the corridor and singled out two more keys on the ring he held. She took them from him and went to the door. He followed and rested against the wall as she inserted first one key, then the other, wondering why she had come all this way to his home. It seemed like Hugo Poggs and his family were not going to let him go so easily. Yet what the hell did they expect from him?

Diane opened the door and stood aside. 'Can I help you?' she asked.

'I'm okay now,' he answered brusquely and went through to the apartment.

She followed without being invited and quickly took in her surroundings. The place was tidy without being fussily so. Filled bookshelves rose on either side of the fireplace; a small-screen wall television set was mounted opposite a wide comfortable-looking sofa; an assortment of magazines and newspapers were stacked on a low coffee table; on a long sideboard behind the sofa were framed photographs – two of an elderly couple, another of a youngish family, a man and a woman seated on a garden swing-seat, two boys kneeling on the grass before them, all of them smiling brightly at the camera. The bleakness of the living room's white walls was broken up by three vivid original landscape pastels, all of them easily recognisable as Provence and signed by David Napp. Rivers' hi-fi system was an old-fashioned Bang & Olufsen. The room's drapes were light and too elegantly feminine to have been chosen by Rivers himself. Unless, of course, she had got him entirely wrong.

'Look, I need to get out of these things and into the

157

shower,' Rivers was saying as he turned to her. 'I don't want to be unsociable, but . . .'

She waved a hand at his unfinished sentence. 'You go ahead and let me mix us both a cool drink. Something with a stiffener in them, yes?'

'Can't any member of your family take a hint?'

She smiled. 'Poggsy has taught me to be thick-skinned. Where's your ice-box – your fridge?'

He nodded towards an open doorway. 'Kitchen's through there. There's vodka, gin, Scotch in the sideboard behind you.'

'Vodka Collins sound good?'

'Yeah. I think I've got the makings. I, er, I've got to be alone for a little while.'

'Don't be embarrassed about plugging in around me. I saw you naked yesterday, remember? I caught sight of the point in your knee. Do those things really work?'

'They ease it, sure. The oscillation somehow settles the nerve endings. Don't ask me how.'

'Don't electrocute yourself. I'll fix the drinks and wait here till you're done, okay? Anything else I can get for you?'

He shook his head. 'Will you answer some questions for me?'

'More? When you're feeling better.' She crouched at the sideboard, pulling open a door. 'In here, you say. Ah, I see it. Vodka. My, you keep well stocked. I'll do plenty of ice for us both, right?'

Rivers had already disappeared into the bedroom.

'Right,' Diane said quietly to herself.

'You look better,' Diane said, handing him a tall glass.

Rivers had changed into light chinos and cotton T-shirt. His feet were bare, his hair still shiny wet. He took the drink from her and pulled over a chair from the writing desk by the window. She raised her glass and took a deep swallow. He did the same.

'Tell me why you're here,' he said without preamble.

Diane tucked her legs beneath her on the sofa and leaned against an arm. 'Josh and Eva wanted me to come.'

'Josh and Eva? Why?'

'They knew you were in danger.'

'They saw the earth tremor?'

'Uh-uh.' A negative. 'They just sensed you were in danger.'

Before he could stop himself, Rivers said, 'The light . . .'

She regarded him curiously. 'They sensed something was happening to you. Poggsy thought one of us should find out what was wrong, particularly when we couldn't contact you by phone. I was nominated. No, not quite: I nominated myself.'

'But I thought I saw . . .' He'd said it slowly almost to himself.

'What, Jim, saw what?'

He straightened his shoulders as if reasserting rational thought. 'Nothing. I thought I saw the weird light again, but it was just a mental image, a memory.'

'You're sure of that?'

'I'm not sure of anything. But I know it was like before, in the research plane. Except . . . except it wasn't real this time.'

'Was it last time?'

He rested the glass on the coffee table. 'That's an odd thing for you to say, especially when your own children claim to have seen it.'

'Oh, I'm not saying the light hasn't been seen. I just wonder if it's actually there.'

'You're not making sense.'

'What if it's a warning, a mystical sign of some kind that's only in the mind. Don't you find it significant that it always

159

precedes a disaster? That's when the children sense it, just before something terrible happens.'

'But today . . .'

'A tremor, that was all. Not a full-blown earthquake, it wasn't serious enough for a vision.'

'You really think what I saw in the eye of the storm was only a vision?'

'For want of a better word, yes. And the children saw it again today, but it was unclear, unfocused, not like the other time. I think they saw it in your mind when you were in danger.'

'Mental telepathy. Are you serious?'

'You know I am.'

Rivers reached for his drink again.

'Don't be such a cynic, Jim,' Diane urged. 'For once in your life just accept what you hear, *believe* in the sincerity of others.'

'Oh, I believe you're sincere.'

'Let's not go through the whole debate again. I can't give you any proof, but you know within yourself that something unusual – and that's a pretty mild word – is going on in the world around us. Josh and Eva are part of it, that's all I'm asking you to believe.' She uncurled her legs and leaned towards him. 'And so are you, Jim. So are you.'

12

The ICI-sponsored BBC 24-Hour Television Newsdesk naturally was full of the day's main event: the Great London Earth Tremor (the earlier title of the Great London Earthquake had been revised in later reports). Power lines had been damaged in some parts, quite a few buildings had been left structurally 'unsound', all public and private transport had been seriously disrupted, the River Thames had flooded at its weaker points; yet only four fatalities so far had been reported (one of these being the man that Rivers himself had seen sliced in half by falling glass), although there were many casualties. Rivers flicked through the ten channels, catching another disaster piece on SKY News – a freak hailstorm over Los Angeles had caused multiple collisions on the freeways and many deaths – but had returned to the BBC Newsdesk with its three excited newscasters every few minutes. He smiled as the attractive female of the trio advised that no more disturbances were expected; no doubt a mass exodus of the capital was the last thing the local authorities, with their token-only Civil Defence Corps, wanted to encourage.

Evening had seemed to draw in both early and quickly, no doubt due to the dust and fine sand still in the atmosphere, and if anything, the air was even more sultry than it had been during the day. Voices drifted in through the barred window, many of the street's residents sitting on front steps or on chairs brought to open doorways, a custom of old London that had found a resurgence in these warmer times. The day's big event had enhanced the desire for doorstep gossip.

Rivers switched on a lamp, realising that he and Diane had been talking in the flickering shadows cast by the TV screen for the past half-hour or so.

'D'you mind if I turn this off now?' he asked, indicating the television.

'It'd be a relief,' she replied, fanning herself with a magazine from the coffee table. 'I think we know all we need to about today's little drama.'

He used the remote control to switch off the set. 'Are you hungry?'

'Famished.'

'I could rustle up something unless you want to eat out.'

'I don't think many restaurants will be busy tonight, but let's eat here anyway.' She flapped the neckline of her blouse. 'Do you mind if I take a shower? I feel sticky all over.'

'Go ahead. There's a spare robe behind the bathroom door.'

'You keep a spare?'

'Occasionally it comes in handy.'

'Can I ring home first, check on the children? Come to think of it, they might be worried about me.'

'The main receiver's in here if you want to use it. Just press P for privacy and it won't come through the external speakers. I'll get into the kitchen.'

'No need.'

162

'S'okay. I'll be fixing us something quick. You like omelettes?'

'Fine.'

He rose and took the telephone receiver from its unit on
the wall. 'Come through when you're finished,' he said, handing her the instrument. 'Have your shower after we've eaten.'

In the refrigerator he found enough eggs for two omelettes
and set about whisking them into a pulp, adding some mushrooms and chopped ham for good measure. Diane came in as
he was setting the table.

'They saw it happen,' she said.

'The tremor?'

'No. Later. They saw the hailstorm over Los Angeles.
They saw the light again.'

He lifted the omelettes 'from the pan on to the plates.
'Come on, eat,' he said.

She looked at him incredulously. 'That's it? "Come on,
eat?" Josh and Eva had another vision, didn't you hear me?'

'Sure I heard. But I'm hungry. You are too.'

She sat at the table. 'We're not getting through to you,
are we?'

About to return the pan to the stove, he paused. 'The
truth is, you might be. What you just said didn't surprise me,
that's all. Maybe I'm getting used to the idea.'

'At last.'

'I said maybe. Tell me about your call.'

She picked up a fork and hived off a portion of omelette.
'Mm, not bad,' she said after her first taste. 'You're obviously
used to coping for yourself.'

'Years of practice. The kids – what happened?'

'I spoke to Bibby. She was quite anxious about us both.
Apparently the first reports of the tremor were wildly exaggerated. She calmed down soon enough when I told her the
damage was pretty limited. She was really concerned though
when she heard you'd been in the thick of it.'

163

He joined her at the table, sitting opposite.

'Josh and Eva went into one of their trances – well, not a trance exactly. They just stop what they're doing and become very still and quiet. You'd think they were listening for something if you saw them – their eyes look to one side, never straight ahead, you know, like when you hear something but aren't quite sure of its source? After a while they close their eyes.'

Rivers began to eat, but scarcely tasted the food.

'Sometimes they've "gone" for a few minutes,' Diane continued, 'other times just a few seconds. Today was a quick one. They saw the little light and then what they described as big rocks falling from the sky, killing or hurting anybody they struck.'

'Hailstones.'

'*Giant* hailstones. A freak hailstorm. And in Los Angeles of all places.'

'They knew it was there?'

'They knew it was over the ocean. Don't ask me how, they just seem to sense the distance.'

For a moment Rivers had wondered if the children had confused what they saw with the falling glass caused by the earth tremor in London.

'They described the roads, some high in the air.'

No, no confusion. Another thought struck him. 'They could have seen or heard it on the news.'

'We heard the first reference to it no more than twenty minutes ago, and Bibby swears they only heard it around the same time. The children had their vision well over an hour before, around 5.30 our time.'

Rivers had eaten only a few mouthfuls, his appetite not lost but never really there in the first place. He went to the fridge and took out a can of beer, offering it to Diane first. She declined and he returned to the table pulling the tab. He poured the beer into his empty vodka glass.

'Why Josh and Eva?' he said, taking his seat again. 'What makes them so special?'

'We're not sure they are so special. We think there are others like them. You see, the children themselves are aware of other minds experiencing these . . . these recognitions, whatever they might be called.'

'How many others?'

'It's impossible to know. What frightens us is that the twins also feel a malevolence out there, something harmful to them.'

Rivers was still too exhausted to become irritated again. Besides, he saw no point: nothing he could say would make this woman – and her family – understand how ludicrous their story was. He attempted a slight diversion: 'Tell me more about Josh and Eva. You said they were Romanian orphans . . .'

She realised why Rivers had redirected the conversation and did her best to disguise her own irritation. What in hell did it take to get through to this man? 'Tony and I knew we could never have children even before we married – my fault, not his. I won't bore you with the medical reasons – twisted fallopian tubes and all that. But as the years went on I yearned for kids, maybe because I felt it might stabilise a rocky marriage, or maybe it was natural maternal instincts. Probably some of both. But adoption in this country of yours isn't such a straightforward thing. Council waiting lists are so long, the requirements so tight, and Tony . . . well, Tony had his own problems that, unfortunately, were visible to others.'

Rivers was curious, but did not press her.

'Even private agencies ultimately let us down. Then, as you'll remember, the world began to hear stories of the Romanian children, so many of them abandoned or orphaned, left to die of malnutrition and lack of care in squalid homes. Word filtered through to the West after the Romanian leader Ceauşescu and his wife had been shot by their own people, and things began to loosen up over there. It took time, but I made enquiries, booked a flight and spent two weeks searching the orphanages of Bucharest.'

'Without your husband?'

'Tony's mother, Bibby, went with me.'

'Didn't the authorities over there expect to see a married couple?'

Her smile was grim. 'Believe me, they didn't want to put any complications in our way. As far as they were concerned, one mouth less to feed was okay by them. Despite money pouring in from other countries to help them in their plight, their resources were still limited. And anyway, they hardly cared a damn. Oh, it wasn't as easy as I'm making it sound – if the child had been abandoned, then every effort was made to contact the mother, and that could take weeks, if not months. Once found, she had to be encouraged to sign the release papers. An exchange of cash usually helped the persuasion, although most times it was unnecessary.'

She finished the omelette and pushed the plate away. 'You're not making much headway with yours,' she said, pointing at his plate.

'I'm not that hungry.' He took another mouthful to satisfy her.

'You have water?'

'Couple of cold ones in the fridge.'

She went over and took out a square plastic bottle. She poured the pure water into a fresh glass. 'Like I said, we toured the Bucharest orphanages to begin with, but . . . well, the best I can tell you is something didn't feel right.' She shook her head at his unspoken question. 'Sorry, I can't explain why. Call it instinct, an . . .'

'Intuition?'

'At the risk of straining my credibility even further, yes, an intuition. Then we heard of a place in Outer Moldavia, a particular institution for what the Romanians called the "irrec-

166

uperable". AIDS babies, the physically handicapped, and gypsy children. Have you any idea of what little regard these people have for gypsy children, especially if they've been abandoned? In those days they treated them no better than wild animals, locking them away from the other kids, feeding them last with scraps and leftovers – not that there was much left over in these places. Thank God the new government there has finally taken responsibility for these institutions. In those days, and maybe even now, these kids were regarded as "tainted". We found Josh and Eva in a dirty basement room, the size of a closet, sharing a cot, their little bodies emaciated, their eyes huge and staring. Just babies, tiny babies, four or five months old. The nurses hadn't even bothered to name them.'

There was an edge to Diane's sadness, a suppressed fury that tightened her features.

'But those eyes, those clear blue eyes. Gypsy children with blue eyes. Maybe it was those eyes that drew us to them. No, it had to be something stronger, something inexplicable. Pity? There were so many others to pity. But we knew those two were coming home with us. It took a whole lot of wrangling, a great deal of arguing, but we eventually got all the legal documents signed and sealed. From the town's mayor to the local authority's lowliest clerk – we got them to agree. Within six weeks the babies were on the plane, on their way home with us.'

Rivers sipped the beer. The air was muggy, but also charged, as though a thunderstorm were brewing. He looked through the kitchen window and saw no clouds in the darkening sky.

He examined the rim of his glass. 'Do they know they're adopted?'

'Of course. I told them when they were old enough to cope, but still young enough for it to be no big deal. They're aware they're gypsy children and they have no hang-ups about it. Quite the opposite – they're pleased at the idea.'

'When you found them, were they . . . ?' He didn't quite know how to put it.

'Normal?' she finished for him. 'Even tiny babies know when they've been maltreated. But they adjusted to love and care after a while. Now if you mean were they unusual in their nature, then no. Apart from those sparkling blue eyes that seemed to look into your very soul, they were regular kids, although they had that special affinity between twins, sometimes acting and thinking as one. I guess they were about four when we first noticed the odd things I told you about yesterday.'

'You also mentioned something or someone was trying to harm them. A malevolence, you called it. You mentioned it again a little while ago. What – what *exactly* – do you mean?'

'I wish I could say. It's just a feeling they have.'

He grimaced at the inadequate answer. 'Okay. You also said I'm involved in whatever's going on. Can you explain *that*?'

Elbows on the table, she spread her hands. 'I wish I could. Somehow the children have made a connection between you and the light, maybe because at the moment you're the only live person we know who's witnessed it. Tell me, before the research plane crashed – were you the only person to see it?'

'It was there for anyone who cared to look.'

She was deep in thought for a moment, her face troubled. 'Will you come back with me and talk to Josh and Eva?'

He sat back in the chair, not answering straight away. Then: 'What do we talk about?'

She seemed at a loss. 'Okay, you got me. I just know you three have to get together. Besides, Poggsy still wants your help to convince the right people to do something about the environment.'

'The right people are doing something.'

'Not enough. Desperate measures are needed.'

'And who the hell would listen to me?' He remembered his conversation with Sheridan earlier in the day. Christ, what authority did these people think he had?

'You'd be an important part of a serious movement. Hugo has contacts everywhere and they're not just woolly-minded tree-loving conservationists. How do you think we found out so much about you?'

Yes, how? Obviously there were frustrated people in his own agency.

Diane leaned towards him across the table. 'Look, when you left this morning the children became very upset. Not right away, but an hour or so later. Eva told me they wanted to see the Light Man again.'

'I'm the Light Man?'

'The names they invent are simple and direct, so that's what they call you now. It's another reason why I think you're involved in all this somehow, whether you like it or not.'

He made a decision. 'I don't go along with any of this, but okay. Seems I've got nothing to do with the rest of the week anyway – I've been ordered to take some leave – so why not, what's there to lose?' And that was exactly how he felt about it – what was there to lose?

She grinned. 'Right. What's there to lose?' She tipped her glass to him, then drank the water. 'Your car's out of action, so I'll take you down myself tomorrow.'

'You can't make a double journey, there and back again.'

'I don't intend to. Let me stay here the night. Your sofa looks comfortable.'

'I, uh, I can catch the train.'

'My God, you look flustered. You'll be quite safe.'

'No, I mean, yeah, you can stay. It's just –'

She laughed. 'Your natural English reserve. Quaint, very quaint. I'll phone again and let Bibby know what's happening. Then I think I'll take that shower.'

Rivers could only nod and wonder what he was getting himself into.

It was Rivers who took the sofa.

Diane had declined the offer of his bed at first, but had eventually given in to his insistence. He quickly changed the bedsheets and then had presented her with a spare pyjama top – 'In this heat? You must be kidding' – and toothbrush. While she took a shower, Rivers put through a call to the US Geological Survey's National Information Service in Golden, Colorado, an agency that, with the use of an international telemetry network, measured the planet's every minor or major tremor. With almost 700 stations reporting in regularly and with 3,000 more contributing information on request (around 60,000 seismic readings each month), and all data entered into the centre's computers, the agency provided the most detailed and comprehensive information to meteorologists and scientists throughout the world. Because earthquakes – at least, *major* earthquakes – often overwhelm regional seismographs, precise calculations regarding damage and its spread are usually best gathered by centres some distance from the disruption; however, Rivers' reason for contacting the agency in Colorado was even more practical – he had been unable to get through to his own offices. *All* lines were busy, and had been throughout the evening. The information he required was simple: had a new fault developed beneath London, or had an old, and until that day, insignificant, fault moved? Also, just how widespread was the disturbance? He learned that the initial rupture – it *was* a new fault as far as they knew – had taken place some thirty miles beneath the Earth's surface, and the computer-assisted analysis of multiple seismograms had measured the seismic waves for a distance of some fifty miles. Most of the damage, however, had been sustained within the City of London's square mile. After thanking his special contact at the Earthquake Information Service, Rivers replaced the receiver and lit a cigarette. It made no sense, none at all. It was as if the world were rushing through one freak catastrophe after another, heading towards . . . what?

He was still pondering the question when Diane joined him five minutes later. She wore a bathrobe that was too big for her, and her hair hung lank and dark around her face.

'You know, seeing your grim face I'm tempted to tell you it's not the end of the world,' she said to him.

Then she wondered why he had begun to laugh so hard.

The aftershock came at 1.22 a.m.

Objects around the room began to vibrate – an ashtray on the coffee table, the two empty coffee cups beside it, pens and pencils in a beaker on the bookshelf, the small brass lamp on the mantelshelf. One of the silver-framed photographs on the sideboard slipped to the floor, pictures on the wall tilted, the palm by the window danced a jig.

Rivers jerked awake and felt the vibration through the sofa he lay on. The rumbling noise itself was distant, unlike earlier that day, and seemed to come from somewhere far below. Something in the hall, probably a dislodged picture, crashed to the floor.

'Oh Christ . . .' Rivers said softly.

His bedroom door flew open and Diane stood there, the bathrobe around her shoulders and held together at the front with one hand. Her other hand gripped the door itself.

'Is it another earthquake?' she asked in a hushed voice.

'It'll pass,' he quickly reassured her.

She hurried to the sofa and crouched beside it. Rivers

leaned on an elbow and drew her to him. 'It's okay, it'll pass,' he told her again.

Diane buried her head into his naked chest and her voice was muffled. 'Oh shit, I don't like this.'

She flinched when two or three books tumbled from the shelf and the walking-cane that had been leaning in a corner slid down and clattered against the polished floorboards.

The rumbling became more intense, although it still appeared to be a long way off. The windows rattled in their frames.

Then it was gone. The noise, the vibration, subsided, leaving everything still and quiet again.

Rivers slid his fingers up to her neck, into her hair. She remained pressed tight against him. 'It's over,' he whispered. 'Everything's okay.'

Slowly she raised her head and in the dimness he could see her eyes were wide and frightened. 'You're sure,' she said. 'It's not another earthquake?'

'Just the aftershock. There may be more.'

'Oh God, I hope not.' She straightened, the robe falling off one shoulder. She pulled it up, holding the sides together more tightly. There were shouts from outside in the street, windows and doors being opened. They heard someone in the apartment above run across the floor.

'Well, now you know how brave I am,' she said shakily but wryly.

'You didn't scream.'

'I forgot how to. I guess I could use a drink about now, something strong. How about you?'

'It seems appropriate. I hear brandy's good for steadying the nerves.' He pushed himself into a sitting position. 'Uh . . .'

'Save your modesty. Let me get the drinks. Now if my legs are steady and I have some light . . .'

'Try the lamp on the mantel. Watch out for the coffee table.'

He watched her dim grey shape move around the room, slightly bent, one arm outstretched for obstructions. 'I can just make it out. Yep, got it. Now if I can just find the switch. Close your eyes.'

The lamp came on and, with her back to him, she pushed her arms through the sleeves of the bathrobe. She tied it at the waist. Diane turned and, although her face was pale, she raised a wavery smile.

He slid his feet to the floor, wincing as a sharp pain shot through his leg. Wrapping the sheet around his waist, he leaned towards the coffee table and picked up the cigarette pack. He tapped one out, lit up, and leaned back into the sofa as Diane busied herself with the drinks.

'These your folks?' he heard her say.

He twisted round and saw she had picked up the fallen photograph. 'Yeah.'

'They look nice. Friendly.'

'They were.'

'Oh, sorry.'

He drew on the cigarette.

'And the family group?' She was studying the other photograph on the sideboard. 'Looks like the man could be a brother.'

'Younger brother. He lives with his family in Canada now.'

She poured the drinks, two good measures, and brought them round to him. 'No other loved ones?' she said, handing him the brandy. 'I'd have expected a girlfriend or two, maybe even an ex-wife.'

'No, no wife.'

'Well . . . something?'

The brandy warmed his throat. He took another, longer, swallow. 'I haven't always been on my own, if that's what you're getting at.'

'Things didn't work out?'

'They didn't have a chance to. It happened at a time when

173

no one was aware of how powerful tropical diseases had grown again, some of them completely immune to vaccines. Laura went down with what we thought was flu when we came back from a holiday in Malaysia. Only it wasn't flu, it was malaria. We realised too late: it only took two weeks to kill her.'

Diane knelt alongside him, an elbow resting on the sofa's edge. 'That's awful. Unbelievable . . .'

'Six years ago. Only the sudden swell in the numbers of people dying from the disease put the medical profession wise to what was happening. And it's become worse since – they're having to produce stronger vaccines all the time.'

'Do you . . . do you keep a photograph of her?' Diane did not understand herself why she was curious to see this woman whom Rivers had loved.

'No.' He smiled at her, and she saw a hardness there that before had not been apparent. She waited for him to say more, but Rivers merely sipped at the brandy again. Outside the noises were dying down, people closing their front doors and windows, no doubt hoping the excitement was over for the night. She could just hear muffled voices from the apartment above, but soon these too faded away.

'Now it's your turn – tell me about your husband, Diane.'

She shrugged, realising he was deliberately turning the conversation away from himself.

'I told you – Tony's dead.'

'That's it? He's dead, no more?'

'You want the whole story?'

'Not necessarily.'

'How about the bare details?'

'If you like.'

'I'm going to bring the bottle over, d'you mind?'

He shook his head and Diane went back to the brandy. She topped up her own glass, then held the bottle towards his. He accepted the offer, but pushed the neck up with the rim of the glass when the level rose too high. Diane rested against the sofa again and he couldn't help but notice the white smoothness of her thigh before she flipped the robe back over it.

'Tony was an alcoholic,' she began baldly enough. 'Have you ever known one of those two-headed monsters, Jim? I mean really known them, not just been aware they seem to be soaked a little too often?' She didn't wait for a reply, nor had she honestly sought one. 'We met when I was a student nurse at the Massachusetts General Hospital in Boston. He was brought into Casualty one night with a cracked jaw – seems that he and a few of his friends had chosen the wrong bar to celebrate the end of their Finals. The barman there didn't care much for students or their high spirits, and when Tony's behaviour got too out of hand he was shown the door the hard way. No one was sure if he'd broken his jaw when he landed on the sidewalk, or if the barman's fist had done the damage. Tony's friends were in no condition to judge.'

'I don't understand – what was he doing in Boston?'

'Oh. Exchange student. Very popular in those days. He was trying for a degree in languages at Boston College. Got it too. Tony was very bright, if not much else. Anyway, although he couldn't talk very well, we struck up a relationship while he was recuperating in hospital. We dated, and in those days the good head was the dominant one; the bad one didn't take control till much later.' She gazed reflectively into the bottom of her glass. 'I didn't meet his parents, Hugo and Bibby, till Tony brought me here to England, and by that time we were married.'

'Did they approve?'.

'Approve?' She tapped his knee. 'You really *are* quaint, aren't you? Oh, I think they were pleased enough. I learned later that Tony had never been easy to handle, although there was no real malice in him. I guess he just liked the good times too much. And I did too in those early years. But gradually I got interested in his father's work. Even in those days Poggsy was fighting for the environment, long before it became such a popular issue. He realised the urgency. Pretty soon I was so involved I didn't pay attention to much else, and that hardly improved my relationship with Tony. A relationship that had already begun to falter. Maybe the work was my refuge from his drinking. It certainly became a vicious circle, because the more he drank, the more I buried myself in Poggsy's work, and the more I did that, the more Tony hit the bottle. But at least I began to understand part of Tony's weakness. It wasn't only that he failed to live up to his father's achievements, but he couldn't live up to his family's ideals either. And I was quickly becoming in tune with those ideals. Okay, so this is the simplified version, but what the hell, we only have till morning.'

Diane smiled, but Rivers could tell she was masking a lot of hurt.

'We all made excuses for him. People do for drunks they love. I'm no psychologist, so maybe it wasn't inevitable, but eventually his frustration showed up in other ways.'

'Violence against you.'

She looked up in surprise.

'There had to be something more for you to be so bitter towards him.'

'It shows that much?'

'Hardly at all. Earlier you didn't seem so saddened by his death.'

'Grief doesn't stay around for ever. Besides, in some ways Tony's death came as a relief. I know that sounds awful, but you had to know how destructive he was, to himself and to others around him. I had hoped that once we adopted the children, he would change – and I think in his more lucid moments, he felt the same. But when I came back from Romania with the babies, something worsened inside him. Don't ask me why, how; perhaps he realised they represented another ideal for him, something more to live up to. Maybe it was all too much.'

The soft light reflected in her moistened eyes. 'As they grew, became little persons, be began to hate them. He was never cruel, I don't mean he hated them in that way. But he never . . . *cherished* them, he was always cold towards them. And angry. I understand the anger least of all, but it was there, a kind of simmering resentment. There was something in the children that made him too aware of his own feelings, and somehow he feared them. Then one day, when they were five years old, he tried to hurt Josh.'

She stopped, as if seeking reassurance to continue. Rivers spoke quietly, with no pressure: 'Tell me.'

Diane ran stiffened fingers around the rim of her glass, her thoughts far away for the moment, reliving the anguish she was reluctant to reveal. Finally her hand ceased its movement and her eyes focused on Rivers. 'We were all living at Hazelrod then. Tony and I had tried to make it on our own more than once, but he was so unstable and his drinking was even worse when he was away from Hugo and Bibby's influence. And naturally, the more I became involved in Hugo's work, the more sensible it was to live under the same roof. Bibby was able to look after the children more and, well, frankly, the atmosphere was a whole lot healthier at Hazelrod.

'Poggsy and I were in the study when we heard Eva screaming. We found her on the stairway, her face white with terror, and we could hear Tony's shouts from above, coming from our bedroom. When we got there he was holding Josh off the floor, against the wall. He was holding Josh by the throat.'

'Christ . . .'

'Yeah, Christ.' Diane stretched over and placed her glass on the coffee table. She laced her fingers together, one elbow still resting on the sofa. 'Tony had been sleeping off one of his drunken rages when he woke to find the children in the bedroom, apparently just staring at him as he lay on the bed. We gathered that much from Tony himself, although he wasn't too coherent. Why should that have upset him so? God, I wish I knew. He was raving, screeching something about the children "raking his soul". His words. They made no sense at all.

'Josh was rigid, not struggling, not trying to defend himself, just still and passive, his body flat against the wall. For one dreadful moment we thought he was already dead. I grabbed Tony by the hair and pulled his head back, while Hugo tried to prise Tony's hands away from Josh's throat. It was a battle I thought we were going to lose, because Tony had a mad-man's strength. Then suddenly he stopped of his own accord as if he realised what he was doing, the rational part of him at last recognising the insanity.

'He let Josh fall to the floor and stood over him, staring down at the little body for what seemed a long time. We still had hold of Tony, afraid to let go, but then he crumpled to his knees and buried his head in his arms, wailing like a baby.

'We took Josh from the room and comforted him, but he was quiet, not even trembling. He was pale though, as pale as death itself. When he saw Eva they clung to each other as if no one else in the world mattered. They shut us out totally, and that hurt. It brought home the harsh fact that these kids were not my own flesh and blood, that I'd never know that closeness, no matter what.

'After that we never allowed Tony to be alone with the twins. I was all for packing our bags and leaving with them there and then, but Bibby managed to persuade me to stay. And besides, Tony, himself, was so contrite. He sank even further into his misery and self-loathing and begged us to forgive him. But it was the end of the road for me – I couldn't cope with our wretched life together any longer. The idea of

178

the children being in danger . . . no, enough was enough. It was time to cut loose and I began to make my plans.

'But divorce proved unnecessary. Within two weeks Tony was dead, killed in a car crash. Yes, he was drunk at the wheel – what would you expect? Fortunately he only managed to kill himself, no other vehicle was involved; somehow he managed to smash his car into a flyover pillar on the motorway. And maybe that was a blessing, who can say? What would his life have been without us? He would have been the one to get out after, or before, the divorce, you see – Hugo and Bibby would never have let us go. Tony was the one to leave, and he knew that.'

Diane's voice became firmer. 'I know what you're thinking and no, I don't believe it was suicide. Full of remorse he may have been at the end, but Tony was too selfish to take his own life. I think he simply fell asleep at the wheel; or maybe he was just incapable of keeping the car in a straight line. According to the coroner's report, he had so much alcohol in his system it was a wonder he could remember how to switch on the engine.'

She let go her breath and her body sagged as though relieved of a burden. 'So now you know the full story. Aren't you glad you asked?'

His own glass empty, he leaned forward and put it next to hers on the coffee table.

'You're a man of few words, Mr Rivers. Anyone ever tell you how infuriating that can be? Sometimes –'

He kissed her, a soft touching of lips.

Diane was too surprised to respond.

His face remained close to hers. 'The only thing you haven't told me is what you saw in him in the first place.'

She shrugged. 'We were young, he was charming. Never underestimate the blindness of youth. I need another drink.'

He caught her arm as she stretched for the brandy. 'No, you don't.'

179

She was almost angry. 'Don't worry, I'm not like him, not like Tony. God, he was example enough. Maybe you're right though – I don't need another drink. What made you kiss me?'

It was his turn to be surprised. 'It seemed like the right thing to do.'

'Out of sympathy?'

'No, nothing like that.'

'I'm not looking for anyone else, Jim. Josh and Eva need all my care and besides, there's so much to do. Poggsy's so exhausted by his efforts to make people face up to the truth of what's happening around us and he needs all the help I can give him. His health isn't that good.'

Rivers rested a hand on her shoulder. 'Forget I kissed you. Why don't we both get some sleep now?'

She bowed her head slightly so that he could not see her eyes. 'I don't want to forget.' Her hand touched his. 'But you're right, let's get some sleep. Something tells me we're going to need it.'

A tiny yet startling *frisson* ran through him, somehow emanating from where their flesh joined, a subconscious acknowledgment perhaps of a thought too subtle, or too vague, to recognise. For an instant, the soft image of the white orb flitted through his mind, this abruptly overwhelmed by something darker, an ominous shadowing that welled sullenly, only to wane almost immediately, resurge again, then disappear.

He sat back in shock, although the impression had been neither forceful nor demanding; a faint yet sinister dip in perception, that was all, a mild but baleful trespass. Rivers took in a breath and the moment passed, barely to be remembered, let alone understood.

'Are you okay, Jim?' he heard Diane say.

And he was unsure of the answer.

NEW ORLEANS, LOUISIANA – *French Quarter*

O yea, sing in praise and beg forgiveness.

The upraised voices filled her body, spread through her big bones.

O yea, Mother of Earth, shine through me.

The congregation, a confused mixture of whites and blacks and those who could be described as neither, clapped in time, shuffled their feet in rhythm, and sang from their very souls. Behind them, the doors to the Temple were locked and bolted, for this sanctum was for the *truest* of believers and not for idle worshippers, guarded from interlopers who sought only the foolish religions and who wilfully disregarded the one true source.

She towered over them, her immense body garbed in dark robes, and most were afraid to gaze squarely into that obese face. Those who dared quickly averted their eyes for fear their looking might gain her attention. Enough to have heard the stories; no need to test their validity. Rumours, the foolishly brave or stupidly ignorant murmured; not so, warned the aged and wiser ones. *Mama* possessed the old powers, and those powers were acquired through the ancient magics, the obscure but timeworn rituals. Some whispered they were from the Black Ceremonies themselves.

It was to the Earth that the assembly sang, to the Blessed Mother of All Life that they beseeched to be spared the disciplines of Her wrath, and those passing by outside these gloomed confines might well have thought that this church was filled with fervent Seventh-day Adventists; had they been able to see what lay beyond the screened windows and had they been able to distinguish the words of those vigorous hymns, then they might have wondered exactly what religion could invoke such darkness of spirit and liturgy. The altar itself was draped with black cloth, the single vessel on its surface was of grey stone. There were no candles and no ornaments, other than the stone altar cup, of any kind. There were no pews: hard benches and chairs seated the congregation. And there were no painted images, no icons, no crucifixes. The interior was darkly austere, the poor light cast by lamps hanging low from the high ceiling. This Blessed Temple of the Sacred Earth tolerated no distractions.

Many New Orleaneans knew of the Temple's existence in this crescent city (it had, after all, been there for as long as the cathedral only a few blocks away; longer, in some respects, for fire had destroyed the St Louis Cathedral three times during the last 300 years) though very few spoke of it. The building itself, wedged inconspicuously between others of similar appearance, was unremarkable. The wooden steps led from the *banquette* to stout double doors; on either side were two sets of long, ornately barred windows, their heavy shades permanently closed; the apartments above were served by a filigreed gallery, on which the tall and obese figure of a black woman occasionally could be observed watching the jostling crowds below. Even the locals knew little of this sombre gargantuan, except that she was called Mama Pitié by her followers and that she was some kind of high priestess of this veiled sect. It was rumoured that she performed miracles (such fancies flourished among the rich nationality 'stew' of the old city, these descendants of bonded servants and slaves from the French Caribbean settlements, of French and Spanish nobility and mixed race whores, of German farmers and Acadians from Nova Scotia, blended with other latter-day European immigrants).

Mama Pitié inspected her flock with an impassive eye. Some of these followers sang their earnest hymn with eyes closed, while others sang with eyes staring fixedly into the shadows of the ceiling. A girl of no more than sixteen years, light-skinned and pretty, her Negro mother lost in the glory of worship beside her, allowed her attention to wander; she gaped at the woman who stood before the plain altar. Mama Pitié's eyes snapped on hers, trapping her gaze as a spider might fall upon some foolishly bold fly. The young mulatto tensed rigid, unable now to look away from that gross face with its one nostril trenched beneath the flattened nose, from those bulbous eyes that held such stark dread, and the scars on her broad cheeks. Her mother sensed the sudden fear in her daughter and quickly turned the girl's head away; gratefully the daughter closed her eyes and whispered the hymn, swaying slightly against her mother, who silently willed her not to faint.

The singing came to an untidy finish and the congregation sat on benches and chairs, the sound of their movement echoed by the unadorned walls. Now, together, they could look at their priestess without fear of gaining her consideration on themselves alone. Mama Pitié raised her arms and the assembly intoned: *'O yea.'*

'O yea, my brothers and sisters.' Her voice was as dark

as her features. 'The' – it was said as De – 'Mother of All do bless her children.'

Some called out loudly, while others murmured their gratitude.

'The Mother of All will take care of her babies in times of tribulation. They shall not starve, they shall not perish. But if they suffer, then it be Her will.'

'Right,' someone called.

'It's true, Mama.'

'O yea.'

Mama Pitié let her arms fall to her sides. 'In the bad times that come, Mother will sustain they who believe. Mother will replenish the land when those dark days have come and gone, an' only the truest of her daughters and sons will know her mercy.'

'Yea, Mama Pitié, Mama Mercy.'

'Fo' She be the One, there can be no others, no gods, no devils, no angels, no demons. An' She keep the power in Her breast to deliver us up when the chaos is died away and the ground, it heave no more, and the oceans and the rivers, they rush and they roar fo' the las' time!'

'Yea, Mama!'

'Mother Earth will be at peace wit' the chosun. An' we is the chosun, we will be the keepers of this paradise, an' they is no others! You *know* the truth of what I say!'

Applause filled the hall and there were moans of rapture.

'Because you seen fo' yo'selves the ways of Her wrath! You seen the earthquakes and the rains and the great tidal waves that sweep over the lands of the sinners! You seen that fo' yo'selves on the news programmes! You seen that!'

'We seen it, Mama!'

Her voice lowered from the peak it had reached. 'An' so you will see yo' own salvation if you seek it in me an' mine.' She waved her hand at the row of silent men who stood behind her and the altar. Gleaming white shirts and plain ties could be seen at the neck of their black robes; underneath the robes they wore dark grey business suits. 'So you will find yo' liberation from the rest of mankind through my supplications to the Divine Mother on whose Body we breathe, an' yo' atonement to me shall be yo' atonement to Her!'

The Temple resounded with their praise and the clapping of their hands, their shouts of jubilation and acceptance.

Rather than command it, she waited for them to quieten. Then, her voice low again, she said, 'Bring the po' little one to me.'

A collective sigh swept round the assembly. Near the back, a Negro woman stood, a baby of perhaps seven months in her arms.

'Bring him to me, child,' bade the priestess once more.

The woman with the baby came forward, haltingly at first, then with more conviction as others in the congregation lent their encouragement. Her steps became hesitant again as she drew near the black-garbed woman before the altar.

Mama Pitié glared impatiently, holding her huge hands out for the swaddled baby. The mother held her bundle forward to be received, her head bowed. The baby was taken and the swaddling unfolded to reveal the boy's twisted and withered arm. Mama Pitié held him aloft so that all could see, and a moan of sympathy spread through the gathering.

'This mark is the outward sign of inward sin,' the priestess told them. 'The shame of this mother is this child's pain.'

Distressed, the baby's mother sank to her knees, her head hung low to her chest, her shoulders bowed.

'You left this church, Sister Angeline, and listened to the lies of those who call themselves holy. How they help you now in this child's need? Will you listen agin to them Ursuline' – she pronounced it *Urslahn* – 'nuns who worship the false mother an' her unholy son, they who preach wicked lies an' fornicate wit the men who call theyselves priests?'

The kneeling woman shook the whole of her upper body

in denial. Never again would she visit the uptown convent of the Sisters of Ursula – the Sisters of Evil, Mama Pitié called them. No more would she clean their convent, launder their clothes, heed their untruthful words. 'Forgive ma foolishness, Mama. The Divine Mother has punished ma son for ma wrongs.'

'*Yea,*' from whose who watched.

'Ask fo' ma forgiveness, Mama.' She wept loudly.

'You'll stay faithful to this Temple,' the priestess stated, rather than questioned.

'Oh yes, Mama.'

Mama Pitié stood proud, surveying the rest of her flock as if to make sure they bore witness to this wretched woman's promise. 'So shall you all be faithful,' she told them.

'Amen, Mama,' they eagerly replied.

Mama Pitié turned from them and laid the lame baby on the altar. 'Hear us this day, O Divine Mother of All. Lend us yo' powers to heal this sick one who suffers through no fault of its own. Hear us an show us yo' Divine Mercy.'

She reached over the wriggling bundle for the stone cup that rested on the altar. It was filled with a liquid that had the colour and consistency of beetroot mixed with mud. No one but the high priestess knew what the potion was made from, but those who were closest to the altar swore it smelled of goat's blood and excrement. Mama Pitié faced the congregation once more and held the rough chalice aloft before bringing it to her lips.

The people murmured; some moaned; some sighed. She drank.

Dark liquid ran in two rivulets down from her mouth on to her chin and they heard her swallow, the sounds loud and guzzling in the Blessed Temple of the Sacred Earth. When she lowered the cup again, her full lips were slick and glistening, her teeth smeared with red.

She replaced the cup on the altar and picked up the child

once more, unwrapping the cloth that bound the small body so that it was naked and exposed to everyone in the hall.

'Behold this child,' she intoned, her eyelids drooped as if she were in trance, only slits of whitish-yellow seen beneath them. 'Behold this child,' she repeated, 'an' be witness to its mama's punishment. But now she renounce this badness and the child, it suffer no mo'.'

She lowered the baby, who had begun to wail, its scrawny chest throbbing with the upset, and held it in the crook of one massive arm. With her other hand she lifted the twisted limb by the fingers. The baby screeched.

Mama Pitié paid no heed, making no attempt to pacify or comfort the distressed child. The mother looked on helplessly, her face damp with her own tears.

The priestess drew out the atrophied arm, ignoring the screeching protests. The arm began to straighten.

The boy's mother stopped her weeping and held her breath. Small gasps and mutterings ran through the gathering. Whispered exclamations: 'Yea'; 'Mama Mercy'; 'Praise be.'

It seemed as though the tiny bones themselves were unbending and slowly re-forming, moulding into a correct shape. The deep creases and folds of scant flesh began to shrink away so that the brown skin was smoother, less stiff and rutted. The baby's cries ceased.

Mama Pitié continued to run her broad fingers along the arm, her face expressionless, eyelids still drooped. Her breathing was laboured, swelling her chest, rasping in her throat. At last she allowed the little hand to drop away.

And now the baby lifted its own, almost perfect, arm by itself. The fingers curled and uncurled in the air and the limb jerked erratically, but only in the natural way of all babies.

The crowd erupted into roars of approval and applause as Mama Pitié held the healed child aloft once more. The baby's mother leapt to her feet and rushed forward to collect her offspring, her tears now of joy and gratitude.

Mama Pitié's eyes blinked open and she looked down at the mother and child. Her lips parted in what might, had there been any warmth to it, have passed for a smile.

'Mama Pitié, Mama Pitié, Mama Pitié,' chanted the crowd led by the six attendants behind the altar. Yet although the miracle these people had just witnessed should have warmed their hearts, their adulation was tinged with something more than devotion: unease was also in their praises.

Mama raised her hands, palms towards the congregation as if in blessing, and they stamped their feet all the more loudly. A young woman who had hitherto stood quietly at the side of the hall near to the altar began a fresh hymn and the congregation quickly joined in. The unaccompanied music swelled rapidly, filling the Temple.

The high priestess, arms still raised, turned her head to one side to catch the attention of her black-garbed cohorts. The signal she gave them, a slight jerk of her brow, set them in motion. They briskly walked to various stations in the hall and passed cloth pouches with metal openings and handles among the singers to be filled with monetary offerings. The flock duly obliged, even the poorest of them, and no purse and no pocket was overlooked.

The laden pouches were brought back to the head of the hall where a cohort took charge of them and slipped through a door. Mama Pitié stood like a solid black rock throughout the hymn, not joining in, but ever watchful, taking in every face present without once moving her great head. She waited until the hymn – like the others sung that day, a hymn for their Temple alone – was almost over before turning away and slowly walking to the door through which her cohort and accountant had disappeared with the evening's collection. One of her attendants smartly opened the door for her and, without a backward glance, she left the hall.

Some sighed to see her go, while others sang all the louder as if hoping she would hear their individual voices over the others and know who it was that sang for Mama Pitié and the Great Mother Earth, and that she – that *They* – would look kindly upon them. *Blessed be the Mother of All and Her Handmaiden, Mama Pitié*. For her will had licked the baby child's affliction, just as it had licked the wounds and illness of countless others. *Praised be the Mama of Miracles.* Unnerving to the eye she might be, with her great bulk, her disfigured face, and those huge all-seeing eyes, but her saintliness was renowned, and her spiritual benevolence legendary. *Glory be to this Blessed Saviour.*

Beyond the closed door, the high priestess paused for a moment, closing her eyes and putting a hand against the wall of the narrow corridor for support. She rested there, her breasts rising and falling beneath the robes in great heaves, the music from the Temple now muted. A fine sweat had broken out on her forehead and she dabbed it away with her loose sleeve.

From the half-open doorway further along the corridor came the sounds of coins being counted and Mama Pitié gathered herself, controlling her breath and straightening her spine. She moved on to the doorway and stood outside, looking in.

Inside, Nelson Shadebank looked up from his chore, fingers enclosed over a small heap of coins. 'Not bad, Mama. A good miracle inspires generosity, wouldn't you say?' His accent was New York Bronx rather than the Southern Brooklynese so prevalent among the various dialects of New Orleans. He pushed back the gold-rimmed spectacles that had been perched on the end of his nose and leaned back in his chair. Placing the counted money next to the other stacks of coins and notes on the round table before him, he waited for a reply.

None came. Mama Pitié passed on out of sight and, with a shrug, Shadebank resumed his counting.

The high priestess climbed the wooden staircase near the end of the corridor, her breath heavier again as she rounded its head. There was scarcely room for her broad hips to manoeuvre.

At the top of the stairs she paused again to listen to the distant strains of the hymn as it drew to a close. Soon her flock would be leaving the Temple, each one returning to a world of abuse and despoilment, most of them forgetting the words of her sermon within a day or two, impressed only by the healing miracle she'd performed at the end. Was this the only thing that truly bound them to her? Did her words mean so little? The woman, Angeline, had turned away from the Almighty Mother's protection, until the punishment of affliction had visited her third-born; then, oh yeah, *then* she had scurried from the clutches of the false Church back to the merciful embrace of the Almighty Mother. But if the Powers had failed to cure the infant, what then? Would Angeline have turned away again? If she, Mama Pitié, had not straightened the unsightly limb, would her followers have doubted her teachings? Was their faith so thin? Mama Pitié felt the rage burn inside.

Only the next question that came to mind calmed her. Did it matter any more?

In the gloom of the stairway she smiled.

Did *they* matter any more?

Did *any* of it matter any more?

For the human race had fucked up, and the Great Mother would no longer tolerate it.

Mama Pitié's smile bloated to a grin. An unpleasant grin, there in the shadows.

And one that froze instantly when an image intruded upon her thoughts. It was the image of a certain man, his features unclear, a psychic manifestation of someone she did not know, but someone with an infirmity like the child's.

Mama Pitié raised a hand to her temple, concentrating on

the projection, aware somehow that this person was important to her. Or he would be. Perhaps soon. Then it was gone,
faded like the music below.

She wondered at it, disturbed and, irrationally, angered by
the vision. In some way this man was connected with the
children whose thoughts interrupted her own. And somehow,
all three were going to play some part in her own destiny.

She could sense their threat, and she loathed them for it.

Mystified and considerably troubled, Mama Pitié continued
along the corridor towards her living quarters that were
above the very Temple itself. In there her needs would be
satisfied, her appetites would be filled.

And screamed protests would be stifled.

13

'Jim.'

He stirred, but did not wake immediately.

Diane shook his shoulder gently.

Rivers opened his eyes and quickly put a hand to them as though the light hurt. He squeezed his temples with fingers and thumb tips, then focused on Diane who was kneeling beside him.

'I've made you some coffee,' she said, holding up the cup so that he could sniff the evidence.

He mumbled a thanks and groaned when he pushed himself up on to an elbow. His back and limbs ached with stiffness.

'You're in bad shape,' she told him unnecessarily. 'Maybe a shower'll help.'

'I wouldn't bet on it. What's the time?'

'A little after nine. I let you sleep – I thought you needed it.' She handed him the coffee and he blinked away the last of the tiredness. 'I borrowed one of your shirts – hope you don't mind.'

He didn't; the light blue chambray hanging loose over her skirt looked better on her than it did on him.

'I'll make us some breakfast and then we can get on our way.'

Rivers remembered he had promised to go back to Hazelrod with Diane. 'I'm not hungry,' he said, sipping the coffee and relishing the bitter taste.

'Maybe not, but you're going to eat. We've got a long drive ahead of us. Now, I'll get on with the cooking while you take a shower. I've managed to scavenge enough from your fridge to make something decent.'

She leaned forward and her lips brushed against his cheek. It was unexpected and she had risen and disappeared into the kitchen before he could react. Voices from the portable television drifted through the kitchen doorway as he wrapped the bedsheet around his waist and limped towards his bedroom, the coffee taken with him.

His bed had been neatly remade and he sat on the corner for a moment to reflect on last night's conversation with Diane. He thought of the twins, their background, her alcoholic husband and his death – his suicide? And the light. A mystical sign, she'd suggested. Nonsense or . . . Or what? Get real, he told himself. Telepathy between twins was one thing, he could handle that; but a mystical sign? A sign of what? He drank the last of the coffee. A sign of their paranoia, maybe. And Poggs and his family were dragging him in. He shook his head, annoyed at himself. Annoyed because there was something about these people – perhaps it was their earnest sincerity – that made him half believe.

He grabbed the bathrobe hanging over the back of a chair and slipped it on before realising it was the spare that Diane had borrowed. Her faint scent was still in the material and he breathed it in, unaware of his own smile. Rivers went through to the bathroom, his mind busy.

*   *   *

Breakfast of ham, mushrooms and grilled tomatoes was on the table and Diane was fiddling with the small TV when he came into the kitchen fifteen minutes later.

'Can't get rid of this damn interference,' she said, glancing in his direction. 'Hey, jeans and sweatshirt – doesn't fit the Met Office image.'

'I'm off duty.' He went over to the television and saw the picture was broken up by now, the sound itself fuzzy. 'The aerial must've shaken loose last night.' He checked the leads at the back anyway.

'I don't know – your radio's got problems as well.'

He was surprised. 'Atmospherics?'

'Could be. Sit, before your breakfast gets cold. You're out of eggs, by the way.' She switched off the set.

Rivers realised he was hungry, ravenously so. He sat at the table and Diane joined him, although all that was before her was a glass of orange juice.

He pointed with his fork. 'Is that all you're having?'

'I found a couple of apples earlier. A lot healthier than what you're about to eat, but I didn't figure you for the health-food type.'

He nodded agreement. 'You'd be right. So tell me the plan today.'

She poured him fresh coffee. 'No real plan. We go back to Hazelrod, you talk to the children, we see what develops.'

'What are you expecting?'

She shrugged. 'I have no idea. I'm as puzzled as you are about this whole thing. We all are.'

'Okay. We take it as it comes. But I think you'll be disappointed.'

'We'll see. I'm just glad you've decided to go along with us.'

'Let's say I'm curious. My own investigations have got me precisely nowhere so, like I said last night, I've got nothing to lose.'

194

'Thank you anyway.'

It was his turn to shrug.

'Why is it so busy?'

Rivers, in the passenger seat of Diane's Ford Escort, studied the heavy traffic. 'It's the rush to get out of London. They're scared of another earthquake.'

Ahead, the ramp leading up to the M4 flyover was blocked with motionless vehicles.

'I hope they've all got somewhere to go.' Diane inched the car forward, progress on the roundabout beneath the motorway painfully slow.

'I don't think they care,' Rivers replied. 'These people just want to be out in the open, away from falling buildings.' He leaned forward and tried the car radio again, but the static that broke up occasional moments of clear reception was too painful on the ears. He quickly switched off and gazed out at the sky. Overhead there appeared to be one massive sheet of white cloud, the sun visible only now and again as a vapid and ineffectual disc. The air itself was uncomfortably warm and humid.

Someone behind thumped impatiently on his horn, and naturally others joined in the chorus. So much for alternate weeks, thought Rivers, as he observed the different colour stickers on windscreens all around. But perhaps these motorists weren't so wrong to panic, for who could say there would not be another tremor? Who the hell would have predicted the first one?

'We should have taken a quieter road out of London,' Diane said, her hands tense on the steering wheel.

'There won't be any quiet roads out of London today. Relax, we'll get there eventually. Once we're on the motorway things'll be smoother.'

'I'm not so sure. I bet it's packed solid up there as well.'
The car moved forward a few more inches.

A police traffic helicopter passed low overhead and veered
away to the left, heading across to the south side of the
nearby river. Rivers watched it go, envying its freedom. He
made up his mind. 'Okay, it might be better to try another
way. Rather than make for the ramp, ease us over so we
can take the next exit. It'll take us down to Kew Bridge and
over the Thames. Traffic might just be a little easier on the
other side.'

She flicked the indicator switch without further discussion
and began to edge the Escort over to the left. Other drivers
were not keen on the manoeuvre, and Rivers stuck his hand
out of the side window in a placating gesture. It took some
time, but eventually they drove off the roundabout and
headed south along the Chiswick High Road towards the
bridge. Soon, however, Diane had to bring the car to a halt:
traffic ahead was backed up from a busy junction, the lights
there apparently having failed.

'Getting out of the city is going to take the best part of
the day,' Diane complained resignedly.

Rivers grinned, although he hardly felt relaxed himself.
'Until a few years ago, rush hours in London were like this
all the time.'

'I remember, although we've always avoided the place.
Dirty, smelly, about to collapse in on itself – and that was
before the earthquake.' She laughed, then became serious
again. 'I still don't understand how it could have happened.
Surely a fault would have shown up before now.'

'Probably a fracture so minor no machine could detect it.
Then something happened deep down in the Earth – an eruption of some kind – to disturb it, make it worse. That sort
of thing is happening all over the world every minute of the
day. This one happened to be more serious than most and
in a very vulnerable place.' He frowned. Something was going

on up ahead, a disturbance of some kind, but he couldn't make out what. Distant shouts came through the open windows of the car. Then he understood.

'Wind up your window and lock your door,' he ordered Diane sharply.

She looked at him in surprise and he saw it was already too late. A large brown-skinned face had appeared behind Diane's shoulder.

For a second or two Rivers was unable to react – *the face was familiar, the huge staring eyes, the broad, strangely disfigured nose* – but he blinked and the face changed. It was still that of a black person, but the features had altered instantly. Confused – and with a deep dread remaining – he stared back into those hate-filled eyes.

Diane cried out when a muscled brown arm shot through the window and the youth's head and shoulder followed. His eyes quickly scanned the car's interior and came to rest on Rivers' overnight bag on the back seat. The man made a lunge for it, throwing himself halfway through the window and pinning Diane against her seat.

Now Rivers moved, anger overcoming his fear. His left fist smashed into the side of the would-be thief's face. He followed up with another swift blow, this one aimed at the bridge of the sprawling youth's nose, sending him scrambling backwards to get clear. Diane pushed frantically at the intruder, helping him on his way.

Once outside, he recovered enough to scream abuse at Rivers, then yank the door open and hurl himself inside. Diane tried to push him away once more, but he was too strong for her. This time, though, Rivers was ready.

He had picked up his cane, which had been resting beside his leg in the footwell, and he aimed it at the looming face. The blow was short, sharp, and very hard. The black youth's broad nose became even broader, flattening itself with a cracking sound. The youth grunted and spittle shot from his mouth. Rivers used his hand to shove him backwards out of the car and the would-be thief fell into the road, a thick ooze of blood trickling from his broken nose.

'Pull your door shut!' Rivers yelled at Diane, but realised he had left himself unprotected when his own door flew open and rough hands reached in to grab him by his neck. He was dragged backwards out of the Escort and, as he sprawled in the space created by Diane's car and the one next to it, sneakered feet began to kick at his body. He managed to hold on to one of the legs that was inflicting the damage and he pulled hard, sending his assailant crashing to the ground. Someone else grabbed him by the hair and shoulders and lifted him. The other man – fair-haired, T-shirted, wearing the usual mugger's mask of snarled hatred - came at him again, aiming a punch at Rivers' exposed gut.

It hurt, it hurt badly. He doubled up, the man behind unable to hold him upright such was his reflex action, and sucked in air, his throat rasping with the effort. A knee aimed at his face sent him flying backwards against the neighbouring car.

'The Filth!' he heard someone shout close to his ear and, as he steadied himself against the car's roof, still drawing asthmatic breaths, a body roughly pushed by him. As the fair-haired assailant squared up to him, Rivers saw uncertainty on his pock-marked face. This one was either wondering if he had enough time to do more damage, or if he had time to grab the wallet bulging in Rivers' jeans pocket before the police arrived. Someone else rushed between them shouting another warning.

Rivers didn't wait for the man to make up his mind. He struck out with a bunched fist, putting all his weight behind the blow.

His opponent was quick enough to dodge the full impact, but the punch caught him nevertheless. He staggered backwards, recovered his balance, and ran without even looking at Rivers again. For his part, Rivers leaned back against the car, his chest still heaving, glad to see the thug go.

Diane had jumped from the Escort the moment the black man had run off and now she flattened herself against its wing as a policeman pushed by. She was relieved to see other uniformed men dodging between vehicles, chasing after the scattering mob. She shook her head in bewilderment.

'Steamers.'

Rivers had come to the other side of the Escort's bonnet and was leaning against it, his breathing still laboured, one hand held over his midriff.

'What?'

'Gangs used to do it in subways or shopping arcades, now they go in for highway robbery. They get together and wait for a good traffic jam, or even wait at busy road junctions – they know the best places – then run between cars snatching wallets, handbags, anything that's easily available. It's usually over so fast the motorists don't know what's hit them. The police call it "steaming".'

Diane walked around to him. 'I hadn't realised what I've been missing all these years down in the country.'

'We were lucky. The police probably already had them spotted – maybe from the traffic helicopter – before they really got started. My guess is mobs have been in action throughout the night and morning, taking advantage of power failures and the chaos after the quake.'

Other motorists and their passengers, some of them in obvious distress, were climbing from their vehicles to watch the chase.

'Are you okay?' Rivers asked, his breathing finally beginning to ease.

'A little shaky, that's all. Thanks for getting rid of the brute.' She noticed a small trickle of blood from his lips. 'Did they hurt you badly?'

'They did their best.' He dabbed at the blood with the

199

handkerchief. 'Come on, let's get back into the car and be on our way. I'm beginning to hate this city.'

For some reason she hugged him, resting her head on his shoulder for a brief moment. He regarded her with surprise.

'Just glad you're with me,' she told him before breaking away and getting back into the car.

14

He sat on a rock not far from the open doorway, his dry leathered face raised as though seeking the sun's rays. But the sun was hidden by the vast sky mist, although its power was scarcely diminished.

The old man had brooded this way for almost three hours now, as if awaiting some empyrean message, perhaps listening for the fleet wings of a carrier.

Despite the sultry heat he wore a threadbare jacket and trousers so faded their colour was inferred rather than stated. His grey shirt, a size too large, was buttoned to the neck, as though he distrusted any rare appeasement to the chill breezes that usually inhabited this great strath.

He waited.

And he waited.

Until a recognition whetted his cloudy grey eyes. A recognition of thoughts.

A thin shivering hand touched his brow and his eyes closed.

His shoulders bowed forward and wisps of fine white hair hung almost to his bent knees.

A single-breath sigh winnowed past his dry old lips.

So many, so many others.

And the jeopardy in that, the danger to themselves, and to all.

His shoulders hunched. Oh so many. And the minds so young. Save for one.

'Ah.' A sharper sigh this time, provoked by a swift vision of her, a grazing of thoughts, an awareness again of each other's presence.

This time the awareness would not so easily fade: the iron in that frangible link had been set.

And a momentum was gathering pace.

Pity us all, he silently implored. But pity the children most of all: they have not known their time.

He bunched the collar of his jacket over his chest, even though the warmth remained and the wind was still quiescent.

Bibby stepped out the back door on to the uneven red-stone path carrying a tray containing two glasses of lemonade and a small bowl of mixed nuts and raw carrots. As she trod the well-worn path she cast a maternal eye over the summer vegetables, the soil around them already dry and crusted, despite the recent downpour. At least the earth beneath the topsoil would still be good and damp, she reassured herself, then glanced towards the heavens for signs of more rain. Although a layer of cloud filled the sky to the hilly horizon, there was no bruising, no indication at all of rain to be shed. At least the big watertank at the back of the house had been replenished, so there was no need to worry about the usual summer hosepipe ban. Now, where were Josh and Minnie

Mouse? Probably feeding the ducks judging by the half loaf left on the kitchen table.

A shadow seemed to pass over her broad and generally good-natured features as she opened the rickety gate at the end of the path. The twins troubled her so, with their visions and their dreams. She feared for them, yet could offer no specific reason for that fear. Except, perhaps, that these visions seemed more frequent nowadays, with less and less interlude between them; it was as if they were taking on their own momentum, the events speeding up, heading towards . . .

She stopped, a hand resting on the top of the gate. *Towards what?* Would there be an answer? Would it be soon? A bee droned by as she pondered. There was a heaviness in her heart that was unaccountable, a sudden dread that caused her to sway and grip the gate more tightly. In a panic, Bibby scoured the area for the children and, when at first she could not see them, the anxiety almost caused the drinks to spill from the tray.

With relief, she heard their voices from somewhere nearby, behind the shrubbery and trees that screened the pond from the garden. Of course they were there, she had *known* they would be there. Bibby chided herself for her foolishness. Their shouts and giggles were perfectly normal, the careless cries of children with no real concerns for the gravities of a stricken world. The notion strangely cheered as well as saddened her.

'*Where are you, my little dryads?*' she called, knowing well that they would be at the water's edge teasing the ducks with bread morsels, luring the bigger ones away from the less hardy so that all would receive their share.

Josh, or it might have been Eva, returned the call. '*Here, Nanny Bibby. Have you got more bread with you?*'

Bibby let go of the gate and her stride was forceful, buoyant even, just the sound of those little gypsy-haired delights

203

dispelling her dark mood. 'I've got something nice for you,' she said loudly as she made her way through the trees.

They watched her approach, eager smiles on their faces. Although softened by the cloud layer, sunlight enhanced the fine blueness of their eyes so that even at a distance Bibby was startled by their lucent beauty. She scoffed at herself, for the light was always catching their gaze just so, and this indeed was no new experience; nevertheless, she took pleasure in her own surprise, happy that she could still be thrilled by the children's bewitching presence.

'What have you got for us, Nanny?' It was Eva aka Minnie who broke ranks and ran towards her, the last of her bread-crumbs hastily scattered among the avaricious ducks.

'Lemonade,' Bibby announced, 'and nuts'n'things.'

Both children's mouths drooped at the latter.

'Now you know they're good for you. Just because Grandad spoils you with sweets and chocolates . . .' She grinned at their arched eyebrows. 'Oh, I know what he brings you back from town and sneaks into your pockets when he thinks I'm not looking. Grandad Poggsy hasn't fooled me once since we've been married and believe me, kiddoes, that's been a long, long time.'

Eva smiled up at her. 'We won't tell him you know, Nanny.'

She laughed. 'Oh, I see. That would spoil things for him, wouldn't it? Yes, I bet he enjoys the subterfuge. And so do you two.'

Eva frowned at the unusual word, but nodded agreement anyway. She looked to her brother, who was clapping bread-crumbs off his hands into the pond, the ducks quacking their approval. Josh joined his sister and grandmother, taking the lemonade from the tray as if it were vital that he drink immediately. He gulped down half of it before tendering thanks; then he did so with a smile.

The twins were dressed in white T-shirts and shorts, their feet bare. With their grandmother they squatted in the grass and dipped into the bowl of nuts and carrots set between them. Eva began to tell Bibby of their morning's adventures, Josh chipping in when he felt the tale needed more detail, and Bibby began to relax in the peacefulness of the setting: the pond rippling lightly with the movement of the ducks, the graceful cascade of the willow on the opposite bank, the low lush hills in the distance. A chaffinch landed close by in the hopes of a morsel or two from the bowl, and the twins willingly obliged.

After a while, the chatter faded, the bowl was empty, the lemonade gone. Bibby lay back on the grass and stretched her arms, content to rest there in blissful quietness until it was time to prepare lunch. An extra place would be needed, for Diane was bringing James Rivers home with her. He was an interesting man in some ways, there was a depth to him that initially wasn't obvious; but did he have any relevance to what was happening? Bibby was not as sure as Diane and Hugo appeared to be that he did. Did the mere fact that Rivers had witnessed the peculiar light – and survived – really have any importance? The children seemed to think so, but she could only wonder.

As she lay there, lost in her own thoughts, she slowly became aware that the world around her had become even quieter.

She raised her head to look at the children.

They were sitting perfectly still, Josh's head cocked to one side as if listening for something.

Bibby sat up. She had observed them like this many times before, so she was not unduly concerned. However, there was concentrated expression on their faces that was different to anything before, as if the thoughts in their minds were more elusive on this occasion.

A shiver ran through Eva and, as though it were contagious, it was taken up by Josh a moment later.

Bibby wanted to interrupt this odd contemplation for,

unlike other times when the twins adopted this trance-like state, now there was a clear edge of fear in Josh's eyes and a slight trembling of Eva's lower lip. Bibby felt the need to draw them back from whatever imaginary abyss they were approaching, yet her hand stayed itself in mid-air, her call remained behind her lips, as an instinct warned her not to interfere.

The children's eyes were cast to one side and focused on some unseen spot as they listened to voices of no substance. They sat with their backs straight, their ankles crossed, hands loose in their laps. Suddenly they stiffened, froze for a moment, then scrabbled towards each other in one instantaneous movement. They clung together, arms entwined, hugging each other close.

It was heartrending for Bibby to watch them and she moved towards them, ready to engulf them both in her arms, to offer them the protection of her plump bosom. But once again she hesitated, aware that there could be no physical risk to them, that the danger – if there was such – was within their own minds and entirely beyond her reach.

Eva's tousled head was against her brother's shoulder and her eyes, as were his, were wide and staring. She could feel the presence of so many others like her and Josh, and so many others who were not like them, those with thoughts that were malign and misshapen. And one was stronger than most, and its thoughts were foul and full of ill-intent. They conjured up an image that caused the children – and these mind-aberrations – to whimper in fear. The instigator seemed huge and swollen in their thoughts, a power with a terrible loathing of humanity, and with the sensing came the essence, a vague visualisation, of the being itself, something dark and brooding, something gross . . .

Now Bibby did enfold the children within her arms, for their small bodies were shaking and tears flowed from eyes now closed. She drew them close, but felt they were still far away, out of reach for the moment, in a place where she had no power to follow.

Josh and Eva were inside each other's mind and together they confronted this awesome thing whose image could not sustain itself, but fluctuated with the beat of a slow heart. It had no edges and no character, and it bloomed and withered, withered and bloomed, with rhythmic pulsing. They recognised it, for it had touched them before, although never like this, never with such strength and so blatantly. They felt weakened, almost overwhelmed. They felt at its mercy.

Until another's thoughts announced themselves and undermined this malignant, pervasive growth and the cohorts that had gathered behind it. This new presence was full of light and was wonderful, and it exhumed all shadows. And it was one they knew, for it had visited them before: Josh and Eva called it the 'Dream Man'.

Instantly the connection was broken: the children – and others with them – were released.

Josh and Eva collapsed against their grandmother and she held them as tightly as she could without crushing their little bodies, rocking them to and fro so that they would feel safe again, aware that she, herself, could never realise the true nature of their fear.

Candlelight filtered through the lace veils that screened the bed from the rest of the gloomed room, lending soft illumination to the violations within, only sounds escaping the concealing shrouds, although movement inside might occasionally ruffle their textured folds. The room itself was locked and on the outside two guards slept, one on a hard-backed chair, the other prone on the floor. They would be needed later.

Mama Pitié rose over the glistening bloodstained body that lay mute and helpless on the soiled sheets, her massive

207

thighs straddling the drugged man's hips. Her fingers groped beneath her to find his swollen penis, its size still immense, sustained by the potion she had poured between his murmuring lips hours before, and she fed it into herself, her own capacity and moisture helping to smooth its absorption. She pressed down, feeling its swift journey, relishing the ascent, her knees straining, thigh muscles stretching pleasurably. She moaned, a deep grumbling sound, and shifted her buttocks, pushing harder, crushing the man's pelvis into the bed so that he uttered a protest, wheezed for release, his vocal chords traumatised by the needle inserted before his rape had begun.

Mama filled herself with him, thrusting hard so that the bed shook, the veils swayed. She lifted his enfeebled hands to her great heavy breasts and forced them against the protuberant nipples, guiding him as a woman might guide a shy lover, but harshly, squeezing his fingers so that they squeezed her, leading them down over her gross belly and through the mass of tough black hair that curled between her legs, making him touch her there at her body's hidden entrance, pressing his hands against his own root. She sighed with the sensation, but was soon frustrated by his inactivity. The man was almost spent, the power of her potion dwindling rapidly.

Almost four hours had passed since he had been brought to this room and laid semiconscious on her bed. And his youth had served her well during those hours. But now there was little vigour left in him and he was beyond any brew she could administer. Soon his carcass would be taken to the swamps up in Cajun country and left to putrefy or be devoured by the 'gators, probably both.

His kinfolk might miss him, would pester the police some, but young bucks like this were loose shots, they came and went as they pleased, loyal only to their pushers. Mama Pitié had an alliance with the best pushers in town.

Naturally, she chose carefully – no victim could ever be associated with the Temple, or traced back to it – be it a prime stud from Lafayette's black community, or a Bourbon Street whore. And she liked them young, young and tender, the men hard-fleshed where it mattered, the girls soft and fragile-boned. Each sex had its own delights and various ways of use. Mama was very inventive.

The man's head rolled to one side, and his eyelids were drooped with only white slivers where his pupils should have been.

Mama Pitié grunted and settled herself. Sweat ran between the gully of her naked breasts and trickled over the swell of her stomach. She regarded her unwitting lover and a pink tongue slid across her broad lips.

'You not done yet, boy,' she told him in a low rumble of a voice. 'Now come the *real* pain, the pain that bring you back to life 'fo' you proply dead. The pain that make you wiggle and writhe and try to buck me. But that on'y make me feel good, boy, it on'y give me mo' pleasure. An' when you done, when yo' blood begins to cool, why that give me even mo' pleasure, 'cos you one last scab on this good Earth, one mo' piece of excrement that don' trash on the Great Mama. That give me ecstasy, honey, that give me jubilation.'

Without losing him, she stretched over and lifted one of the lace drapes, reaching beyond to the bedside cabinet on which three candles glowed. She slid out a drawer and brought it into the bed, its metal contents clinking together as she laid it by her side.

Inside the drawer were ten rings, their bands wide enough to take Mama Pitié's stout fingers and thumbs up to the first knuckle; a long curved blade extended from every one of them so that when worn they appeared on the hands as talons. She took her time to fit them on her fingers and smiled when she had finished. It was a brutal smile.

Mama held her arms above her head, wrists bent, claws

209

pointed downwards at her prey, a dramatic gesture incited by her own weary exhilaration and, as if sensing something worse was about to happen, the man straightened his head and opened his eyes. His mouth widened to scream, for even a drugged mind will recognise death's approach, but only a high wheezing sound issued from those parched lips, a muted squeal that held no vitality.

His recognition delighted Mama Pitié and she squeezed her haunches together, sucking him into her gross body, holding him there tightly lest his fear cause an unfortunate spasm. Her hands commenced their lethal descent.

His eyes closed again as the metal talons pierced his chest, sinking to the bone, the pain raging through the stultifying drug-haze. The claws were drawn downwards, over his rib-cage and his stomach, towards his groin. There they stayed and blood spurted out, bubbling on to her wrists so that her brown skin was quickly concealed beneath a thin red coating. Her fingers dug deep.

But then her head jerked upwards and her eyes rolled from side to side, until her eyelids dropped just as suddenly and she became perfectly still, oblivious to the near-corpse that feebly struggled under her.

Voices, whisperings, inside her head. Images, vague shapes, unformed spectres floating by, gathering speed, spinning into whirlpools of light. All familiar, but this time . . . this time different. Stronger, yet more confused.

Unconsciously her claws sank deep into the meat before her. The victim's scream was almost soundless.

Children. She saw children. Many – hundreds, thousands! And they bleated at her, like sheep, afraid, cowering. They feared her, they all feared her. And others like her. She could feel the energy of those others, but they were not as powerful as her; they seemed to loiter in the shadow of her own presence.

There came a double image, a child's pallid, anxious face

210

and its mirror-reflection. Dark, dark hair which on one tumbled over high cheekbones and down to curl around a delicate neck. That was its difference from the other and Mama realised it was two faces she could sense, two children with the brightest blue eyes that could only be dreamed of.

Wrath began to replace the awe that had transfixed her so. Her fingers curled inside the body she had invaded and blood spilled over on to the sheets of the bed.

She felt them waver at her fury, these sensings, these cloudy images, felt them cringe from her displeasure as they had before when she'd sent the storm, these motherless beings . . . these motherless . . . Motherless . . .

Understanding of her own anger glimmered.

Mama had sensed them on other occasions. These *things* . . . were against the changes, resistant to what had to be. And slowly she was beginning to comprehend what it was that *really* had to be . . .

She, too, became frightened.

'*Oh, Mama . . .*' she moaned aloud.

The body on the bed quivered as life ebbed.

'*Oh, Mama . . .*'

Another presence imposed itself, something . . . someone . . . as powerful as her, perhaps more so. And familiar. She had known this one for some time, and its potency was intimidating. She mentally backed away, for the moment was not yet right; the confrontation would need stealth, cunning, it would need . . . thought.

Mama Pitié withdrew, closing her mind to the sensing, opening her eyes so that the visions' obscurations were aided by the reality of her sheltered resting place. The connection was swiftly and easily broken.

Her breasts heaved with exhaustion, for it had been a long night, though not one without interest. She pulled her hands from the corpse, the interior flesh squelchy, streaky slivers caught in the claws, and raised them over her head again.

211

Blood trickled down her thick arms and small pieces of gummy matter fell into her bushy hair.

She stared solemnly at the glow from the candles beyond the veils, the mesh causing a ring of light around them, a dull ball of incandescence. She smiled, and this time it was almost sly.

For she realised that in her mind – and in *their* minds – a meeting had taken place. Introductions had been made.

15

It was with relief that they pulled into Hazelrod's courtyard, for the journey had been long and wearing. It seemed that all routes from the capital were jammed, the extra traffic caused by people anxious to leave a potential disaster area; the chaos was further augmented by those journeying *in* to view for themselves the damage already caused. Alternate travelling regulations were ignored. Once on the open road, however, the journey was easier, but two hours at least had been lost in just reaching the suburbs.

Throbbing pain in Rivers' leg indicated that a bruised stomach and bloody nose wasn't the only damage he'd sustained during the attack earlier; he must have knocked his old injury during the scuffle, although not hard enough to have noticed it at the time. He had swallowed a couple of dihydrocodeine to ease the discomfort, and the slight euphoric effect of the pills had made him more receptive to conversation. During the journey they had talked of consequential and inconsequential things and both had learned a little more about each other. Rivers decided he liked what he learned about Diane.

She appeared strong-willed, even tough in some ways, but there was an underlying and opposing gentleness about her, a sensitivity towards others, that rendered her susceptible to all kinds of concerns. It was obvious that Josh and Eva meant everything to her, and when she spoke of her failed and ulti- mately tragic marriage her prime regret was the effect it had had on the children rather than the hell her late husband had forced on her. Her bond with parents-in-law was firm – perhaps her strength compensated for their own son's failings; and of course, she had provided grandchildren, even though they were adopted. Oddly enough, Diane herself was an orphan, raised in a home in Springfield (whose only claim to fame, she told him with a wry smile, was that basketball was first played there), not far from Boston. She confided to Rivers that as a child she had often dreamed of her mother, but never her father, and once or twice recently those dreams had returned. On awaking, though, she couldn't remember her mother's face, only her eyes, soft and blue, paler images of Josh and Eva's. These new dreams left her quietly weeping, as they had when she was a young girl, and lonely and frightened for herself.

There was no such sadness in Rivers' background: his had been a standard middle-class English upbringing. The correct but commonplace schools, a First at university, and a longish career with the Met. Pretty dull, he had all but apologised, the highlight being two years' travelling after university, across Europe first and then Australia. Since then it had been a steady career and a few broken love affairs until the last, more painful, one. Not very exciting, he admitted.

Several years investigating extreme weather and ecological phenomena, she reminded him. Flying through storms, visiting disaster areas, advancing the methods of climate pre- diction, and a near-fatal air crash. Not so humdrum, she sug- gested.

214

En route, and more than halfway to Hazelrod, they stopped at an inn for a short break and for Rivers to exercise his aching leg. It was there, while she sipped orange juice and Rivers quaffed a pint of bitter, that Diane spoke of her few years as a nurse and how her experiences – for some time on a cancer ward – had taught her the real value of life, and even more, the value of *living* it while it was there for you. She talked of the inevitable goodness, as well as dignity, of the human heart when physical adversity became overwhelming, those qualities never more distinguished than when death was at its closest. That time working in hospitals had served to shape the rest of her life, for she had come to appreciate the precariousness of existence, the sheer caprice of life itself, and that self-survival was never enough: the good of all was what mattered, and the well-being of the individual followed from that.

Rivers might have been embarrassed by this unabashed sentiment had not Diane uttered it with such pragmatic naturalness. She also grinned at him immediately afterwards, letting him know that she was well aware of how precious she had sounded. But, she went on to admit, that was why her work with Hugo was so important to her: she felt that she was playing some tiny part in helping the planet survive, seeking solutions that might ensure the continuance of the human race itself. 'Preoccupied, I may be. But not obsessed and certainly not deluded. We've already discovered so much.'

The rest of the journey had been easier, the mood between them comfortable and inquisitive. Although at first Rivers was reluctant to reveal too much of himself, Diane soon had him talking of matters he had never discussed with anyone before. The death of his lover years before had devastated him inwardly and for a while he thought he might go quietly crazy. Apart from grief, concentration was the main problem. Concentration on work, briefings, conversations, or even just

215

reading the newspaper. Executing detailed reports was almost impossible and only his past reputation and the surreptitious help of colleagues enabled him to hang on to his job. But the time of mourning had eventually passed and then his work had taken on a new importance; in fact, it had become all that was important to him. He buried himself in it.

She understood completely, for the loss of her own husband, despite the circumstances, had had a similar effect. Ecology and its many mysteries had become almost a calling to her, a pursuit rather than an interest. As it was for Hugo Poggs and many others who worked closely with him, although in their own situations. Odd, she reflected, how personal loss had driven both Rivers and herself towards a greater effort in their chosen agendas. And now they had joined – she hoped – together in a mutual quest for knowledge of the Earth's failing condition. (She thought it prudent not to mention this to him lest it arouse his natural cynicism.)

The first person they saw within the confines of Hazelrod's courtyard was Mack. He was pushing a wheelbarrow overloaded with roof-tiles across the cobbles and he stopped to give them a wave of welcome. His bare sun-browned arms were ridged with old muscle and the smile between his multi-toned beard was tinged yellow. Rivers took a moment to study him before climbing from the Escort, for the opportunity to appraise Hugo Poggs' helper had not presented itself on his first visit to the family.

Mack could have been in his late fifties or early sixties, the climatologist surmised, although his burly body gave this less credence: it appeared unshackled by the aches and slowness of age. No, it was the lines of his face and the worldliness in his eyes that reflected the passage of years; together, perhaps, with the calmness of his demeanour and the relaxed certainty of his movement. The man had an earthy stability about him that was reassuring. He appraised Rivers just as the climatologist appraised him.

'Good to see you back safely,' Mack said, addressing Diane. His mild West Country burr was as comforting as his presence. 'News yesterday were full of the earthquake.'

'We're fine, Mack.' Diane closed the car door and smiled back at him. 'We ran into a little trouble leaving London this morning, but that's all. Where is everybody?'

'Jus' finished lunch. The, er, the twins were a mite upset earlier.'

Diane's smile dropped away.

'Oh, they're all right, no need for you to be concerned, Missy. Mrs Poggs took care of 'em. One of their funny little dreams, s'far as I can make out.' He eyed Rivers again. 'You look as though you been in the wars, Mr Rivers.'

Rivers touched a hand to his nose, realising it was swollen as well as sore. 'Rush hours are never much fun at the best of times.'

The other man did not pursue the matter. He lifted the handles of the wheelbarrow. 'Jus' replacing some of them roof-tiles we los'. Had most of the broken windows done yesterday and this morning. Glazier and his man could hardly believe it. Damn storm.'

He meant the freak wind that had whipped around the house and shattered windows, Rivers assumed.

'Okay, Mack,' said Diane. 'Don't go falling off any ladders.'

He nodded at her, humour in his grey eyes. 'I'll watch meself, don't you worry. And don't you worry about them little ones – they're tougher than they seem.'

He trundled his load away, leaving Diane and Rivers to glance across the car's rooftop at one another. 'You do look as if you've been in the wars,' she commented. 'Your nose must have swollen up during the last hour and the cut on your cheek from the other night still looks sore. Let's get inside and put something cold and wet on both.'

She led the way, and, taking his overnight bag from the car, Rivers limped after her, wearied by the journey and the sharp pain of his leg. Something cold and wet might do for his parched throat as well, he thought. The sun was still hidden behind the thick blanket of cloud, but the afternoon heat had increased uncomfortably.

As Diane turned in the doorway to wait for him to catch up, she saw him wince and his leg nearly give way under him. He seemed embarrassed by her attention and she quickly went through into the shade, leaving him to follow. They met Hugo Poggs in the hallway.

'Diane, James.' He gave his daughter-in-law a hug and stuck out a robust hand towards Rivers. 'We expected you before lunch. Did you have problems?' He wheezed in a breath while awaiting an answer.

Diane kissed his cheek. 'We ran into some hooligan trouble on the way out of London,' she explained.

'Hence the disrupted physiognomy. You really must put something on that, m'boy.'

'I'm just going to get an ice-pack,' Diane told him. 'Mack said there was a problem with Josh and Eva.'

'Oh, nothing to worry about. Bibby soon calmed them. She's upstairs with them now trying to get them to take a little nap. Now why don't you let me attend to our man here, while you go on up.'

'If you don't mind, Jim?' She looked askance at Rivers.

'Of course not. I'm fine, really.'

She took to the stairs, her ascent swift.

'Jim, is it, rather than James?' Poggs said. 'Good. Very stuffy name, James, I've always thought. Now look, I've still got half a bottle of Macallan left, so what say we treat ourselves to a stiff one? If I may say so, you look as if you need it.'

'A long drink would be more appreciated.'

'Both then. A whisky and a chaser. How's that?'

'It's a fine idea.'

The geophysicist harrumphed with satisfaction. 'Tell you

what – you go through to the sitting room and pour us both a drop of the hard stuff and I'll fetch you a cold beer from the kitchen. Oh, and an ice-pack. I expect you're hungry too, but Bibby will arrange something shortly.'

He gave a wave towards the sitting room door and disappeared into the kitchen. Rivers walked through taking a pack of cigarettes from his overnight bag as he did so. He paused to light up, then tucked the pack back into the side pocket of the leather bag. He found two tumblers and poured whisky into each, making Poggs' more generous than his own, then took his to the large window, whose glass was still smeared with fresh putty, overlooking the courtyard. He stared out while he drank.

The first sip and first few inhalations of nicotine soothed him a little, although the throbbing in his leg was not so easily pacified. 'Good health,' he toasted himself quietly, and took a longer drink.

Hugo Poggs soon appeared again, a glass of beer in one hand, a tea-towel wrapped around ice-cubes in the other. 'Here you are, m'boy. If you don't feel a lot better in five minutes, then there's not much hope for you.'

Rivers placed the tumbler on a side table and accepted the beer and ice-pack gratefully. He took a long swallow of beer, put the glass beside the tumbler, and sank down into the sofa, lifting the ice to his swollen nose as he did so. He winced, then let out a sigh.

'Feel good?' Poggs enquired.

'Feels cold,' Rivers replied.

Poggs brought his own whisky over to the armchair and sat, catching his breath before taking a drink.

'Bliss,' he said as he settled back. His tone, and his expression, became serious. 'How bad was the tremor? We had reports on TV last night, but today's reception is so bad with both television and radio we're not at all up to date.'

Rivers, his legs stretched out before him, shoulders sunk

deep into the sofa's cushions, raised the ice-pack momentarily to look at the other man.

'You've had bad reception too?'

'Almost nil. Lots of static in the air.'

'We had the same problem in London. Later, too, on the way here.'

'Ah.' It was a non-statement from Poggs. He took another swallow of Macallan, his attention fixed on the carpet at his feet. 'Do you suppose this means something? Heavy atmospherics, and all that?'

'It's unusual.' Rivers let his head fall back and returned the damp towel to his face. 'Disturbances to the airwaves over an earthquake area aren't rare, but this is different. I doubt that the two are related.'

'Another enigma, then,' mused Poggs. 'Something else our planet has decided to mystify us with.'

'It'll clear soon enough. I don't think it's anything dramatic at all.'

'Perhaps you're right.' Poggs let out a huff of impatience. 'We're in danger of blowing every slight deviation from the norm totally out of proportion. God knows, nature is constantly breaking its own rules.'

'Not quite. It breaks the rules we try to impose on it to create some kind of order for ourselves.'

'You're absolutely right, of course. Still, we have to work to some kind of pattern, otherwise everything is chaos.'

'Weather men work with the chaos theory: we've come to understand weather changes with our computer models, but we'll never be able to predict it with absolute certainty; there are just *too* many variables.' Rivers changed the subject, not in the mood for a lengthy debate on the nonlinear equations of turbulence and how they complicated, if not completely frustrated, the laws of physics. 'What was the problem with the twins?' he asked. 'Mack said they'd been upset by a dream.'

'What? Oh no, not a dream as such. That's just the way we refer to it. They were down by the pond feeding the ducks this morning when it seems they were lost to one of their trances. It's become a regular thing with those two little imps, too regular for my liking.'

'What happened?'

'Bibby was with them, thank goodness, although I don't believe anything terrible would have happened to them physically. But she was there to comfort them when they became upset.'

There were voices on the stairs.

'If that's my wife on her way down she can tell you for herself.' Poggs drained his glass and slipped it out of sight by the side of his chair. He grinned at Rivers. 'She doesn't like me drinking this early in the day unless it's a weekend. Says it's bad for my liver. Lot of nonsense, of course. Nothing finer to keep the blood flowing if taken in moderation. Ah, my two wood nymphs. Come along in.'

The two children were in the doorway staring at Rivers. Diane and Poggs' wife arrived behind them and ushered them forward. Curiously the twins walked straight across the room to Rivers.

Once again he removed the ice-pack and returned their gaze, uncomfortable under their scrutiny. Unconsciously he rubbed at the ache in his knee.

'Hello.' His greeting sounded awkward even to him.

'Does your leg still hurt?' Josh asked.

'Uh, yes. I had an accident once . . .'

'There?' Josh placed a finger on his knee.

'Kinda . . . All around there, actually. It's okay though, nothing to . . .'

Josh clasped both hands around Rivers' leg, his small fingers reaching behind the knee. He slowly pulled his hands away, as though wiping them against the denim. He repeated the motion. 'Your leg was hurting last time you were here,

221

wasn't it?' the boy said. 'I saw you limping. The pain's really bad, isn't it?'

Taken aback, Rivers replied, 'Sometimes it is.'

'Let me do it, Josh.' Eva moved in eagerly.

Rivers looked around at the adults as if for help. Bibby smiled back at him while Diane merely offered him an ashtray for his cigarette. When he took it her look asked him to be patient with the children.

Eva was giggling as she touched his knee. Astonishingly, as the twins repeatedly brushed their hands against his trouser leg, taking it in turns, the throbbing began to ease, the pain began to subside. Rivers opened his mouth to speak, but no words came to mind.

'They're good with headaches too,' Bibby said proudly. 'They've given me the treatment more than once. They can't take away all the pain, not yet, but who knows what they'll be capable of when they're older? Now, how's it feeling?'

He was almost afraid to speak in case it broke the charm of what they were doing. He dogged his cigarette in the ashtray. 'It feels . . . it feels . . . What is this?'

'Psychic healing, I guess you'd call it,' said Diane. 'Sorry, Jim, Bibby persuaded me to let the children attempt it when we were upstairs and I mentioned you weren't feeling too good. We didn't mean to surprise you so.'

'I still don't understand – how could they stop the pain?' There was only a dull ache in his leg by now, an ache where before tiny demons had tormented him with red-hot needles.

'They're not. They're merely opening your energy channels so that your own body can help itself. There's no medical way of explaining this, Jim, you just have to go along with what's happening. Don't question it.'

'My apologies for springing this on you too,' said Poggs' wife as she sat on the arm of her husband's chair. 'I wanted you to experience a part of Josh and Eva's uniqueness for yourself, so I asked them to come down and show you. As

222

a matter of fact, they were very anxious to help you; for some reason you're important to them.'

The children stepped away, pleased with themselves, and Rivers gingerly touched his leg. 'That's unbelievable,' he said, and flexed his knee, expecting the pain to come shooting back. When it didn't, he shook his head in wonder. 'Unbelievable,' he said again.

Diane sat next to him, her pleasure at his incredulity evidenced by her smile. 'It must be hard to take for someone so practical. You haven't been drugged or hypnotised, yet your pain has been eased by two kids who don't even know the nature of your injury. How does someone like you cope with that?'

His attention was still on his leg. 'With difficulty, I suppose. And with gratitude. How long will it last?'

Diane shrugged. 'No way of knowing. Maybe for an hour or so, maybe for the rest of the day. Like medicine, more than one dose is needed if the cure is to be effective.'

'These two could make a fortune.'

Hugo Poggs and his wife laughed. 'There are plenty of other healers in the world without putting pressure on Josh and Eva,' said Bibby. 'Besides, their talent hasn't been developed yet.'

Rivers gave his attention to the children. 'Thank you for stopping the pain,' he said. 'Do you know how you do it?'

Both shyly shook their heads.

'Do you feel anything when you do it?'

Josh spoke up. 'It sort of tingles a bit.'

Eva nodded agreement. 'We pull the hurting out. It comes very easily if we think hard enough.'

'Doesn't it hurt you?'

They giggled at one another. 'Of course not,' replied Josh scornfully. 'We just throw it away.' Eva giggled again.

'Your mother said you wanted to see me. Is that right?'

They nodded as one.

'Will you tell me why?'

'Oh yes,' said the boy.

Rivers waited, but was forced to prompt them when they offered nothing more. 'So tell me why.'

This time it was Eva who spoke up. 'You've got to find the Dream Man,' she said.

16

The children stood on chairs before the large map of the world on Hugo Poggs' study wall, while Poggs himself, with Diane, Bibby and Rivers crowded behind them.

It had been Diane's idea to bring them in there and confront them with the map, for persistent but patient questioning of the twins had failed to reveal the identity of their Dream Man, or where he came from. He was just there in the dreams, they insisted, and he was kind, not like the other person. They refused point blank to talk about this 'other person'. The kind one was old, they said, although they had never actually seen him. They had only *felt* him being there, but they knew he was very old and wise, and that he wanted to help them. Rivers had asked why they felt *he*, of all people, could find this very old and wise man. Because you're part of the light, had come the baffling reply.

Rivers had let the others continue with the questions after that, for the children's simple statement had left him full of unease. What the hell did *that* mean? How could he be *part* of the Light? He had witnessed it, but it had nothing to do with him. Noticing his discomfort, Poggs had poured him another drink.

Eventually Josh and Eva had grown tired of the interrogation and that was when Diane had suggested the game with the map. It would be similar to a game they had played a few times before, she explained to them, when something had gone missing around the house and she or Bibby drew a rough room sketch of Hazelrod so that they could point out a particular place where the lost article could be found. Seven times out of ten when they went to the room Josh and Eva homed in on the missing item, she assured Rivers.

He had followed them through, taking the whisky with him and lighting another cigarette on the way. This was ridiculous, he reminded himself as if afraid of falling under the spell of Hazelrod's residents. They were good people, sincere people, of that he had no doubt; but they had to be misguided, surely? What they were doing – what they were dragging *him* into – had nothing to do with reality. Yet the children had stopped the pain in his leg. At least temporarily. And they had been aware of the world disasters as they happened. According to Diane. It was with mixed feelings that he gazed at the map with the others.

'Look at all the countries,' Diane was instructing the twins, 'and clear your minds of everything else.'

Josh and Eva stared at the map, looking from left to right, up and down.

'Ignore the coloured pins,' she told them. 'They're just where bad things have happened in the world.' Her voice became low and soothing. 'Now, take your time and think of the Dream Man, not what he looks like, but the kind of feeling you get when you know he's there. Can you do that?'

They indicated that they could.

'Okay. When you're ready, point at the map where you think the Dream Man is.'

They hesitated only a second or two; Josh pointed at Africa and Eva pointed at India. Then Josh pointed at Brazil and Eva pointed at Russia. Then they pointed at Bulgaria together.

Rivers watched Diane's concerned expression turn into one of triumph.

Then Josh pointed to Sri Lanka and Eva pointed to Japan. Josh changed position and Eva's finger went to China. They laughed when their separate fingers sought out Mexico and Portugal.

Diane looked round at Rivers in dismay.

'He's all over the world, Mama,' Eva exclaimed delightedly as she singled out Pakistan and Josh indicated Cuba.

VARANASI (BENARES), INDIA

Young Salim Prabhu reached for another battery from the pile before him and brought the short-handled hammer smashing down on the casing. His body and shorts were covered in carbon dust; even his face was smeared with the red powder. His back ached and his head throbbed with the incessant hammering – not just *his* hammering, but that of the other seven boys who shared the work in this cheerless lock-up set between a rickshaw mechanic's shop and a butcher's. He had arrived even earlier than his workmates – just before dawn – so that he could take up a position close to the open doors where he could at least enjoy the daylight and breathe air that was slightly less clogged with the dust of their labours. Those boys at the back had to work by the light cast by a single clay lamp and their eyes were white and ghostly in the cavernous gloom. For every battery broken for its carbon they received one paisa, and each of them hoped to have earned at least nine rupees by the end of the day or, as Salim knew it, by cow-dust hour (he lived outside the city where the farmers herded their cattle home from grazing at dusk). Not that any dust would be raised in this third month of the monsoon season, he reflected as he hammered, for the rains had arrived early and the *pandas*, the Hindu priests, predicted they would leave late. As they had the year before, and the year before that.

At that moment, however, the rain was at rest, and outside in the streets the populace went about its business regardless of the brown floodwaters of the Ganges that swirled through the city. The Ganga Flood Control Commission had striven to improve drainage over the years, and had built dams to lessen the flood's impact, but soon now the deep-cut streets would no longer be able to cope with the rising levels and even the platforms on which goods and food were stored would be under threat.

Salim hoped that his sister, Nergish, a year younger than his ten, would find garbage dumps high enough to scavenge plastic and tin to fill her huge bag this day. Their father would be displeased if the bag was not bulging with recyclables for the greedy scrap merchants and he would take his anger out on them all.

Salim had left Nergish just before dawn at the edge of the shanty town where they lived with their parents and baby brother, Tipu, he journeying into the waterlogged city, his sister taking a short cut through the jungle scrub to the dumps on the outskirts. Their father, Rakesh, had been in a drunken rage the night before and even at this mid-morning hour probably tossed in his sleep and dreamt of his glory days as an officer in the Indian Army. He had been a proud man then, a short service commission officer, serving his country gladly only to be cast aside like a bonded labourer after ten years, without pension, medical cover, or subsidised ration, but with a young family to feed. For a while he had worked as a pandal builder, but such toil was not to his liking, nor did it suit his dignity as an ex-officer. Now Salim and Nergish laboured to keep him and their tuberculosis-stricken mother, Rajnee, and Tipu, while he consoled himself with cheap liquor and railed against the fates that contrived so spitefully against him, sometimes his language so crude and his mood so clumsily violent that his family would flee across the sewage canal that ran by their shack to wait until snores took the place of his ramblings.

Ignoring the immense black flies (they had become known as the beasts of the air) that swarmed while the rains regathered their strength, Salim briefly looked up from his labours to watch the teeming activity outside. There were no yellow Ambassador taxis to clog the streets today, for they kept to the city's higher ground, but cycle rickshaws and camel-driven carts waded in abundance through the waters, while enterprising boatmen drifted by, their small boats and gondolas filled with fare-paying customers. Pilgrims and worshippers were everywhere, making their way through the bazaars and narrow alleyways to the Mother Ganges, mourners among them bearing shrouded burdens, lamented loved-ones whose bodies would be purified by flames on the banks of the great river and their ashes cast into the flow. Some seasons before, an even greater multitude of worshippers had flocked to this city of the dead to witness the miracle of the goddess' menstruation, for the river had suddenly begun to run red; not even when the Grasilene factory further upstream was prosecuted for using rayon grade pulp in its manufacturing process and discharging its effluence into the river, did the fresh influx of pilgrims diminish. Sacred cows wandered at their will, and *dhobi-wallahs*, on their way to the river carrying their laundry, scrupulously avoided them, afraid to even brush by the lumbering beasts with their bundles.

Across the street a tea-seller called out *'Chai! Chai! Chai!'*

and Salim's dry mouth ached for the thick sweet cardamom taste. Someone else called his name and he looked up to see Rekha waving down at him from one of the small individual balconies that graced the top floor of the building opposite. Below her, a covered wooden gallery ran the length of the building, and below that, at ground level (but still raised from the street itself) was a line of shops. Rekha was a *hijri*, a eunuch whose manhood had been removed at the age of twenty-one (she had been known on occasions to lift her skirts and reveal the castration scars to any passerby who might be interested) and she lived among others of her kind with their guru in the top-floor brothel. They proclaimed themselves the chosen guardians of the prophet's grave and would often descend on marriage and birth ceremonies dancing and singing and demanding money for their blessing, a curse taking its place if no rupees were forthcoming. Her sari was of the brightest yellow and even from where he squatted Salim could see her lips were painted the deepest rouge and her eyes were kohl-lined, her skin lightened with turmeric paste. She pouted her lips at him and lowered her eyelids in seductive manner, screeching with laughter when the boy quickly lowered his gaze and became intent on his work.

She called his name again, a tease with no spiteful intent, for she liked the boy and would often, when the streets were dry and she flaunted herself among the tourists and pilgrims, stop to talk to him and sometimes toss him a boiled sweet as he pounded away at his batteries. Salim sneaked another look and grinned from ear to ear; he returned the wave. An itinerant barber shaving a customer in a doorway nearby caught the exchange and hawked phlegm in to the muddy water his lower legs dipped into, for the *hijra* were reviled as well as respected, not just because they had power to bless or curse as they pleased, but also because their lifestyle was considered disgusting by the pious of the community.

He growled at Salim, who busied himself with his task once more. Rekha waggled her tongue at both the boy and the barber and swanned back into the room she had come from.

As Salim hammered, his thoughts drifted to things less dull, the thoughts becoming daydreams: of celebrations with elephants wearing flower garlands and painted with vegetable dye, of tiny bells tinkling on chains over soft beds, of tiger hunts (now banned) and polo matches, of fresco painters high on bamboo ladders adorning virgin walls with India's past glories, of bejewelled dancers dressed in brocade and transparent veils, their ankle-bells tinkling to their rhythms, of flaunting peacocks and colour-transient chameleons. He dreamed of such things because the world outside these very doors held none of them; save for the occasional glimpse of Rekha and her lurid companions, his daily vista was drab and unexciting. So his mind presented him with things bright, adventurous and beautifully gay.

Sometimes he daydreamed of the little ball that glowed like a sun-filled pearl and floated as a petal on the breeze.

It filled him with joy, this vision, and was as welcome as a visiting friend. In night-dreams, for he saw it in those too, the light brought others to him whose companionship was utter, their bonding supreme. Usually he sensed them, those other children, but occasionally he saw them and they were of all races and creeds. And all were charged with the same unfathomable yearning as he.

Yet recently he had begun to wake from such dreams in a burning sweat, for now there was something to fear in those wondrous slumbers, something that loomed and spread like the blackest of clouds to subdue the glory; it came as a dark threat that possessed no substance. This thing frightened Salim, but the mundanity and hard toil of his waking hours soon shooed away such terrors. What always remained, however, no matter how harsh this regime, was the urge to reach beyond the mere dream and to touch the haunting light.

The strains of the five-stringed tanpura interrupted his wanderings as the *Ustad* played from the dark recesses of his shop across the street and Salim's skin prickled as the old music guru's chant rose above the other city sounds, for the words sang of fire mingled with heaven's tears. The cooling rains that followed the scorching, dry heat of April and May had always been welcomed, even when they gave cause for the goddess Ganga to overflow her banks and flood the plains; but the *Ustad*'s words warned of the horrors when fire and water combined their might. Two *pandas* who squatted on stone blocks above the flow not far away, their loins wrapped in muslin, the sacred thread denoting they were twice-born in Hinduism's endless wheel of life worn over their naked shoulders, paused from their *puja* to listen. Salim caught trepidation in their eyes before they bowed their heads and renewed their devotion with greater intensity.

The hammer Salim wielded hovered over its mark as he heard a distant thunder, and passersby paused to listen too, some cocking their heads to one side in attitudes of unease. The boy saw a bright flash of colour as Rekha returned to the balcony. She first peered down into the street below, then up at the heavy skies as if curious about both. The *Ustad*'s song ceased when the sluggish waters that drifted through the old city began to agitate.

Salim felt the floor beneath him quiver. The pyramid of batteries belonging to the boy behind him collapsed, the cartridges rolling loose among the powder.

The floodwater was now stippling as well as surging through doorways it had been unable to reach before. Everywhere people were looking around in dismay.

At that moment the clouds decided to discharge their load and the rain struck so forcibly and with such suddenness that several of the people fell or tottered beneath the impact. The downpour swiftly turned the flood ooze into a bubbling sea so that small boats and gondolas rocked in the storm.

Salim hurriedly moved back from the open doorway, his skin and shorts already soaked with the spray and his black hair flat against his forehead. He prayed that his sister was not caught on the garbage dumps, for torrents of this intensity would create quagmires of the tips, drenching everything into a swampy mass that was easy to sink into and be lost. The other boys huddled together at the back of the room, the candlelight sputtering on its shelf, while Salim stayed to view the teeming sheet of greyness, his mouth gawped open at such a wondrous deluge. The floor trembled, sending up clouds of fine dust and Salim marvelled at the rain's power.

He could just discern the colourful robes of Rekha high on her balcony, those shades now reduced to pale pastels by the deluge between them; the buildings opposite were no more than dull shapes, as were the figures scurrying before them.

Salim shivered, although the air was not yet cold; he shivered because a strangely exhilarating fear was stirring within him. He was suddenly both afraid and excited, and neither emotion held the upper hand.

He felt the presence in his senses before his eyes caught sight. He stared at the precise place where the small globe was to appear seconds later.

It emerged from the rains like a single headlight, its incandescence scarcely muted by the downpour, the halo around it close to the undetermined surface, and it floated gracefully above the erupting floodwater, the drenching having no influence on its journey.

It came to a shimmering halt directly in front of Salim, although some distance away still, close to the building opposite. A rainbow formed around it, a complete circle whose lower edge dipped into the unsettled water below, and the boy's smile widened in recognition. This was the light of his dreams.

He gave a cry of delight, and the boys behind him cowered

further back, gaining no such joy from this odd sight. But soon even Salim's smile withered on his lips.

The structure around him had begun to tremble. The lantern fell from its shelf, its glow snuffed so that half the room was cast into further darkness. The batteries jiggled and twitched on the floor, their piles disassembling, their sound that of a thousand chattering teeth. The boys wailed.

Outside in the rain, the pearly light started to spiral, its sweep limited at first, then opening out as it rotated faster. No raindrops bounced from the light's soft-edged face as it cut its circular swathe through the downpour. It spun faster, rising slowly, and licks of water rose with it like lizards' tongues snatching at a taunting prey, until the water swelled as a mass towards the glowing orb.

Salim watched mesmerised, oblivious to the shaking of the building around him. He craned his neck as the light and the spume-flecked water beneath it rose higher, and his breath was held and his heart beat faster. He fell back among the scattered casings when a roar rumbled from the earth below the street and the very foundations of the ancient city seemed to shudder. Mud and thick clods of earth abruptly spewed from the rising heap of water and almost immediately a great fountain of dirt burst through, an immense geyser that quickly ran clean as boiling liquid soared skywards to claim the shining orb. Steam hissed and billowed around this giant white tower, whose edge drove through the sidewalk and gallery above, rising to take some of the small balconies, on one of which the *hijri* stood gaping. Rekha screamed in agony and surprise as the scalding column flayed the skin from her flesh and took her with other flotsam to the heavens. Her cry was swallowed along with her body.

The waterspout expanded as it flowed, its crest unfurling high in the sky, showering droplets that sizzled with the rain, and at its base steam rolled outwards in great clouds, creating a searing fog that spread with lightning speed.

The noise was shattering as Salim fled to the back of the room to join his friends who huddled together in a tangle of bodies. But no one was safe from this unleashed behemoth.

Within seconds the whole façade of the building it was closest to was dismantled, only the rear walls containing the furious steam; the jet rapidly spanned the whole street, instantly boiling the merchants, holy men, pilgrims and animals in its path.

The terrible scalding heat felt by Salim and his companions crouched there in their dusty refuge lasted but a moment, for its shock alone was enough to destroy any sensing. And as their frail bodies blistered and broiled, another part of them, a part that could never be touched by physical pain, was released.

As Salim's spirit sailed it seemed that he was heading for a bright light, far brighter than any he had ever known in his short life.

More radiant even than the sunlit pearl of his dreams.

17

It was a beautiful place, a garden that stretched for miles, with sweeping lawns and tree-topped knolls, and immense flowerbeds full and vibrant with every shade of colour. Palest blue snow-capped mountains rose over the distant hilly forests and the untainted azure of the cloudless sky governed all. Like spectral sentinels around these cherished and organised pastures stood many white pillars, tall yet unobtrusive, and set in no definite order. High in the clear air a golden eagle soared, its flight graceful and supreme. A stream that reflected the blueness above ran through this nirvana into a great lake, dazzling jewels of sunlight dancing on its ripples.

The twins held hands as they wandered through the flower displays, Eva stopping them both as they walked to stoop and observe a holly blue butterfly that had settled on the head of a poppy, or to watch a furry bee skit among a cluster of dandelions, gathering pollen on its way. A light breeze made the warmth pleasant and stirred the leaves in nearby trees. The twins dropped to their knees to study a green caterpillar scaling a blade of grass, and when they raised their heads again they found the lawns busy with other children, many playing together in groups, some chatting or singing to one another, quite a few lost in solitary thought; and although their appearance was instant, they carried on as if they had always been there. Josh guessed there must have been at least a thousand of them, probably many more, and he glanced at Eva in astonishment, for never before had they met with so many. Her eyes sparkled and she dragged him towards a bunch of boys and girls playing blind man's buff around the pillars. The twins were not so much welcomed as accepted naturally and were soon giggling with the others as a blindfolded boy, arms outstretched like antennae, searched for dodging friends.

Josh and Eva enjoyed returning to this dream for here they joined with children like themselves, familiars who shared a common bond: the One-Thought. None of them understood what the One-Thought was, they were only informed that it belonged to them alone by the old man who sometimes roamed among them, and that it enabled them to come together in this way. One day they would realise its potency as well as its source, the old man, the *Dream Man*, promised; one day that perhaps was not too far away.

Eva laughed as she ducked beneath the waving arms of the blindfolded seeker and slipped behind a nearby pillar. The pillar's smooth surface was warm to her touch and she gave a small squeal of surprise as she hopped away. Curious, she approached it again and put her fingertips to it, and this time, perhaps because there was no surprise, she found the mild heat pleasant. She leaned her cheek against the column and took pleasure from its warmth.

Josh came scooting around the other side, glee shining from his blue eyes, and snuggled close to Eva, using both sister and column as a barrier between himself and the hands that sought him.

The blindfolded boy appeared, having followed soft fleeing footsteps and the giggles that went with them. The twins moved around the pillar as if glued together, and tried to hold their breaths in check.

But the boy halted and looked about as though his eyes were not covered. He pulled the mask away and there was such abject misery in his expression that Eva's lip trembled in sympathy. Other children had ceased their activity now and they, too, were looking around as if searching for someone. Josh and Eva felt the grief with them, for they were suddenly aware that, although their numbers had grown, one of them was missing. The loss was in the collective-consciousness, and they all shared the thought that soon many more would fail to arrive at this place. Some of the children began to weep. Others looked towards the sky and saw the storm clouds gathering over the far mountains. Their sadness was replaced by a crawling dread.

The clouds began to move rapidly towards these green fields, dark and furious, lightning stuttering through them, the low rumble of thunder rolling over the forestlands.

The breeze quickened, ruffling the children's hair and catching their clothes. Some cried out, others whimpered their distress. Lightning flashed again, still distant, but bleaching the landscape; the crack of thunder that came after caused the children to cringe, their shoulders hunching to their ears and their hands curling into tight grips. They huddled together in groups or in pairs.

Boiling clouds sped towards them, ragged and threatening, filling the sky, and as they approached parts seemed to form into vaporous claws that sank downwards as if to pluck the children from the lawns, only to lose substance and wither away as they neared the ground.

As Josh crouched beneath another thunderclap, something moving in the grass caught his attention. He stumbled backwards, taking Eva with him. She screamed when she spotted

239

the worms wriggling from the earth, for they were every-where, oozing from below. Spiders, bugs and shell-backed creatures came with them and soon the grasslands pulsed with this teeming unbidden life. Children shrieked and stamped their feet when they discovered what they were standing in, then began to scatter in all directions. As they did so, more shapes appeared in the storm clouds that were now over their heads: mouths and eyes formed in the tumbling mists, not necessarily together, and long tongues snaked towards the ground; whole arms appeared, only to be dispersed on completion by the angry winds. And there were monstrous configurations whose place could only ever be in such nightmares; these too dissolved as soon as they were fashioned.

'Run, Eva,' Josh urged, spinning her and propelling her towards the nearest cover, the woods that bordered the vast gardens. *'Run!'*

The children bumped into each other as they fled, many of them falling into the filth exuding from the ground, their panic intensified by the sharing, and Josh and Eva were knocked over several times before reaching shelter. They hesitated before entering, for none of the other children had chosen this way, and besides, the nocturnal shade offered by the leafy canopy was uninviting.

Josh stared back at the darkened lawns filled with running, tumbling friends and wondered if he and Eva would be better off among them – at least there might be safety in numbers. But Eva tugged at his arm and pointed.

Inside the woods shone a small light.

The boy cried delightedly and drew his sister over the forest threshold. Immediately they found themselves on a narrow footpath.

The light twinkled among the trees not far away.

They exchanged glances and did not need to speak; both knew the way ahead was towards the light. They ran, Josh in front, for the width of the path did not allow them to travel side by side, and the moss and debris of the forest floor was soft and comfortable beneath their feet. The upper branches of the trees shook with a wind that seemed to follow their progress.

'Wait for me,' Eva pleaded, and Josh was forced to slow down. Impatiently he reached back for his sister's hand so that he could pull her along at a brisker pace. They sprinted that way for a short while, Josh awkwardly half-turned so that he could keep hold of Eva, low branches and bushes lashing at them as they went, and stopped only when they were getting no closer to the light. It hovered ahead of them, shimmery in the dusky air. It retreated, then returned, as if encouraging them onwards.

'It wants to take us somewhere safe, I know it does,' Eva insisted.

Josh smiled: he knew it too. 'Come on,' he said, and they were off again, racing through the trees with the graceful speed of wood nymphs.

The small ball of light led them on, a flittering will-o'-the-wisp that was sometimes lost from view, but never for very long. Eventually the path widened and the twins ran side by side, their breathing often broken by chuckles of excitement as the little glow played hide and seek with them, disappearing into thickets to reappear in another place some way off, orbiting trees to shoot off, straight as an arrow deeper into the forest. And deeper into the forest the children followed.

They began to grow weary.

'I'm tired, Josh,' Eva complained as she rested against the gnarled trunk of a twisted old tree. She looked around warily, for the forest was even thicker here and the foliage more wild and prickly.

'We can't stay here,' Josh told her, although he, himself, collapsed on to the leafy path and rested.

241

'But where are we going?' Her manner was mournful.

'After . . . after the light.' He drew in quick breaths and searched ahead.

'I don't want to follow it any more.'

'We've got to, Eva, we –' He squinted his eyes.

Night had swiftly and inexplicably descended upon the forest, blending with its shadows in a dark conspiracy. The way forward was sinister, but another kind of light filtered through the trees, one that was somehow warmer and steadier.

'It's a window,' he whispered.

'It's a house!' Eva exclaimed, following his gaze.

They burst into a run again, ignoring the cruel barbs that snatched at clothes and scratched their flesh. Eva screeched as she stumbled over a tree root, but Josh was there to save her from falling and to pull her onwards. As they drew nearer to this new light, they became more cautious and slowed their pace. The winds rustled leaves and caused upper branches to sway and creak. A disturbance nearby made them jump, but whatever animal had become entangled in the undergrowth freed itself and hurried on, its path plotted by quivering foliage.

The twins finally broke through into a clearing. The black clouds roiled above the treetops and lightning bathed the scene below with silver. Two tiny windows of the old stone cottage were aglow with a soft welcoming light and smoke curled lazily from the chimney stack in the thatched roof before it was seized and dispersed by the blustery wind. Climbing roses took the harshness from the walls, although they themselves were rendered bleak then dulled in turn as the light variegated. There was no garden, for the forest itself was just that, but bluebells shivered on either side of the path that led to the doorstep. The door itself was slightly ajar, a thin seam of flickering light beckoning from within.

Josh and Eva recognised the tiny dwelling from storybooks

they had read and, although there were variations in those stories, the promise was always the same: such a sweet place always offered sanctuary. Sometimes there was more, but at that moment the children could not remember what it was. They were tired and frightened, and despite their exertion, a chill was in their very bones. They needed comfort.

'Come on,' said Josh, boldly leading the way. Less confident, Eva followed.

They heard a quiet lilting song as they drew close to the open door, but the wind scooped away any meaning to the words. The fiercest thunderclap yet and, finally, the first raindrops, sent the bluebells into a frenzy of shaking and the children scooting the last few steps to the door.

Yet still they paused at the threshold and listened as the reverberations of thunder rumbled away. The song was more easily heard, but they realised it was in another language, one that was alien to them yet strangely familiar. They shivered there on the doorstep, afraid to go in, afraid even to knock, when abruptly the singing ended and a voice as sweet as the song itself bade them enter.

'Kom inside, children, there iss nothing to harm you here.' It was a woman's voice.

The twins looked at each other for a decision. The voice was not an English one, but the message was precise.

'Please kom, there iss warmth and food for you.'

It was Eva who pushed the door wider.

A figure sat in a rocking chair by the fireside, one side of it lit by the flames, the other side cast in deepest shadow. An oak dresser filled with hanging teacups and painted plates stood against one wall, and a small round table covered over with a lace cloth stood near the room's centre; there was a low stool opposite the rocking chair and a black pot hanging over the fire; curtains dotted with tiny flowers decorated the small windows and a soft-coloured rug covered much of the wood flooring; a rickety corner staircase led to the room or rooms above. The children stayed where they were, encouraged by the fire-lit cosiness of the room, but wary of the stranger who welcomed them.

She raised a hand towards them. 'Don't be afraid,' she said in her strange accent. 'I em som-one who knew you once, som-one who loves you.'

A shawl was around her shoulders and thin, laced boots rose above her ankles into the petticoat that showed beneath her long skirt. Ringlets of wild dark hair hung around her face, shadowing her features even more. It was Eva who conjured the word 'gypsy' in her mind and the thought was as swiftly passed to her brother, who drew in a sharp breath. The connection was as swift again, for assumptions have a strong hold in dreams and challenges are for waking hours.

Josh remembered the picture-book where they had first seen this place. The story had been about . . . about . . .

To and fro went the rocking chair, to and fro, creaking all the time . . .

He couldn't remember, though he knew it was important, and Eva wasn't even trying: she was moving closer to the figure.

'Kom, little one,' the gypsy lady entreated, 'we haf things to tell each other. So pretty . . .'

Josh was uncertain. The story – what had it been about? Something was nagging at him, jigging up and down in his mind, annoyed at him for not remembering. *There once was a tiny cottage hidden away in a dark and terrible forest* . . .

Eva looked back at him, smiling, before continuing towards the lady, who now sat with her arms outstretched to receive her.

'So much to tell . . .' she was saying, her accent distorting the words, somehow making them heavy. 'Soooo moch . . .'
And in the cottage there lived . . . there lived . . .

'Where are you from, little one, and what do they call you?'

Eva hesitated. 'But you're our mummy. You know my name.'

'Ah, yes, bot it has been so long. Won't you tell me where you lif now? Kom closer and whisper it to me.'

There lived an old witch . . .

Eva stood before the shadowed lady.

. . . who tempted wild animals and birds, and the pixies who lived in the forest . . .

His sister was about to be enfolded in the lady's arms.

. . . and little lost children to come to her . . .

But instead the lady had gripped Eva's wrist and was rising from the chair, her shape still half in shadow.

. . . to come to her so that she could boil them in her stew . . .

A mighty thunderclap shook the cottage and the door behind Josh flew open wide.

. . . and eat them!

'Eva!'

Josh dashed forward as his sister turned towards him, but the dark shape was still rising over her, rising and growing huge, the shawl slipping from her shoulders as they broadened, just as her hair had slipped away to reveal a face so black and cruel that Josh almost fell to the ground in terror.

Eva swung round to see what could frighten her brother so and she screamed when she saw the giant that towered over her. She tried to back away, but the monster held her tightly by the wrist and drew her in.

'No!' cried Eva, her resistance futile.

Josh flew into them both, flailing madly at the monstrous figure – a woman still, he realised, but changed now into a huge evil-looking black woman with a single long hole beneath her flattened nose and scars on her face, who swatted him away with her free hand as if he were no more than an irritating fly.

'Leave her alone!' Josh yelled and jumped to his feet to

charge at her again. So fierce was his kick – and more importantly, so violent was the intent in his mind – that, whether in surprise or real pain, the monster released her grip on Eva. The boy grabbed his sister and dragged her towards the open door.

But just as they reached it, it slammed shut.

He let Eva go so that he could pull at the handle, but as he strained at the unnatural force that held the door there, a shadow loomed on the grainy wood. Eva helped him, their hands yanking at the handle together, and without warning the door swung open again just as lightning stuttered outside and blinded them all.

With terror in his heart Josh plunged out into the rain and ran and ran as the night returned and the wind swept against him as if to slow him down. Through the shrivelled bluebells he pounded, crashing into the undergrowth without a backward glance, his chest raw with fear and the harshness of his own breathing. And as he fled blindly from the dream he called to Eva: *'Run, Eva, run, run . . .'*

He called even though he knew she was no longer with him.

As usual, the evening news was grim. A dust storm had swept across highways in America's Midwest, causing vehicle pile-ups and many deaths, a cyclone had whipped across the Bay of Bengal, and there had been an earthquake in Kazakhstan, one of the Commonwealth of Independent States.

Rivers lit his fourth cigarette of the night, aware of Bibby's disapproving glance, but not deterred by it, and watched the small two-dimensional television perched on a corner of the kitchen's dresser. The others sat around the kitchen table with him, their attitudes sombre despite the almost-empty wine bottle before them. Unwashed dishes from a hastily

246

prepared supper lay stacked in the sink. The television's reception was bad although not, they suspected, because of the set's age: the night air was still troubled by atmospherics.

At that precise moment they were watching a giant boiling waterspout on the screen, at least 300 feet high and filmed from some distance away, its spray cooled by heavy rain into blustering clouds. It had erupted in the middle of an ancient Indian city.

From time to time the picture faded and fuzzed with snowy blemishes or double images, but just then the picture was clear – and awesome. 'The wrath of the inner Earth,' Poggs remarked over the newscaster's voice as though quoting an aptly remembered text.

'But it's so high,' his wife said, a hand to her face in alarm.

'The pressure must have been extraordinary,' replied Poggs. 'It must have –'

He was interrupted by scampering footsteps on the stairs outside the open kitchen door. They heard Josh's frightened voice calling for his mother before he appeared in the doorway clad in pyjamas, his eyes filled with tears and his narrow shoulders shaking. Diane was already halfway there to meet him.

'Josh, what is it?'

He threw himself into her arms and buried his face into her waist. 'It's Eva,' came his muffled answer. 'The bad lady's got Eva.'

Diane gently held him away from her and crouched to look into his face. 'Who do you mean, Josh? What lady?'

He began to sob. 'The . . . the big lady . . .' He pointed back at the stairs.

Diane was out of the room before the others had even risen. Bibby quickly followed her.

Poggs went to the boy. 'Calm down now, Josh. You've been dreaming, haven't you?' There was no accusation in his words, only a mild prompting.

Josh shook his head vigorously. 'No. We ran and ran, Grandad, and . . . and we found a place. The lady was inside . . . but, but she . . .' He choked on a sob.

'It's all right, Josh, you're safe now.' Poggs sat on another kitchen chair and drew the boy in between his plump knees. He put an arm around Josh's shoulders. 'It's only one of your nightmares, Josh, nothing to be afraid of. You're awake now.'

The boy snuggled against his grandfather's chest, his head shaking in denial. 'Not a dream, not a dream . . .'

Bibby's voice came from upstairs. 'Hugo, come quickly.'

Poggs rose at once, startling Josh, who blinked through his tears. Poggs led him by the hand through the doorway to the stairs, while Rivers wondered if he should follow. He compromised by waiting at the foot of the stairs while Poggs and his grandson climbed them.

He listened to their urgent muted voices for a while before deciding to join them. Halfway up he met Bibby, her features tightened by concern.

'What's happened?' he asked.

'Eva. We can't wake her up. She appears to be in some kind of coma.'

She left him there and soon he heard her in the hall phoning for an ambulance.

NEW ORLEANS, LOUISIANA – *French Quarter*

Jumpin' shit, things were gettin' hot.

Nelson Shadebank wiped the perspiration from his gold-rimmed spectacles, then dabbed the same from his wrinkled brow as he climbed the creaky wooden staircase at the rear of the Temple. The steamy weather caused the sweat (although his only concession to it was the removal of his jacket; his tie was tight against his neck, the cuffs of his pin-stripe shirt unrolled and boasting bright gold links), but the visit from the two NOPD officers instigated the anxiety.

Hell with it, she hadda be told.

He turned at the top and walked back along the landing, his armpits damp and staining the otherwise immaculate shirt, undershorts clingy beneath the precisely creased beige trousers, and stopped outside the door of Mama Pitié's private – *very* private – quarters. 'Oh shit,' he mumbled, reluctant to knock. What the fuck would she be up to in there this

249

afternoon? He guessed she was alone – her last 'requirement' had been dispatched in the early hours of the previous evening, and he himself had organised it – but that didn't mean it was okay to disturb her. Fuck no. Last time he'd done so her glare had made him trickle his pants. Least she hadn't whopped him – he'd seen those huge paws at work on one of her zombies and they were lethal.

Shadebank had thought he'd struck paydirt when he'd fled New York four years ago and had wandered into the Temple, drawn by the music rather than spiritual need. He'd been curious because those hymns hadn't been in praise of the Lord, but in celebration of Mother Earth, Herself, and sung with revivalist passion. Nor was the crowd, the congregation, all black as he'd expected; he'd entered just before the doors were locked from the inside and found that the worshippers were a mixture of white, black and Cajun. His eyes had shone with their same fervour when he saw how full the offering pouches were after the collection, and it was not from nickels and dimes. Even the poorest-looking among them were more than generous, while Shadebank himself had contributed a twenty, and he was only there out of curiosity.

But it was more than just the scam value that attracted him to this church. His last employer, one of the Big A's major crack barons, had turned state's evidence to save himself the inconvenience of five life-terms, consecutive, for murder, mutilation, torture, rape and, of course, dealing, and had sung high soprano about anyone and everyone connected to the drugs trade. Fortunately, Shadebank had been tipped off by one of New York's own finest, a cop who'd benefited to the tune of a few hundred grand over the years for services rendered to the gangs, and he had skipped before being clapped. He'd headed south, gravitating naturally towards the cesspit area of New Orleans.

It had taken a few days to find out about Mama Pitié and her Blessed Temple of the Sacred Earth after his first visit, but all along he'd known it was a small-time racket – instinct, not his college degree, had told him that. The hurdle had been getting past her over-protective goons – zombies he called them – but he'd managed it by dropping a note in the offerings pouch and hanging around the front door after service. When he finally got to know her, two things surprised him: Mama Pitié's brainpower and the fact that there was no scam – the lady was sincere; weird, but sincere. She was also very evil.

She had been interested in his ideas of how she could reach so many more people by travelling the country and advertising her arrival in local newspapers and radio stations, and he, personally, could guarantee that donations towards the Temple would triple, quadruple, quintuple and whatever the goddam next one was. Wealth, he assured her, meant power, and power, he added, meant *influence*. And to influence the hearts and minds of the people would lead eventually to their spiritual union with the Blessed Mother of Earth, Herself. Whether she believed in his sincerity or not he wasn't sure, but that wasn't really important to either of them: what was important was how useful they could be to each other. Shadebank had worked well for her, keeping check on the Temple's incomings and outgoings, organising Mama's visits to other states, and keeping some order among the zombies, who were as stupid as they were devoted to their high priestess. He also became expert at covering up Mama Pitié's occasional 'aberrations'. Unfortunately, she had been careless about one of her more recent 'choices', and Shadebank had been careless in letting it happen.

He raised his hand to knuckle the wood, but again hesitated. Was that voices he heard from inside Mama's room? Couldn't be – no one had passed his room downstairs where he'd been attending to the Temple's accounts for the past couple of hours with the door, as always, open wide. Two of the zombies were cleaning the church and the others were

251

either sleeping at home or working. Maybe Mama was talking to herself. Nothing unusual about that. Well, she had to be told the cops had paid the Temple a visit and they'd be back to talk to her direct. He'd played the dumb nigguh to their Southern bigotry and told them *she out, offsuh*, but they weren't fooled. Oh no, they didn't like his sharp duds and shiny shoes one little bit. If they could have busted him for looking cool they would have. *Okay, apeshit*, they'd said, *we'll be back later*, and one of them had spit on the church floor. What Shadebank resented, what he *really* resented, was that one of the cops was black himself.

A kind of groaning from inside now. Shit, was this bitch alone or not? What the hell, she had to be told the cops were looking for a missing kid, a young chick who'd disappeared some weeks ago. The kid's folks had mentioned she liked to visit the Temple, so maybe Mama Pitié knew something about her – like where the fuck she was. They hadn't said the last part, but Shadebank could see it in their suspicious pig eyes. Cops didn't like religious freaks – they knew the scams, too.

Maybe it was time for him to move on. Before this degenerate bitch screwed up the whole operation. Yeah, get the hell out before the shit really hit the fan. There was enough in the safe downstairs to set him up somewhere else. Somewhere a long ways from this crazy woman. A long, long ways. He lowered his fist.

But the door opened before he touched wood.

The image of the child was still strong in Mama Pitié's vision even though it was the bookkeeper, Shadebank, who cowered before her. Soon it would fade, though, and she would have to cling to what she could, hold on to part of the girl, keep an element of her locked away inside her own will.

Mama had risen from the bed, sensing the presence outside the room, Shadebank's inner trembling upsetting her thoughts, interrupting her pleasure. She had lumbered over to the door, a huge shadow moving among other shadows, and when she had opened it she scarcely saw the man standing there.

Shadebank, this unknowing fool, muttered something that was incomprehensible and Mama Pitié closed her eyes to hold on to the child. Keep her there, she told herself, trapped within. The boy had escaped, but the girl was hers. For now. And the girl had things to tell. So many, many things.

18

'Eva!'

In the dream his voice echoed back across the great lake from the forests and mountains on the other side. The last sound faded and Josh called Eva's name again.

The lawns and pasturelands were empty, only the silent pillars reminding him of the times when he and his sister had played with the other children among them, their laughter enhancing the paradise. Memories echoed like her name, gently fading and leaving him alone and desolate.

He scanned the woodlands at the gardens' edges, seeking the opening into which he and Eva had fled, but the foliage was uniform and offered no breaches. Again he turned towards the silver lake and watched an eagle swoop low, feathers golden in the sunlight, then rise high into the heavens until it became no more than a speck and eventually nothing at all. The loss saddened him even more.

Josh sank to the ground, his head bowed almost to his chest, his shoulders hunched. 'Please come back,' he said quietly and as if to himself. His body spasmed with the first sob, but before grief could take complete hold he became aware of a change in the very air around him, a charging of ions that might forewarn a thunderstorm.

He sensed the Dream Man's presence and smiled when he looked up to see he was there . . .

Hugo Poggs hooked the receiver and went back into the kitchen where Rivers was sipping his third coffee of the morning. It had been a long night for both of them, although they had dozed where they sat for some of the time. The ashtray on the kitchen table was full and Poggs retrieved the pipe resting on its rim. He got the burn going again and sat opposite Rivers.

'Well?' said Rivers anxiously.

Poggs drew on the pipe before replying. 'No change since last time Bibby rang. Eva's in some kind of shock, but there's no indication of catatonia, thank God – she can move and, as far as the medics can tell, she's functioning normally. Even responds to stimulation.' His whole frame shook with a wheezing cough, but the pipe never left his lips. He thumped his chest once with his fist and looked across the table at Rivers. 'Unfortunately, they can't wake her – her sleep appears to be too deep.'

'Sleeping sickness?' Rivers ventured somewhat lamely.

Poggs refuted the idea with a brief shake of his head. 'I know there have been some such cases in England since the climate changes, but the tsetse fly hasn't managed to flourish over here yet. At least, that's what we've been assured. Besides, Eva has none of the symptoms. She's . . .' he removed the pipe as if suddenly interested in the stem '. . . she's sleeping, that's all. Bibby says the doctors think she'll wake naturally when she's ready to, although personally

I believe they're taking it much more seriously than that.'

'How's Diane coping?'

'She was still with Eva when Bibby and I spoke. I think she's afraid to leave her side in case Eva simply slips away. No reason for that to happen, of course, but . . .' He tucked the pipe back into his mouth and waved a hand helplessly. 'It's all so bloody strange, isn't it? Josh claims they both had the same nightmare, but he escaped from it by running away. Now Eva appears to be stuck there, held by something monstrous – a dream witch, d'you suppose? – that won't let her go. Can a nightmare, no matter how traumatic, really have that kind of power?'

'Not as far as two healthy kids are concerned.'

'Then what's the answer?'

Rivers shifted in his seat, aware of the other man's scrutiny. 'Josh and Eva are different from any other kids I've known. You've told me they have unusual mental powers and, judging by the healing treatment they gave my leg yesterday, I'm inclined to believe you.' He didn't mention that the pain had returned with a vengeance during the night.

'What's your point?'

'Their mental – sorry, psychic – powers might have a downside. The twins could be vulnerable psychologically.'

'To what exactly?' There was no criticism in Poggs' tone, only interest.

Rivers shrugged. 'That's the mystery. But it might help Eva if a psychologist found out.'

'While she's asleep?'

'Through Josh.'

'I don't think Diane would agree to that. The implication would be that there was something mentally wrong with the children.'

'That's an old-fashioned view.'

'Nevertheless, a very real one. And particularly so for someone whose children are adopted. It takes a long time for such parents to lose the feeling that their little ones can be taken away from them, irrational though that may seem, and remember, Diane has already lost a husband. No, there has to be another way.'

'That may be so, but in this case –'

They both became aware of Josh standing in the doorway at the same time. He was wearing his Peter Pan nightshirt, his feet bare on the wood floor, and he was smiling triumphantly.

'I know where to find the Dream Man, Grandad,' he said.

19

Josh squirmed excitedly in his seat as Diane endeavoured to strap him in. Next to them Rivers clicked in his own seat-belt, then did his best to relax, allowing his gaze to drift around the aircraft's cabin. The flight was packed with 500 tourists and businessmen and he had been lucky to book passage for himself, Diane, and Josh at such short notice. As it was, they had been forced to take the flight to Glasgow out of Gatwick rather than London Heathrow, which meant a longer drive from Dorset, but at least marginally less congestion at the airport itself. He longed for a cigarette and silently cursed the worldwide airline ban on smoking; mercifully the journey would take little more than an hour, maybe less if they had a tail wind behind them.

The European Airbus trundled smoothly towards the runway and a smiling stewardess offered Josh a boiled sweet. He sucked it with relish, another part of the flying experience for him to enjoy. Rivers wished his own nerves were as untroubled, but one crash-landing in anybody's lifetime was enough to curb any such pleasure. He gripped the armrests as the engines gathered power. Then they were rolling forward, picking up speed, the battle between gravity and excessive weight swiftly reaching its climax. They were airborne, but Rivers did not breathe a surreptitious sigh of relief until the plane had banked and the engines had taken on a steady drone. He felt a hand over his and realised Diane had noticed his unease.

'Thank you, Jim,' she said.

'For what?'

'Helping. It must be difficult for you to believe in us.'

'I'm still not sure that I do. But at least . . .' he searched for a reason, as much for himself as for Diane '. . . at least I feel I'm doing something positive instead of standing by while the world carries on destroying itself – or rather, destroying *us*. Besides, if our trip will help Eva . . .'

'It will. I just know it will. We may not understand what's happening, but there are definite links that we can't ignore. If we locate this man – this Dream Man, as Josh calls him – then maybe we'll have some answers.'

'You're sure he'll be where Josh says?'

She nodded and her soft brown eyes were earnest as they looked into his. 'I know it, Jim.'

Rivers wondered as he glanced past her at the boy, then out at the thick layer of clouds they had risen above. It could be a wild-goose chase, a completely irrational and desperate one at that. When Josh had claimed he knew where to find the Dream Man the day before, his grandfather had led him to the world map in his study once again and there the boy had stood on a chair and immediately pointed to the country where he believed the man in his dreams to be. Rivers had assumed this person was a fantasy, someone the twins had merely dreamt about or invented; but no, Josh had insisted he was real – real and living in Scotland. He had almost laughed aloud when the eight-year-old had jabbed his finger

259

at the map, and only weariness from the sleepless night filled by lengthy discussions with Hugo Poggs, plus the seriousness of Poggs' interest, had prevented him from doing so. The geophysicist had searched among his many old Ordnance Survey maps and produced several covering various areas of Scotland – 'The Scottish Highlands have been carved from some of the most complicated geological structures on Earth,' he had said to explain his past interest to Rivers – and Josh had leaned over them on the study table, his face puckered up with concentration, his small shoulders almost touching his ears with the tension. He had found a place, or at least an area, that seemed to have some significance in whatever intuitions his latest dream had evoked.

An extensive volcanic rift, linked by a series of long deep waters from the Firth of Lorn to the Moray Firth, and known as the Great Glen, split Scotland in half, and it was to the mid-region of this that the boy drew their attention. 'He's here!' Josh had exclaimed, showing them a region of smaller lochs at right angles to the larger ones. 'The Dream Man lives here.'

It had been Diane's decision when she returned from the hospital later that day to take her son to this place. Eva did not appear to be suffering physically and the doctors were sure there was no danger for the moment; nevertheless, the unusual sleep persisted. She had asked Rivers to accompany them to Scotland while Bibby kept a vigil at the hospital and Hugo Poggs stayed at Hazelrod to liaise between both parties, and he had agreed.

The A320 was over the Midlands when Rivers saw the light outside the aircraft window.

Josh had just finished breakfast – Rivers and Diane had refused theirs, preferring coffee and biscuits – and the climatologist had been talking to Diane when the small brightness outside had attracted his attention. She saw him stiffen and turned to see for herself.

'Is that it?' she said breathlessly.

Rivers squinted his eyes, now unsure. There was a rainbow effect around the ball of light as it hovered above the cloudbank.

'Oh, they're quite normal, sir.' An air hostess was leaning over Rivers to retrieve Josh's tray. 'It's only an aureole of light reflecting off the clouds. It's pretty, isn't it?' She took the tray handed to her by Diane and went on her way to attend to other passengers.

Rivers let his breath go. 'She's right – it's not the same. I've just got the jitters.'

'You and me both,' said Diane.

'Me, too,' Josh admitted brightly enough. 'I keep thinking about the Dream Man.'

'Can you describe him, Josh?' It was Rivers who wanted to know.

'He's not clear when I really try to make a picture of him. He goes sort of fuzzy. His voice sounds old, though. And I'm sure he's got white hair. I can sort of see that.'

'Tell us about the dreams again, Josh,' Diane urged.

'*Mama,*' said Josh meaningfully.

'Just once more. It's important.'

With an exaggerated groan the boy re-related the dream he'd shared with Eva, then went on to his own subsequent dream, describing both the events and the surroundings in great detail, as if taking them from a picture-book laid out before him. By the time he had finished and they had questioned him further, the plane was beginning its descent.

They had only hand luggage with them, so there were no delays once they landed. Formalities for the hiring of a car were minimal and within twenty minutes of arrival they were crossing the bridge over the River Clyde and then on the main trunk road that would take them right to their destination. They travelled alongside Loch Lomond for many miles and, despite their quest, were able to appreciate its dark

261

beauty. Soon they were driving through a range of mountains whose snow-topped peaks were unaffected by the season's sultry heat. The lowest clouds seemed to snag on their points before drifting off in fleecy tatters.

Although the road was busy with tourist traffic, their progress was good, and two hours later they had passed through Fort William and were approaching the little town they had decided would be their base. The towering hulk of Ben Nevis loomed large on their right as they drew near.

Spean Bridge was a hamlet rather than a town, with shops and houses built along the roadside and with a tiny railway station tucked away at the back. Diane spotted the small hotel as they drove through and Rivers pulled over to park by the front entrance. Fortunately, there were a few rooms available and they booked two next door to each other. After a quick snack they went to Rivers' room where he spread a map on one of the twin beds.

'Take a good look, Josh,' he told the boy, bringing him over to the map. 'This is the area you pointed at before. You said the Dream Man is somewhere here . . .' He circled his finger around a region of parallel lochs. 'This is where we are now . . .' He indicated the town. 'Can you be more specific, Josh?' The boy screwed up his face. 'I mean can you point out exactly where you think the Dream Man is?'

'I think . . .' Josh frowned, his eyes intent on the map. 'I think . . . he's . . . here.' He dabbed at an area where three lochs almost joined together in a straight line.

'You're sure?'

The boy leaned his elbows on the bed and tapped at his lower lip with a finger. He murmured noncommittally, drawing out the sound. He looked up at his mother. 'I only think so,' he said apologetically.

'That's all right, darling,' Diane assured him. 'We just want you to do your best, okay? Now take another look and see if you still feel the same.'

262

He scrutinised the map once again, his face cupped in his hands. 'It's not clear any more,' he complained.

Rivers and Diane exchanged glances. 'What do we do?' she said. 'I thought Josh would be even more definite when we were closer to the source.'

'We'll take him for a drive around the lochs and stop here and there to let him walk. It may come to him then. If we find any houses or cottages we'll just knock on the door.'

'And say what?'

Rivers shrugged. 'Whatever comes to mind. Are you tired, Josh? D'you need a rest after the journey?'

The boy jumped up from the bed. 'I'm not tired at all. Can we go out on a boat?'

Diane drew him to her. 'There's no time for that. We're here to find the Dream Man, remember? It might just help Eva if we do.'

'He will, Mama. The Dream Man always looks after us. He watches over us while we play.'

Like a shepherd? Rivers mused. He studied the boy and wondered what went on in these dreams. Did they mean anything at all, or were they merely the fantasies of two imaginative and oversensitive kids? And if there was nothing to them, and this person, this *Dream Man*, did not exist, did that mean everything Diane and Hugo Poggs had tried to convince him of had no validity? With all the other phenomena – the freakish weather patterns, the inexplicable earth ruptures, and the mysterious light itself – that wasn't necessarily so. But there *was* a test ahead of them that might disperse or strengthen his doubts. He guessed Diane was aware of the conflict still raging within him, although they had not discussed the consequences of failure; but now she had other reasons for seeking answers up here in the Highlands, for success might mean that Eva could be drawn from her unnatural slumber. On that score alone, Rivers hoped the Dream Man was real.

'Are we ready?' he asked, the significance of the simple question not lost on Diane.

She nodded and, unnoticed by Josh who was already scooting towards the door, touched a hand to Rivers' cheek. He caught her fingers and held them briefly before allowing them to drop away.

'It's going to be fine,' he said, with no conviction at all.

As they passed through the hotel's comfortable lobby the man now on duty behind the receptionist's desk bid them good-day and introduced himself as the owner.

'Will y'be sightseein' or will y'be walkin' this afternoon?' he enquired. 'Because if it's the sightseein' from your car, ye'll be fine, but if it's the walkin' ye'll be needin' something stronger on your feet.' His heavy brogue was barely comprehensible to Josh, but he followed the hotelier's pointing finger.

Rivers looked down at his tan sneakers also and then at Diane, who nodded her head in agreement. She had provided walking boots for herself and Josh, but had had nothing at Hazelrod suitable for Rivers.

'Now, if ye don't mind my suggestion, there's a wee store doon the road where they'll find something for ye.' The hotelier, a strong-faced man with a nose and cheeks full of broken veins, grinned broadly. 'On th'other hand, ye kin tell me to be mindin' ma own business.'

'No, you're right,' said Rivers. 'We came away in a rush. I'll take your advice.'

'It's just that the tracks tend t'be rocky and the moorlands are treacherous here and there with the bogs. We've had some awkward mists appear with this kind o' weather too, but as long as ye don't wander from the main paths ye'll be fine.'

They thanked him for his concern and drove down to the store he had mentioned. Rivers emerged five minutes later wearing a tough-looking pair of walking boots, his jeans tucked into their tops. He tossed his sneakers into the back of the car as he got back into the driving seat.

'Sure you don't want me to drive?' Diane asked, anxious that his leg might be causing pain after such a long journey.

'Better that you keep a lookout with Josh. If he reacts to anything at all, let me know and we'll investigate. Okay, Josh?'

The boy's enthusiasm had faded. He observed the hills beyond the town gravely and said, 'I'm a little bit afraid.'

As Diane reached over and pulled her son towards her, Rivers, too, stared at the distant hills. The summer's sun had burnt much of the rugged slopes to a golden brown, and the weighty, yellow-tinted clouds that hung over them diffused the light to a mellow glow. Yet there was something ominous in the landscape, an idle broodiness that was unnerving. Rivers was afraid too.

He drank brandy, Diane sipped white wine. They were in the hotel's spartan lounge bar, with Josh sound asleep in the twin-bedded room he shared with his mother. Every ten minutes or so, Diane quietly looked in on him, then rejoined Rivers at their table in the corner of the bar.

They examined the map spread out before them yet again as if attempting to sense some clue therein.

'I didn't expect us to find him right away,' said Rivers, straightening a crease in the paper. 'One afternoon of searching doesn't mean very much.'

'Josh seemed so certain before we started.' Diane ran her fingers over the terrain as if a braille message might be contained within. 'He was weeping with disappointment when I put him to bed.'

'Tomorrow he'll be rested and maybe more receptive.'

'But he was so sure of the area.' She withdrew from the

map and glanced around the bar as though there might be someone there who could help with their hunt. The room was full, although not crowded, and conversations were conducted in moderate tones, for the hotel was the kind used by dedicated ramblers and climbers rather than fun-seeking tourists. The local sights were the fun, but much of it had to be earned by some hard walking, whether around loch sides and moorlands, or along mountain tracks. The bar next door, used mainly by locals, was livelier and occasional bursts of laughter would drift through.

While Diane was putting Josh to bed earlier, Rivers had taken the opportunity to chat to the plump middle-aged barmaid, and then the hotelier himself, who had wandered through. His questions were necessarily vague, but the hotelier assured him that the glens and hillsides were dotted with lonely abodes, the inhabitants of which were rarely seen from one year to another. Many of the croft cottages were now deserted, bleak hardship a discredited mistress in this day and age. Certainly there were still those who lived a life apart, reclusives who shunned civilisation and most of what it offered, but these people were generally known only by their closest neighbours, and 'closest' could mean several miles away. The post office or the town's grocery store, which still made deliveries to some of the more remote parts, might be of some help, 'but then ye'd nid a name,' McKay, the hotelier, had advised. Rivers offered no explanation for their search, nor was any sought; they did gaze at him with some curiosity, though, as he made his way back to his table.

Rivers lit a cigarette, then reached into his jacket pocket for the tin pill box he carried there. He swallowed two pills with an adequate amount of brandy, then inhaled on the cigarette as though it were part of the ritual.

'Are you supposed to drink with those painkillers?' Diane was watching him doubtfully.

'No, but somehow it makes them more effective.'

266

'I'm sure that's only in the mind.'

'Yeah, like a lot of things.'

She stiffened and he added hastily, 'Hey, I didn't mean anything by that. They say all pain is in the mind anyway, so maybe alcohol helps me to forget.'

'Tony used to say he drank to help him remember.'

'Remember what?'

'How much he enjoyed being drunk. His sense of humour was morbid at the best of times.' She looked down into her lap, avoiding his eyes. 'This isn't going to work, is it?' she said quietly.

He couldn't find the words immediately to reassure her and he noticed tears glistening in her eyelashes.

'We haven't given it a chance yet,' he said, laying his cigarette in an ashtray and lightly touching her arm.

'We've driven for miles and we've walked and walked.' Her fingers wiped away a tear before it fell. 'I suppose I just assumed Josh would lead us straight to this man. Have we been foolish all along, Jim? Have we been carried away with our own stupid imaginations?'

'A few days ago I'd have said yeah, no question. Now I'm not so sure.'

'But you're not certain.'

'How can I be? Let's just say my mind's been opened to ideas I'd have considered crazy before.'

Her cheeks were damp, but she managed a flicker of a smile. 'You're a good man, Jim,' she said.

'No, I'm a curious man. The truth is, I've gone along with you and Hugo because I've got nothing to lose and maybe – just maybe – something to gain.'

Her expression asked the question, but he gave a shake of his head. 'I don't know yet, that's the hell of it.' His smile was grim. 'Sometimes I wonder if it's not only the world that's changing but people too. Maybe I'm looking for more than just an old man with white hair.' He shook his head

267

again, perplexed by his own thoughts. 'Maybe,' he added as a footnote.

Later, she called Hugo from the phone in Rivers' room so that Josh would not be disturbed.

'How is she?' he asked as Diane replaced the receiver.

'Little change. Bibby's still with her at the hospital and she'll stay with Eva overnight. Oh Jim, what can we do?'

Rivers left his chair by the dressing-table and sat next to her on the bed. 'If she's no worse it's a good sign.'

'That's what Hugo said. But why *is* she sleeping like this? Josh says someone is holding her, but how can that be possible? How can a dream hold on to someone?'

Rivers might have put the same questions to her, but he had no desire to upset her further. Instead he put a comforting arm around her shoulder and said soothingly, 'You need to rest. We'll cover a lot more ground tomorrow and knock on every door we come to if necessary.'

She turned to him, burying her head against his neck. 'What if we do find him and he can't help? What if he's real enough, but has no power to help Eva?'

He felt a shiver run through her as though how incredible their undertaking was had finally hit her. He pulled away and lifted her chin. 'I'm the unbeliever, remember?' He kissed her, gently at first then, when she responded, he pressed his lips harder against hers and his arms held her tight.

Although Diane was vulnerable in her despair, she was also anxious. She broke away and he let her go, aware that the timing was all wrong, that her emotions were already stretched to the limit. Concern for her child could not allow for other distractions.

'I'm sorry,' she offered.

He brushed a lock of hair away from her cheek. 'No need.

268

You've got enough on your mind.' He drew her to her feet. 'Get some sleep now – we've got a heavy day ahead of us tomorrow.'

She went back into his arms and held him close before going to the door. When she looked back at him before slipping through, her eyes revealed her confusion. She closed the door quietly.

20

Gardenia's face touched his own, an embrace from someone already dead, and Rivers pushed the body away with a scream that was lost in the roar of the aircraft's engines. Gardenia floated to the ceiling, the grin beneath his thick black moustache mocking the climatologist.

'It ain't so bad, Doc. Dyin' ain't so bad once you get used to it.' The dead man laughed and drifted away to haunt other members of the research aircraft's crew.

The aeroplane fell again and the storm outside endeavoured to flip it over. This time the pilot didn't seem able to pull it up from the dive and Rivers felt himself pressed back against his seat, his stomach several yards behind him. The plane was going down, down, down, and everyone on board was screaming. He ripped off his headphones, but the noise was worse, the screaming more real, the cacophony of storm and raging engines almost unbearable.

His head snapped round to look out the window and he saw there was land out there now and it was rising up to meet them, fast, too fast, a great solid mass hurtling itself at the plane which began to revolve sideways, spinning, spinning, out of control, and the screeching from the crew was mingled with the rending of metal as the aircraft began to break up, began to disintegrate under the pressure, shedding a wing and an engine, and Gardenia was floating back to him, only this time he had the others with him, and some were weeping, and some were grinning, and some were looking at him with horror on their faces, and the ground outside was only feet away and drawing closer and closer . . . and Gardenia and his friends were reaching for him because death had its claim on all of them and nobody should be left out, they were all in this together, all for one, and all for oblivion, and they touched him, fingers already cold even though they were not yet dead, pawing at his face, his eyes, his lips, tugging at his clothes, urging him to give in, to join them in what had to be . . . and the light shining through them just before the impact, becoming larger, stronger, absorbing the corpses that, apart from Gardenia, were not yet dead, incorporating them in its radiance, consuming them and dazzling him with its glare of absolute purity, entering him and seeping through every tissue and tendon and every part of his flesh and his mind so that he, too, was consumed . . .

He heard the crash, the explosion of tons of metal grinding into earth and concrete, and for the briefest moment felt the terrible, the awful, searing pain that seemed to emanate from his leg, but which soon – no, quicker than soon: immediately – dominated every nerve and sensation in his body.

But the pain's passing was as swift as its beginning as the light enveloped his mind, clearing it of any thoughts and any discomfort, and somehow he was travelling through it, neither sinking nor rising, but journeying in a straight, although indefinable, line and the bliss was immense, the joy was supreme, and the destination was unimaginable . . .

And he emerged into peace.

And this, too, was brief.

Just before he woke he glimpsed soft green pastures, pillars of white set among them, and a silver lake with pastel hills and forests behind. An eagle flew over the lake, the beat of its wings silent, its flight slow and sure. He wanted to stay there; if this was death he craved its tranquillity. But a glimpse was all he was allowed.

The vision faded rapidly, his own consciousness its subjugator.

Rivers' eyes opened, and someone from the dream called to him.

He sat up, and the voice that was not a voice but a thought, continued to call to him, its exhortation persuasive even though the message was obscure.

He pulled back the sheet and sat on the edge of the bed, remaining there awhile, staring into the shadows, his hand vaguely rubbing at his aching leg. The slight pre-dawn chill caused a shiver, but still he sat there, preoccupied with the dream. The dream and the soundless but persistent call.

Only light from the slit beneath the door gave the room substance; without it furniture and Rivers' own naked body would have been lost to the void. Suddenly he became active, switching on the bedside light and snatching up his jeans lying on the twin bed opposite. He dressed quickly and silently, not wishing to disturb Diane and her son next door. Collecting the car keys from the dressing-table he lightly padded to the door and opened it. Light from the hallway was uncomfortably bright and took a second or two to become used to. Closing the door behind him with as little noise as possible, he crept down the corridor, away from the hotel's small lobby and towards the rear fire door. He slipped the bolts and stepped outside.

A creeping pink flush was beginning to colour the darkness

behind the faraway hills and a breeze snagged at his thin jacket. He waited a moment, his own sound logic questioning his motives; such reasoning soon passed, however, and he moved on, walking through the hotel's car park around to the front of the building where he and Diane had left the hire car the evening before. He climbed in, switched on, and reversed out into the main road. He headed north-west.

The Great Glen was formed some 350 million years ago when the land convulsed and split from coast to coast, the upper mass slipping more than sixty miles to the south-west. The long valley that was created was filled by the waters of Ness, Oich, Lochy and Linnhe, these lochs later linked from sea to sea by the Caledonian Canal. There are smaller though no less impressive lochs among the mountains and glens that govern the great divide, these mainly along the north-west edge, and it was into this beautifully wild hinterland that Rivers drove. Ironically, the particular loch he headed for was close to the areas he, Diane and Josh had already searched, although it was even more off the beaten track. The road he travelled was rough and stone-patched, its course through forest of pine and birch crooked and dipped.

The sun had not yet crested the ragged horizon and in the grey darkness Rivers needed all his attention to negotiate some of the sharper turns along the route. He was forced to brake sharply on rounding one of the more acute turns when he came upon a red stag blocking the narrow roadway. Proud head, with its fine spread of antlers, cocked, it regarded the bright lights of the car without alarm but with some curiosity. Rivers waited patiently, for he considered the deer had more right to this path than he, and when the animal's interest was satisfied and its authority asserted, it wandered off to mount the slope with short, twisting leaps. Soon it had disappeared from view, only the sharp thrash of leaves indicating its progress. Within a minute, even the sounds were gone.

The moment had given Rivers another chance for reflection. But he ignored it. He transferred his foot from brake to accelerator and the vehicle trundled forward again, its progress slow as it bumped over ridges and tilted into dips. He realised he did not want to analyse the situation, that he did not want to ponder the rationality of this journey for fear that the certitude of his instinct might be disturbed by considered thought.

He came upon the loch he was searching for almost by surprise. One moment he was driving alongside a small, swift-flowing river, the next, the sky having lightened, he saw that the landscape had opened up to reveal a long loch stretching into the distance, contained by steep hills on one side and a mixture of hills and slopes on the other. Both boundaries were filled with mixed woodlands or dark shades of heather and bracken. An old bridge on his left crossed the river, but there was no allure for him in that direction, no compulsion to cross; he kept to the road he was on, passing the bridge without a second glance.

The wooded area on his right quickly gave way to inclines of moorland and as the sky began to lighten he caught glimpses of small dark shapes, rabbits these, hopping from grass tussock to tussock. Occasionally he heard the bleating of sheep, or passed a lonely whitewashed house set back off the road, lights on in only one to suggest someone other than himself was about at that unholy hour.

The loch seemed endless as he drove doggedly onwards, his speed slow not because of the unevenness of what by now was no more than a rough track, but because he was looking for some sign that would tell him he'd reached his destination, whether it be a suggestion in his mind or a biding figure by the roadside. But no such intimation or sign came to him and doubts allied with reason began to declare themselves. His confidence faltered and he started to wonder if he might be undergoing some peculiarly lucid form of 'sleep-walking', a semiconscious continuance of his dream. Once more he brought the car to a halt, this time leaving it to stand on the grass verge.

The breeze that had begun to unfurl the mists over the loch stirred the reeds, their rustlings coming to Rivers like cautionary whispers. The heads of white cotton-grass leading down to the water's edge bobbed and swayed as the light wind passed through them, and Rivers felt its sharpness as it ruffled his hair, its keen aroma carried inland from the northern seas. He shivered as he looked about him, searching the lake, the hills, the moorland for he knew not what. The bleak call of the curlew reached him, but he failed to see the bird itself.

'What am I doing here?' he murmured aloud as if full consciousness had only just arrived to catch him unawares. But he knew this to be self-deception, for his actions thus far had been acceptable to him if not understood, and guidance had come from an intangible yet insistent source that drew him to it like some transcendent beacon. The assertion returned, too stealthy for conviction, yet persuasive enough to cast aside his doubts.

Woodland once more closed down the panorama on this side of the lake, and Rivers peered into the shadows under the trees as he drove on, nervous of his own impulse and perhaps even afraid of what he might find. In a perverse way, he was glad of the pain in his leg, for it offered a reality to what otherwise might be mistaken for a dream.

Open land again, and black-faced ewes watched his progress from the slopes. Through the car's open windows came the scent of bog-myrtle and heath flowers, and peewits dived suicidally across his path in their morning search for sustenance.

He stopped by a small fank – a sheepfold – at the side of

the track, for beyond it stood the shell of an old building. No doubt at one time it had been a crofter's cottage, solidly built with ancient stone and firm against the elements, but now dilapidated with half its corrugated-iron roof blown away and its windows glassless voids. He left the car and limped towards the ruin, not because he thought this place might be his destination, but because his bladder was full and this humble abode would provide privacy. He scolded himself for such an unwarranted concern in an area so deserted, but nevertheless, his modesty prevailed. The interior was dank and unpleasant, the floor littered with wood and rubble, so he made his way round to the rear of the building, stumbling awkwardly over debris and twice straining his knee slipping off damp stones. The wind hurled itself at him with some gusto as he turned a corner and he touched the rough wall for balance. Satisfied he was well out of sight from the track, he unzipped and began to urinate, the breeze untangling the flow and spreading it so that it spattered the wall and ground. He angled his body to avoid being splashed himself and as he did so, something in the distance caught his eye.

The mists had all but gone from the loch and lower slopes of the hills by now, and just beyond the far end of the great stretch of water a tiny pinpoint of light glowed.

At that distance he could not judge its size or shape, but it seemed to have some strength, for its brightness was clear and unwavering. A lamp, a lighted window? Rivers doubted it, for the distance between did not seem to weaken it at all. A small mirror reflecting the sun's rays might have been the answer, except that the sun was still dawn-pink and this light was almost white. Rivers became afraid: such light had terrible connotations to him. Could it be the same, a harbinger of disaster, a portent of something cataclysmic? No, no, that was absurd. The thing was too far away to tell, and besides, it was perfectly still, unlike the mysterious ball of light he'd observed from the research aircraft just before the crash. It could be anything – a powerful torch, a single headlight. He told himself this, but somehow was not convinced.

He straightened and wiped his hands on his jeans. What the hell, there was no going back now. Besides, the light might be a beacon of some kind, a guide for him. Rivers returned to the car and looked back along the loch to find the light had disappeared. Maybe the angle of vision had changed, he told himself, and the light was hidden behind trees or hills. He drove off, keeping the rough locale of where the light had been clear in his own mind.

The sun held more sway over the sea-blown breeze by the time Rivers reached the end of the track; it warmed the air currents and brightened the underbellies of the clouds that swept high over the landscape. He found a flat area, probably a vehicle turning point, and swung the car into it, switching off the engine but remaining in his seat for a few moments to take note of his surroundings. Something small dashed through the long couch grass and heather nearby, startling him with its thrashing. He settled back and reached into his jacket, taking out the pill bottle and unscrewing the lid as he looked around. He swallowed two tablets, then lit a cigarette. What now? he asked himself silently.

'What the fuck now?' he said aloud.

The loch became a narrow stream at this point, hills of mixed woodland rising up from its banks to define its route. There were moorlands to his right, these soon became steeper heather-clad slopes and hills. There were no build- ings, nor any light, in sight.

He finished the cigarette outside the car, the smoke whipped away instantly by the strong breeze funnelling through the river valley. He turned a complete circle, search- ing back down the loch, over to the other shore, following the course of the river, and then back to the open moorland where he stood, all the while studying each piece of territory intently, looking for a sign, anything at all that would give a hint of which direction to take. Exasperated, he dropped the remains of the cigarette and ground it into the dirt with his foot.

Although his visual search had provided no answer, he decided to make for higher ground in the hope he would be able to see further. He began climbing the gentle rise of the moorland.

It was rough going and he regretted having left his walking-cane back at the hotel. The ground was firm one moment, pitted the next, and his progress was both painful and laborious. More than once one of his feet became immersed in water and he soon learned to move from tussock to tussock as the rabbits he'd observed earlier had.

His advance was erratic because of it, but with every few steps he paused to scan the hillsides, often turning round to look back down towards the loch itself. He leapt across a fast-flowing hill burn, its water almost clear amber from the peat it had filtered through, and when he landed on the other side he gasped at the pain that shot through his weakened knee. He bent over it, clasping the joint with both hands, his eyes shut tight.

He stayed that way until the pain eased, then fumbled for more painkillers, even though it was too soon to take them. Kneeling, he scooped up water from the burn to wash down the pills, then rubbed the dampness over his face as he stood upright once more.

Other than this beautifully wild terrain, there was nothing to see – no house, no people, not even an animal in sight. Nothing but a dark speck wheeling in the cloudy sky.

The bird swooped, its broad wings flattening to ride the airstreams.

It was hopeless, Rivers decided. He'd been drawn to this impressive yet empty place by the vagaries of his own mind, his dream, and his subsequent response to it, no doubt encouraged – or *induced* – by the events and the discussions of the past week. He'd been a bloody fool to follow such a nonsensical impulse.

The bird was headed in his direction. Its wings, caught by the sun, were golden brown.

Rivers was undecided. Return to the hotel, where perhaps by now Diane would be waiting anxiously, or look further? But look for what? There was nothing here, for God's sake. Just hills, and mountains in the distance, a great loch meandering away from him, its far end out of sight. He shook his head in despair. His journey had been so definite, so . . .

The flapping of the bird's great wings overhead caused him to wheel about and look towards it. The golden eagle flew past him with an easy grace that belied its speed. It dropped low and disappeared behind a ridge just twenty or thirty yards ahead of him.

Rivers remembered the eagle of his dream and it was this thought that drove him to scramble up the steeper incline, grabbing tufts of grass to pull himself forward. The ridge was not particularly high, but it was deceptive when viewed from the track below, for although the rise was gentle at first, it suddenly veered upwards at an angle, screening what lay beyond it.

He was on his knees when he reached the crest, panting hard with the effort and the pain it caused; such discomfort was soon forgotten when he discovered what nestled in the shallow dip of land beyond.

The walls of the crofter's cottage were of rough granite and whinstone, its roof of weathered blue slate. It was a solid, single-storey structure with a line of rowan trees protecting its western flank, and a metal water-butt standing at one corner. A single blackened window faced him and a door, open and just as black, was next to it. There was no light, and no sign of occupancy.

Rivers felt his body go cold, and it had nothing to do with the stiffer breeze on the exposed ridge; this was a coldness from within, a chill that prickled at the inside of his flesh. This was the place, he was certain. This was where he would be given answers to the mysteries that had plagued him not just over the past few days, but since the crash of the research aircraft. He did not understand why he was certain, but then he did not even understand what had drawn him here. Perhaps that, too, would be answered inside. He hoisted himself over the ridge and limped towards the old dwelling, his eyes focused on the dark, open doorway.

He called as he approached, not wishing to startle anyone who might be in there – and perhaps wanting to be confronted while he was still a distance away. No one came to the door, nor answered his call.

He noticed the eagle again, beyond the rooftop of the house, a fly-speck once more, disappearing towards the far horizon of hills. He briefly wondered if the sighting of the great bird was no more than a coincidence, or if this too was part of the mystery, a dream vision materialised to lead him here. A little while ago he would have laughed at the idea.

Rivers lingered before the cottage and watched the open door with not a small amount of trepidation. Many thoughts ran through his mind, but these were intrusions rather than considerations, for the situation was perfectly straightforward: his search, perceptual though it might have been, was over and the expectation or, more truthfully, the aspiration, of that search lay a few feet away inside those four walls; to enter was simplicity itself. However, it took some resolution to do so.

He had to force himself to limp to the door, his breath held for a moment, and look inside.

There was only one room and the light that filtered through its three grimy windows was dim and sepulchral. The floor was of stone slabs worn smooth, and a cooking range housed within a wide hearth faced the door. The lintel over this was blackened with peat-reek, as were the walls. Against a wall was a settle that might have doubled for a bed, and a small table and chairs stood beneath one of the windows. There appeared to be no frivolous comforts in this home.

Disappointed – yet oddly relieved at the same time – to find no one there, Rivers stepped through. There was a sour smell about the place that not even the draught from the open doorway could dispel, a scent of age, although not decay, a blend of ashes from the hearth and the staleness of a cell. At first he thought the cottage might have been abandoned, but jars and pots, some full, others half full, on a shelf by the cooking range and raw vegetables lying on the table as if about to be prepared, told him otherwise. He scanned the room again, an exercise that took little more than three seconds, and saw no other human touches – no pictures or photographs, no books, no phone or radio. The austerity was chilling and Rivers couldn't help but think of the witch's cottage in Josh's dream and the horror that awaited the children inside. It was difficult to keep his imagination in check inside such a place.

He wasn't sure what to do – what he was *supposed* to do. Was he to wait here? Was he to go outside and look for whoever had guided – or *lured* – him to this lonely spot? He winced as sharp pain shot through his leg again and he stumbled over to the settle to take the weight off his knee. He sat there nursing the old wound, his eyes downcast, when a shifting of shadows across the floor caught his attention. He glanced up towards the window above the table and its clutter of mixed vegetables and saw the small light shining from outside, its glow muted by glass stained with old rain-spots and dust. Rivers thought it was the sun coming into view until he realised the window faced west, away from the morning sun. Besides, the light was moving.

It sank to the centre of the window before becoming still, a little circle of light diffused by the dirt on the glass that nevertheless shone with a steady intensity.

Rivers rose and backed against the wall beside the fire-place, his head swivelling round to keep the phenomenon in view. He became aware of drifting shadows again, this time creeping across from the other side of the room. His head snapped around to discover another light shining through the opposite window. It hovered outside, seeming to watch him like some incandescent eye.

'What . . .' he heard himself say, the question taking no further form because his thoughts were in too much disarray.

And then, 'Oh Jesus . . .' he said when he realised another ball of light was descending just outside the open door to fill the entrance with a glare so blinding he was forced to shield his eyes from it. He pressed himself back against the wall as if to meld himself into it, to become an unobtrusive part of the stone and therefore unnoticed.

He blinked, not just against the blaze, but to clear his vision, for now there appeared to be something moving within the effulgence, a faint, insubstantial shape emerging, growing to become more material, looming up from behind the floating orb itself to move through it, then beyond it, becoming an indistinct silhouette in the doorway.

THE MARIANA TRENCH, *Pacific Ocean*

It was hours until sun-up, but the two men, Lieutenant Henry 'Hank' Whitesell and Scientific Officer Carl Fricker were alert and keen to go.

'Wind's freshened during the night,' the lieutenant advised Dr Victor Brenman, the scientific director of the project, a man whose hair-deficient head was humbled before his lush curly beard, 'and the swells are getting meaner.'

'Where you're going, Lieutenant, it won't bother you.' Brenman turned to Fricker. 'How are you feeling this morning, Carl? A little better I hope.'

Fricker saw no reason to disguise his discomfort: Brenman knew him too well. 'I'd rather be beneath it than riding on top – and please don't make anything out of that statement, Hank.'

The lieutenant, a tall lean man who modelled himself on the young good-looking captain who played second banana to

Richard Basehart's admiral in the old, old TV series *Voyage to the Bottom of the Sea* still playing on some of the networks, grinned and raised his binoculars to study the lights of the Navy tug some distance away. Behind the vessel and attached by a few hundred feet of steel cable bobbed the *Dauphin*, a bathyscaph built four years ago to withstand all the pressure that the oceans could test it with. Its purpose today was to take Fricker and Whitesell into the abyss known as the Challenger Deep, one of the deepest underwater regions ever explored by man. The bathyscaph, Whitesell considered, would be more at home underneath those waves than rolling around on top, just like his companion Carl.

He rested the binoculars against his chest. 'Whaddaya say, Buddy? Ready to take the plunge?'

'You make it sound like a wedding,' Fricker replied, steadying himself as the ship pitched to starboard.

'Well, we'll be spending a long time together.'

'I'm not sure about this weather, gentlemen,' said the commander of the USS *Quayle*, on whose bridge the men had gathered. 'This wind is beginning to look real mean.'

'The latest reports tell us there's nothing untoward heading our way,' Brenman reassured him. Pressure from important quarters was on him to complete this mission with the minimum of fuss and delay, and a little rough weather was not going to deter him. He turned to his scientific officer. 'It'll take several hours for you to reach bottom, so I suggest you get under way as quickly as possible.'

'That suits me fine,' replied Fricker looking across at the lieutenant to see if he felt the same way.

'Sure,' said Whitesell. 'Let's get to it.'

They left the escort destroyer's bridge with a good-luck wave from Commander Jessel and made their way down to the lower deck, Fricker and Brenman using handrails to steady themselves wherever they could, the lieutenant strid-

ing along before them completely at ease. The waiting whaleboat pitched and tossed alongside the steel hull of the *Quayle*
at an alarming rate.

At the rail Brenman pulled Fricker close. 'You're going
down more than 38,000 feet so take it slowly and carefully.
We don't know what you're going to find and we don't even
know what to tell you to look for, but there has to be an
answer to this, so keep your eyes peeled and take fresh
footage at every five thous. Naturally that's just a guideline
– film anything you feel might be important.'

'You got it.' Fricker wiped moisture from his spectacles,
then turned to face the whaleboat that now was at least ten
feet below him. He felt his stomach sink with the little craft
itself.

Brenman clasped his shoulder. 'Good luck, Carl. Remember – it's a routine operation, but it might provide some
invaluable answers. We've got to know what's making that
stuff come up like this.'

From the desk, and even in the poor light, Fricker could
see the billions of tiny plankton floating on the ocean's surface; individually, most were microscopic, virtually invisible,
but massed together like this they formed an abnormal coating over the rough water. He nodded to Brenman, then felt
the lieutenant take his other arm as the whaleboat rose up
swiftly to meet them.

'*Now!*' Whitesell shouted over the boom of the water.

They leapt together into the rubber boat and were caught
by the firm hands of its crew members. Fricker quickly sat
and waved back at Brenman as the small craft veered away
from the mother ship and headed through the swells towards
the waiting bathyscaph. He pulled his Detroit Tigers cap
down tighter and wiped spray from his glasses again. The
rust-stained submersible they were approaching looked far
too frail and unstable for the task that lay ahead, but in the
six years he had travelled in such vessels not one had ever

given him cause for alarm. Certainly leaks were not unusual, but inside pressure always took care of that.

Waiting for them on the *Dauphin* were Lieutenant Chris Nelligan, assistant officer-in-charge of the bathyscaph, and Joseph Bundy, its master mechanic, both of whom would carry out the topside work before the dive.

'Welcome aboard,' Nelligan called out as he extended a hand towards Fricker to help him transfer. *'Everything's shipshape, not a thing to worry about.'*

Fricker clung to the conning tower and waited for Whitesell to join him. *'This weather gonna cause any problems?'* he shouted to Nelligan.

The young lieutenant shook his head. *'None at all as it is. If it gets worse – and I mean a lot worse – we'll call you and you can haul yourself outa there. We'll be waiting right here for you, x marks the spot.'*

'You're a prince, Chris,' said Whitesell, holding on to the conning rail.

'You know it, Hank. Take it easy down there.' He slapped Whitesell's shoulder. *'Don't go chasing mermaids.'*

'Only the pretty ones. Everything in order, Bundy?'

'It'll hold.'

'Glad to hear it. After you, Carl.'

Fricker climbed into the conning tower and down the ladder of the access tube into the passenger gondola attached to the bottom of the bathyscaph. The smell of rubber and solvent wafted over him as he raised the sphere's hatch and slid through. Relieved to be out of the wind and spray above, he quickly scanned the instruments inside the cramped capsule, checking the batteries first, and then the bilges and the oxygen and air regenerators. Satisfied that all was well he switched on the tape recorder and announced the date and dive number, the operation's division and title, and his and Whitesell's name and rank.

The lieutenant soon joined him, squeezing his tall frame

into the tiny compartment without a groan or grumble, eager to get on with the mission.

Bundy had followed him down the access tube and his head poked through the open hatch. 'Ready to go in ten minutes,' he said to them both. 'Have a pleasant day.'

'So long, Bundy,' bade Whitesell, preoccupied with checking the same instruments that Fricker had moments earlier. 'Thanks for doing a good job.'

'You're welcome, Lieutenant. Now don't go scratching my baby on any rocks down there.'

'We'll avoid 'em, don't worry. You set, Carl?'

'Ready.' Fricker reached for the steel hatch and all three of them, Bundy on the outside, lowered it into position. They heard bolts being tightened, and then the master mechanic shone a flashlight through the hatch's porthole to let them know it was secure. Bundy disappeared up the ladder to open a valve and within a few minutes the vertical passageway through the main body was filled with water.

That was the beginning of Fricker and Whitesell's isolation, for now they were entombed inside the sphere until the voyage was over. They listened as the ballast tanks were opened and two tons of sea water was allowed to flood the float. Above them, Nelligan and Bundy were already scrambling aboard the rubber boat that would speed them away from the sink area. The depth gauge needle began to move downwards and as the *Dauphin* sank deeper its rocking motion lessened. Fricker waited a few minutes before reporting in on the underwater telephone.

The descent was frustratingly slow, but necessarily so if the bathyscaph was to adapt correctly to the mounting pressure. At 300 feet it passed into the thermocline where the water dropped sharply in temperature and became denser. Their journey stopped for the moment because of the renewed buoyancy and the two men took the opportunity to discard their damp outer clothes and, caution being the

287

by-word of such dives, re-check all the instruments. After a few minutes had passed, Whitesell released gasolene from the manœuvring tank to get rid of the excess buoyancy and the dive continued.

Before long they had entered a zone of deepening twilight where colours became monochromic and distance was indiscernible. By 1,000 feet there was no light at all.

'Let's see what's out there,' Fricker said, switching on the forward lights and turning off those inside the cabin.

'Will you look at that shit,' said Whitesell in a low, amazed voice.

It was not unusual to see formless plankton streaming past at that depth, but this was different: there was almost a solid wall of minute aquatic animal and plant life rising past the observation window.

'I've never seen anything like this before,' said Fricker in hushed tones, his eyes alight behind his spectacles.

'We gonna grab some of this stuff?' Whitesell wanted to know as he moved closer to the glass.

'No need. We've collected enough from the surface to realise it's no different from any other plankton. What we'd like to discover is what exactly is causing this uncommon mass rush to the surface.'

'There's gotta be an upheaval down there.'

'If there is, it's not showing up on any of our surface instruments. Besides, this is not the only place that this is happening.'

Whitesell turned his head sharply. 'Say again?'

'Plankton's rising to the surface of other oceans and seas like this around the globe, it seems.'

'You're kidding me.'

'Uh-uh. Something's going on, Hank, that's got us all guessing. There has to be a reason, but so far we're baffled.'

'That's why this mission has been kept so secret?'

Fricker shrugged in the darkness. 'Not quite secret, but

our lords and masters are keeping it pretty close to their chests.'

'Any particular reason for that?'

'Yeah – habit. Okay, I'm going to take some film, then we'll souse the lights and concentrate on getting to the bottom.'

It was getting cold inside the sphere, but the two men were too busy re-checking instruments and making adjustments to notice much. Fricker triggered the camera again at 5,000 feet and reported their progress to the waiting destroyer. At around 10,000 feet a small leak started.

'It's coming through one of the hull connectors,' Whitesell informed Fricker, his voice quite unconcerned. 'It'll stop when we go deeper and water pressure packs the sealer more tightly.'

'I hope you're right.'

'Trust me.' Whitesell grinned.

At 20,000 feet Fricker used the underwater phone again. 'We've lost them,' he said after attempts to make contact with the *Quayle*.

'We may pick 'em up later,' said Whitesell. 'You know how freaky conditions can get. Let's take another look outside.'

'I want to check out the sonar transducers first to make sure we haven't drifted too close to the trench wall.' He touched buttons and watched the lighted panel before him. 'Hell, that can't be right.'

'What is it?' Whitesell's question was sharp; for some inexplicable reason, the lower they sank the more uneasy he was becoming.

'I'm not getting anything that makes sense on the sonar.'

'Let's get the forward lights on again.'

Fricker pressed the switch.

'Holy Mother . . .' he heard Whitesell say.

At this depth, Fricker knew he might possibly see anything from red shrimps to flat fish swimming through the midnight waters, even though any such activity was rare; but on this occasion there was just a thick wall of what looked like moving sludge.

'That's mud out there. We must have stirred it up from the bottom of the trench,' said the lieutenant.

'No way,' Fricker replied. 'We've got at least another 15,000 feet to go before we touch bottom.'

'I'd check the fathometer if I were you.'

'I already have and I'm right.'

'Okay, Brains, you tell me what it is.'

'It's the plankton,' Fricker said quietly. 'Now it's mixed with silt from the ocean bed.'

'Impossible.'

'Not really. Like I said, recently our weather satellites have been discovering plankton blooms rising to the surface anywhere and everywhere. It's quite a phenomenon. In this case we figure the plankton's been gathered and swept along the Mariana Trench by fierce currents and for some reason is being pushed to the surface right here.'

'That's interesting, Carl, but at this point in time I gotta tell you I'm not entirely happy about being down here in this slime.'

'You know how valuable this life form is to the Earth's atmosphere.'

'Sure. It exchanges carbon dioxide with the atmosphere. That doesn't make me feel any better.'

'It absorbs carbon dioxide at higher latitudes and releases it nearer the Equator. The point is the oceans store about fifty times as much carbon as the atmosphere, so the more manmade gas it soaks up the better to counter-balance the greenhouse effect.'

'But we're in a warmer latitude here. All this shit is going to upset the balance.'

'No, most of the blooms are in the northern and southern regions. This one's a freak.'

'And we're here to find out why.'

'We're just here to take a look.'

The bathyscaph was abruptly buffeted and both men grabbed hand-holds.

'Yeah, well it seems obvious to me something's happening below to disturb the normal – or should I say abnormal? – flow. Are you thinking of going lower to find out what?'

'That's the idea.'

'I don't think I like it.'

'You have to make the decision; I'm only a passenger. But it could help a lot to know exactly what's going on.'

'The hell you say.' Whitesell thought for a moment. 'I guess the commander wouldn't be too happy to hear I'd chickened out, and if it starts getting rough we can always turn about. How deep d'you want to go?'

'Another 10,000 at least. Ideally I'd like to get down to the floor, but that may not be possible in all this.'

'You got it. Ten thousand and then we have another conference, right? Let's keep the forward lights on as we go – these currents are getting tricky and I'd hate to hit the trench wall.' He grumbled softly to himself. 'Not that we'd have much chance of seeing it through that stuff.'

'I'm switching on the camera – I want to get a visual record of all this.'

A long time went by with Whitesell using the directional propellers constantly to resist the strong currents and keep their descent on course. Because of the bathyscaph's unnatural buoyancy in the upflow, more and more gasolene had to be released. Conversation was at a minimum as the occupants of the sphere concentrated on the job in hand, and the deeper they sank the more edgy Whitesell in particular became.

At nearly 30,000 feet visibility outside was a little clearer. 'It's mainly silt out there now,' Fricker said. 'I think we've passed through most of the plankton.'

'At this depth that's hardly surprising.'

'So – do we keep going?'

'You realise how long it's taken us to get to this point?'

'Almost six hours.'

'Right. And it'll take us quite a while to get topside again. Think about that if we get into trouble.'

'I'm thinking about it right now, Hank. Just a little deeper, huh?' There was still nothing to see, nothing worthwhile for Fricker to report back with. He'd get Whitesell to take them to the ocean bed even if it meant persuading him foot by foot.

'I'm gonna dump some more shot ballast to slow us down again.'

Fricker smiled. 'Fine. No rush at all.'

They busied themselves with instruments again, both of them happy to be occupied as they sank further into the deep. Fricker tried the underwater telephone once more to no avail; the mess above them was making contact with the surface even more difficult than usual. Between checks and adjustments Whitesell glanced out of the observation window, his unease mounting to a distinct nervousness. There was something wrong but he didn't know what. Years of similar dives and the few odd scary moments had seasoned him well, and he had the reputation of being one of the most relaxed and capable bathyscaph divers in the service; but something was spooking him on this voyage and it irritated him not to know the cause.

Fricker turned on the sensitive fathometer. 'That's strange,' he said and waited for Whitesell's groan to fade. 'We're not getting a steady reading. It's as if –'

He was about to say it was as if the ocean floor was fluctuating when the lieutenant gripped his arm.

'D'you see what I see?'

Fricker peered through the circular window. There was something whitish out there in the murk, something that was rising smoothly and slowly, unaffected by the currents that rocked the sphere to and fro.

'Is it a fish or a luminous plant?' Whitesell wanted to know.

'Beats me.' Fricker flipped off the cabin lights and then the outside forward lights.

The glow became stronger, and continued to rise steadily.

'It's a light,' said Whitesell in almost a whisper. 'It's – a – God – damn – light.'

'That's impossible,' Fricker said incredulously.

Yet it did appear to be a light of some kind. Its soft radiance was unchanging, although shadows of eddying silt curled around it. Because of the thickness of the glass and the distortion of the dense water, its size was difficult to judge, but Fricker thought it might have a radius of between six inches and one foot. They craned their necks to follow its progress, but it was soon gone from view.

In the small glow of the cabin's console lights they looked at one another.

'I got no idea what it was, but it scared the shit outa me,' said Whitesell.

'It . . .' Fricker was almost lost for words. 'It was fantastic.'

'Yeah, incredible, but I still didn't like it.'

'Let's go after it,' said Fricker, already reaching for the switch that would release more ballast.

'Wait, it's moving too fast, we'd never –'

The terrible muffled rending that emanated from somewhere below the bathyscaph caused both men to freeze. The sound came again, only this time it was a roar that the layers of water did little to mute. Other sounds followed, the cracking of rock, the thumps of objects striking the steel of their vessel. The sphere began to tremble, then to bounce, and Fricker and Whitesell were thrown against the curved walls and instruments.

'Get the forward lights!' Fricker shouted. *'Let's see what's going on down there!'*

Trained to act on command no matter what, the lieutenant struck the switch. Unfortunately, before they could look outside, the bathyscaph was hit by a sudden upwards surge; it tilted violently, throwing the two men together in a tumble of arms and legs.

'*What's happening?*' yelled Whitesell.

Fricker had a strong notion as to the cause of the turmoil, for deep ocean trenches such as this often lay close to rows of active volcanoes and had always been areas of powerful geological activity. Many earthquakes occurred within their vicinity.

'*Get us up, fast as you can!*' he shouted at his companion, aware that 'fast' could only be a relative term when inside pressure had to adapt to that of the outside throughout the ascent.

And anyway, it was already too late for them.

Through the sphere's observation window, and because the bathyscaph's lights were shining directly towards the ocean bottom, they could see what looked like a huge bubbling grey cloud hurtling towards the *Dauphin*, turning the freezing waters around it to steam as it came and bringing with it tons of broken bedrock.

The submersible was pushed upwards before the rising spume at a tremendous speed and blood was already pouring from Fricker and Whitesell's eyes and ears and every other orifice when the bathyscaph flipped over.

Strong as it was, the steel hull of the *Dauphin* cracked, the glass of the observation window burst, and the two men inside imploded.

21

The sun was tinged red and nearly touching the tips of the furthest mountains when Rivers drove back through the long glen.

He was tired, drained almost. But there was a wonderment in his eyes that had not been there since his childhood.

A deer ran ahead of him along the bumpy track, only scuttling up an embankment when the car drew too close.

Clouds that were now golden-edged swept over the landscape, driven on by westerly winds, and the waters of the loch rippled that same gold, while the hillsides were burnished a false autumnal brown.

Rivers drove the vehicle skilfully enough, but his thoughts were on other matters, for it had been a day of learning, of understanding. A day of revelation.

It had also been one of confusion and anxiety, for the lessons learned had not come without debate or initial fearful rejection. The old man had been patient with his pupil's cynicism as well as his trepidation, and had explained with enormous care and gentle warmth.

Yet this wise man had not claimed to know all the answers, for there were mysteries that the human mind could never comprehend in its present state of evolution. There was one certainty that he impressed on the climatologist, however: whatever turmoil lay ahead, they were not alone in the struggle; unity was their ally, and the force it brought with it was their champion. Change was about and there were many to be tested; Rivers was but one of their number.

Shadows were long in places along the valley way and the coming dusk teased visibility; with his mind far from the movement, Rivers switched on the car's headlights. A jack-rabbit, followed by another, and then another, bounded across the track in front of the car, quickly disappearing into the undergrowth and reappearing further up the slope, their speed as fast as Rivers' and their direction the same. Soon they were swallowed by the tall grass.

The loch was narrowing, coming to an end, and the track was beginning to rise. As he rounded a slight curve Rivers glanced over his shoulder at the long valley. His foot jammed on to the brake and the car skidded into a small area levelled out as a tourist viewpoint. He pulled on the handbrake and stared back down the length of the glen.

There must have been at least a hundred of the glowing orbs hovering over the great stretch of water, each one a tiny shimmering star enhanced by the gathering dusk.

22

Josh angled his head to give his drawing a new perspective. He added a few more touches with his crayon, then held the picture up. He smiled and turned towards his mother who was still on the telephone.

'You're sure, Hugo?' he heard her saying.

A tinny sound from the old-fashioned receiver, his grand-dad speaking.

'Give her our love, won't you?' His mother smiled over at Josh. 'Yes, he's fine. I bought him a little sketch pad today to keep him occupied. He's busy with it now. Jim? I still don't know – he hasn't returned. Yes, I'm very anxious. I can't understand why he didn't leave word.' A pause while Grandad Poggsy spoke. 'Yes, Hugo, soon as I know myself. We'll be back soon.'

Diane said goodbye to her father-in-law and replaced the receiver. 'Grandad sends his love, Josh,' she said to the boy who was sitting at the dressing-table in his pyjamas. She went to one of the single beds and sat on the edge. 'You got a cuddle for Mama?'

Josh slipped from the stool and ran to his mother's out-stretched arms. She hugged him close and kissed his cheek. 'Eva's going to be okay, Josh,' she told him, curling her fingers through his tousled hair.

'Is she still awake?'

'Uh huh. Not even sleepy now. How did you know earlier, Josh? When I rang this afternoon?'

He shrugged. 'I just felt her wake. I told you she wasn't sleeping any more, didn't I?'

'Yes, yes, you did.'

'Is she going home from hospital?'

'They want to keep her overnight for observation.'

He pulled his head back to look at her face.

'To see if she's still all right in the morning,' Diane explained. 'Then I think they'll let Grandad and Grandma take her home.' She pulled him close again and rocked his little body in her arms. 'I wish I understood how it works with you two, this link you have with each other. It's very precious, Josh, that kind of closeness, to know what the other one's thinking, how they feel.'

'Sometimes it's horrible.'

'When you get upset with each other?' She felt him nod. 'All brothers and sisters fight from time to time, Josh, even twins like you. It's okay so long as you make up and don't let the bad feeling last.'

'But I left her in that bad place, I let the bad lady get her.'

'No, it was only a dream. It didn't really happen. And anyway, she's awake and talking ten-to-the-dozen now. She's going to be fine.'

'I'm glad Eva's better, Mummy. It's been lonely.'

She squeezed him. 'You've always got me.'

'It's not the same.'

Diane felt a tiny pang of sadness, a regret that no matter how much she showed her love for the children, she would never be quite as close as they were to each other, and although they loved her in return, she would always be just on the outside of their mutual bond. Perhaps if she had been their real mother . . .

'Can I draw again, Mummy?'

She released him, lest he sense her anguish. 'Sure.' She followed him back to the dressing-table. 'That's good, Josh,' she said, looking down at the crayon drawing. 'Is it the garden from your dream?'

'Yes. See, there's all my friends.'

The figures, with their matchstick limbs, were colourful and their dot-and-line faces were happy. He and Eva had drawn this same picture time and time again: the bright blue sky crayoned in as a kind of ceiling with a definite end, the round spiky sun beneath it; half a lake jutted in from the left-hand side, and broad green strokes depicted the grass and hills; the matchstick children themselves ran about and waved their arms among tall uncoloured posts. More than once in the past Diane or Bibby had enquired what these posts or pillars were meant to be, but each time Josh and Eva would jerk their shoulders and say: 'They're just there.'

Diane turned away and went to the window, arms folded beneath her breasts. There wasn't much to see out there – only the car park against a backdrop of now darkening hills – but she had gazed from the window several times through-out the day, hoping to see the hire car pull in and Rivers step out from it. Where could he be? Why would he leave before she and Josh had even risen without knocking on their door or pushing a message under it? It didn't make sense. But then she had felt since the day she met him that Rivers was unpredictable. Oh, he appeared normal and sensible on the surface, but something was going on deep inside him that was as puzzling as it was disconcerting. She wondered if he had been different before the plane crash. Or maybe he'd been a different kind of man before his lover had died. Was he still grieving for her? If only he wasn't so self-contained, if only he would be more open with his feelings. And how much did his physical pain affect him? Sometimes she could see the tension there, the furrowed brow, the tightening of his lips, as pain from his injury bothered him. He disguised it well enough most of the time, but it was always evident in his eyes. The change in his demeanour, the expression of immense relief, when the twins had soothed away the pain had been so notable. Did he, himself, realise that constant hurt was debilitating to the soul as well as the body? Oh Jim, where are you? She felt anger. Why are you doing this?

Diane made an effort to calm herself and looked back towards Josh. 'Are you tired, honey?'

Josh laid down his crayon. 'A little bit.'

'Come on, then, let's tuck you into bed.' She had bathed him earlier after they'd eaten in the hotel's small and, because of the children's early dinner hour, lonely dining room, glad to be distracted for a short time.

The boy skipped over to his bed and yanked back the cover. Diane folded it down neatly so that only a sheet was over him. Once he was settled she would go to reception – not for the first time that day – and see if there were any messages. It wasn't very logical, but he just might have phoned the hotel without wanting to speak directly to her. Maybe then she'd go to the bar and order a stiff drink; a Scotch and soda would be very welcome right then.

Josh, who had already snuggled down on to the pillow, suddenly raised his head. He looked past her at the wall as if he could see through it.

'What is it, Josh?' she asked, laying a hand on his shoulder.

'He's back.'

'What?'

'He's back, Mama. And . . . and he's sort of . . . sort of funny.'

'Stay there now.' She laid him down again. 'Just stay quiet, Josh, and try to go to sleep. I won't be long.'

Josh closed his eyes when his mother left the room, but sleep was far away. His thoughts travelled to an older mind than his, the mind of an ancient who sat in darkness not many miles away and who wept for the world.

NEW ORLEANS, LOUISIANA

Shadebank shot his cuffs so that at least three-quarters of an inch showed beneath the sleeves of his linen jacket. He fingered one of the gold cufflinks, his morose gaze fixed on the window of the stretch-limo he and the three other passengers were travelling in. There were not many people on the streets of the city at this time of morning.

Beside him, and taking up most of the seat, sat Mama Pitié, her eyes closed and fat lips twitching as if she were deep in prayer. The limousine's air-conditioned coolness seemed to provide her with little comfort: she stank of sweat and cheap perfume and her breathing was so laboured she might have been powering the vehicle's engine herself. Was the big woman scared of flying? Shadebank sincerely hoped she was.

Opposite and facing them were two of Mama's zombies, their eyes lowered but not quite closed, as if they, too, were lost in prayer.

302

Crazy. Fuckin' crazy.

Drivin' to th'airport at this godforsaken hour, skippin' town – *'skippin' the fuckin' country!* – when the cops were this suspicious! But on a return ticket, that was the craziest thing!

A body had been found out in the swamps (Mama's goons had forgotten the swamplands were mostly dried up nowadays and had dumped the corpse – or what was left of it – where the 'gators no longer belly-walked) and word had reached him from impeccable and well-rewarded sources that Mama Pitié was in for some severe questioning. Seemed like the dead guy had been last seen in the company of one of her disciples, a loose enough connection, sure enough, but not when linked with the girl who'd gone missing weeks ago.

We shoulda stayed cool, Shadebank told himself, and hung around until the dumb cops got tired of askin' the same dumb questions. This way it looked like we was runnin' out.

Not that he, himself, had intended to remain at the Temple for very much longer anyway. In fact Shadebank had decided only last night that it was definitely time to move on. Things're gettin' too dam' hot, he'd told himself not for the first time over the last day or two. No packed suitcases, justa quick dip inta the safe, then long-gone. Sweet. You might say he was now an old hand at the game.

But the bitch had spoiled his plan. It was still dark outside when she'd phoned him at the run-down hotel where he rented cheap rooms and told him to reserve four seats on the next plane out of New Orleans. 'Anywhere partic'lar?' he'd enquired testily down the phone, not quite sure if she was kidding him or not. 'England,' she'd said, her voice suddenly quiet and breathy.

England! What the fuck was there for them in England? And why the hell did she want him to go with her? The last question he already had an answer to. Shadebank was an 'educated niggah'; he knew about flying and foreign countries and things. Mama Pitié, for all her wiles and ways, was not experienced in such things. Truth was, she was plain dumb in such matters. That's why she'd taken him in in the first place. She was aware of her own limitations, and she knew he could be useful. He tugged at his cufflink and wished her freakish heart would collapse under the strain of keeping her big body functioning before they reached the airport.

23

The first thing that Diane noticed about Rivers was that he was no longer limping. She had reached the hotel's lobby when he came striding through the entrance, his footsteps hurried and an urgency in his expression that stopped her in her tracks.

He saw Diane immediately and made his way towards her, skirting round a middle-aged couple in walking boots and carrying canvas backpacks who were leaving the reception desk. He raised a hand towards her as he approached.

Relief followed by anger swept through her.

'Where . . . ?' she began to say, lips tight, eyes blazing, but instead of finishing the sentence she stepped forward into his arms. 'We've been so worried,' was all she managed.

His fingers ran through her hair at the back of her neck and he drew her close against his chest. 'We've got to ring the airport and make reservations,' he said, his voice breathless and tense. 'We've got to get back as quickly as possible.'

She lifted her head away from him. 'There are no late-night

flights – I checked when I booked tickets for the journey up. But why, Jim? What's this all about?'

'D'you know the first morning flight?'

She shook her head. 'Why the rush?'

'We have to get back to Eva.'

Still shaking her head, Diane smiled up at him. 'She's all right, Jim. She's awake now. Poggsy says . . .'

'Yeah I know. But we've got to get to her before it's too late.'

Diane drew away completely. 'How could you know?'

'The old man told me she was fine.'

'The Dream Man? You saw him?'

'I've been with him all day. It was me all the time, Diane, not Josh. I was the one the old man needed to see.' He took her by the arm and led her out of the lobby into the corridor.

'You're not limping any more,' she said through her confusion.

He smiled grimly and she saw his weariness, an exhaustion that was mingled with something else. Anxiety? Yes, it was certainly that, but there was more to it. She realised it was a guarded kind of elation that shone from his eyes.

'He's a healer,' Rivers said to her without slowing his step. 'Like Josh and Eva. Like thousands of children of their generation.' Now he stopped to look directly at her and for the moment any elation she might have imagined in his gaze was replaced by another emotion. His words echoed the sadness therein. 'They're our only hope, Diane. Without the children we're lost. The whole bloody world is lost.'

He walked on and Diane hurried after him.

24

Diane examined the sky as she held open the rear car door for Josh to scramble in. The clouds, so dark and brooding, concealed the early morning sun and shadowed the very air itself.

Everything was still.

There was no birdsong.

And no breeze.

The long road was deserted.

And even the houses seemed devoid of life.

It wasn't cold, yet Diane shivered. She looked across the car's rooftop at Rivers, wondering if he, too, sensed the unearthly mood. The look he returned assured her that he did.

'Ready?' he asked her.

She nodded and climbed into the passenger seat. She touched his arm when he joined her in the car. 'Can it be true?' she said.

'We'll know soon enough,' he replied, reaching for his seat-belt.

'I'd like to see for myself.' It was more of a request than a demand.

Rivers was firm. 'No. He insisted that we had to get away from here.'

'To protect Eva?'

'Not only that.' He switched on the ignition before turning to Diane. 'We have to trust him.'

'You don't feel any different this morning? You still believe in him?'

'Did you think I wouldn't?'

'Cold light of day and all that . . .'

The car rolled forward from the hotel's parking bay into the road and swiftly began to pick up speed as it headed towards Fort William. Because of the morning's greyness, Rivers switched on the headlights.

'Did you manage to sleep last night?' Diane asked because her own sleep had been so fitful.

'Like a baby, even though it wasn't for long. I guess I was too exhausted to think any more.' He didn't bother to add that it was the first time in months that pain had not disturbed him. 'And I woke this morning without a doubt in my mind. Don't ask me how or why, but I knew everything he told me was true. Incredible, fantastic – *unbelievable* – as it is, I *know* it's right. Even if I hadn't been convinced by his words the lights I saw over the loch showed me something extraordinary was happening.'

'But what can we *do*, Jim?'

'Not much. It's already too late to change anything.'

Josh, who had been strangely quiet since Diane had roused him that morning, spoke up from the back. 'Are we going home because of Eva?'

'Yes, Josh,' Rivers answered.

'Is something bad going to happen to her?'

Rivers hesitated. 'I'm not sure, Josh.' *Leave this place and protect the children*, the old man had told him. Keep the innocents from the harm that seeks them. There had been no explanation, no reason given, just an insistence that Rivers return to Hazelrod without delay.

'You heard me speak to Nanny Bibby before we left our room,' said Diane, leaning over to touch her son's hand. 'They're collecting Eva from the hospital this morning if the doctors say it's okay, so you see, there's nothing to worry about.'

The ominous bulk of Ben Nevis loomed up on their left, its Delphian presence even more forbidding in the grim light. Today the mountain seemed more sinister than majestic, more threatening than impressive.

'It might have been better if Eva had stayed in the hospital,' Rivers said quietly to Diane.

'They don't keep anyone in longer than necessary, you know that. They feel she can just as easily be watched at home as in hospital.' She had the uncanny feeling that the mountain was observing them and she tore her gaze away, chiding herself for such foolishness. Rivers' disclosures last night – true *or* false – had spooked her. 'Jim,' she said, 'I'm not sure about any of this.'

Despite his own deep disquiet, Rivers couldn't help but smile. 'There's a turnaround,' he said. 'I thought I was the cynic.'

'It isn't easy, can't you see that?'

'Oh sure, I can see it, and I don't blame you at all.'

'This is just *so* extraordinary. You're asking me to . . . to . . .'

'Have faith? Right, that's what I'm asking. But it makes no difference what you or I or anybody thinks: the process started a long time ago and nothing's going to change it now. It's too late, we've all been too bloody stupid.'

They had reached the town of Fort William and as they drove through Diane watched the houses and hotels, imagining the people inside, perhaps just waking or having breakfast, many no doubt still sleeping, all of them unaware of what was happening to the world around them, complacent, irresponsible, even negligent in their ignorance. And totally unaware of what was going to come.

'God help us,' she said softly, and Rivers wondered if He would bother.

They were a few miles past Crianlarich when Rivers brought the car to a juddering stop.

Diane, whose eyes had been closed, a hand resting across her brow, her elbow on the sill, jerked forward with a start. Josh, who had been so quiet throughout the journey they thought he was asleep, shot forward too, only the seat-belt preventing him from banging his head against the back of Diane's seat.

All three stared through the windscreen at the road ahead.

Diane blinked, then screwed up her eyes, unsure of what she was seeing at first. The highway cut through moorland and valleys whose slopes led to mist-laden mountains. Silvery flows fell from the craggy steeps, becoming rushing, rock-filled streams, burns, on the lower stretches. Trees were sparse here but vegetation, although browned and dried by the season's sun, was abundant. It was from these grasses, shrubbery, and gorse that the small animals poured, making their way across the roadway in their hundreds it seemed; mostly it was rabbits and hares, but among them ran smaller creatures, voles and fieldmice, and the occasional fox and deer. They teemed over the highway in a mad dash for other territory.

'What are they running from?' Diane said in dismay.

'It's started,' was Rivers' reply.

Diane tore her gaze from the fleeing animals. 'What's started? What do you mean?'

'The old man said there'd be panic among man and beast. The animals are frightened of something we're not aware of yet, something we can't see.' He began to move the car forward, quickly reaching the edge of the flow.

'Jim, you can't.' She grabbed his shoulder.

'We can't miss that plane, Diane. We've got to get through.' He thumped the car's horn and the nearest animals veered away, but nevertheless carried on their charge across the road. The vehicle bumped over something and Diane shuddered, imagining the tiny crushed bones beneath the wheels. Rivers continued to press the horn as he eased the car steadily through the stream of furry bodies. A fox startled them as it appeared against the windscreen and scrambled across the bonnet without even glancing in their direction. It leapt from view and they listened to the thumps against metal and frequent squeals as other animals dashed themselves against the bodywork on Rivers' side. He remained resolute, closing his mind to the sounds and the bumps, keeping progress steady, resisting the urge to accelerate, to get it over with, to get beyond this tide of suicidal creatures as quickly as possible.

He braked only when two red deer bounded in front of them, and advanced again immediately they were clear. Josh curled up in the back seat, hands over his ears so that he wouldn't hear the tiny screeches, while Diane closed her eyes and bit into her lower lip as the car slowly eased forward. Rivers took advantage of clear patches here and there, speeding up then slowing to snail's pace when more animals blocked the way.

It was a protracted and distressing journey, but eventually they were through. Anxious to make up time and relieved to be free of the relentless drove of fleeing beasts, Rivers stepped on the accelerator and quickly gained speed. Diane looked back through the rear window, upset by what Rivers had done and curious to know why the animals were so frightened. She scanned the land behind them, but there was nothing evident that could cause such panic. She faced the front again and concentrated on the road ahead.

Last night when she had finally returned to her own room, leaving the exhausted Rivers to sleep, she had been both terrified and bewildered by his revelations. Even though it was very late, she had phoned Hugo and warned him to keep a watchful eye on Eva when she came home from hospital. She told him that she, Josh and Rivers would come back the next day and then they would explain everything that had happened. Naturally Hugo had plied her with questions, but Diane had been too confused – as well as wearied herself – and had bade him wait for their return. Now there were so many more questions that she, herself, needed to ask, for there had been too much to take in before, the concept too immense to be absorbed at once.

She checked on Josh, reluctant to ask Rivers questions in front of her son. Josh was still awake, knees curled up, his shoulders hunched; his head rested against the back of the seat, and he was staring at nothing in particular. Occasionally his eyes would blink, but otherwise he was still, almost lifeless.

Diane shifted her attention to Rivers. His profile was grim and the weariness was still there in his eyes. He was unshaven and the dark stubble emphasised a gauntness in his cheeks she hadn't noticed before. She was glad she'd insisted he ate something the night before, for there had been no time for breakfast that morning. Her fingers touched his face, tentatively, for she was a little afraid of him now. His own hand reached for hers and squeezed it.

'Will everything be all right?' She spoke in a quiet voice, hoping Josh was too preoccupied to catch its tremor.

'It's got to be,' he said simply, and she took her hand away, wondering if the power he had spoken of last night could possibly exist. Could he have dreamt his encounter with the

312

old man who lived in a crofter's cottage by the side of a loch? Or had it been a weird hallucination brought on by all kinds of pressure? Was he still traumatised by the plane crash and the pain he'd suffered since? Pain, she reminded herself, that had abruptly, *miraculously*, gone? Yes, the twins were healers of a kind, but just how much of that healing process was due to the power of the sufferer's own mind? Then there was the constant strain of his work, the ever-increasing demand on him to come up with answers or predictions for a world climate that had become bizarre and out of control. Add to that the grief he must have suffered over the lover he had lost through an illness that had at one time been considered to have virtually died out, but which had risen again, like other such tropical diseases, to epidemic proportions because of the radical change in the planet's environment. (It was ironic that this bygone disease should return so lethally while cures or near-cures had been found for relatively new ones like AIDS and cancer.) Was it possible for anyone to carry such burdens over such a lengthy period without it affecting them in some way? And then, of course, she and Hugo had added to his problems.

Diane immediately became angry with herself over this last thought. Angry and guilty. She studied him again and he became aware of her scrutiny. He turned to her, curious.

'Jim . . .' she began to say, then hesitated. She shook her head and said, 'I'm sorry, there's just so much . . .'

'To take in? Yeah, I know. You could say it's overwhelming.' Now he grinned and in that moment she recognised the strength deep within him that had pulled him through these past ordeals. No, there was nothing wrong with the balance of his mind, despite what he had been through. She believed the story of his meeting with the old man – Josh and Eva's Dream Man – even though he had not allowed her to see him. But what had come from their discussions was a whole lot harder to swallow.

And yet . . . and yet it was only two steps further on from Lovelock's hypothesis that planet Earth was a living, self-sustaining organism, and one step further on from Hugo's theory that their world was simply a huge interstellar life-support system created specifically for the human race. The Dream Man's premise was considerably more profound than either of the first two, but was it any less believable? The answer was possibly no, it wasn't. But did it matter now? According to the Dream Man only a special few would take part in the changes the world was about to endure. In their hands – no, in their *minds* – lay the destiny of mankind and the planet it dwelled upon. The signs were there to warn us, as they had been for many decades; now they were transformed into tiny psychic markers, portents, precise but enigmatic indicators of environmental disruptions. The early warnings – the warming of the Earth's atmosphere, the holes in the ozone layer, pollution's massive annihilation of sea creatures – these and others had been ignored until it was too late; now the warnings were of a more inscrutable, perhaps even mystical nature, and were precursors of immutable perils rather than distress beacons of things that might be altered. Diane silently began to pray.

Very soon they had reached the northern tip of Loch Lomond, the twenty-four-mile-long lake whose narrow end cut deep into the Highland mountains. They drove along its shore and on this return journey Diane took little note of the spectacular scenery, the mountain ranges and the lush mixed woods that climbed steeply up the flanks of Ben Lomond from the water's edge. Further south the loch broadened to accommodate a scattering of wooded islands in its calm, slate-grey waters, and more gentle slopes led up from its distant, wide southern shore. They were passing through the point where the Highlands of Scotland met the Lowlands.

At first Diane thought there was something wrong with the car's suspension, for the vibration initially came from below their seats; it felt as if they were travelling over a thinly spaced cattle-grid, or a surface full of tiny bumps. But then the bodywork itself was oscillating and Rivers' hands were visibly shaking on the tightly gripped steering wheel.

He swung the car over to the side of the road and quickly turned off the engine. The vehicle continued to vibrate; a tube of sweets bought for Josh on the outward journey rolled off the dashboard shelf and fell at Diane's feet. A lorry coming in the opposite direction had also stopped further down the road and they could see the driver looking about his cab as if it were his vehicle at fault.

'Look at the water,' Rivers said over the rattling of loose parts and shuddering metal.

Diane followed his gaze and saw the great loch, a moment ago so calm and smooth, now choppy and bubbling with spumy ripples. 'What is it?' she asked without turning away.

Rivers knew, but did not answer. He jerked open the driver's door and stepped out on to the roadway. Nearby, a pyramid of old stones, piled there for use on a wall that was being reconstructed, clattered to the ground. The leaves in the trees shivered and rustled. A loose wooden post that had long lost its sign quivered. Rivers felt the vibration run through the soles of his shoes and up his legs into the whole of his body. His hand rested on the top of the car to steady himself and the tremors from the metal buzzed through his muscles up to his shoulder. He remembered that they were close to the Highland Boundary Fault.

Diane emerged from the other side of the vehicle, her face pale with apprehension. She was now aware of what was happening without being told. A deep rumbling sound came from below, steadily rising in intensity as the disturbance increased, and Diane suddenly pointed at the sky behind them.

To the north the air was filled with tiny black specks that were approaching fast. Birds wheeled and dived over nearby treetops, screeching their alarm as they awaited the advancing flocks.

Rivers and Diane watched with both trepidation and astonishment, while Josh peered out the car's rear window, his eyes large, his mouth agog. Gradually the tremor began to ease and the rumbling subsided to become a low slow-vanishing drone. The sound that now came to them was the beating of thousands of wings and the shrill ululation of the birds as they drew nearer. It was only seconds before their mass was darkening the sky over the loch; their numbers seemed endless, their species undeterminable, as they were joined by others in the locale, and the wind their wings created stirred the trees once more and ruffled the water's surface.

'Incredible,' Diane said, her voice unheard over the noise. She craned her neck, looking from end to end of the great flock as they filled the air above. The birds' cries echoed off the mountains, their sound swelling to such a pitch that she clapped her hands to her ears and leaned against the car's roof, her eyes closed. Over they passed, more and more so that it seemed every species of bird in the Scottish Highlands was on the wing and heading south, deserting their habitat, the season playing no part in their migration.

It was a full seven minutes before they were gone from overhead and had become a black feverish cloud in the distance, with only a few stragglers left behind striving desperately to catch up. The silence that followed was unnatural and somehow sinister.

Diane watched until the birds were no more than a broad wavering smudge on the horizon before turning to Rivers, awe in her expression and in her question: 'Where are they going?'

Rivers opened the car door before replying. 'Away from here,' was all he could tell her.

* * *

316

The storm broke as they were crossing the Erskine Bridge over the River Clyde. The wind was already powerful, but now it threw rain at the windows and buffeted the car as it crawled along the toll bridge behind heavy traffic making its way into Glasgow. By the time they reached the airport car park the wind and rain was merciless and quickly soaked them to the skin as they dashed across the road into the air terminal itself. There was some delay in departure time for Gatwick and Diane took the opportunity to call Hazelrod once more on a public payphone. Mack answered, and informed her that Hugo and Bibby had left for the hospital to collect Eva some time ago and should be back soon. Everything was fine, he assured her, and indeed just the sound of his steady, dependable voice with its slight rustic burr was comforting, for it was the sane voice of reason and constancy in a time of doubt and grand disorder.

Josh was unusually quiet when eventually they boarded the European Airbus, displaying none of the excitement of the outward journey, and Diane felt his brow as she settled him into his seat, wondering if he might be coming down with something. His forehead was cool to the touch, though.

She kept an eye on him as the aircraft gathered speed down the runway and was surprised that even at lift-off he remained listless, his attention fixed uninterestedly on the seat in front. On her other side, Rivers was scanning the morning newspaper handed out by one of the blue-uniformed stewardesses. A glance over his shoulder at the headlines confirmed the worst for, whilst any normal day's national journal covered at least one disaster somewhere in the world (and over the past few years there had always been two or three), in this edition there were several: floods in Italy, Thailand and Korea; earthquakes in Armenia, Japan, China, Afghanistan, and the northern tip of Antarctica; a hurricane currently making its way across America's Midwest while tornadoes had devastated parts of New Guinea, Indonesia and Tahiti; a number of low-lying islands in the South Pacific had disappeared completely under the sea, and a massive tidal wave had wrecked a long section of Sri Lanka's coastline. There were smaller events that nevertheless shocked Diane: at least a hundred dolphins had deliberately battered themselves to death on the rocks just off Cornwall's shores; there was a small photograph of a great 300-foot tower of steaming water that had erupted in the main street of a city in India called Varanasi; huge belts of plankton were rising to the surface around the world's oceans, these mainly, but not solely, in the northern and southern regions. Rivers' face was grim when they exchanged glances, and Diane remembered the strange atmosphere she had been aware of but had taken little notice of in the airport earlier; there had been a buzz of anxious conversation and it was now obvious to her that its cause was the magnitude of these global calamities.

'You were right – it has already started,' she said to Rivers.

He shook his head. 'No, it started a long time ago, Diane. I think what's happening now is a kind of metamorphosis. The planet's beginning to change itself, just as the old man said it would.'

She leaned closer and lowered her voice almost to a whisper. 'I'm so afraid, Jim. What's going to happen to us?'

He laid the newspaper down in his lap and linked his arm in hers. 'He said it all depends on the children – Josh and Eva, and many like them. We mustn't let Josh see how afraid we are.'

'But what can they do, how can they help?'

'He told me we had to trust in them. Trust in them and protect them, because they're our salvation.'

'I still don't understand how.'

'But you're beginning to believe in him?'

'The Dream Man?' Her smile was almost wan. 'I wasn't at all sure first thing this morning. I thought maybe you hallucinated the whole thing – you sounded pretty crazy last night.

Then later I witnessed the earth tremor and the migration of birds for myself. Add that to the bizarre world catastrophes over the past decade, Poggsy's own version of the GAIA theory, the way Josh and Eva have been acting for some time now – adding it all together makes taking the next step not quite so difficult. Let's just say I'm not entirely convinced, but I'm not rejecting what the Dream Man says either.' She quickly checked on Josh, who was now gazing out the window. 'But what really worries me,' she said, turning back to Rivers, 'is how much damage will be done to the human race itself. Are we going to survive this?'

Diane caught the slight tremble of his hand as he took it away from her arm, but otherwise Rivers appeared calm, and even resolute.

'I asked him the same question,' he said, 'and he could give me no answer. He told me he couldn't foretell the future, he could only sense the shift both in human consciousness and in the Earth itself.'

It was a breathtaking concept, and one which she had not yet come to terms with.

'I'm not . . .' Her voice faltered and she shook her head as if rejecting a multitude of thoughts. Then: 'What makes this man so unique? Why – *how* – does he have such knowledge?'

Rivers actually smiled. 'He told me there are many like him, spread around the world, there to serve as some kind of guide to the special children.'

'Special like Josh and Eva?'

He nodded. 'It seems some of these others, although similar to him have, well let's say, different values, divergent, even deviant, perspectives on the order of things. It's from these people the children have to be protected.'

Diane felt the chill dread of fear run through her anew. 'But *how* does he – and these others – know these things? You still haven't told me.'

'Apparently the knowledge is inherent within all of us, but

319

we each have different psychic levels. A few of us choose to develop this extra sense – no, that's wrong, it isn't an *extra* sense at all. It's a very old one that's been obscured by centuries of civilisation and scientific progress. I guess the human race eventually considered it unnecessary. Our sense of smell is no longer as keen as that of our forebears who had to hunt to live, nor is our eyesight as sharp. We're not as strong and probably not as fast. No doubt our hearing isn't as good as when we lived in caves and our enemies were the animals around us. God knows what else we've lost in our so-called development.'

Out of habit he was massaging his knee, but he stopped when he realised the pain was no longer there. 'Although we've never completely lost this ability – this *sensing* – it's oddly consistent that it should begin to revive itself to a noticeable degree during the last hundred years when the threat to our world has grown more and more critical. Clairvoyants, healers, mediums, psychics – they've almost become an industry in their own right.'

'You're implying something has triggered it off?'

'Oh yeah. Our own subconscious. Somewhere deep down in the human psyche the power still exists, and maybe now our natural instinct for self-preservation is drawing on it, gradually bringing it to the fore again.'

'But why hasn't it happened to all of us? Why aren't we all like the Dream Man or the twins?'

'According to him, it doesn't work that way. It can't be instant, it has to evolve again. It's like learning to walk after years of debilitation. The faculty's there but we've forgotten how to use it. It'll come easier to new generations once its presence is accepted, and to many, those like Josh and Eva, it'll come naturally. I suppose the Dream Man is a forerunner of the children who have the ability, a kind of combined prophet, sentinel and protector. An advance guard, if you like.'

Diane was silent as she tried to absorb what Rivers was

saying to her. The psychic link between individuals had certainly become a proven fact over the past fifty years or so, and within the last decade the existence of the human mega-psyche, the collective consciousness, was beginning to be accepted both by scientists and academics alike. Even the once discreet government-backed organisations set up specifically to investigate such possibilities were no longer so coy in publishing their findings, most of which were positive if not absolutely conclusive.

She was distracted by a passenger across the aisle and two rows ahead who was calling urgently for a stewardess. One quickly attended him, listened to his complaint, took a peek under the seat in front of him, then went away. She returned moments later with a small canister and began to spray the floor beneath the seat in question. There was a shout when the cockroach was spotted and a further roar as the offended passenger himself brought his heel down hard on the scuttling creature. The air hostess swiftly swept up the remains with minimal fuss and everything returned to normal once more.

'Incidentally,' Rivers continued as if nothing had occurred, 'there's something else you should know about our friend up there in the Highlands.'

'Give me some relief and tell me he's crazy.'

Despite himself, Rivers grinned. 'I'm afraid not. I think he's the sanest man I've ever met. No, this is something else. He's blind.'

She looked at him incredulously. 'But how could he survive up there on his own?'

'He seems to manage. He has groceries delivered every month from the nearest village – about twenty miles away that'd be. They're left at the end of the track where he collects them for himself. And then he has his own small vegetable plot at the back of his cottage, as well as a goat for milk, hens for eggs.'

'But if he can't see . . . ?'

'He gets by, that's all I can tell you. He told me his other senses more than compensate for his lack of sight. People from other crofts in the area help him out from time to time and they also bring him food – the Highlanders are well used to hermits.'

'Surely he needs money to pay them though?'

Rivers shook his head. 'He's a healer, Diane. Animals, sick children from the village, bunions on toes, bronchial complaints, infertile livestock – he treats them all and is paid in kind. The old barter system still thrives in those parts.'

The plane was suddenly rocked by a violent gust of wind and several passengers looked around anxiously. A hostess, at that moment pushing a drinks trolley down the aisle, smiled sweetly and said to no one in particular, 'Bumpy ride today.' The comment, light enough to be soothing, drew nervous laughter from those within earshot.

Rivers peered past Diane to check the weather conditions outside for himself. Rain lashed the windows and the clouds were a deep, tumbling grey. He folded his newspaper and tucked it into the back pouch of the seat in front, then unbuckled his seat-belt. 'I'm going to call the Met Office and talk to Sheridan.'

Diane held on to his arm. 'You can't discuss all this on the phone.'

'I don't intend to – he thinks I'm neurotic enough already. I'll arrange to see him, then he can tell me I'm mad to my face. At least I'll have done all I can to warn them.'

She was about to say more, but he was already gone, making his way towards the nearest of the Airbus' passenger cardphones.

She put an arm around Josh, who was still quietly staring out the window, and asked him if he would like a drink or anything to eat. He gave a desultory shake of his head. Diane brushed hair from his forehead, a guileful way of checking his temperature again; his skin was still cool to the touch.

The soft announcement chime of the PA system preceded the pilot's relaxed voice: 'Good morning, ladies and gentlemen, boys and girls, this is Captain Linacre, your pilot for flight 484, Glasgow to London Gatwick. Sorry about the rough weather out there, but our current altitude is 33,000 feet and I'd hoped we'd be above the storm. I'm reliably informed it's even more disagreeable up ahead, so I think we'll make a small detour to miss the worst of it. This will only add a few minutes to our expected arrival time which, as you know, was going to be a little late anyway because of our delayed departure. I hope you'll bear with me on this one, but it'll ensure a smoother flight for all of us. Uh, this means we'll be flying over the eastern seaboard, so for those of you who haven't already observed it from the air before, it'll give you a chance to see the damage the winter floods of '96 did to our coastline. Thank you for your patience, and if there's any more news to report during the flight, you can be sure I'll let you know. Might I suggest you'd be more comfortable with your seat-belts on. Thank you, enjoy the rest of the journey.'

A buzz of conversation among the passengers followed the announcement, with many of those in the middle or in the aisle seats leaning over fellow-travellers to view the weather conditions for themselves. Diane did the same, but there was nothing other than a continuous mass of rolling grey to see.

By now the drinks trolley had reached her and she ordered a vodka and tonic for herself and a Scotch for Rivers, with coffee for them both to follow. She insisted that Josh had a glass of milk and some biscuits and he reluctantly acquiesced, nibbling uninterestedly at the biscuits and gulping down the milk as if to get it over with quickly.

Rivers returned and accepted the whisky gratefully, but declined the choice of biscuits or nuts.

'You heard the announcement?' she asked.

'I caught some of it while I was on the phone. It won't delay us much.'

'Did you speak to Sheridan?'

'He wasn't at the Met Office. His secretary told me he's over at Pilgrim Hall today, so we could go straight there from the airport – it's not far out of our way.'

'Shouldn't we get back to Hazelrod as quickly as possible?'

'It won't take long, Diane.'

She didn't argue: if the Dream Man was to be believed, then the environment was about to go through – no, according to that morning's newspaper, it was already happening – a massive upheaval, and it would have been selfish of her to persuade Rivers not to at least warn someone in authority first. Rivers, of course, was right – he'd be considered insane; but at least he would have done *something* to warn them. Perhaps they would soon begin to believe him when things really got out of control. She took a long swallow of her drink and still, in a corner of her mind, a tiny doubt nagged at her. It was all so fantastic, so incredible. Maybe both the Dream Man and Rivers were consumed with some kind of divine madness, and maybe she was catching it too! Oh God, she silently prayed, let that be the truth of it.

Rivers recognised her fears, as well as her doubts, and he spoke quietly to her, talking of things other than the danger the world was facing, whispering feelings he had not expressed to another for a long, long time; and Diane responded, reaching for his hand, entwining her fingers in his, revealing her own concerns for the children and eventually, her growing affection for Rivers himself. Perhaps it was the circumstances they found themselves in that had drawn them together so swiftly; or perhaps the attraction would have been there anyway. Either way, it didn't matter, for it had happened, there was a bond between them and only time could test its strength. *If* there was to be any time for them.

She became aware that Josh had moved when his feet brushed against her thigh. She turned to find her son had freed himself from his seat-belt and was kneeling in the seat so that he had a better view out the window.

'What is it, Josh?' she said, sensing something was wrong and moving over to him. Rivers leaned forward too, curious to discover what had shaken the boy from his lethargy.

Josh did not reply and Diane released her own seat-belt so that she could look over his shoulder and find out what interested him so. She drew in a sharp breath and instinctively put her arms around him.

The Airbus had just passed over what had once been known as the Humber Lowlands, most of which was now under the sea, and was now beginning its descent approach to Gatwick somewhere over the flooded regions of East Anglia. Although the sky was still filled with turbulent clouds, there were clear breaks through which Diane could see the floodlands and new coastline below. Rising from them was a small but clearly defined pinpoint of light.

At first she thought it might be sunlight reflecting on the water itself, or perhaps from glass on a boat deck, but she soon realised that the light was way above sea level and the sun was concealed by thick overhead layers of clouds anyway. And there was no doubt that this small ball of light was moving steadily upwards.

'Jim,' she said urgently. 'I think . . .'

Rivers was already on his feet and leaning forward. She moved aside a little to give him room.

'Is it an aureole again?' she asked hopefully. 'Like the one we saw on our journey up.'

It took a second or two for him to answer. 'No,' he replied, 'not this time. It's a warning. Oh Jesus . . .'

Diane pressed close to the window again, for Rivers was now looking in another direction. She saw a further light to the north of the first.

Passengers in the seats behind them had noticed their concern and were peering out their own windows. As surprised murmurs rose up, yet others followed suit and it wasn't long before even the cabin staff were leaning across seats to watch the strange lights that by now were performing a weird ballet together in the sky.

'Mama.' Josh was pointing at the water below the dancing lights.

It was still a long way down, even though the plane had begun its descent, and the area was gradually being left behind, but Diane and Rivers could plainly see a point in the water below bubbling white foam. At once the surface erupted and, because their angle had changed as the Airbus travelled onwards, they saw what looked like a huge fountain shoot into the sky.

Although it appeared small to them, both Rivers and Diane realised the jet must have been hundreds of feet high to be so visible.

HILLER HIGHLANDS, *above San Francisco Bay*

They had emerged from their homes to watch the strange
lights that danced over the wooded hillsides, one neighbour
alerting another that there appeared to be UFOs in the night
sky. And the bright little lights had put on a dazzling display
for them, skimming over the treetops like pearly fireflies,
rising high into the air, then swooping gracefully to loop
around each other like alien extras in an old Spielberg movie.
Sometimes it seemed that they would collide, so fast and so
set was their trajectory, but they would avert course at the
last moment, leaving the observers below to gasp, then
whoop with glee. The lights spread as they passed over Oakland, Berkeley and Piedmont. Students of Berkeley's University of California were provided with an extra attraction as
they left their summer prom, the music long since over, but
the loitering afterwards still in full swing. They stood around
in groups, the girls wrapping their date's arms or jackets

327

around their shoulders against the strong winds that blew in from the bay, watching the weird and exciting phenomenon with either cries or murmurs of amazement, depending on how deep was the effect on them.

Many of the residents of these areas watched from the balconies or patios of their luxury homes and, indeed, they were afforded a fine view. Others, like Fire Lieutenant Antonio Degrazza watched from less flourishing quarters and with much more apprehension, for he knew that five months of continuous drought had left the surrounding woodlands tinder-dry. The lights – there appeared to be at least sixteen of them – were beautiful to watch, but he distrusted them for their fulgent glow. If they were hot, if they should spark . . .

He had gone back inside to phone his chief and voice his concern when the lights did precisely as he feared.

Their aerial ballet ceased and each glowing orb hovered twenty or thirty feet above the treetops, dispersed there in the night like twinkling stars, a heart-lifting sight that at last rendered the onlookers silent. Then they dropped, the paths of each directed to one spot a foot above the highest tree.

When they converged – for this time they did not veer from their chosen course – they exploded in a blinding shower of sparks.

The leaves and branches below ignited instantly as if the trees themselves had long awaited this fiery touch. The flames *whoomphed* into life and, urged on by the winds, spread through the dry timbers, ripening into a living thing that sucked in the dark air and devoured its own host.

The fire became a rolling inferno and the residents of Hiller Highlands fled before its fury, taking little with them, for to delay was to burn alongside everything they owned. It swept through the homes that lined the hills and canyons of Oakland, becoming a monstrous conflagration, a napalm nightmare, that moved down into the seaport itself. The heat was so intense that water mains shattered, towers bearing high-voltage power cables melted, and propane tanks and electricity transformers exploded. Pumping stations soon failed and the emergency planning coordinator wasted no time in calling a squadron of air tankers and water-dropping helicopters, but all to no avail. The fire was too immense, and it was too powerful.

It hurried towards the sea, a rampant beast that destroyed everything in its path and filled the sky with churning black clouds that obliterated both the natural and the false stars.

COX'S BAZAR, BANGLADESH

They stood on the beach and watched with amazement the single light that hovered over the fishing boats, the distant bad weather providing an ominously dark backdrop which emphasised its brightness. The little light, with its subtle purplish corona, seemed to gleam a pureness that was dazzling to the eye, and the people wondered at its serene stillness. Not even the stiff breeze that came off the ocean could stir the light from its position ten metres or so above the boats that had gathered beneath it.

Some of the sturdier boys on the beach swam out to cling to the fishing boats so they had a better view. They called out along with the fishermen and gesticulated for the wondrous glowing sphere to descend into their boats so that they could take it back to the shore where they might pay proper and due homage. But the divine light paid them no heed.

Word swept rapidly through what had once been a small fishing town but which was now a bustling resort and residents and tourists alike left the coolness of the buildings to hurry down to the quaysides and beaches to witness this curious phenomenon for themselves. The evening took on an almost festive air and officials and photographers were sent for so that this unearthly event could be properly documented. The world would soon hear of the miracle of Cox's Bazar.

A street hawker among the spectators, who had been deaf for half his lifetime, suddenly claimed he could hear, while another, this one a rickshaw-puller whose livelihood had been ruined by crippling arthritis fell to his knees in the sand and weepingly blessed the light for releasing him from the pain that had plagued him for so long. Women among the crowd fainted; a father carried his sick child to the water's edge and pleaded with the light to eradicate the cancerous blood cells from his dying daughter's emaciated body; further along the shore a holy man who denounced the light as a devil's evil eye was castigated by those around him when his rantings became too vociferous.

All chatter, all motion, and all prayer ceased when other lights surfaced and slowly rose to the height of the first light. At least twenty metres apart, the same distance from the shoreline, they spread along the eastern side of the Bay of Bengal for as far as the eye could see. It was almost as if they had been pulled up by a single and endless invisible thread so uniform was their ascent, and now they hung there like the well-spaced fairylights that adorned the city streets in times of celebration.

After the initial shock a great chanting broke out among the crowds. Some, particularly the children, clapped their hands in delight, while others stepped back in awe. Still more rushed into the sea where they fell to their knees or waded further out to offer up their arms in supplication. The more cautious hastened back to their abodes and locked the doors behind them. Many of the tourists busied themselves photographing the phenomenon.

Neither the jubilation nor the adoration lasted long.

The breeze abruptly transformed into a wind that tugged

330

at their hair and clothing, and a great shout went up when the huge wave approaching from the ocean behind the extended row of lights was noticed. And emerging from the blackness beyond the wave itself was a sight all too familiar to the people who lived along the coasts and the islands of Bangladesh. The swirling white tower of vapour and water rushed towards them with incredible predatory speed (at almost 200 miles an hour, it was later calculated).

The crowds lost all interest in the 'miraculous' lights and fled inland, making for their homes or hotels, the wisest of them fleeing further with the hopes of reaching the sparse high ground.

The preceding tidal surge gathered up the swimmers and the frail fishing boats and swept them on to the land to be smashed against resisting trees and buildings. The cyclone, itself, swiftly followed.

MOUNT PINATUBO, PHILIPPINES

It was as if the night had lost patience with the setting sun, for the land was in gloom even though the day was not yet over. The thick, angry clouds from the mountain cast their shadow everywhere and dust muted the natural colours of vegetation, buildings, vehicles and even animals within a radius of a hundred miles. In Manila, fifty-five miles away from Mount Pinatubo, the people who had ignored the Philippine Institution of Volcanology and Seismology's warning to vacate the city watched the great mantle of smoke with considerable trepidation; tremors had shaken the buildings two days earlier and more were expected to follow. High winds and torrential rain had compounded the fear as well as the damage, but such alarmism could not be allowed to intimidate commerce. Then came the rumour that more than 30,000 Filipino Aeta tribesmen had fled their homeland by the old volcano because a shining omen had been seen above the rim just before smoke and ash had belched forth. While the more sophisticated businessmen of the capital dismissed such primitive superstitions, many of them arranged for their families to spend some time with friends or relations further south or even on one of the other islands. Sensibly (even though these kinds of superstitions had even less effect on them), the Americans were already evacuating Clark Base, headquarters of the US 13th Air Force some fifty-five miles north-west of Manila, and the Subic Bay naval base near Olongapo on the coast. The unease was widespread, the simmering sense of panic barely controlled.

But tribal farmer Micker Ramos ignored all such hysteria and continued to tend his crops at the very foot of the volcano. The rich soil here had served him well over the decades even though he had been forced to flee at the last moment more than once in his lifetime. Damage could often be severe, but always the cycle of replenishment continued. It was true that his family had gone, his two girls and one boy taken by a wife who could no longer suffer the strain of living under this mounting threat. They had both seen the star hovering just above the volcano's lip before the earth had grumbled and black sulphur fumes had obscured it, and he had told her that it was a good sign, a *holy* sign, and that such a thing of radiant beauty could only be a symbol of hope and good fortune. Nevertheless, while he celebrated, she had left, and with her the children and his prize pig. How he would miss that pig.

The day was drawing to a close and the poor light no longer allowed him to work his field anyway, so he rested sitting on the running board of his old Ford truck and gazing up at the great black mountain that he refused to fear. Pinatubo was an old friend who, despite its occasional bouts of tetchiness, should be revered, not dreaded.

For only a second or two the smoke from the crater thinned and Micker jumped up in surprise. *Yes, yes, it was still there, the star was still there!* It was only a tiny pinpoint of light, but it was fiercely striking as it glimmered in the fumes just twenty metres or so above the edge of the volcano. When it had first appeared two days ago, Micker had watched it through a long telescope borrowed from a friend and had been able to see that in reality it was a small, glowing ball, not unlike a wonderful giant sea pearl. And here it was once more, letting him know that all was well, that there was nothing to be afraid of. Oh yes, this was an omen, but it foretold of good things to come, not bad, and perhaps . . . yes, perhaps, like the star of 2,000 years ago, it announced a new birth, the coming of a holy saviour! Micker dropped to his knees in the dirt and clasped his hands together on the truck's running board as if it were an altar rail on which he could pray. He bowed his head and his lips moved with the silent prayer.

He raised his head again when his hands began to vibrate. And he hurriedly pushed himself away from the truck when the whole of its aged bodywork began to rattle.

A strange warmth flushed through his bare feet and lower legs and he stared down at the ground in amazement. The evening was cold and the rolling cloud of smoke above had screened the earth from the sun's rays all day; the field should not have held such heat! Then he heard an ominous groaning.

It seemed to come from below, but Micker faced the true source, Mount Pinatubo itself.

The groaning developed to a bellow, the bellow to a roar, the roar a scream, after which a poisonous shower of ash, mud and pumice stone was expelled from the volcano. The explosion that followed was like a thousand bombs set for the same moment and the farmer clapped his hands to his ears. The sky lit up and the dark rolling clouds turned a furious gold as fire and stone erupted into the atmosphere.

333

Micker was rooted to the spot, too overwhelmed to run, too frozen with fear even to cower. He did not stay rooted for long though: a fissure opened up in the field he had lovingly tended for so long, snaking from one end to the other, across the bumpy, rock-strewn track where his truck continued to shake, and into the jungle beyond; Micker was swallowed along with his truck and burned to nothing by the fiery lava below.

Debris from Mount Pinatubo was thrown fourteen miles into the air and the people of the closest towns used umbrellas and towels around their heads to protect themselves from falling ash and rubble as they fled through the streets. Those who had refused to leave the cities of Angeles, San Fernando and Olongapo before now tried to do so as tremors shook the buildings and pavements and mud slides, made worse by the recent storms, threatened bridges and roads.

But terrifying as the first eruption had been, it could not be compared with the one that swiftly followed. Mount Pinatubo simply blew apart.

The heavens lit up and the blast was heard almost 3,000 miles away. Scientists later calculated that the explosion's force reached more than 30,000 megatons – one million times greater than that of the atomic bomb that had destroyed Hiroshima at the end of World War Two. With this second devastating explosion, rocks and ash were hurled fifty miles into the air and pressure waves circled the globe. Earthquakes and tidal floods quickly followed, and the same fissure that had swallowed up Micker Ramos and his truck stretched another three miles. The cities of Angeles and Guagua, as well as other smaller towns and villages, were reduced to dust-coated rubble, while many buildings in Manila and as far north as Dagupan collapsed under the weight of fallout ash.

The people of the Philippines thought that the end of the world had finally arrived.

25

Hugo Poggs looked in on Eva from the doorway. She was tucked up in bed, pillows fluffed up behind her so that she could sit and scribble on the pad in her lap. She was very quiet and although she responded to his and Bibby's attention well enough, there was a distinct lack of verve in her reaction. Perhaps it was to be expected. In fact, the consulting physician at the hospital had warned that although she appeared perfectly normal when they had arrived to collect her, some form of mild inertia might follow once she was back at home.

Bibby, in a comfortable armchair that had been moved close to the bedside, laid down the book she was reading and peered over her bi-focals at him. 'Shall I make us all some lunch, dear?' she asked.

'Is our Minnie hungry?' Poggs looked expectantly at the child. 'Eva?' he enquired when she offered no reply.

This time she ceased drawing and looked up at him, her face pale, but her eyes still a sparkling blue.

'Would you like something to eat, darling?' Bibby reached for the little girl's hand and held it lightly.

'No thank you, Grandma.' Eva wriggled her hand free and went back to her drawing.

Poggs exchanged glances with his wife and Bibby gave a tiny shake of her head. She rose, kissed the top of her granddaughter's head, and joined her husband in the doorway. 'Eva might try some soup,' she said quietly, looking back at the girl with a troubled frown.

Poggs gave her an encouraging squeeze, aware of just how much she worried about her grandchildren. The loss of their only son, Anthony, for all his faults, had been hard for both of them and, like all such bereaved parents whose offspring had turned out less than perfect, they wondered how much they, themselves, were to blame. He knew that the question had never fully resolved itself in Bibby's mind and the thought of the twins being harmed in any way – particularly because of their horrid start in life as orphan babies in Romania – was the cause of constant concern to her. Diane's phone call early that morning had raised their fears to a wretched level, even though their daughter-in-law had been unable to explain her alarm.

Bibby had grasped the cloth of his shirtsleeve. 'Do you think we should let the hospital know how she is?' she whispered.

He shook his head and kept his own voice low. 'They said to ring if she seemed to be acting strangely, or if she suffered a relapse. The mood she's in at present isn't at all strange for Eva – we've seen both her and Josh like this on other occasions, haven't we? And she doesn't appear to be sleepy, just very subdued, I'd say. Tell you what, old thing, let me see to the food and you go back and sit with her. If she's out of your sight, even for a moment, you'll only worry all the more.'

Bibby smiled at her husband, this big, bluff, *kind* man, who was lost so often in a world of science and geology, yet who

336

cared so much not just for his loved ones but for his fellow-man also. Perhaps it was tiredness compounded by the anxiety over the last forty-eight hours that caused a wave of deep sadness to sweep through her; she laid her head against her husband's broad chest for a moment. He patted her back as though she were a melancholy child and allowed her to rest against him until the mood passed. She listened to the wheeziness of his lungs and was quickly reminded that Hugo was not a fit man despite his superficially robust appearance. Bibby straightened up immediately and gave him a smile that belied her concerns.

'You go ahead then,' she said, 'while I stay with our little dryad.'

'Good girl,' he said, not in the least fooled by her change in manner. Their years together had instilled a natural instinct for each other's feelings and in this circumstance they both shared a sense of foreboding. 'I'll do us a sandwich as well, shall I?' he said, patting her ample bottom as she turned towards Eva again.

'I'm not hungry,' Bibby insisted.

'Neither am I, but I'll make us something anyway.'

He left the room and Bibby heard his heavy footsteps fading down the stairs. She leaned over her granddaughter to brush tousled hair from her forehead and glanced at the picture Eva was drawing at the same time.

It was the usual one. The green lawns filled with playing children. And of course, the pillars they played amongst, just two straight lines with no top.

Wind shook the bedroom window and Bibby noticed rain had begun to fall.

Poggs was at the bottom of the stairs and passing the front door when he heard a noise from the other side. He stopped to listen, holding his wheezy breath in check for a moment so that he could hear better. It sounded as if a vehicle had drawn into the courtyard.

He went to the window in the sitting room and pulled the half-drawn curtain back. 'Good Lord,' he said under his breath when he saw what was outside.

A large, grey Granada was parked out there and three men were climbing out. They were all black, although one, the most smartly dressed of them, had a lighter skin tone. This one opened the rear door on his side and out stepped the largest and blackest woman that Hugo Poggs had ever seen.

He jerked back as a gust of wind rattled the window in its frame and shuddered when he remembered the freak wind of a few nights before that had shrieked through the house as if seeking out those inside.

He leaned forward again and saw that Mack was approaching the group.

26

It was a relief to be out of Gatwick and heading north towards London, for the airport had been chaotic. The information boards were announcing more delays than arrivals and departures and frustrated would-be travellers milled around beneath them, complaining to airline staff and anyone who would listen. From brief snippets of conversation Rivers managed to catch as he and Diane hurried Josh across the concourse, the problems appeared to be with other airports around the world rather than Gatwick itself.

The brown-tinted Surrey fields and woodlands spread into the distance on either side of the motorway and to the west black clouds rolled across the horizon. Insects the size of small stones – and some considerably larger – splattered against the windscreen of Diane's car and she had to use the wipers and water jets frequently to clear the glass. Although still subdued, Josh wanted to know if they were going back to Hazelrod.

Aware that Josh was concerned for his sister, Diane

reassured him that Eva was okay now and safely at home with Grandma and Grandad. His silence told her he was still troubled.

'What is it, Josh?' she asked him. 'Why are you worried so?' She shifted in her seat to see him in the rear-view mirror. He was looking down into his lap.

'I don't know, Mama,' was all he would say.

Rivers reached round and jiggled the boy's knee. 'We'll be back at Hazelrod soon, Josh. Just some business to take care of first, okay?'

There was little response and Rivers faced the front again.

'Do we need to stay long at Pilgrim Hall?' Diane asked as she pulled out into the fast lane to pass a heavy artic that was hogging the centre stretch.

'No,' Rivers promised. 'I'm not sure how I'm going to tell Sheridan, but it'll be brief.'

'What if he needs you to stay there?'

'There'd be no point. There's not a thing any of us can do.'

'But if he insists.'

'I've been looking forward to a career change for some time now.'

She took a quick look at him. 'You don't mean that.'

He sighed. 'Maybe not.' He touched her hand on the steering wheel. 'While I'm talking to Sheridan try and get through to Hugo again.'

Before she could reply she felt a vibration running through the car and, when Rivers' hand dropped away, she could see her knuckles juddering on the steering wheel. 'Not again,' she began to say, 'not here . . .'

They had passed the long lorry and on their left, less than a hundred yards away from the motorway, they saw a steep, grassy knoll. Small clumps of earth were breaking away from it and as they drew closer they noticed deep cracks appearing on its slopes.

The whole car was shaking now and traffic ahead was slowing down as if the drivers thought the problem was with their own vehicles.

'Keep going, Diane,' Rivers urged. 'Keep in the fast lane and don't stop.'

They were almost level with the small hillock when small clods of earth started to erupt from its top. Other vehicles were pulling over on to the hard shoulder as the road itself began to quiver visibly.

'Don't stop,' he said again, his voice low and urgent, as he felt their own speed reduce.

She overtook the Volvo in front on the inside as it slowed down almost to walking pace. Control was awkward and her hands were rigid on the wheel, but she managed to swing back into the fast lane once past the Volvo.

The hillock exploded with the sharp cracking sound of prolonged thunder and steaming water jetted from it in a fountain of raw, pressurised energy. Earth and stones were expelled hundreds of feet into the air.

'*Move!*' Rivers yelled and Diane slammed her foot down in a reflex action. The car shot forward as sizzling droplets of water cascaded down on to its roof and bonnet. She kept going, not daring to look back, avoiding cars, lorries and coaches that were screeching to a halt ahead of her.

'*What the hell is it?*' she shouted over the gushing roar.

'It's impossible,' was all Rivers could reply. He craned his neck and watched the great gusher scream towards the sky, a hundred feet, two hundred, rising and rising. 'Jesus . . .' he said in an exhalation of breath.

Much of the traffic behind them had stopped and the more foolish drivers and passengers were leaving their vehicles for a better view of the phenomenon. He watched them stagger and try to cover their heads with their hands as scalding water rained down on them; those who could frantically clambered back into their vehicles, while others ran through the lines of stalled traffic and across the motorway in pain-stricken panic. He closed his eyes as several of them were struck and flung into the air by oncoming cars, their limbs loose and lifeless before they even smashed back on to the concrete.

The terrible and wholly bizarre scene was quickly left behind as their car sped onwards, although the great water-spout itself, with its blustery clouds of steam spread by the wind, could still be seen rising higher into the air. At least, Rivers reflected grimly, the sight would serve as an ominous warning beacon to other approaching traffic on the motorway. He felt their own speed beginning to slow again.

'Keep going, Diane,' he snapped. 'There's nothing we can do here.'

Diane accelerated once more, but kept glancing into the rear-view mirror. She noticed that Josh was paying no heed at all to the spectacle: he leaned against the side of the car, his eyes on nothing in particular. Her attention was drawn back to the jet of steaming water.

'That can't be a natural geyser,' she said to Rivers.

'It isn't a broken pipeline, I can tell you that. Ordinary pressure could never push it that high – it must be 300 feet or more. Besides, it's coming from a high rise and no frac-tured pipe could cause water to burst through like that from such a deep level.' He paused for a moment, studying the diminishing scene behind them. 'Wait a minute. D'you remember that piece in this morning's paper about the water geyser that had erupted in the middle of a city in India? And what about those things that looked like waterspouts we saw from the plane when we passed over the east coast floodlands?'

'Natural hot water geysers?'

'In unnatural places.'

From her work with Hugo Poggs over the years Diane had a good idea of the areas in the world where such break-throughs could occur, these mainly in volcanic regions, par-

342

ticularly along the edges of continents. Neither India nor England were contenders for such activity.

'This isn't possible,' she said. 'Most of the world's geysers and hot springs are in places like New Zealand, Italy and Japan. Scientists here have been trying to tap this country's geothermal energy potential for years, but with very limited success. Even that's confined to a few areas in the south-west and northern regions where granite formations are suitable for the dry rock development.'

'You're right – this *is* impossible. But look behind you and tell me it isn't happening.'

With that, both of them lapsed into silence, their own thoughts a turmoil of possibilities. Rivers broke that silence only when he had to give Diane fresh directions to Pilgrim Hall.

They left the M23 to join the M25, soon leaving it at the first ramp and taking a circuitous route that led them across a bridge back over the motorway. They followed the narrow, winding lane through thick woodland which led to the long ridgeway that looked over both northern and southern counties. However, he told her to stop the car before they reached the top and the road to Pilgrim Hall.

'Look,' he said, pointing at a break in the woodland that had been cleared for the fine views it offered. From that point they could see straight across the counties as far as the South Downs, beyond which was the sea.

Diane stiffened at the sight below them.

She only saw three of the white towers of water at first, their spray caught by the increasing winds, their height impossible to judge from that distance; then she became aware of others further away, tiny columns that gleamed white against the landscape. There were six at least that they could see, but even as they watched another broke through somewhere near a town that must have been Westerham.

They left the car to see more clearly and, as they walked

further into the clearing, Rivers realised there was something odd about the woods around them. He had often strolled through this area during his lunch-break, for it offered a tranquil respite from the general bustle of the research centre, and he had always enjoyed the sounds of the forest, the singing of birds and the sudden rustle of hidden animals. Now the woods were silent.

He saw no point in mentioning this to Diane, but instead nodded towards the vista below, part of which was once renowned as the Garden of England. 'Don't you see what they look like?' he said in a low voice.

She turned to him, puzzled for the moment.

'Don't you see?' he insisted. 'Those white columns among the fields and woodlands, don't they remind you of something?'

She understood and turned her gaze back to the land below them. 'The pillars in Josh and Eva's gardens,' she said almost to herself. 'This is what they were drawing all along.'

Now they both looked back at Josh's pale face pressed against the car window.

'Where's Sheridan?'

Yet again the secretary who doubled as receptionist at Pilgrim Hall was surprised to see James Rivers standing in her doorway. 'I thought you were . . .' she began to say.

'Yeah, I am on leave,' he interrupted impatiently. 'Just tell me where he is, Margaret.'

She looked past Rivers at the attractive dark-haired woman standing behind him and was further surprised to see a little boy with the most incredibly blue eyes clinging to her skirt.

'*Margaret!*'

She jumped at Rivers' fierce tone. 'I think Mr Sheridan is just about to leave, but he's with Mr Marley at the moment.'

She pushed back her large-framed glasses to the bridge of her nose.

'Is he in Marley's office?'

'I'm not sure.'

Rivers wheeled away and took Diane by the elbow, leading her down the corridor. She gripped Josh's hand tightly and he trotted to keep up with the two adults.

A door opened ahead of them and a short, tubby man dressed in baggy cords and a shortsleeved shirt stepped out. 'Jim.' He sounded both pleased and startled to see the climatologist.

'Jonesy,' Rivers greeted.

'You've come at the right time, boy.' The Welsh lilt was slight, but the excitement in his voice was extreme. 'All hell seems to be breaking loose.'

'I know.' Rivers indicated a room further along the corridor to Diane. 'Use the phone in my office. Dial nine for an outside line.'

She hurried Josh away and Jonesy took a moment to watch her go, an appreciative grin on his broad-cheeked face. 'Very nice,' he said to Rivers.

'I need to see Sheridan.'

'He's pretty involved right now. We've got reports of cyclones, flooding, earthquakes and any other God-awful disaster you'd care to mention coming in from all over. It's as if the bloody world's gone crazy.'

Not quite that, Rivers thought. The room beyond Jonesy was a hive of activity, figures moving about without their usual passive efficiency, voices raised as new pieces of information came in, telephones ringing, computer keyboards tapping. Celia appeared in the open doorway just in time to see Diane and Josh disappearing into Rivers' office. Her expression was quizzical, but before she could even speak, Rivers had brushed past her into the room.

He had caught sight of Sheridan and Marley standing in

front of a bank of television screens whose visual images appeared to be plagued with interference. He stopped only to ask Celia what the problem was.

'Atmospherics,' she told him, still wondering why he had returned to the centre and who the woman and child were. 'We've been having problems with our satellite signals for most of the day.' She had no chance to question him, for he was already making for Sheridan across the other side of the room.

Marley saw him first and muttered something to Sheridan. The Research Director, who was in shirtsleeves and anxiously scribbling notes on to a clipboard, turned to meet Rivers.

'Didn't expect you back this soon, Jim,' he said, slipping his pen into a sheath attached to the clipboard's side. 'But you've arrived at the right time – we need all the help we can get. There's one hell of a mess going on out there and unfortunately some of our communications systems are proving less than reliable.'

'I'm not staying here, Charles. I just need to talk to you.'

Sheridan consulted his wristwatch. 'I'm afraid I don't have time. I've a briefing with the Minister and the Chief Executive in less than forty-five minutes, then we're off to Downing Street for a meeting with the PM. I'm running late as it is.'

'This is important.'

'No can do, Jim. You heard my schedule.'

'Just give me five bloody minutes!'

Marley looked shocked and others in the data room looked up from their computer screens and monitors, or broke off from telephone conversations to see what the extra commotion was about. Sheridan, however, looked no more harassed than he had a moment before.

His voice was calm but had a curt edge to it. 'I've spent all night and most of the morning at the Met Office, assimilating information and dealing with frantic phone calls from ministers

346

and various government officials. I then rushed here to gather up as much first-hand predictive intelligence before my first appointment this afternoon. Bluntly, I'm in no mood to waste time, so if you've anything to tell me you'd better make it quick.'

'In my office.'

'I don't have time . . .' The words were emphasised individually.

'It has to be in private.'

Sheridan brusquely handed the clipboard to Marley. 'Finish up here. Get any information down as it comes in, then bring it along to Rivers' office. Just short, concise notes – the Minister doesn't want anything fancy. I'll read everything myself on the way over to him.' He reached for his light cotton jacket hanging over the back of a chair. 'Okay, Jim, let's get on with it.'

They went to the door together and Jonesy and Celia, who had been watching the whole exchange with bated breath, hastily stepped aside to let them through.

'Do you need us?' Celia asked Rivers as they went out into the corridor.

'No.' The answer was short and the girl flinched. Rivers paused and said more softly, 'There isn't a thing you *can* do, Celia.'

She nodded without understanding and watched the two men stride down the corridor to Rivers' office.

'Did you notice,' she said to Jonesy when the door had closed behind Rivers and the Research Director, 'that he isn't limping any more?'

The Welshman drew his chin into his plump neck and his eyebrows arched. 'I'll be buggered,' he said.

Diane had just switched off the videotape when Rivers and Sheridan entered the room. Josh was sitting quietly in a chair by a filing cabinet.

'Diane,' the Research Director said and, to Rivers'

astonishment, walked round the desk to plant a kiss on her cheek.

'You know each other?' Rivers asked.

'Hugo Poggs and I have been friends for many years,' said Sheridan, sitting in the chair behind Rivers' desk.

Diane went over to Josh and Rivers noticed her face was a little flushed. He returned his attention to the Research Director, his eyes narrowed with puzzlement.

'All right, I may as well tell you now,' Sheridan said. 'I gave Hugo permission to approach you for help. He wouldn't say why it was you in particular he needed, but I have enough respect for the man – and his work – to know he had good reason.'

Rivers was stunned. 'You insisted I take a week's leave . . .'

'Yes, so you could help him. Let's face it, Jim, you weren't being much help around here at the time.'

'I don't get it, Charles.'

Sheridan waved his hands helplessly in the air. 'I couldn't involve myself officially. I'm the Meteorological Office's Research Director, for God's sake. Can you imagine how I'd look if it got out that I was lending one of my own people for an investigation that had more to do with metaphysics than scientific enquiry? I'd be a laughing stock! But frankly, not one of my departments was producing sound results, and I was prepared to try anything.'

'You knew about this?' Rivers' question was directed at Diane.

Her eyes were downcast, but now she looked up at him. 'I'm sorry, Jim.'

'Don't blame her,' Sheridan cut in. 'It was one of my conditions that you shouldn't be told of my connection. I wanted you to go into this without being influenced by the fact that your own boss might believe there was some kind of mystical reason for so many things going wrong with the planet. Hugo and Diane had to agree to that before I gave my consent.'

348

He leaned back in the chair, his hands flat on the desktop. 'Do you really think I would send my best man, no matter how worn out he'd become, on a week's holiday at a time like this? I thought it would be the best way to use you, given the circumstances.'

While the truth sank in, Rivers continued to stare at Diane. Then he shook his head and gave them both a weary smile. 'I suppose it makes what I'm going to tell you a little easier,' he said to Sheridan. 'At least you're prepared for something that might not sound too rational.'

'I'm not sure of that,' Sheridan replied bluntly. 'Hugo never fully explained his reasons for seeking your help and I certainly didn't press him. The truth is I've had problems with some of Hugo's more fanciful theories in the past, but in this instance his great knowledge might have proved useful.' He glanced at his watch and groaned. He tapped a number on the desktop videophone. Because he was using the internal non-visual circuit he announced himself to the receptionist when she answered. 'Have my car outside with the engine running in four minutes.' He broke the connection by touching another button and said to Rivers, 'Okay, you know how long you've got.'

'There's no way –'

'Just get on with it.'

Rivers ran both hands down his stubbled jaw as if composing himself, then swiftly let them drop away. 'You're not giving me enough time to explain everything, but no doubt you're aware of Hugo Poggs' theory that the Earth is a living organism that adapts itself solely for the purpose of sustaining human life.'

'Sure, and I'm aware it's severely damaged Hugo's reputation as far as most scientists are concerned. To be honest, I'm not very happy with it myself.'

'Then now's the time you've got to believe it, because that's what's happening at this very moment. The world is changing itself because of the terrible damage we've inflicted upon it, particularly over the latter half of this century. You might say we finally broke the camel's back and now we're being given a harsh lesson.'

Sheridan was already shaking his head in disbelief, but Rivers pressed on, unperturbed.

'The worst part is that there's nothing we can do now to stop it. We've fucked up our planet and we're paying the price.'

'You said the Earth exists to sustain us. Why isn't it doing just that?'

'You've missed the point. It is. There was a report in this morning's newspaper about plankton rising to the surface of the world's oceans.'

'Yes, yes,' Sheridan said impatiently. 'It's mostly in the northern and southern regions. We're quite mystified.'

'Don't you see? Think of the change it will make to the atmosphere. The planet has increased its own method of controlling the poisons in the air. And maybe it's even showing us a way of helping ourselves. If we could actively encourage the growth of plankton in the seas – mass introduction of fertilisers and iron filings are two ways – then *we'd* be improving the balance by our own efforts.'

'We'd still have to burn fuels for the energy every country needs. We can never escape that vicious circle.'

'No, we're almost within reach of the answer to that problem. Right at this moment we're being given time to develop a limitless source of pollution-free power without using up diminishing natural resources.'

'I take it you're referring to nuclear fusion.'

'That's it.'

'The anti-nuclear lobby wouldn't agree with you.'

'They're misguided. Nothing can prevent our scientific progress and the real truth is that only a small part of it has been harmful.'

'But we're years away from solving the problems of nuclear fusion.'

'And we're being given a breathing space until we do. Just another example of the changes taking place is happening not a couple of miles away from this office. You must be aware of the hot water geysers that are breaking through in places we would have thought impossible before today.'

'Yes, we've had reports of them coming in from all over the world for the past twenty-four hours. It's even happening in desert areas.'

'Then don't you understand? They're a purer source of energy for us, something we can harness and use. We'll no longer be so dependent on fossil fuels. And there'll be other ways of channelling natural energy, I'm sure of that.'

A sharp knock on the door startled them all. The door opened and Marley's head peered round. 'You're going to be awfully late, Charles. I've finished your notes and your car's ready and waiting.'

'Thank God for small mercies,' Sheridan snapped as he quickly rose from the desk. He strode briskly to the door and snatched the clipboard and other papers from Marley. His tone was severe when he turned back to Rivers. 'I'm sorry. I made a big mistake in assigning you to Hugo – as debilitated as you were, you'd have been more use here at the centre. Hugo's a good man, with a fine brain, but he sent you off on a wild-goose chase.' He held up a hand to stop not Rivers', but Diane's protest. 'I don't know where you got these ideas from, Jim, and frankly, I don't want to know. All I can tell you is that they're beyond all natural comprehension.'

'Charles, listen to me . . .'

'*Enough!* How do you think I could explain what you've told me to the PM? For God's sake, he'd not only think I've gone off my rocker and dismiss me instantly, but he'd shut down the whole department also. No, I made a mistake – you've been working too long and too hard and you still haven't got over the trauma of your accident. Now not another word! We'll talk again when things have settled – *if* they ever settle again.'

With that he left the room and they listened to two sets of footsteps receding down the corridor, Marley obviously accompanying the Research Director right to his waiting car. Rivers could imagine the smirk on Marley's face.

He turned to Diane and breathed a resigned sigh. 'And I didn't even tell him all of it,' he said.

27

'You don't seem angry.'

They had reached the research centre's porticoed entrance and Diane and Josh were hurrying to keep up with Rivers.

He stopped before going through the glass doors. 'I spent most of last night thinking over everything the old man had told me, and all this morning worrying about it. But now I've warned Sheridan and given him the opportunity to pass on the information to higher authorities it's as if a weight's been lifted from my shoulders. I didn't expect him to believe it anyway – it sounded crazy even to me. Yet somehow I feel free. Whatever's going to happen will happen and there's nothing anyone can do to stop it. All *we* can do is look after ourselves.'

Diane felt Josh tugging at her skirt. 'Mama, Eva's frightened,' the boy said, his sad eyes piercing into hers.

'I still couldn't get through to Hazelrod,' she said to Rivers. 'Either there's a fault, or the phone's been left off the hook. I know something's wrong, Jim, and so does Josh.'

Rivers crouched so that his face was level with the boy's. 'Okay, Josh. We're going home now. Everything's going to be okay, you'll see.'

He straightened and pushed the door open. The wind hit them immediately and Diane had to grip Josh's hand tightly to help him along.

'I'll drive,' Rivers said when they reached the car. Diane handed him the key and helped Josh into the back seat. She belted him in and hugged him.

'Let's hurry, Jim,' she said as she climbed into the passenger seat. 'I've got a bad feeling about Eva.'

Rivers switched on the engine. 'Josh is spooking you.'

'The Dream Man said the children have to be protected.'

It was pointless to try and comfort her with assurances he hardly felt himself; the main thing now was to get back to Hazelrod as quickly as possible. Rivers checked the petrol gauge and swore under his breath. 'We should have filled up at the airport. Look, there's no service station on the motorway so I'll have to find a garage before we get on to the best route. It'll only take us ten minutes out of our way.'

'Just hurry, Jim.'

Ignoring the grounds' speed restriction, he put his foot down and the car roared along the tarmac drive. He pulled out into the main road with barely a glance to the right and took the road leading down towards the great metropolis. There was a garage he often used not far away and it was this he was headed for.

Less than a minute later it was Diane who was telling him to stop the car and as he slowed down and pulled over he realised why.

They had reached a rare vantage point on the ridgeway that offered a limited view of the sprawling city in the distance. Rivers wondered if there were any more shocks in store for him and the answer was in front of him.

'Oh Jesus Christ . . .' he said, closing his eyes momentarily against the sight.

A great black cloudbank filled the northern sky, its approach steady and plainly discernible. Within it there was shadowy movement as huge vapours tumbled over each other, their turmoil lit by occasional lightning flashes. But as awesomely threatening as was this tenebrous, nocturnal backcloth, it was what it highlighted that sent a chill through Rivers and Diane.

Hanging in the air above the city were seven tiny portents of light.

As Rivers opened his door and stood beside the vehicle, one arm leaning against its roof, he remembered the light he had imagined just before the earth tremor struck and he wondered now if this had been some kind of precognition.

Lightning flashed again inside the disordered clouds, brightening their underbellies, and he heard the thunder rumble among them. Birds in the trees around him took to the air, their cries shrill and piercing as they scattered here and there, swooping and soaring in disarray, some of them plummeting to the ground where they dashed themselves against the road.

The thunder, barely audible under the shrieking of the birds, faded. But a new kind of thunder had roused itself. And this was from the earth itself.

The city below began to quiver.

Lightning flashed again and this time it escaped the confines of the cloudbank to capture the small lights below in its glare. For a brief moment the seven lights disappeared, absorbed into the mass, becoming one with it; but when the lightning's force had been spent, they were left with tiny flickering lines of electricity emanating from them, jagged lines which grew bolder and stronger so that they stretched through the sky to join with each other, linking the shining orbs and forming a thin web of light over the city.

The low rumbling swelled and sky thunder joined its roar once more.

To Rivers' eyes it was as if the whole city had become unfocused, the buildings and towers shivering in a paroxysm that failed to ebb.

The first tall building began to topple.

GUMRI, ARMENIA

A cloud of dust hung over the shattered city as rescuers dug into the rubble with bare, bleeding hands, occasionally stopping to listen for the faint cries of survivors buried below. They used crowbars to raise the steel girders and pickaxes to smash through collapsed woodwork and debris. From the northern city of Kirovakan to the Turkish border near Kars, towns, villages and the land itself had been devastated by the earthquake's savage force. The deeply religious Armenian people had thought that the tiny star that had appeared just before the tremor began was a sign that God would end the persecutions and misfortunes that had blighted their and their forebears' lives for the past century, and the earthquake that followed told them they were wrong.

Yet still they prayed as they tore and scratched at the ruins; and screamed in terror when the first aftershock struck.

357

PESHTIGO, WISCONSIN

Nobody could remember a longer drought in the history of America's Midwest and for months small and, at least, containable fires had plagued the pine forests along Green Bay near the borders of Wisconsin and Michigan. But on this day, when star-like lights had appeared over the treetops, high winds had united the scattered blazes into one huge conflagration that advanced on the lumber town of Peshtigo as a massive wall of searing heat. As the townfolk fled, their houses crumpled like paper and rooftops flew into the air to become fireballs themselves. Many of the people tried to escape in cars and trucks, but the fierce heat melted tyres and cracked windscreens; others took to the Peshtigo River, submerging themselves but perishing the moment they surfaced and inhaled air that had, itself, become incendiary. The driven fire created an enormous updraught and hurricane-force winds whirled through the region, destroying everything in their paths. Onwards they sped, vortexes of wind and fire, hungry for nourishment, bent on total destruction.

Above it all a vast cloud of smoke darkened the morning sun, changing its brightness to a dark red hue, the colour of running blood.

KASHI, CHINA

The city had once been an important oasis on the Silk Road trade route to central Asia, but was now the economic centre of Xinjiang. Before it sprawled the great Taklimakan Desert, 130,000 square miles of shifting sands, and reports had arrived with desert-travellers of a strange light that glowed above the dunes. It shone, they said, with the pureness of a star and the glitter of a rare jewel. The more curious citizens set out to discover this wondrous thing for themselves, unconcerned that the way would be dark; those too idle, or too sceptical, to embark on such a mission bade the wanderers to bring back proof of the phenomenon – photographs or even the object itself, if that were possible.

Many watched the great desert from balconies or high windows, waiting for the bold ones to return with tales and evidence of this marvel, and as they watched they became aware of an immense yellowish wall that loomed out of the darkness to advance on the city like some colossal tidal wave. But this was not from the distant ocean; this was from the desert itself. This *was* the desert itself.

It was as if the strong winds from the east had coaxed the sand to rise up as a whole and transport itself through the night to smother every town and village in its path in an avalanche of grit and dust. Even the hills around the city could not contain its force and when the sandstorm, a mile high and many more across, struck Kashi, frail buildings collapsed and people and vehicles still on the streets were tossed into the air to be buried by sand within seconds wherever they came to rest. Soon only the top lights of the hardiest buildings could be seen and these too were extinguished when the spinning sand clogged the city's power stations.

CALABRIA, SOUTHERN ITALY

They thought the sun had found a playmate. The smaller sun – much too high for its size to be determined – spiralled around its larger counterpart and the workers in the olive groves shielded their eyes from its glory. Only when clouds scudded across the natural sun's face did they understand that the smaller one was within the Earth's own confines and that it was not some faraway playful planet. A spaceship, they murmured. Others disagreed. A fire devil, they opined. An Angel of Death, muttered an old woman whose hands were gnarled and disfigured from more than seventy years working the fields and orchards, and whose face was leathered and wrinkled from those same years under the burning sun. The peasants (and peasants they were, for Calabria's three provinces, Cosenza, Catanzaro and Reggio di Calabria, had never caught up with modern industry and even the mountainous terrain sought to hinder their mainstay olive trade) looked on as the mysterious light suddenly dropped to a point just above the treetops.

It was then that the very ground began to moan. A donkey grazing beneath the shade of the trees raised its old dusty head, then spread its legs as if bracing itself. The noises from the earth faded and everyone was very still and very quiet. The old woman deftly touched her forehead, chest and shoulders with her thumb, the self-blessing a protection against the horror she suspected was to come. The moaning resumed, this time instigating wails of fear among the tremulous peasants. One of them broke away, an idiot son of an idiot father, and ran for the dirt-track that was the olive grove's only access, but the others were weakened by their own fright and could only watch as shrubs and trees began to move from their roots. The ground rose and fell in orderly furrows like the waves of the sea. Now they screamed and the donkey brayed as they lost their balance and fell. A fissure opened beneath them and several of them plunged into it. Trees leant precariously, their roots exposed and those in line with the fissure plunged into its jaws only to be spat out again on scalding geysers of gaseous mud, for the rupture had tapped into deep springs of boiling water.

The tremors spread throughout the three provinces and the earth erupted, releasing more springs and blistering mud. Before long the entire region was moist from rolling steam mists.

TOPEKA, KANSAS

The tornado hit the capital city of Kansas in the early hours of the morning just as the state assembly was gathering for its emergency debate on the UFOs that had been clearly sighted here, there and everywhere over the territory for two consecutive nights. The building was hurriedly evacuated as the storms tore in and the Kansas National Guard stood by on full alert, not to help the worthy citizens, but to prevent looting from the damaged stores and private dwellings once the worst had passed. It was not a single tornado that swept through the Midwest, but a series of them, all wreaking their own separate havoc and demolition, one flattening a whole caravan park, another destroying the hospital wing of a military base, all of them carrying people, lampposts, hoardings, cars – anything caught out in the open – hundreds of feet into the air, wrecking the less sturdy buildings, sweeping away livestock and turning rivers, some of which had almost run dry, into raging torrents.

As well as Kansas, the winds and rain roared through Oklahoma, Nebraska and Louisiana, deadly swathes of destruction that for the time being obliterated all thoughts of weird flying lights and strange encounters.

TOKYO, JAPAN

While the citizens of Tokyo observed the three mystic lights that had appeared in the cloudy night sky over the city, nineteen miles below them a part of the Earth's crust was shifting dramatically. The shockwave that rose to the surface was equal to thirty Hiroshima-sized nuclear explosions. Great chasms opened up in the roads, trains were derailed, and thousands of panic-stricken people were killed or maimed by falling masonry, glass and even water tanks (mercifully, the newer buildings of the city had been built to absorb and withstand the worst of tremors, so damage to property was limited) or crushed by the fleeing hordes. But it was the fires caused by broken gas pipes, oil storage tanks, Calor gas heaters, vehicle petrol tanks and cooking stoves that inflicted the worst damage.

Soon the shanty slums of Hongo were ablaze, as was the Shitamachi area of the city, whose narrow lanes of wooden houses fed the hungry fires so that they spread and merged with those of other districts. It wasn't long before a huge wall of flame was moving through the city and many of the people were forced to leap into ponds and rivers. And so were boiled alive.

ZAFFERANA ETNEA, SICILY

The procession made its way up the mountainside towards the advancing lava flow. The people from the village chanted their hymns while at their head four of the menfolk concentrated on keeping the statue of the Madonna upright on its makeshift wooden platform. The route was winding and arduous, but Zafferana's priest resolutely led them onwards. Hundreds of mines detonated by the Italian military, aided by the US Marine Corps, had failed to redirect the lava flow and even the two-ton concrete blocks carefully placed by American helicopters were unable to divert the unremitting advance. Padre Giuseppe Pacello, however, was undaunted, for faith – and holy statues – had stemmed the burning tide's advance twice before in years gone by. Mongibello (the mountain of mountains) was the villagers' name for Mount Etna and less

than a decade before the white-hot lava from openings in its rugged slopes had stopped only metres away from the first few houses. The Blessed Virgin had saved them then and on another occasion, and so would she this time. Much of the chestnut woods and orchards further up was already covered by pulsing black molten rock and the smell of sulphur was so thick and pungent that the children and old folk, whose lungs could not cope with such pervasion, had been evacuated to other places far away from the danger zone.

They halted just twenty feet from the oozing lava, hands shielding their faces from the hot glow, and followed their priest's example by dropping to their knees on the stony track. They sang the Lord's and His Virgin Mother's praises, voices swelling with emotion, eyes shining with desperation. It had taken the flow a matter of weeks to reach this point after the initial eruption, the fastest advance in their recorded history, and they knew their homes would be threatened within days. Padre Giuseppe indicated that the Madonna should be placed alone between his flock and the lava and, their backs turned towards the heat, the four men shuffled forward to set down their burden a mere ten feet from the flow. Bushes nearby burst into flames as the men retreated. Now the priest urged his people to pray even harder for their salvation, and this they did with vigour and fortitude, some of them covering their mouths with handkerchiefs and scarves against the acrid stench, others edging to the back so that their companions' bodies would protect them from the worst of the heat. Together they beseeched their Lord and His Mother for divine intervention.

The statue of the Madonna began to blacken. Its face grew dark, the hands, held palms outwards in supplication, began to crack. Wisps of smoke began to rise from the wooden platform. But the miracle they prayed for started to happen. Or so they thought.

The tiny halo appeared over the head of the Madonna, a

white radiance whose centre resembled a round communion wafer. Now the eyes of the farmers and villagers shone with joy and wonder and their mouths opened in silent cries of adoration. The priest raised his face to the heavens that at present were soiled with smoke and ash, for here before them was the sign they had been waiting for. Zafferana and the land around it would be saved!

He was stretching his arms towards the blackened sky in gratitude when the Madonna disappeared before them. But this was no mystery, for the ground had opened up without warning, without even a sound or a trembling of the earth, and swallowed the statue and platform whole. The bright halo light, however, remained where it was. Until a jet of white-hot lava spewed from the newly created hole and consumed the light as it rose high into the air.

The people of Zafferana and their priest scuttled back down the mountainside, but very few escaped the searing rain of fire that fell from the terrible burning fountain. And the lava moved doggedly onwards towards the village.

LAKE NYOS, CAMEROON

They had flocked there from the village to see for themselves the little star that flittered over the big brown lake. It was mud and iron hydroxide that stained the surface of the normally blue Lake Nyos during this part of the season, but the villagers were unconcerned with such explanations, preferring to believe that the waters had grown old and weary with the passing of the year and were about to die only to be reborn, fresh and clear, when the days grew cooler. That phenomenon had been witnessed many times, but this god-light had never played a part in the rebirth before. They pointed at the light as it flitted here and there and they jabbered and nudged each other excitedly. The word spread and their numbers swelled to 2,000 or more as others heard the tale and journeyed to its source. They uttered a great collective sigh as a bubbling and belching breath emanated from the lake, then cried and held their noses when a white cloud smelling of rotten eggs rose from the depths. An ever-widening ripple swept towards the shore and those at the water's edge stepped back in fright.

The light was faint and ghost-like through the mist that drifted towards them. The cloud soon enveloped them where they stood and they began to feel a warmness spread through them; one by one, men, women and children, they began to fall to the ground as a pleasant drowsiness overcame them. They were not to know that the gases, which included carbon dioxide, had seeped into the water from below, for the lake occupied what had once been a volcanic crater. Those gases remained at the bottom of the lake, trapped in the cooler water there, to be released during the monsoon season when cooling surface water sank to the bottom and displaced the now warmer water which, along with the gases it contained, rose to the top.

They weren't to know this, nor did those few who survived wish to hear it, for they preferred to believe that the Death Star had visited their people and warned them to mend their ways. No one could tell those left alive that they were wrong in this, and not too many tried.

. . . And so it continued, throughout the day and throughout the night, upheavals that would irrevocably change the planet's environment. California's San Andreas fault finally lived up to its full and lethal promise, the golden state torn asunder from Cape Mendocino to Imperial Valley, destroying

365

the cities of San Francisco and Los Angeles, as well as Daly City, Hollister and Bakersfield. A tidal wave hit Osaka in Japan, not even its sophisticated system of storm barriers saving the port city from devastation; another *tsunami*, caused by seismic faulting on the sea floor, swamped the Hawaiian island of Oahu, the waves returning again and again until not one building or tree on Kawela Bay was left standing. Another convulsion beneath the sea, this one in the English Channel, fractured the long and much-troubled tunnel rail link between England and France, causing the deaths of hundreds as they travelled through on high-speed trains. Hurricanes swept along the whole chain of Leeward and Windward Islands, the worst damage rendered to Antigua and Barbuda; storms also tore through Cuba, flattening buildings and vegetation, killing people and animals in their thousands. Earthquakes rocked Armenia, Iran, Afghanistan, Thailand, Indonesia, Peru, Chile and, more surprisingly, South Africa and Madagascar. Chicago and the Pyrenean village of Rébénacq were pummelled by hailstones as big as footballs, while Yellowstone Park's Mount Jackson shrugged off thousands of tons of rock in dusty torrents in the aftershock following a tremor that shook the whole state of Montana. Three mountain islands rose from the depths of the Indian Ocean, their emergence causing tidal waves along the southern tip of India, Sri Lanka and Somalia. Mount St Helen's, never entirely dormant after its last eruption only a few years before, shot a blast of ash-filled steam and gas into the air at a speed of 700 miles per hour, snapping off trees from its slopes to scatter them like straws over a vast area, while a molten lava stream arced from the side of Hawaii's Kilauea volcano into the sea before the entire top of the open mountain sank into its own bubbling centre. A volcano in Iceland known as Laki tore open a thirty-mile-long fissure, lava pouring from it into the Skafta River, replacing water with molten rock that overflowed the river valley; twenty miles wide, the lava

366

moved on at incredible speed, filling a large lake and two other river valleys, melting huge quantities of glacial ice which flooded the land, the steam created causing torrential rain that contributed to the flooding.

In many regions the sky was full of lightning and thunder, bolts strafing the air, joining earth to cloud with numerous simultaneous streaks. New York's Empire State Building was struck no less than sixty-five times during a single hour-long thunderstorm; eleven sightseers on an observation platform in one of Kenya's game parks were hit by lightning, six of them killed instantly, the others burned severely; a hole was melted through a bell inside a church tower in Ohio; in Ireland potatoes were cooked in their fields; many fires were started in forests all over the world, particularly in Canada, and a great ring of fire threatened the city of Sydney, Australia, and its suburbs when lightning set the surrounding woodlands ablaze. Lightning penetrated a reserve fuel tank in the wing of a 747 jetliner over Miami, igniting the vapours and sending the aeroplane plummeting; all passengers and crew were killed. An immense ethereal aurora appeared over Canada's Yukon Territory and auroral fires lit up Alaska's skies, their colours a beautiful blue-green merging to purple and mauve. High above Kiruna in Sweden, the northern lights swirled in a spectral 'folded ribbon' shape of blues, greens and indigos, and this during sombre daylight hours.

Tremendous gushers of boiling water burst through the ground everywhere, many of them in the unlikeliest, if not impossible, places: towering geysers erupted in Africa's Sahara and Namib Deserts as well as in Monument Valley and the Sonoran Desert, Arizona; geysers sprang from the Bande-e Amir lakes *10,000 feet above sea level* in the Hindu Kush Mountains of Afghanistan as well as from the limestone plateau in Chad's Tibesti Massif: smaller, but no less impressive, springs bubbled from the almost dry Valley of Antarctica, while giant geysers appeared in the Thar Desert

in north-west India and the bleak Denakil Depression of north-eastern Ethiopia; others, some as high as 380 feet, appeared in Australia's Gibson and Great Victoria Deserts, at the edge of China's Altyn Tagh range and the Taklimakan Desert in the Sinkiang Province. In these places and countless others the great geysers jetted into the air, each of them having the power to change the environment and the quality of the land around them.

And prior to all these calamitous and astonishing events, strange lights were observed. Some claimed to have seen only a single but wonderfully bright star, while others swore there were clusters of lights performing in odd ways, skimming erratically through the sky, circling each other, soaring up to the heavens to glide earthwards again without ever touching the ground; a few said the stars had joined together as one mass of shining light . . .

28

The journey to Hazelrod was long and arduous. The roads near to London were jammed with traffic as those who were able to fled the ruined capital, afraid of the aftershock that might follow the earthquake. Emergency services called in from the closest counties rushed by in the opposite direction, lights flashing, sirens wailing. Private vehicles headed towards the disaster area too, and Rivers could only surmise that the drivers were either ghoulish sightseers or those who had family or friends caught up in the earthquake. Perhaps others merely wanted to help.

After filling up with petrol, Rivers had avoided the motorway completely, deciding the minor roads might be less congested. And so they were, but only relatively so.

In exposed stretches the wind, which had strengthened considerably, rocked the car and bent the branches of trees. The sky had darkened even more as the clouds hurried south: they were black turbulent masses that hid the sun and turned daylight into dusk. Rain had begun to fall in torrents and was

whipped by the wind into a driving force that beat at the windscreen and roof of the car. Thunder rolled in the distance and each time they heard it, Rivers and Diane wondered if the sound was from the skies or the earth below.

They drove past accidents more than once, cars jammed into each other because their drivers had been distracted by their own concerns or by the pelting rain. More fire engines roared past them in both directions and at other times it was ambulances or police cars. Sometimes it was all three together. Diane switched on the radio, but interference was so bad from local radio stations that they soon gave up trying to listen. From the main London frequencies there was nothing at all.

When they had travelled quite a distance and were approaching the town of Guildford, the car began to vibrate. They pulled over to the side of the road but the tremor did not last long. It hadn't been strong, but it increased their tension.

Diane checked on Josh to find him sleeping. His face was pale and occasionally his lips moved as if he were carrying on a conversation in his dream. She thought it wise to leave him be even though his sleep seemed troubled.

Their journey took them through country towns and villages, some of whose streets were deserted as if the residents were hiding from something more than just the storm. In a few of the larger towns the roads were blocked solid with traffic with perhaps one policeman or traffic warden trying to sort out the mess and inevitably making it worse. Rivers asked Diane to try the radio again and this time, although static was still bad, they managed to catch snatches of news. The obvious topic was the London earthquake, but the newscaster on the local frequency they had picked up gave reports of other global disasters, many of them as cataclysmic as England's.

'Now perhaps they'll understand,' Rivers had commented

and Diane was not sure if he meant Sheridan and those he had to advise, or the world in general. She switched off when the interference worsened and they drove on in silence. It took a long time to work through some of the traffic's snarl-ups, but after a while they found themselves on open roads. Diane tried to reach Hazelrod again from a remote telephone box in one of the lanes they were passing through; she returned to the car frowning and shook her head when Rivers raised his eyebrows at her. By now she was desperately worried and urged him to make better progress, but because of the conditions there was little he could do to hasten their journey.

They saw lightning flashes, mostly on the horizon, and the clouds were low and heavy. Now and again the rain eased, but this was due to shifts in the wind rather than an alleviation in the downpour. Once or twice they saw in the distance more of the white steaming towers of boiling water rising from open countryside or cultivated fields. The thunder was moving closer and a cornfield they were passing suddenly blazed as a lightning bolt struck it; the persistent rain soon doused the fire, but the event triggered something in Rivers' mind.

'The lights we saw over the city,' he said, diverting Diane's attention from the still-sleeping boy.

'The warnings? What about them, Jim?'

'Lightning rises from the earth or grounded object to the sky, not the other way round as most people imagine. It's caused when the negatively charged base of a cloud induces a positive charge from the ground and the current leaps up along the conductive channel of negative particles from above.'

'The energy came from the lights themselves?'

'I think so.'

'But the lightning also joined them together.'

'Some kind of chain reaction between positive and negative. The lights must contain both.'

'You're saying these things are more than just pretty illuminations?'

'They're full of concentrated energy, don't you see?'

She did see, but wasn't sure where the notion led them. The Dream Man had told Rivers that the lights were portents, warnings that something was about to happen, without explaining their origin. 'Then I don't understand where this energy comes from,' she said. 'They have to have a source . . . don't they?'

Rivers did not reply. He kept his eyes on the road ahead, but Diane could tell by his expression that his mind was a turmoil of thought. Then he said, 'I think they come from us.'

The main street of the next village they came to was blocked by fallen masonry; they soon learned that the area had suffered an earth tremor powerful enough to demolish the spire and tower of the village's ancient church. It took quite a time for Rivers to reverse and find another route that would lead them back on to the right roads again.

The blackened sky was lit up by lightning flashes every few minutes or so by now, with no indication that the storm would soon pass, and Diane began to wonder just how much longer Rivers could continue this nightmare journey; he'd had little sleep the night before and had been exhausted when he had returned to the hotel. She offered to take over the wheel, but he declined; he told her he preferred to be doing something while the world around them went to hell.

They had to stop several times and use other roads when the way ahead was flooded; and sometimes the sheer force of the rain obscured their vision totally, despite the overworked wipers, and they were forced to halt and wait for the worst to pass. Eventually they were within a mile of Hazelrod, but by now night had fallen and added to the darkness around them.

And before they had reached the muddy track that would lead them to the house, Josh started screaming.

He steadied himself as the walls around him, the roof above him, and the ground beneath him shuddered. He felt the vibration course through his thin legs, but he was no longer afraid. At least, he was not as afraid as he had been.

The final moment was nearly here.

The final moment for him.

But perhaps a new beginning for mankind.

If those who laboured towards a different outcome were defeated.

And if they learned the lesson of this terrestrial holocaust.

A deeper judder nearly sent the old man backwards, but he recovered and staggered to the door. Once outside he took five steps forward and stopped. From above he heard the shrill cry of the eagle. Was it leaving this valley in search of a safer abode as the other birds had? Surely it was protected on the high ground? But no, rocks would have tumbled, crevasses would have opened, and nowhere was safe. Better to seek new ground, for food alone would be hard to find for some time.

The roaring was from both directions, his keen ears told him, a seething maelstrom of sound, a rushing storm of water; but one was closer.

The Great Glen had finally succumbed to the wise man's prophecy. The Earth itself had shifted along the massive trench rift and the seas from both shores were pouring in to fill the deep channel it had created. Ah, pity those who had perished either in the eruption itself, or now, under the deluge as ocean and sea raced to join with each other. He prayed for their souls, and he prayed for the lives of those left behind, not just here in these rugged regions of the north, but for those who would survive the Earth's grand tragedy, for there would be much for them to accomplish once peace returned and the terrible forces were rested once more, much for them to sow, and much for them to learn again. The world, they would find, was to be a different place.

If . . .

He shuffled around to his right, wind and rain pounding at his upturned face, for there the noise was loudest. It was from there, along that long and thin gulley that eventually led to the western coast and the Atlantic Ocean that the waters would arrive first.

The trembling of the land had ceased, but it was the old man himself who trembled now as fear returned. Yes, he knew fear, for death itself was invariably painful and the paradise that was waiting was hard to contemplate at such a time. Still he prayed, and not for himself: he prayed for those who, at this very moment of earthly metamorphosis, fought the evil that sought to destroy. The evil that endeavoured to end it here. In the hands – in the minds – of the innocents lay mankind's destiny and only their champions could deliver them from the physical malevolence that conspired against them. He thought of the one who had found him only yesterday, a man who knew suffering, and one who bore the frailties and weaknesses so inherent in the human race, yet still had the goodness in him

374

to achieve so much; and he wondered if this man was resolute enough to succeed. His task, like that of so many others around the world, was to help the little ones to assert their power. But would he – would they be firm enough in spirit? Some would lose, the law of uncertainty decreed that. But others would win through and he prayed there would be enough of them.

Yet the answer to this he would never know. At least, not in this world would he know.

He heard his animals bleat their terror as they fled or sought false sanctuary within the walls of the cottage and he felt sadness for them. Just as he felt pity for every living creature in this wonderful but abused planet. His blind old eyes wept for them even though it was too late for such pity.

He fell to his knees as the waters rushed into the valley towards him, and its booming terror took any other sounds from his ears.

And when they crushed his weary body he welcomed the oblivion and hoped for the paradise.

29

'Hush, Josh, it's just a bad dream. Everything's okay now, we're nearly home.'

Rivers had stopped the car so that Diane could climb into the back and comfort her near-hysterical son.

'The witch . . .' Josh was saying over and over again '. . . she's waiting . . . she's here . . .'

The interior light was on and Rivers could see the stark terror in the boy's eyes and the drawn whiteness of his face.

'There's no witch, Josh,' Diane told him soothingly. 'You've had a nasty dream, like the one you had the other night, that's all.' *On the night they had been unable to wake Eva,* she reminded herself. *Had they both had the same nightmare?* 'Not far to go now, Josh, just a little ways. Don't you want to see Eva? I bet she's wide awake waiting for us to come home.'

Josh clutched his mother even more tightly. 'The witch lady, Mama, Eva knows the witch lady.'

Diane looked at Rivers in desperation.

'Maybe he'll calm down once he's back in familiar surroundings,' he said quietly to her. 'It's hardly surprising he's in a state with everything we've seen today.'

Diane nodded. 'Let's get him home.'

Rivers swung round and engaged gear once again. Although the wind still nudged the car, the rain had become a drizzle, and the headlights cut through the darkness, rendering the trees and shrubbery peculiarly one-dimensional. Josh's cries had become a weary whimpering by the time Rivers turned the car into the muddy track leading down to Hazelrod. By the time they pulled into the courtyard, he was quiet.

Rivers slammed down on the brake just inside the entrance, sending Diane and her son sliding forward in their seats. She stopped them both from slipping on to the floor by pushing her elbow against the back of Rivers' seat. She looked at him in surprise, then followed his gaze towards the house. In all there were three cars inside the courtyard: Hugo Poggs' Toyota, Mack's pick-up parked across the yard outside his apartment over the stables, and a metallic grey Granada. But it was something lying close to the porch steps that Rivers was staring at.

Diane spoke with a flat kind of dread in her voice. 'It looks like a body,' she said, then added, 'Oh God.'

Advancing slowly, his foot soft on the pedal, Rivers swung the car around slightly so that the lights played fully on the object on the ground. He brought the car to a gentle halt.

'I think it's . . .' Diane began to say, but he had already switched off the engine and opened the door.

'Wait here,' he told her.

'No, I'm coming with you.' She was out of the car and moving towards the body before he could protest. Rivers turned before he got out to warn Josh to stay where he was and it was at that moment that flash lightning lit up the car's interior. Josh was frozen in that brief, flickering blaze: he could have been made of white marble, he was so still and pale, his eyes wide but not moving. The light was soon gone, but the thought lingered on: with his shock of black hair against his pallid skin, Josh had looked like a tiny elfin-creature from a child's storybook. Thunder rumbled somewhere in the distant hills.

Rivers left the car and quickly caught up with Diane who, by now, was standing over the slumped body. Something – perhaps her own apprehension – was preventing her from stooping to see who it was.

Rivers gently drew her aside, then knelt beside the body. 'It's Mack,' he said before he had even touched a shoulder to roll the body face up.

'Dear God . . .' Diane quickly knelt beside Rivers. 'I thought it was Mack, but how –'

'Oh shit,' said Rivers as the burly handyman's eyes stared sightlessly up at them. Rivers had moved slightly so that the car's headlights were unimpeded by his own body, and now they both saw the neat dark line beneath Mack's throat where blood drained mostly from one corner to run like a small river between the cobblestones of the yard, the drizzling rain diluting the flow.

'Get back into the car,' Rivers ordered Diane as he pulled her to her feet.

'Mack . . . oh my God, why . . . who would –?'

He gripped her tightly above the elbows and pushed her towards their car. Josh's small face was watching them from behind the glass. 'I want you to wait in the car, Diane.' Rivers' command was calm but insistent. 'Sit in the driver's seat, switch on the engine, and wait for me. Understand?'

'No, I've got to –' She tried to break away, but he held her firmly.

'Do as I tell you. Let me find out what's happened inside first.' He opened the driver's door and, using considerable force, pushed her in. He bent over her, a heavy hand on her shoulder. 'If you hear anything that doesn't sound right, or

378

if you see there's trouble, I want you to get away from here to a neighbour's or a phonebox and call the police. *Listen* to me, Diane.'

With an effort she looked away from the body and stared up at Rivers. 'I'm afraid, Jim. Eva . . .'

'It's important that you stay out here. D'you understand me?'

She nodded her head slowly, but he still kept his hand on her shoulder.

'Turn the car around so you're facing the gates. Remember, if you see or hear anything you don't like, get out fast. Josh, I want you to watch the house too.'

Josh regarded him gravely and all Rivers could see was the boy's eyes staring out at him from the shadows.

He squeezed Diane's shoulder and left the car, closing the door quietly even though he knew it was too late for such a gesture – if there was anyone inside Hazelrod they would have heard the car drive up, or at least have seen the headlights sweeping in. Lightning flashed through the night sky again and the thunder that followed was nearer, and louder. Surprisingly, lightning flared again, even as the thunder rumbled on and the house was lit up in an eerie strobe effect. The sight reminded Rivers of all the clichéd horror movies he had seen when that particular cinematic trick had seemed laughable rather than scary; unfortunately there was nothing funny about this moment.

The porch door was swinging slightly in the wind and he held it steady as he went through. Although there was no light on inside the porch, a faint brightness came from behind the lace curtains of the entrance door. He moved forward, gripped the door handle, turned it, and pushed.

The soft light from a small lamp on a hallstand lit the scene inside and Rivers' first instinct was to close the door again and get the hell out of there. His next instinct, however, was to help Hugo Poggs, who was slumped against the wall, his eyes closed, but his chest heaving as he drew in shallow wheezing breaths. His wife's prone body lay across his lap.

Rivers opened the door wider and quietly stepped inside. Another body was propped up against the bottom steps of the stairway, the wooden handle of a knife – it looked like a kitchen knife, one of those with a strong broad blade that was used for carving meat – sticking out of one shoulder, just above the man's chest. The blood that stained his shirt and ran down between his outstretched legs was congealing into a slick dark mess, and only the whites of his eyes showed beneath his half-closed lids. These looked whiter than normal, for the man himself was black. To Rivers he looked very dead.

More than ever he wanted to retrace his steps back to the car. More than ever he wanted to leave Hazelrod and take Diane and Josh with him. But he knew he couldn't leave Poggs like that, nor Bibby. And besides, Eva was somewhere in the place. Unless, of course, she had been snatched away. He remembered Josh's dream – the little cottage in the middle of a darkly weird forest, the witch lady who waited for the children inside – and quickly chided himself for the foolishness. A child's nightmare was one thing, the situation here another. Rivers went in and, keeping his attention solely on the black man's corpse, edged his way over to Hugo Poggs.

He was almost beside the geologist and his wife when he thought he heard a noise from upstairs. He paused and listened. No other sounds. Save for Poggs' wheezing breath. Rivers crouched next to the geologist, who opened his eyes in alarm. The fear stayed there in his eyes for several moments and it didn't quite leave even when he recognised Rivers.

'Hugo, what happened?' Rivers kept his voice low without knowing why.

Poggs' lips moved, but the window at the end of the hall blazed silver-white and thunder, so near and so loud that the window frame rattled, boomed through the night. Rivers leaned closer to catch the half-conscious man's words.

'Eva . . .' Poggs rasped. 'Upstairs . . . she has her . . .' He began to cough and for the first time Rivers saw the blood seeping from the geologist's plump stomach into Bibby's grey dishevelled hair. He tried to turn her head, for her face was buried deep into Poggs' lap, but something felt wrong, the head was too loose, somehow too flexible. He let go, then put his hands beneath Bibby's shoulders and lifted.

Her plump breasts flattened against his own chest as he held her, and her head fell backwards as if she were in a lover's swoon; the angle of her neck was too acute, too distorted and he grimaced as he realised it was broken.

'Barbara . . .' Poggs murmured, and one of his hands fluttered in the air as he tried to touch her. It fell uselessly back to the floor, palm upright, fingers curled. Rivers laid Bibby's heavy body to one side and turned back to her husband.

'Who did this, Hugo?' he asked urgently, his voice still low.

Poggs tried to raise himself to a sitting position, but only managed to push himself further up against the wall. He drew in a long, hoarse breath, the wind whistling into his lungs. His shoulders hunched against the pain and one hand, lifted now in reflex action, clutched not at the bloody wound of his stomach, but at his chest. 'Oh God, it hurts,' he said feebly.

When Rivers pulled away the buttons of Poggs' shirt so that he could examine the wound, he began to understand that it was not the cuts to his body that had left the geologist in this state, for although there were several slashes, they were mainly small and superficial, but the man's belaboured heart that was causing the problem. The draining of blood from Poggs' usually ruddy face, the purplish tinge to his cheeks and the slight blueness of his lips confirmed his suspicion that the injured man had suffered a heart attack. He leaned closer to listen as Poggs tried to speak again.

'Help Eva . . . upstairs . . . we tried to . . . to stop . . . her . . .'

He said more, but lightning bleached the sky outside once again and thunder cannoned directly overhead and seemed to rush through the very house itself. And as it slowly rumbled away, somebody came out of the room at the end of the hall.

Nelson Shadebank had flushed the toilet as the thunder struck. The sound from overhead had made him jump and he cursed the country, the weather, and the plane journey over that had upset his system so. But most of all he cursed Mama Pitié for draggin' him halfway 'cross the world to terrorise a kid that knew doodlesquat. What the hell was she playin' at? Three people dead, one of them their own, another on his way: and for what exactly? What the fuck were they doin' in this place? He had zipped his fly and was hoisting one strap of his red braces over his left shoulder as he opened the toilet door. Shit-scared he might be of Mama, but enough was enough. He was goin' to split soon as the right moment came, soon as she was too busy to see him go. Like right now, mebbe. Take the hire car and blow. Mebbe stay in this country, find a new life. No, wrong move. Git out, sure, but don't hang around, git back to Harlem, boy, where you kin lose yourself, be jus' another buck. Murder over here wasn't took so light.

He walked out into the hall. The fat ol' guy was probly dead by now, his fat ol' lady sprawled 'cross him with lame-brain George – not Chicken George, but Chicken-shit George, he'd named the zombie – layin' dead as a bug by the stairs with eight inches of steel buried in him, stuck with some balls by the ol' lady when Chicken-shit George had whopped her ol' man; Mama had taken care of her after that and the ol' bag had squawked like an ol' hen when her fat neck'd been broke. That was what he'd expected to find, but never a *fourth* body, this one very much alive.

Shadebank gave a whoop of alarm and stared at the newcomer who was crouched beside the fat man. *Fuck*, he said to himself, *it jus' had to start goin' wrong!*

Rivers stared back as the black man slowly lifted the strap of his bright red braces over his right shoulder. It was a long, long moment in which he was able to take in the intruder, who seemed just as startled: the shiny brown and cream shoes, the light-coloured linen trousers whose creases were there by design rather than the material's natural flaw; the immaculate blue pin-stripe shirt with its neat double cuffs and gold cufflinks. Perhaps it was bizarre to notice so much under the circumstances, but moments of shock were often full of such incongruities.

Rivers' question was not quite so incongruous, but it was fairly close. 'Who are you?' he asked.

The other man pushed back gold-rimmed glasses to the bridge of his nose and replied: 'The fuck you say.' Then, to Rivers' amazement, he called out: '*Mama!*'

Rivers took a wary step backwards and then another.

'*Mama Pitié!*' the black man yelled again, but even louder. '*We got comp'ny!*'

The car's headlights had lit up the room, swinging across the walls and ceiling like a searchlight, chasing deep shadows that sunk back into the overall gloom when the illumination had passed. Mama Pitié bent over the child on the bed, the gown she wore as dark as those shadows. Her temples throbbed with the probing, her giant's fists clenched with the tension.

The girl was resisting her. No, not that, not resisting. Young as she was, the wretch had realised her weakness and her mind had run from Mama, had found a place inside her own self where no one could touch her. *Oh blessed child, don't mess with Mama! Your power is useless on its own, it needs the thoughts of others to give it worth. Come back to me, l'il girl, come back to Mama an' let me show you the way. The right way. The way fo' Mama Earth to rise above her tribulations an' reign supreme agin. Don't fool with me, child, you cain't escape, ah'll drag you back an' tear your skinny arms 'n' legs off 'til you give up the power you don't deserve to have. Ah'll make you holler an' scream an' all the other l'il ones will feel your pain an' taste your fear an' they'll tremble an' shake an' their minds will wither an' die an' they'll stop what they're doin' an' they'll scream for their own mamas an' their mamas won't be there no mo' an' the whole wor . . .*

Mama Pitié's head jerked up. She looked towards the big window that overlooked the courtyard, but the intrusion was in her mind, not out there in the rainy night.

The other one is here! Sweet Mother, they conspire against me. She leaned over the girl again and pulled the limp body into her arms. *Ah won't leave you alone, l'il pretty one. You kin sleep, but you cain't escape me. Ah've followed yo' befo' an' ah kin do it agin. Your days is done, oh yay, they's done . . . sing Her praises, lift your heart with joy fo' the One Mother shall be whole agin . . .*

She nuzzled the white skin of the girl's cheek. *When I start eatin' your flesh, child, you'll return soon enough. You'll come back quick as a flea.* Juices from Mama Pitié's lips drooled on to the pure and icy cheek beneath her and her teeth grazed the flesh. Her jaw began to tense.

Someone callin'! Mama Pitié raised her head, her eyes alert and darting like those of a predator disturbed from its meal. The faintest tint of blood stained her teeth. *Shadebank was callin', the dam' fool.*

She went to the open door of the darkened room, the comatose child still held in her arms.

There was movement from above and Rivers backed away even further so that he was almost at the entrance door. Someone had appeared up there in the gloom of the landing. No, there were two of them. The first, another black man in white shirt and dark trousers, the other . . .

Lightning seared all the windows again and continued to flicker long after the initial flare, the thunder joining with it, so loud and so violent that Hazelrod itself seemed to shudder.

Rivers staggered back against the door he'd left half open, knocking it closed with a bang that was lost under the thunder. The lights of the house – the hall, the sitting room, and from the open kitchen door – dimmed momentarily as if power lines somewhere had been struck by the lightning, but the flash still strobed, filling the interior with its curious silver glow. He held up a hand before him as though protecting his eyes from the sun, and through his open fingers he watched the immense – the *gargantuan* – figure standing beside the man in the white shirt on the landing overlooking the hall. Never in his life had he seen a woman so huge, her shape alternately silhouetted by the stuttering light from the window behind her. The halo that was her hair looked as if it was constructed of curled silver wire, and when the lightning finally fluttered away he was able to gaze into her cruel and mad eyes.

He suddenly remembered the day in London when he and Diane had been attacked by thugs as they waited in a line of traffic. The visage that had appeared at the car window – for a moment only he had seen the image of this woman and then it had dissolved into the brutish face of their would-be assailant. It had been a premonition, and now that face was real. It glared down at him from the top of the stairs: the crazy staring eyes, the thick, savage lips, the dark, pock-marked skin – and the flat nose with its deep shadow beneath. Even from that distance and in that gloomy light he could see – he could *feel* – the hatred of her gaze.

And a recognition seemed to flicker in that gaze for a moment, and he wondered if she had had the same precognitive moment on that day, but in reverse, with him as the subject.

Her expression changed to one of curiosity and she moved to the first step and now something registered in his own mind, something that only shock and fear could have made go unnoticed before. In her arms she carried a small, curled bundle, a figure made even smaller – and infinitely more vulnerable – by the immensity of the black woman's own bulk. She was holding Eva.

He thought the woman was coming down to him, perhaps to goad him with the child she held tight against herself, perhaps to reason with him using Eva as a shield, or even a threat – those powerful hands could easily snap the little girl's neck (had they done exactly that to Bibby? he wondered). But no, she would not goad him, nor would she threaten him with the child; she looked strong enough to snap Rivers, himself, in two, and that, he thought, was her intention.

Instead she gave a jerk of her head and the man with her slid by and started down the stairs towards him. As he came he was fixing something to his forefingers and when lightning blazed again it picked out the tiny curved blades of the ring knives.

30

Rivers had known deep fear before. Three months ago when the research aircraft had begun its spiralling dive over the Gulf of Mexico, tossed and shaken by the hurricane with only the pilot's experience and innate skill pulling the plane out of the dive, his dread had been all-consuming. That was the moment he had thought he was going to die and it stayed with him during the long and rough flight back to the mainland, the crippled aircraft's remaining engine spluttering and stalling every inch of the way. Captain Heckart – the poor courageous pilot who was to die anyway – had crash-landed the plane just outside Galveston and all but three on board had been killed instantly. Of those three, one had lost the fight to live six weeks later, one was now little more than a vegetable with no memory at all of the accident, and Rivers himself, while recovering physically – apart from the leg he had thought would never heal – had been left with scars of a different kind. For him the memory of the storm, the terrible journey after the research aircraft had sustained severe damage, the dead body of Gardenia pressing itself against him almost in a lover's embrace – and the light, the tiny, beautiful ball of light that had warned of the disaster that was to follow. That deep and appalling fear returned each time he thought of, and each time he saw, the portent.

Then there was the other kind of fear, the sort that could be so dreadful because it left you helpless and without hope. He had felt that debilitating fear during the last few days of Laura's desperate struggle for life, when the perniciously new form of malaria had swiftly claimed her, wasting her body within such a short span of time, taking her finally when no contact could be made, her confused and tormented senses denying communication, refusing that last contact when death was inevitable and only words could comfort. She had gone and he could only pray that his words of love would be heard beyond her life.

There had been other times when he had been afraid, naturally, but none were so significant, none felt with such desperation; until now.

The sight of this man descending the stairs, fixing these wicked blades to his fingers, and the strange giant of a woman on the landing above, aroused a terrible fear, for he was presented with a choice: he could either escape through the door, or he could face the horror. It was the choice that made this fear so desperate.

He almost chose the craven way, but he knew Diane would never flee from Hazelrod with him, not when she was aware that Eva and her family were inside the house. Besides, he had seen Eva stir, a tiny frail hand waving listlessly in the air to flop over the massive arm that held her. That small gesture – together with the contemptuous look the black woman had given him before disappearing from view – helped him decide.

The advancing man was halfway down the stairs, his eyes fixed on Rivers, no expression, no sign of any emotion whatsoever in them. His hands were slightly raised, thumbs supporting the sides of the ring knives' blades. Could they kill? Rivers wondered. They looked lethal – were these the weapons that had cut Hugo? – but the blades were short. Perhaps if they were sunk into an eyeball, or scythed across an exposed throat . . . He moved with a speed that gave no time for further thought.

As his foot found a step between the torso and right arm of the corpse on the stairs, Rivers gripped the carving knife sticking from the body and pulled. The knife came free with surprising ease and he continued the motion, twisting his wrist and bringing up the blade in one fluid movement so that it plunged deep into the groin of the assailant above him.

The man uttered a peculiar kind of strangulated yelp and fell on to Rivers, the ring knives flailing the space behind as if he were a non-swimmer out of his depth. Rivers lifted him, jerking his shoulders back at the same time so that the intruder slid over him and tumbled down the rest of the stairs to fall in a heap at the bottom, his body entangled with that of the corpse. He writhed there, knees drawn up, shoulders hunched, his hands around the knife handle as if to pull it free. To do that would cause more pain and he was afraid of suffering any more than he had to; but soon he had no strength to do it anyway, and before Rivers had reached the top of the stairs the man's throat was gurgling its death rattle.

There were two doors on that side of the landing and one of them was open. The room was in darkness, but he could sense the big woman's presence, could smell her sweat-soaked stench, as soon as he entered. And then he saw her standing by the dim light that came from behind. He became still as blinding light swept through the room, the thunder almost instant and shockingly close. As the light flickered he caught sight of Eva's little body, dressed in her nightgown, lying on her bed, her arms and legs outstretched, her eyes now open and staring up at the ceiling. The bedroom must have belonged to Hugo and Bibby, for the bed itself was full-sized, a curving headboard of dark wood at one end, a footboard of similar shape at the other. He had a chance to take in the room's layout before the light faded: there was a dressing-table to one side of the window and a huge old-fashioned wardrobe against a far wall; small cabinets stood either side of the broad bed, a lamp on each one. The position of the nearest lamp still in his mind as the room plunged into darkness once again, Rivers made for it rather than scrabble at the wall near the door for the light switch. He found the switch and clicked it on; the glow was barely adequate.

The thunder had died away moments after the lightning and he could hear the wind and rain outside the window. The woman there had not moved, but now she let a hissing breath escape her. Rivers straightened up from the lamp and faced her.

He could not help the shudder that ran through him when he moved aside to allow the light to reveal her, for this close she was even more awesome. The smock-like dress she wore was dark-coloured, black or perhaps navy blue, and it reached down almost to her thick ankles, the arms loose and split at the elbow so that her broad and powerful-looking wrists were plainly visible. Her hair was in crinkly curls around her face and there were scars, not pockmarks, that seemed almost tribal on her cheeks. Her nose was flat, mis-shapen, and there was something else odd about it; maybe it was a trick of the light that caused the shadows to be so deep, but it looked as if she only had a single nostril. Instead of a shudder, this time a cold ripple ran between his shoulder-blades to the base of his spine.

Still she did not move.

'Eva,' Rivers said urgently. 'Eva, come here to me.' He didn't dare take his eyes off the woman in case she made a move towards him. There was no response from the child on the bed. 'Eva,' he said again, this time raising his voice so that it was almost a call. Still there was no response. He

390

risked a glance towards her and for one heart-stopping moment he thought she was dead. Although her eyes were open, he could tell they registered nothing. He breathed a short sigh when there was a slight stirring as her chest moved up and down.

'She cain't hear you.'

His attention snapped back to the tall woman. It had sounded like 'cain't *heyar* you'.

'She ain't dead.' Ain't *daid*. 'But she's not with us.' The voice was low and gravelly, almost like a man's.

'Who are you?' Despite the tension, he wanted to know.

'Git away from her.'

He remained where he was, but a feebleness, an almost nauseating weakness swept over him, as if this woman's voice had a power of its own. Her accent was that of the southern states of America, he was sure, but the knowledge only added to his confusion. The man he had come face to face with in the downstairs hall had called her Mama Pity – no, Mama Pitié, he had used the French word, its accent plain (and *his* accent had been pure Bronx). Just what was she and those others doing here, and what did she want with Eva? At once he remembered his conversation with the old man – the children's Dream Man – in the crofter's cottage in the Highlands. The old man had told him there were many forces at work in this time of change, some for the good, but others committed to chaos and destruction, opposing influences whose sole purpose was to wreak havoc against mankind. Their motive was unclear, but these latter forces had been ever-present throughout mankind's evolution (and long before that, he had added enigmatically). Rivers had assumed the old man had spoken metaphorically, that these other forces symbolised the contrariness of the human psyche that was natural and innate to everyone; but now he understood it must assume a physical identity, that this woman, this Mama Pitié, was the word made flesh. This debilitating weakness that was

391

nothing more than fear of her told him the truth of his considerations.

More in desperation than curiosity he asked, 'What do you want with this girl?'

Mama Pitié stared at him for long seconds, her ample breasts rising and falling as if with exertion. Then she said, *'She's the parasite that feeds off Mother Earth.'* The words were spat at him, their rage stinging him like hot pellets. But in her eyes he caught the merest hint of frustration.

'She's just a kid,' he said as coolly as he could. Could it be possible? he thought. Could someone so small and frail stand in the way of whatever crazy ideas this woman had for the future of the world? But then Eva wasn't alone; she had Josh, and if the dreams were true, if the old man's words had meaning, there were many others – thousands, perhaps – like them, all psychically joined in the battle to shape the Earth of the future. Some, those of a religious nature maybe, would refer to it as the age-old battle between Light and Darkness, while others who took the Bible even more literally might say it was the eternal war between God and the Fallen Angels. Yet others would declare that mankind held its destiny in its own hands and now was the time for all voices – all minds – to be heard. The old man had said the human mega-psyche, the neglected sense that linked us all, had been revived, or reclaimed, by the children of the new evolution, and it was this special power that linked us to the planet itself. The thoughts crowded in and Rivers had to still his own mind.

'Every man, woman and child is the parasite,' the big woman was saying slowly, 'an' it's time for the clensin'.'

He wondered if he could reason with her. 'You've got it wrong,' he said, the calmness in his voice a lie to the paralysing fear he felt. 'We *are* the Earth. We're part of it and the Earth is part of us.'

'Mother Earth is destroyin' us.'

392

The inner turmoil he had felt over the past twenty-four hours had begun to evaporate. The old man's testimony had been difficult to accept, especially for someone as pragmatic as Rivers, but because his predictions that Josh and Eva were in mortal danger and that he, Rivers, was the one who would help them had become true, the realities had somehow become starker, the truths more plain. Since yesterday he might have acted as if he were convinced, but a grain of doubt had remained; now this bizarre creature before him had flushed away that last dissenting speck of disbelief. Lovelock and Hugo Poggs were partially right, but they had both missed the essential truth: mankind was born *of* the Earth, its earliest life forms crawling from the muddy depths of the oceans and seas, the light giving it energy, taking away the darkness, the part that was the absence of energy. The light became part of the human psyche, for the light was hope, it was faith, it was life itself. Its warmth was the very essence of feeling. It became the metaphorical symbol for love, for compassion, for the *spirit* of life. The light had enabled mankind to rise above the underworld, to become more than a mindless organism existing in the world's crust. And even now, the light was mankind's focus, it was showing the way, just as some believed it showed the way at the moment of death.

Mama Pitié was still speaking and her voice had risen to evangelical tones. 'Mother Earth is shakin' us off Her back, gettin' rid of the bugs that have been eatin' away at Her heart. She will no longer be the tormented one an' Her wrath shall be great.'

'No, that's wrong,' Rivers argued, hoping that Eva would soon rouse from her frozen state. His own tone was reasonable, his voice moderate. 'We're being shown the results of centuries of abuse, we're being chastised, if you like. But it's us, we're the ones who are doing it. Our own collective psyche is causing this havoc. Please try to understand what

I'm saying. We control our own destiny.' As he looked at this strange woman he knew he was wasting his breath: not even a single glimmer appeared in those black staring eyes to indicate she was even listening, let alone comprehending what he had told her. It was, however, giving him time to edge closer to Eva. One knee was now on the bed. 'Don't you see? We've found our own way to change the Earth. Our minds have been led by these' – he indicated Eva – 'innocents, these children who are the new order of things. Much of their power is as old as mankind itself, but it's also part of our own evolution. Eventually the whole of the human race will become as they are. The disasters – the earthquakes, the floods, the storms, droughts, fires, diseases – are all part of our own punishment. Enduring them will make us understand we have to change, they'll make us appreciate everything we have, everything we've taken for grant –'

'*No more of this bullshit!*'

He almost overbalanced at the ferocity of her yell. She moved away from the window, her steps surprisingly light for one of her size.

'Mama Pitié!' he shouted in desperation.

She hesitated and that encouraged him.

'You mustn't interfere with them, Mama Pitié.' Out of the corner of his eye, Rivers caught movement on the bed. 'You mustn't oppose the children, it's too dangerous.' It occurred to him that conditions had become so catastrophic precisely because of the opposing forces and remembered the old man had suggested as much. 'You must leave them alone; they're here to lead us through all this destruction.'

'That's exactly why *I'm* here.' The black woman reached over the foot of the bed and grabbed Eva's ankle. She glared at Rivers. 'Don't *you* see that, boy?'

Eva screamed as Mama Pitié pulled her towards the end of the bed, a tiny shrill sound that cut through the night like a knife.

'*No!*' Rivers shouted.

Eva was conscious enough to clutch at the bedclothes as she was dragged down the bed and they went with her. Rivers lunged forward and grabbed the big woman's arm, but he might have been a child himself for all the effect he had. Without wasting further time, he drew back his fist and struck at the black woman's disfigured face.

His knuckles stung like hell, but at least Mama Pitié released her grip on Eva. Instead she seized Rivers, who was half sprawled across the bed, and lifted him. Rivers was helpless as her vice-like fingers dug into his arm and although he tried to pull away she raised him up, then grabbed him by the waist with her other hand. She tossed him over the bed and against the wardrobe on the other side of the room. The wardrobe rocked back against the wall behind as he crashed into it.

His senses swam as he tried to pick himself up from the floor. He clutched at the side of the bed and pulled against the covering there, hauling himself on to one knee, shaking his head to clear the dizziness. In a blur he saw Eva sit up as her body, shifted by the bedclothes, moved towards him. She gaped at the mountainous creature at the end of the bed, her neck sunk low into her hunched shoulders.

The black woman saw the movement towards Rivers and lunged at the bedsheets. Her fingers locked through the material and she began to draw the little figure towards her again, her eyes two glittering orbs in the lamplight that revealed the nastiness of her intent. She showed her teeth in an expression that was more canine than pleasured.

Blood ran down Rivers' cheek from his ear, but he barely noticed it or the pain; he was still stunned, but nevertheless thinking fast. He yanked at the bedclothes so that Eva fell on to her side and when Mama Pitié reached for her ankle once more he scrambled to his feet, stretched for the unlit lamp on that side of the bed, yanked it from its wire and smashed it into the side of the woman's massive head.

She roared and let go of the child to deal with him. She lifted him easily again, dragging him over the bed and crushing him against her own body. The air left his lungs as she squeezed and he gasped against the pain, sure that his spine would break at any moment. Lightning lit up the room and the thunder that accompanied it was softened by his own blood rushing to his head. He dug his fingers into her fleshy neck, squeezing her throat just as she squeezed his body. He felt his grip weakening, his head spinning, but he renewed his efforts, afraid for himself, for Eva, and for the world.

It was no good; he could feel the bones of his back bending inwards and the last dregs of air leaving his lungs to emerge from his throat as a last rasping sigh. The gloom seemed darker, the shadows blacker. Mama Pitié's face was only inches from his own and, oddly, his eyes focused on that deep slit beneath her nose, the wide nostril that was like a second toothless grin, mocking him for his feebleness. It began to blur as vision and strength slowly drained away from him. His senses began to go.

He struggled against her, his head dropping forward as he strained his back against the pressure. His moist lips slid over the scars of her cheek, and then against her big lips in a kiss that held no passion. He bit down hard and she flinched away, releasing him only slightly, but just enough for him to draw in a short breath through his nose. He felt disgusted, sickened, but he sank his teeth harder into her lower lip, tasting her blood, grinding his teeth together to cause maximum damage. He felt himself raised in her arms, his body pushed away from hers; still he clung to her lip, biting down, drinking her blood, fighting the nausea that threatened to choke him.

Mama Pitié tried to thrust him away. She shook him as though he was no more than a rag doll. But still he hung on to her.

He felt her relax for the briefest of seconds as she gathered all her strength; then she gripped him beneath his shoulders, straightened her arms and tossed her head to one side in the same movement. Her howl filled the room as the flesh of her lip came away from her face and Rivers felt her bloody meat inside his mouth. He choked, then spat out the thick sliver, bile rising in his throat as he did so. But she had him still and, despite her pain, she held his elbow and yanked at his wrist at the wrong angle, snapping the elbow joint as easily as one might snap a wishbone.

Rivers screamed with the pain and she threw him aside, leaving him there in a heap on the floor while she turned back to the little bundle on the bed that had been too shocked to move. Mama Pitié would deal with this man when she had more time for pleasure. Blood gushed from her torn lip and flooded her chin and chest with its slick crimson flow, but she ignored the agony and the wetness just as she ignored her antagonist slumped in the corner. There were more important things at hand.

She wrenched the child from the bed and turned to face the window, her burden held high over her head, her eyes bulging with rage.

Rivers heard Eva's scream and he looked up, his whole body, and not just his broken arm, a mass of pain.

'*Noooo!*' he shouted as lightning lit the tableau before him, the huge black woman, her lower face a gory mess, holding the screaming child aloft, ready to hurl her through the big window.

Thunder drowned Eva's screams.

31

Her arms were straight and powerful as she stood poised to throw Eva out into the stormy night. The lightning flickered still and the thunder shook the house to its very foundations.

But Mama Pitié paused.

She stood before the window, the weight she held nothing at all to those mighty arms, staring at something out there in the night.

Fighting against the pain, Rivers shifted from the corner he'd been carelessly tossed into. Blood was smeared across his lips and the taste of her, vile and rotten, was still in his mouth. It was difficult to move, each stirring sending fresh pain streaking through his body, but he did so, crawling to the foot of the bed so that he was almost behind the big woman. He gagged, but fought back the sickness, the short, dry retching sound he made lost in the thunder overhead.

Suddenly it was quiet, the patter of rain on the window the only noise. Mama Pitié remained motionless, her gaze fixed on something outside the window, and although his head still spun with the punishment he had taken, Rivers noticed light continued to brighten the room even though the lightning had faded. The last rumble of thunder died away as he raised himself to his knees and looked past the dark-robed woman before him.

The tiny, shining light was above the courtyard, glowing in the rain, a halo of colours around it, a rainbow circle whose spectrum was soft yet dazzling to the eye. The wind had no influence over the ball of light, for it hovered without movement and not even the rain dulled its blaze.

As Mama Pitié watched it through the glass she felt doubt for the first time. This thing made no sound, it said nothing, but its meaning . . . oh its meaning was so clear. Yet so confusing. Somehow the shining light told her through voices implanted inside her own mind, voices that sounded like a million children singing, that the planet *was* their existence, that it nurtured them and fed them, was their home and their host, and it was *them*. The revelation was overwhelming. Yet Mama Pitié's tortured soul tried to deny it, for to accept would be to reject all her own past teachings, her own affirmations, the beliefs that had given her a goal, that had taken her from the slums of the city and the entrapment of her own brutish ugliness and laid before her a mission that would sustain her through life and set her aside from others, not as some carnival freak, but as a saviour, a saviour of the Great Mother Earth Herself. And the powers she had been born with were the key, for they told her she was special, someone apart from all the rest, not for her size, not for her physical strength, but for her ability to heal, to read the thoughts of others, to travel with her mind. She believed Mother Earth, Herself, *Her Great Self*, had bestowed these powers upon her for one purpose alone, and only in recent months had she come to realise just what that purpose was: Mama Pitié had been blessed so that she could help the Great

Mother in her final hour of conflict – and now that time had come.

She stifled the doubt, she smothered her own wonderment at the shining light outside the window – a light that, after all, was put there by other devious minds to confuse and distract her from her true purpose – and she bent her arms to throw this child with its degenerate thoughts, this child who plotted and schemed with others to dominate and cripple the Great Mother Earth. Her arms tensed and she leaned back. *The child would join the light outside!*

From the floor Rivers watched as those powerful arms trembled with the tension that ran through them. The woman's fingers were open, Eva balanced between the huge hands. Eva screamed again.

And Rivers leapt up, the movement awkward but fast. His one good arm wrapped itself around Eva's waist and his own weight as he fell back to the floor did the rest. Her nightdress tore as Mama Pitié reflexively closed her grip, and the child toppled with Rivers, both of them falling in a heap on the floor.

Rivers cried out as his broken arm struck the bed, but he took Eva's weight on his own chest, breaking her fall. He hugged her to him as he sprawled there, his shoulders resting against the footboard and, with eyes half closed with pain, he watched the huge bloodied woman turn towards them.

Light burned through the windows behind her, dust motes caught in its rays; her massive lumbering body was almost in silhouette as she towered above them.

She was screeching as she reached for Eva again.

32

At first Rivers thought it was thunder that tore through the room, but the sound was too sharp and even its echo was over too quickly. And its brightness hadn't the electric starkness of lightning, nor did it linger and flicker.

Mama Pitié staggered backwards, her bloodied chest now torn and bubbling more blood. She stood inches away from the window and roared her pain and screamed her frustration. Her body was rigid, her arms upraised, her fingers curled into thick claws.

Only when Diane pulled the shotgun's second trigger did Mama Pitié jerk backwards, her arms flailing as she lost her balance. She crashed through the glass, the hem of her gown fluttering in the wind like the wings of some monstrous bird. Her scream was cut short as she hit the cobblestones below.

The rain and the rushing of the wind was louder through the broken window, but there was a deep silence in the room where Rivers and Eva lay, and where Diane stood in the doorway, smoke from Mack's shotgun curling towards the ceiling. There was a look of utter horror on Diane's face as she stared towards the window, the light outside merely a focus point that had no significance in her shocked mind.

Rivers felt Eva squirming against him and he released her immediately. 'Mama?' she said as she scrabbled to her feet.

At first he thought she meant the gross woman who had tried to kill her, the one the man downstairs called Mama Pitié, and he spoke to her, his voice barely a whisper, telling her it was all right now, the bad lady was gone, she was safe; but Eva ran towards the door, her arms outstretched, calling 'Mama' over and over again.

He raised himself to see Diane drop the empty shotgun and sweep up her daughter into her arms. Eva buried her face into Diane's neck, and Diane held her tight, tight, her eyes closed, her lips moving as she repeated her daughter's name.

Pain, almost forgotten for a short while, returned and Rivers rested his head against the curving top of the bed's footboard. It felt as if white heat was racing through the whole left side of his upper body. He clung to the bed with his good arm and resisted the waves of exhaustion and hurt that tormented him.

'Diane,' he managed to say.

She came to him quickly, Eva still clutched in her arms, and as she approached he noticed the room was bright, the light from outside stronger.

'What . . . who was she?' Diane said, kneeling beside him.

He drew in a breath before he spoke. 'Remember what the Dream Man told me? He said . . . he said there were others, others like the children . . . with their power, but opposing forces. He said their beliefs were different . . .' He couldn't go on, the pain was too great. Time enough to talk of it later.

'Jim, your arm . . .'

'Yeah, the bitch broke it.' He winced and leaned his forehead

402

on the bed. He drew in a long breath again. 'Is Eva okay?' he asked when the fresh flush of agony had subsided a little.

Diane looked at her daughter who tried to smile but couldn't quite manage it. She rested against her mother's arm and watched Rivers as he turned his body to sit.

'I took Mack's shotgun from his room before I came into the house,' Diane said hurriedly. 'Oh God, I used to hate him using it . . .'

'You had to do it,' Rivers told her. 'She'd have killed Eva if you hadn't. Probably me, too.'

'Poggsy's in a bad way. I think he's suffered a heart attack. And Bibby's . . . Bibby's . . .'

Rivers nodded. 'I think she stabbed one of them before they broke . . . before they got to her.' He wondered if it *had* been Mama Pitié who had snapped Bibby's neck like that. God knows she had the strength to do it. 'I got the other one with the same knife.'

'I saw them downstairs. Jim, there was another one. I saw him leaving the house as I came back with the shotgun.'

'Let's hope he's long gone. We've got to do something about Hugo, get him to a hospital . . .'

'And you. You'll have to get that arm fixed.'

Eva raised her head from her mother's shoulder and solemnly regarded Rivers, looking from his face to his injured arm. Without a word she stretched out her hand and touched him. She left her mother and knelt down in front of him, her little hand running down the length of his broken arm, starting at the shoulder and moving down to the wrist. He felt the heat from her fingers and the warmth quickly spread through the whole of his arm and shoulder. And as the warmth radiated, so the pain fled before it. The relief was gradual at first, an easing of the pain's sharpness, but soon Eva's magic began to work rapidly, and before long all he could feel was a dull ache. Something clicked and he realised the bones had locked together again.

'Jesus,' he said, staring first at Eva and then at Diane. He tried to move his arm, but it was stiff; stiff but free of pain.

He began to haul himself to his feet and Diane rose with him, taking him beneath the shoulder as she did so. The room became even brighter as lightning lit the troubled sky; this time the thunder followed a moment or two later.

'It's moving away,' Rivers muttered absently as he looked down at Eva. 'Thank you,' he said to her. Tiredness almost overwhelmed him and he leaned heavily against Diane. She held him close and he felt her body jerk with a sudden sob. 'It's over, Diane, the worst is over. Now we've got to help Hugo.'

He noticed the shadows in the room were moving, running back towards the broken window where Eva now stood looking out, the wind whipping at her tousled hair. He realised the light outside was moving upwards. Diane sensed his distraction and followed his gaze. The small light with its ring of colours was about to disappear from view.

'My God,' she said quietly, 'it's beautiful.'

Then it was gone, though its glow still lit Eva's head and shoulders.

'Eva, careful of the broken gla –'

Diane's words were cut off when her daughter screamed, '*Josh!*'

Rivers and Diane moved quickly to the window and peered down into the courtyard below. A small sound escaped Rivers, for he knew it was not yet all over for them, that the horror had not passed. Clouds rolled towards Hazelrod in a boiling mass, sheet lightning flaring in their vapours as if now unable to escape. Thunder rumbled low and menacing. Towards the far hills a bluish tower swayed erratically.

Rivers had barely noticed these things as he'd taken the few steps towards the window, and now his attention was on Josh who was standing in the centre of the courtyard watching the dark shape that was stirring on the cobblestones. A short distance away the bespectacled man, whose red braces were vivid under the light from above, also watched the rising heap. This one stood by the Granada, his shirt drenched by the drizzling rain so that his black skin showed through.

Mama Pitié's broad shoulders heaved with the effort, her head slowly raising itself so that she could look at the boy just a few yards away. She stretched out a quivering arm towards him, its fingers bent and broken.

Even from above they could hear her crazed murmurings as she raised herself to her knees, her misshapen hand still pointed towards Josh. They looked on in dread-filled paralysis as she staggered to her feet and stood there, swaying in the wind and the rain. She took one step forward towards the boy, and then another.

'Run, Josh, run! Get away from her!'

Rivers held on to Diane, afraid she would fall as she leaned forward and screamed at her son.

The boy did not move. He seemed mesmerised.

'Josh.'

Eva only spoke the name, but he looked up at the window instantly. His eyes found his sister's.

Diane turned away, ready to make for the stairs, but Rivers held on to her arm.

'I've got to get to him!' she yelled at him, her eyes damp with tears of fear.

'Look,' Rivers said, pointing towards the sky. 'Look . . .'

The lights were coming from everywhere, moving just below the black roiling clouds, hundreds of them it seemed, the rain causing soft aureoles around each one.

'What are they?' Diane asked in a hushed voice, her body still half turned towards the door. Neither of them could see the smile on Eva's face.

'I'm not sure,' Rivers told her, 'but I think they're help.'

*　　*　　*

Rain washed the blood from Mama Pitié's face and body, but it could not stem the flow. She knew she was dying, and the incomprehension in her eyes was for the lights that approached in the stormy night sky. She could not understand their presence and she could not understand the light that shone from the boy himself, not a visible radiation but an inner glow that came from his very soul. She blinked as raindrops struck her eyeballs and her vision was unclear, her sight blurred, but there seemed to be others with him now, hundreds, thousands, of children and somehow they were part of the light that shone from within him and part of the lights that were arriving above to cluster over this place where Mother Earth Herself had sent her to carry out her duty to Her, to do Her will, to erase the evil that opposed . . .

Mama Pitié stumbled, almost collapsing to the ground. She had to reach him, had to hold the boy in her arms, had to crush the life from him so that Mother Earth could reign in Her true glory . . .

She was in shock and she was dying, but the pain meant little and her life even less. She would shake the boy until his bones broke and his neck snapped. A few more feet, a few more moments, and then she would claim him.

Fresh hatred welled inside Mama Pitié and its strength carried her forward . . .

The lights were drawing closer, converging, becoming more brilliant, their reflections playing as patterns in the drizzling rain, their movement smooth and swift. The light outside the broken window continued to rise and Rivers, Diane and Eva watched its unwavering ascent; the strengthening winds failed to deflect it from its course as it rose into the sky, soon to become a tiny pinpoint of light that might have been a distant fiery planet in the solar system if the rolling clouds could not be seen above. The other stars resolutely moved towards it and within seconds the first few had joined the single light, merging with it, followed by others, growing into a fulgurating body that swelled ever more as other lights fused with its mass, illuminating the sky, the clouds, bathing the landscape below with its white radiance.

Eva clapped her hands together with excitement, her face caught in the incandescent glow. Diane moaned quietly as if in rapture and Rivers felt its brilliance wash through him, the tiredness and the aching leaving him as if routed by some sublime energy.

It became stronger, pulsating there in the sky like a freshly born sun, a vibrant union of infinite power.

And then it began to contract, to condense itself, the light becoming too fierce to look upon. Its movement was so quick and so sudden it was almost an implosion, and within moments it was gone.

Diane groaned with disappointment and Rivers shook his head in dismay. But the children laughed, for they felt something inside them – something that might have been their spirit, their life's essence itself – expand and become firm, become strong. It filled them with elation.

But Josh was unaware of Mama Pitié, the Witch Lady of his dream, only a few steps away.

'Oh my God.'

Rivers turned sharply to Diane, who had uttered the words. She was looking straight ahead, beyond the old stables opposite, and now he saw it too, the cyclone, that had been nothing more than a moving bluish tower in the distance before. It was approaching fast, cutting its deadly swathe through the countryside, coming directly towards Hazelrod.

He drew Diane and Eva away from the window and pushed them down on to the floor, yelling at them to stay there as he made for the door. Diane protested but he was already gone, slamming open the window on the landing

407

as he went by so that pressure inside the house would be relatively equal to that outside. It would have been better if he could have opened all the windows and doors, but there was no time, he had to get to Josh and bring him inside before the cyclone reached them. Even then he didn't know how safe they would be, how well Hazelrod's old walls would stand up to the storm. The noise of the rushing wind was tremendous, building to a terrifying crescendo. And then the noise stopped.

He burst through the open front door and pulled himself up as he reached the porch door, grabbing on to its frame to steady himself.

He could hardly believe his eyes.

A soft blue light, almost fluorescent in quality, bathed an area of the courtyard and within its undulating circle, everything was still, everything was quiet. He could see the bespectacled man, his shirt and trousers sodden, standing by the car; he could see the huge, bent shape of the woman called Mama Pitié; and he could see Josh standing before her, his small body looking even tinier against her massive bulk. But he could see nothing beyond the pale blue curved wall of the cyclone's eye.

It was as if someone had clapped their hands over his ears for there was hardly a sound, not even the faint scream of the storm itself. The porch around him was trembling and he noticed little showers of dust were falling from between the brickwork of the walls behind him. The old toy pram creaked and one of the small bicycles clattered to the floor. The inside door shook on its hinges.

'Oh shit,' Rivers said under his breath as he stepped out into this unearthly realm.

He walked to the boy, his footsteps steady but sounding distant, muffled, as if he were underwater; the cobblestones glistened blue. He avoided the sagging figure of the woman and she watched him with sad baleful eyes. She slumped to her knees, a hand still outstretched to touch the boy. It wavered inches away from Josh's face. Finally the effort was too great and her hand dropped to her side, blood drooling from her broken fingers and making a puddle.

The man, the one whose braces were now purple under the eerie light, opened his mouth, but Rivers could not hear what he called, the sound smothered by pressure inside the circle. He seemed transfixed, one hand still on the car door, and his jaw continued to move as he shouted towards Rivers.

Rivers ignored him. As if in slow motion, he swung the boy up into his arms, then took a moment to look up into the vortex. The smooth wall comprised opaque rings which undulated gently, creating a ripple effect that ran upwards and out of view, the whole of it swaying to and fro. He could see that the upper reaches were partially filled by a blue-grey mist, and inside that mist, a soft light glimmered. He knew that light.

He looked away and walked back towards the house, not speaking to Josh, afraid the strange spell would be broken if he uttered a sound. The boy was quiet too.

As they passed her, Mama Pitié fell forward, her hands holding her there on her knees, while her life's blood drained in a constant stream.

The air was difficult to breathe and his lungs heaved with the exertion; he felt Josh's chest labouring against his own. Almost there now, almost at the porch steps. A few feet to go. Relief began to creep into him.

But with only three more strides to take, the cyclone began to move. It closed in on itself with a grinding shriek of rushing wind, snapping up both man and car at its outer edge and shrinking inwards with great speed. The huge bulk that was Mama Pitié was lifted into the air and her dying screech mingled with the screaming of the wind. She was gone in a split second, thrust into the howling storm, her great black body lost in the furious night.

Rivers lingered not a moment longer. He threw himself and Josh through into the open doorway and into the hall beyond.

33

The rain ceased shortly after the sun appeared over the horizon. The wind had eased and finally stopped some hours before.

Josh and Eva stood in Hazelrod's doorway. Hand in hand, they stepped out.

Only a few broken timbers remained of the porch and they carefully trod over the pieces of scattered wood and walked down the two steps into the courtyard. Diane and Rivers followed, but lingered on the bottom step and looked around them.

The wet courtyard was littered with rubble and tree branches. A complete tree leaned against what was left of the stables and rooms above; roof-tiles and bricks lay everywhere. Hugo Poggs' minibus was on its side at the corner of the house, while Mack's old truck was beyond the gates, its front caved in by the oak it had come to rest against. Diane's Escort had vanished, as had the intruders' vehicle, and Rivers shivered when he thought of the storm's power.

He remembered how they had sheltered together through the night in Hazelrod's hall, himself, Diane, the children, all huddled around Hugo Poggs, protecting him with their own bodies, Bibby's corpse lying only a few feet away. Rivers had thrown the other two dead bodies out into the porch, and now they were gone too, along with the porch itself and its other contents.

It had been a terrifying night, the worst moments when the cyclone was directly overhead. It had sucked at the house, taking new glass from the windows – and even bricks from the walls. But the storm had not entered and they had remained safe, even though Hazelrod had shuddered and strained around them and branches, leaves and objects had flown into the windows.

The bodies of the woman called Mama Pitié and the third man who had been with her had disappeared like the other two. And so had Mack's. Rivers wondered where they would be found.

Incredible though it seemed, those inside the house had all fallen asleep, the twins first, then Diane, and finally Rivers himself. And when they woke, daylight was streaming through the open doorway and they could hear the birds outside singing. It was a sound that Rivers had thought they might never hear again.

Soon they would have to get a doctor to Hugo, although Josh and Eva had worked their special magic with him only a short while ago, touching his chest, soothing his pain, calming him so that now he was sleeping peacefully. Another crisis might arise when he awoke and realised Bibby was gone from him, but Diane would be there to administer sedatives. They had moved Bibby's body into the living room and covered it with a sheet. The twins had wept over her, but for the moment, as with most children of their age and younger, the new dawn had brought fresh promise to their young lives and the bad thoughts were cast aside. They would grieve later, but for now something had happened to them, something that neither they nor Rivers and Diane understood, but its wonderment was there shining in their faces.

He thought of the portents, the lights, and knew somehow he had been right: the lights were from the people themselves, their own inner warnings manifested in this strange form through powers that were still beyond mankind's own comprehension.

He slipped his arm around Diane's waist – an arm that had been broken the night before and was now miraculously healed – and she leaned against him, her hand finding his. They watched Josh and Eva wheel around, their faces upturned towards the other miracle that was in the sky.

The rainbows were everywhere, graceful arches that stretched for miles and miles, some beneath others, some breaking through their neighbours' gentle slopes, their mixed colours creating new shades and hues, all soft to the eye.

Their beauty was uplifting and, although Rivers did not know in what condition the world had been left, how many battles such as theirs had been fought that night, he had hope.

The spectacle of the rainbows gave him that.

*You must teach your children that
the ground beneath their feet is
the ashes of our grandfathers. So
that they will respect the land,
tell your children that the earth
is rich with the lives of our kin.
Teach your children what we have
taught our children, that the
earth is our mother. Whatever
befalls the earth befalls the
sons of the earth. If men spit
upon the ground, they spit upon
themselves.*

*This we know. The earth does not
belong to man; man belongs to the
earth. This we know. All things
are connected like the blood
which unites one family. All
things are connected.*

*Whatever befalls the earth befalls
the sons of the earth. Man did not
weave the web of life, he is merely
a strand in it. Whatever he
does to the web, he does to himself.*

CHIEF SEATTLE'S TESTIMONY, 1854